KING OF THIEVES

BY EVAN CURRIE

Odyssey One series
The Heart of Matter
Homeworld
Out of the Black

On Silver Wings series
On Silver Wings
Valkyrie Rising
Valkyrie Burning
The Valhalla Call
By Other Means

Other works
SEAL Team 13
Steam Legion
Thermals

KING OF THIEVES

EVAN CURRIE

47N RTH

Text copyright © 2015 Evan Currie
All rights reserved.

No part of this book may be reproduced, or stored in a retrieval system, or transmitted in any form or by any means, electronic, mechanical, photocopying, recording, or otherwise, without express written permission of the publisher.

Published by 47North, Seattle

www.apub.com

Amazon, the Amazon logo, and 47North are trademarks of Amazon.com, Inc., or its affiliates.

ISBN-13: 9781477828243
ISBN-10: 1477828249

Cover design by becker&mayer! Books LLC
Cover illustration by Marc Simonetti

Library of Congress Control Number: 2014953859

Printed in the United States of America

CHAPTER 1

▶ Captain Morgan Passer felt his full body weight settle back onto his feet as he landed on the deck of the Space Station Unity One. The new station was three times larger than the Liberty it was replacing, and it was one of seven planned for construction in the wake of the Drasin Holocaust. Over a year had passed since the last shots of the invasion had been fired, and the death toll for the Earth was still being tallied, with numbers already in the hundreds of millions. He was constantly surprised by how little of the devastation was visible from space.

The curve of the Earth was still as awe-inspiring a sight as it had been two centuries earlier, or so he liked to believe. The planet seemed blue and white and pure. Unharmed, untouched by the ravages he personally had experienced, and seemingly peaceful.

Morgan grimaced, looking away from the curve of the Earth and out into the black beyond, spotting the Heroic Class ship settled into high orbit above the station.

It was the *Odysseus*, the Warrior King.

Probably the most lethal amalgamation of military hardware ever assembled in the combined history of Earth and the Priminae colonies, any one of the Heroics could probably destroy a planet, possibly a star if their captain and crew were feeling kamikaze enough. *Odysseus*, in particular, had a growing reputation on Earth and, from what he'd heard, in the colonies as well.

Captained by a man who, by all reasonable rights, should be dead, the *Odysseus* crew certainly lived up to and reveled in their reputation.

Passer's new ship, however, was something else entirely.

He left the observation deck, heading for the briefing room where he was already expected.

The admiral glanced up as he entered, nodding in his direction and motioning him to a chair. Admiral Gracen had never been one to be overly formal in the past, but recent events had caused her to toss out most of the protocol she had left, from what he could see.

Morgan recognized the other man in the room—Lazarus himself, Captain Eric Stanton Weston.

He took his seat, observing the senior captain out of the corner of his eye as he considered what he knew of the man. Morgan had been a Navy man his whole career, but Eric started as a Marine and bounced around like the proverbial grasshopper. No one questioned either the man's competence or his tactical acumen, however, though Morgan had heard more than one snide comment about his strategic judgment.

Eric nodded to Morgan as he settled in, but didn't speak. Morgan didn't blame him. He certainly wasn't going to interrupt whatever the admiral was doing.

Gracen looked up finally, an amused expression on her face as she glanced between them.

"Welcome, gentlemen. I wanted to speak with you both, as you'll be working together on occasion in the near future."

Morgan straightened, not quite leaning forward upon hearing that.

He hadn't been given any hints of his first assignment, but he had known it was coming, of course. His ship had just passed her trials, and the *Auto* was ready, as was her crew. The fact that he was being linked with Weston meant that he wasn't about to be assigned to Solar System Command.

We're getting a deep space assignment.

Weston and the *Odysseus* were assigned to Priminae worlds, and beyond. They were the tip of the spear, but also the explorers and ambassadors who represented Earth. Scuttlebutt had it that the *Odysseus* was about to receive a long-term mission, out beyond even Priminae space.

That was what everyone had signed up for.

"We'll talk about the *Odysseus'* assignment later, Captain." Gracen glanced to Weston, who just nodded. "For now, this concerns Captain Passer and the *Autolycus.*"

The newly commissioned UES *Autolycus* was Morgan's new baby, his one true love, and possibly the finest piece of steel he'd ever seen in his life. The Rogue Class destroyer was also probably the last wholly Earth-designed ship that would ever be built, since the Priminae had offered to help Earth build a new shipyard to colonial specs in the system.

"We want Passer to test the *Autolycus* in deep space," she said. "If it holds up to our expectations, she and her crew will eventually operate as a long-range recon. As you both know, her weapons don't hold a candle to the *Odysseus*, but they're nothing to sneeze at either."

"Absolutely, Admiral," Passer said with a hint of pride.

"Given what we accomplished with the *Odyssey*, with probably half what the *Auto* is packing," Weston said, referring to his old destroyed ship, "I'm not one to underestimate the potential of the Rogues, ma'am."

"I knew that you wouldn't be." Gracen smiled thinly before looking over to Passer and sliding a flimsy across the desk. "Captain, your orders."

Morgan took the device, thumbing it on with his biometrics. A quick read-through of the summary was all he needed before he looked up sharply. "Ma'am?"

"You read it correctly, Captain. There's a list of stars in there," she said seriously. "Stars the James Webb had reported anomalies about. We had passed them off as mistakes, natural phenomena, and so forth . . . but given what we've learned about the enemy and their abilities, we can't afford to do that anymore."

"No, ma'am," he said, reading further.

His orders were clear enough; no questions there.

He was to take the *Auto* out and examine each of the suspect stars, getting as close as he dared, and return with any intelligence he could gather on those celestial bodies that may harbor the enemy that had invaded Earth. They all knew that the Drasin were still out there, but no one had seen a hint of them in the last year since the remaining invaders had been wiped out of the immediate solar system.

Even their one known stellar base was now empty, with only the solar collectors remaining in the swarm orbit of the star they'd once claimed as their own.

That, of course, led to the question of where the hell did the Drasin go? A question every military and political leader on Earth . . . and in the Priminae colonies . . . wanted answered yesterday. It was one hell of an important assignment, and he had to wonder why they were sending the *Auto* and not the considerably more powerful *Odysseus*.

Thankfully, that was one question he didn't have to wonder about too long.

"Ma'am . . ." He glanced up. "Why the *Auto*?"

Gracen sighed, and he noticed Weston shift out of the corner of his eye, which made him all the more curious.

"Eric?" Gracen gestured.

Weston nodded, speaking after a moment. "One thing we worked out quickly in the last battle is that the Priminae power cores have a potentially fatal flaw. Yes, they provide exponentially more power for weapons, gravity, and various other uses . . . but they also warp space-time, and are fueled by planetary masses."

Passer nodded. He knew that much. The Priminae-built ships could literally run on almost anything. They simply dumped whatever mass they could find into the singularity core and functioned on the Hawking radiation produced by the natural "evaporation" of the mass within the singularity. That meant that a single Priminae vessel actually had as much power on tap as the entire planetary society of Earth, and probably a bit more besides.

"Since they use planetary masses as fuel, they're also easily detectable by gravity detection instruments," Weston said with a sigh. "And, much like the old nuclear reactors on blue-water navy ships, you can't turn off a core if you want to sneak around."

Morgan suddenly understood exactly why the admittedly under-powered and arguably obsolete Rogue Class of ships had never been canceled. They ran on a more volatile matter/antimatter reactor, far less powerful, but they certainly wouldn't have anywhere *near* the gravity footprint.

"I see. I'm surprised this wasn't in my original brief," he said, curious.

"We want this information classified," Gracen said, "which is one reason we're going to intentionally limit your interactions with the Priminae."

"I thought they were allies, ma'am."

"They are, and good ones," she said. "However, we know that the mysterious group that dropped the hammer on them with the Drasin use ships that match Priminae specifications in almost every way. We don't know where they got those specs, Captain, and until we do . . . Earth is holding a few cards close to the vest."

"Yes, ma'am."

"Once you've cleared the *Auto* for service, we want you to start inspecting the suspect stars," she said. "Be thorough, be sure, but don't get caught. You won't have much backup out there."

"Will we have any?"

"That's where I come in." Eric Weston spoke up. "The *Odysseus* will be on deep space assignment as well."

"They'll be your contact in case of emergencies," Gracen confirmed. "The *Odysseus* has the power to mount a full-scale FTL transceiver array."

Passer whistled softly, recognizing just how much power was involved in that. More than the abstract, that told him just how much power the Heroic Class of ships really had on tap. FTL arrays were rarely built, simply because the power requirements even on Earth itself tended to be prohibitive.

"The crew of the *Odysseus* will stand ready to respond as quickly as we can," Weston said, "but remember, space is a big place."

Morgan nodded, knowing the truth of that.

"We'll do our best not to have to call," he said, trying to sound as confident as he could.

"Good," Gracen said. "I won't tell you to stay out of Priminae space, but I will ask you not to spend too much time there."

"Understood, ma'am."

"While I know you have your full complement of crew on board already, I've also sent a few specialists to fill out the less common situations you might find."

Eric snorted, almost but not quite laughing out loud, getting a dirty look from the admiral in the process. Morgan gave him an odd look, wanting to ask what was going on, but not sure he wanted to know.

"You have my condolences, Captain," Eric said. "I've seen some of the names on the list."

"They are the best at what they do," Gracen said firmly.

"Oh, no doubt there," Eric agreed. "It's just that some of what they do is drive their associates nuts."

"Wonderful," Morgan sighed, having had to deal with people like that in the past.

Eccentric genius was always a nuisance to deal with on any Navy ship, but the few times he'd been forced to house such a person on one of his commands, he'd been especially aggravated. Submarines, and starships, were exponentially more difficult to work in than an open-air vessel. Being crammed in with someone who actively rode on your nerves was orders of magnitudes worse, but it was something you had to deal with on occasion.

At least the Autolycus *is larger and roomier than any submarine I ever commanded,* the captain supposed. *That's something.*

"I'll deal with it," Morgan said, shaking his head. "What are the odds we'll be walking into another hive like what the *Odyssey* located?"

"Unknown, but you'll have every instrument scan the *Odyssey* took of that thing to compare from as far out as possible," Gracen said. "Whatever you do, do *not* go sailing through it if you do find one."

"She's not kidding," Eric offered. "They'll pick you up on gravity scanners, no matter how stealthed you are."

Morgan raised an eyebrow at that.

In order to pick up a ship the size of the *Auto* on gravity scans, they'd have to have a scanning array the size of . . . He closed his eyes, wincing. Right. A scanning array the size of a solar system.

"He got it faster than I did," Eric chuckled ruefully.

"Thanks for the heads-up," Morgan sighed. "I probably wouldn't have gotten it in the field."

"Trust me, once they start tracking you when you *know* they can't see you . . . you figure it out in a hurry," Eric said dryly. "There's more in the unredacted reports. You'll have them waiting for you on the *Auto*."

Morgan just nodded, electing not to add anything more to that. "Is there anything else, Admiral?"

"No, Captain. I just wanted to introduce you two and give you your orders. You're dismissed, unless you have more questions."

Morgan shook his head. "Not at the moment, Admiral."

He stood up, saluting the admiral, and then offering his hand to Weston to shake. Eric took it quickly, and smiled.

"Take care out in the black," he said. "There are real monsters there."

"I know, Captain," Morgan said. "I think we all know, now."

"That we do," Eric nodded as Morgan stepped back.

"Captain Weston," Admiral Gracen said, "we have a little more to discuss concerning your assignment. Captain Passer . . . good luck and Godspeed."

"Thank you, ma'am," Morgan said, saluting again before stepping out of the office and heading down the hall.

▶▶▶

▶ With his orders in hand, Morgan felt a certain lightness in his step that had nothing to do with the artificial gravity of the station. He'd expected to be detailed to outer solar system patrol, basically just swooping around and watching for another Drasin incursion. Important work, to be sure, but deathly dull.

A proactive mission was an almost literal godsend, in his opinion. Sure, he wasn't supposed to drop by any of the inhabited worlds they knew of, but he could get past that disappointment.

The *Autolycus* was built for deep space; he and his crew had signed up for the same.

He rounded a corner on his way back and caught a glimpse of his ship through one of the observation ports. Morgan couldn't help but stop to admire the clean cut of the destroyer.

Unlike the old Odyssey Class, the Rogue Class had no slop in its design. No rotating drums, no protruding spires or exposed ports. The *Autolycus* looked like it had been designed by one of the skunk works crews of the twentieth century, with angled armor plate and everything recessed and sealed tightly away. Her radar cross section would be small, but it was really all about the visible and near-visible spectrum. The *Auto* could hide three klicks off the bow of any ship in the galaxy and not be spotted. Her chameleon plates and slim profile would see to that, as long as the crew didn't get clumsy and eclipse something noticeable.

More than that, however, the design added to her defensive capacity, since the plates would serve to reflect laser attacks off at glancing angles, improving the life span of the expensive material that protected the ship.

The smaller rear tower housed the observation deck and the bridge, but it too was designed to retract into the angled armor of the ship for when the black sea got a little rough.

Morgan continued past the port, heading for the lock connection to his ship with a spring in his step that he felt the need to enjoy for one last bit before boarding.

One downside of the Rogue Class was glaring, unfortunately.

Even with the added power of the new matter/antimatter reactor, there just wasn't enough spare power to run a gravity generator. That, coupled with the lack of rotating drums, mostly because of the smaller size of the ship, meant that you got to spend the entire cruise in microgravity. Fun at first, to be sure, but it didn't take that long to ride on everyone's nerves.

A Marine was waiting at the airlock and saluted as soon as Morgan came into sight.

"Sir."

"Inform the officer of the watch that I'm back," Morgan said, returning the salute as he passed.

"Yes, sir."

As soon as he passed the red tape on the floor and stepped into the transit tube, Morgan felt gravity fade. He kicked off the deck and directed his fall into his ship with a few nudges on the tube and a couple of overhand pulls. The traverse took a couple of minutes, both because of the length of the tube and because getting a clean glide was hard, and he had to keep from bouncing off the sides.

On the other end, Morgan pulled himself into the clear and floated into the receiving deck of the *Autolycus* moving more gracefully than he had in the tube.

"Welcome back, Skipper."

"Thank you, Chief," he said, noting the officer of the watch approaching from down the hall. "Lieutenant."

"Sir . . ." Lieutenant Burke didn't salute. That was one tradition they did away with in microgravity for a host of reasons. Instead he just slid into the room and cleared the doorway. "I was informed you were coming across."

"I am aware. Permission to come aboard?"

"Granted, Skipper," Burke said with a grin. "Do we have our orders, sir?"

"We do, Lieutenant. I'll brief everyone later," Morgan said, permitting himself a satisfied and, if he were pressed to admit it, more than slightly smug smile. "I think it's safe to say they won't disappoint."

"Outstanding, sir."

Morgan slid past the lieutenant and grabbed a handle in the main corridor, thumbing the biometric switch and speaking a command. "Main bridge."

The handle slowly accelerated off, pulling him through the main drag of the ship a fair bit quicker than he could have moved on his own. The path to the bridge was fairly straight, turning only one sharp corner before he was brought up to the maximum speed of the device.

Other crew members were sweeping past in the other direction, saluting sloppily as they passed. It wasn't a sign of low discipline; it was just an adaptation to how much trouble protocol could be in microgravity or the cramped confines of a ship like the *Auto* . . . let alone both. Saluting was in fact no longer officially required. He'd have a word with his officers and get them to remind the crew of the new protocol later, but it would take time.

The handle vibrated as a reverse acceleration was put on it and he swung forward, his feet moving out ahead of him as he held on. The entrance to the bridge was a large, heavy airlock that was currently wide open. One meter beyond that was a wall that served mostly to keep people from flying into the bridge from the corridor. He landed on the wall, absorbing what was left of his inertia with his legs, and flipped around it to enter the command deck proper.

"Captain on the bridge!"

"As you were," Morgan said, dropping into the center chair and casually looping the seat restraints over his shoulders, but not bothering to do them up.

The tower of the *Autolycus* was extended at the moment, so Morgan and the bridge crew were treated to a panoramic view of local space, including the station they were docked with and the Earth beyond. It was a spectacular view, but he had other things on his mind.

"Did the meeting with the admiral go well?"

Morgan nodded absently as he put his codes into the computer and brought up his orders and the intelligence download. Then he looked up to respond.

"Yes, very well, Commander," he said, deep satisfaction in his voice.

Commander Daiyu Li was his first officer, and despite his original concerns about having Block officers on board, he'd come to respect the striking Chinese woman during the trials. She was even more severe than he was when it came to discipline, but thankfully she understood that what worked outside the hull of the *Autolycus* wasn't necessarily a good idea within.

She was assigned as part of the science team in addition to being the *Auto*'s first officer, and was one of perhaps eight people on the *Auto* who truly understood the space-warp drive that the new class of ship used.

"I presume you received our orders, then?" Daiyu asked.

"I did," he answered, tapping a key to bring the orders up before he swept them from his screen and over to hers with a gesture. "Have a look."

Daiyu was silent as she read, so he took the time to check the *Odyssey*'s brief on the Dyson Construct they'd located some years before.

A Dyson Construct had been, up until then at least, a theoretical megastructure that could be built around a star to capture the energy released by it. In theory, the designs of such things varied from the ringworld concept all the way to a Dyson Shell, which was largely considered fundamentally impossible without access to supertechnologies that would likely render the need for such a construct obsolete.

The Drasin hadn't built anything quite so insane, though it was close in his mind.

The Dyson Cloud discovered by the *Odyssey* had been a two-tier, counter-orbiting swarm of satellite collectors that captured approximately ninety-eight percent of the energy emitted from the Sun. What the Drasin were *doing* with all that power was something no one had quite worked out, but the best hypothesis he was seeing in the report was that they were using some form of energy-to-matter conversion system to help produce more of themselves.

Unfortunately there was no causal data to make that connection, so it remained a guess rather than a real, solid theory.

"Interesting," Daiyu said from beside him. "Very interesting."

"Isn't it, now?" Morgan ceded. "I expected system defense patrols at best."

"As did I. Even the *Odysseus* hasn't been cleared for maneuvers this deep," she said.

Morgan nodded. "I expect that command wants to keep Weston and his crew close to the Priminae for now. They're basically seen as heroes there, so while Earth's rebuilding, it's key to get as much help as we can. And I'd bet that the ambassador loves to trot them out whenever possible."

She nodded, her face closing up a little.

Morgan didn't comment on it, knowing that there was little to be won there. Captain Weston was a polarizing figure, particularly among the Block officers who had fought in the war. There were many who had an axe to grind with the poster boy for the Confederate cause, and some had a personal stake in it.

He thought that Daiyu was one of the latter group, but Passer hadn't found out what had happened . . . yet. Her file was redacted even for his security clearance, which was an annoyance but not entirely surprising, since she had been one of the military officers attached to the Confederation's FTL program. It wasn't like they openly listed the resumes of the people who worked on the transition program, after all.

"Issue the order for the morning shift," he said. "Leave is recalled. We have our orders. We'll depart from Earth space tomorrow evening, third shift."

"Aye, sir," Daiyu acknowledged. "They were all placed on short notice when they left."

"Good. I want to get under way as soon as possible."

Neither of them had to say what he was thinking: The sooner they were clear of Sol space, the less likely they'd have their orders rescinded. Oh, it wasn't likely, but both Morgan and Daiyu wanted out into the black far too much to risk even a slight chance of that happening.

"Aye aye," she told him, with a hint of hesitance at using the Western military form.

Daiyu unbuckled from the acceleration couch and drifted free, grabbing an overhead grip as she pulled herself across to the far board to speak with the officer of the watch. Morgan just settled in and began reading the information packet that had come with his orders.

It became very clear in very short order that the *Odyssey*, to his mind, had been insanely lucky. Unlucky too, of course, all things considered, but just the fact of stumbling through an alien Dyson Construct like the proverbial drunken sailor and living to tell the tale almost destroyed his belief in statistical calculations.

Dyson Constructs were incredibly unlikely to begin with, for the simple reason that by the time a culture had the capacity to build one, it probably had no use for one. The sheer level of technical skill required to build even the most basic of constructs was so far beyond Earth science, or even Priminae science, that to Morgan's mind any species that could build one should have swatted the *Odyssey* like a bug.

That they didn't hinted deeply at unanswered questions concerning both the Drasin and the mysterious people holding their leash. There was a distinct personality separation there, perhaps more than one, and Morgan suspected that identifying the reason for that might be vital to Earth's ongoing survival in a newly hostile galaxy.

▶ ▶ ▶

▶ Commander Daiyu rode the rails down the spine of the *Autolycus*, heading for the engineering deck. Engineering was located amidships on the Rogue Class vessels, buried as deep as possible to protect it from attack or accident. One of the design flaws in ships like the *Wei Feng* was that engineering had been too exposed. Enemy lasers had opened large sections of it to space and made repairs and damage control that much more difficult.

The rail handle slowed, causing her feet to swing forward as she prepared to land on the "bump wall" that kept people from flying right into engineering with what she was sure would be both hilarious and disastrous results. She landed, absorbing the impact easily, and flipped around the barrier into engineering.

The engineering deck was at once the largest and most cramped space on the ship. Daiyu had no intention of delving any deeper into the deck than she had to. It wasn't her domain, and frankly she was terrified of the things housed within it.

"Commander."

Daiyu floated over to the speaker, nodding politely as she caught a hand grip and brought herself to a stop nearby, orienting herself so she could look him in the eye on the same level.

"Chief," she said to the stocky engineer. "The captain wants the ship ready to depart by tomorrow, third watch."

Chief Xiang Feng nodded. "Understood. I will inform my counterpart. We will be ready."

Daiyu nodded, knowing that he was referring to Chief Doohan, the Canadian engineer in charge of the transition section as well as the ship's main reactor. Xiang was one of the foremost experts in the Block's adaptation of the Alcubierre equations that gave the *Auto* her reactionless space drive, but Doohan was one of the Confederation's best technical engineers and specialists in transition technology as well as antimatter generation.

The *Auto* was very much a sum of contrasting parts. Many of the best from two very disparate cultures had been brought together to accomplish something worthy. Daiyu intended to see that they succeeded.

"Very good, Chief," she said.

"That means we have our orders, of course?" Xiang asked.

Daiyu nodded. "Yes. The captain will be making an announcement shortly, but I think you will not be disappointed."

Xiang smiled. "Deep black then, I hope?"

"The captain will say," she told him sternly, and then rolled her eyes with a hint of a smile.

"Of course, I will await the announcement eagerly." Xiang smiled right back, not bothering to hide it in the slightest.

There would be a few on the *Auto* who wouldn't be excited and enthusiastic about the orders, she supposed. No one had signed up to get system patrol duty, though after the invasion there was practically no one who would complain about that either. Still, as necessary as patrol missions were, the only reason to sign up for the Black Navy was to get a chance at the deep black.

▶▶▶

▶Captain Passer settled in some time later, forcing himself to relax in preparation for sleep. He wasn't normally what one might call high-strung and, while he was certainly not lazy by any means, there were few who would consider the word "energetic" to describe him either. However, this one time he would admit to having a great deal of trouble calming himself.

He felt as he had on his first deep sea assignment, something that had passed a good many years before, and again on his first blue-water command. There was a distinct anticipation of the unknown future unfolding before him.

Passer twisted up his lip as he settled into the narrow "bunk" in his nearly equally narrow cabin. The *Auto* didn't have all the frills of the *Odyssey* or the *Enterprise*, to say nothing of the ostentatious luxury of the *Odysseus* and other Heroics. It felt right to him, as someone who'd come up in the Pacific Submarine Fleet, however. Luxury was for shore leave, not for duty.

Sleeping in microgravity was an acquired taste he'd learned, but once you were used to it, you slept better and awoke more refreshed than you could imagine. Of course, he'd be paying for that later, with bone-density treatments and an extremely heavy exercise regimen. For the time being, however, Morgan settled in and lay out as if he were on a real bed. For some reason it felt better to align himself with the ship the same as he would if there were gravity.

With determination bordering on herculean, the irony of that thought amusing him as he drifted off, Morgan Passer closed his eyes and slept.

CHAPTER 2

▶Captain Passer strapped into the command station, paying only partial attention to the buzz of work going on around him on the bridge. Behind the people and the equipment, the curve of the Earth was visible beyond the hard lines of Unity Station and the gleaming sparkles of the weather control network that was being put into place.

One unfortunate side effect of the invasion was the massive alteration of the world's weather patterns due to dust, contaminants, and a whole host of other factors. The new mirror satellite network would, in theory, allow the sun's energy to be focused on areas that needed it and withheld from those that didn't.

He wasn't sure if the network was a good idea, but the mini–Ice Age was wreaking havoc in northern latitudes, while the remnants of the previous heat wave of the past century had mixed with some of the nastier contaminants to throw superstorms at the most populated areas remaining on the planet. He supposed something had to be done. Hopefully any mistakes made with the new system would be small enough to be corrected.

It wasn't his concern. For the moment, he had his own duties to attend to.

He carefully checked the systems reports from his heads of stations, noting that everything was nicely listed in the green. That meant no nasty surprises, which was very much a good thing. If the *Auto* were seriously delayed now, they might see their assignment given to another ship. That done, Morgan reached up and pulled the ship phone down from the ceiling.

Unlike the *Odyssey* and the *Odysseus*, as well as other ships with simulated or actual gravity, the *Auto* didn't have the luxury of a bunch of wireless knickknacks, items that could get forgotten to float around and bean someone in the head. The ship phone was connected to the *Auto* by a decidedly old-fashioned-looking curly cable, though there was no copper inside it, of course. The optical audio cable would keep the phone tethered and, as a nice bonus, couldn't be jammed by stray radiation.

"All hands, all hands, this is the captain," Morgan announced into the microphone, his voice going ship-wide.

"I'm sure most of you have heard some scuttlebutt or other about the nature of our orders, but to avoid you actually believing any of it, here they are," he said with a crooked smile. "The captain and crew of the *Autolycus* have been ordered to proceed to target stars as selected by astronomers directing the James Webb Space Telescope. We are directed to investigate the targets to ensure that the Drasin have not occupied said systems."

He took a moment, letting that sink in. "There are more details, but that's it in a nutshell. After what the *Odyssey* found, and the results of their encounter, we're not letting those bastards set up shop in our neighborhood again. We have *not* been directed to engage in combat. That is not our mission. We will hunt them down, however, and tag them before calling in the cavalry."

The crew members on the bridge were silent, all eyes on him, and Morgan could feel much the same from the rest of the ship, though of course he couldn't see them.

"We didn't ask for a war. Hell, I'm not even certain that those things even understand what war is . . . But if not," he said grimly, "we're going to damn well teach them the concept. That is all. Passer out."

He shut off the comm and slung the phone back to its cradle and locked it in.

"Nice speech."

"Too much?" Morgan asked with a hint of a grin as Daiyu finished something at her station.

She shrugged. "I just wonder if you ever gave a similar one about us."

"More than once," he told her honestly.

She nodded. "Good."

Morgan glanced in her direction, amused. "Good?"

"That means you took us seriously."

Morgan chuckled. "Let's get this show on the road."

"Yes, Captain," she answered, turning to the helm station. "Helm. Bring thrusters to one-third power, heading niner niner eight one zero, negative three degrees."

"Aye, ma'am." The young lieutenant at the helm nodded, punching in the numbers. "Thrusters warming up, new heading entered. We are standby to engage."

"Engage," Morgan ordered. "Take us out, one-third thrust *only*. Do *not* gravitate."

"Aye aye, Captain. Ahead one-third, thrust only. No gravitation."

The *Autolycus* didn't rumble so much as hum as her thrusters began firing, slowly pulling the ship away from Unity Station. As close as they were to the space station, there was no way they could risk using their Alcubierre drive. There was too much chance of throwing the station out of orbit. Even a minor orbital correction would be expensive for something the size of Unity.

So they pulled out of Earth's orbit like the proverbial snail, clawing up out of the well into the more open areas of cislunar space. After twenty minutes they were finally clear of obstructions, though it would have taken another hour if the old satellite network had still been in place, but most of those had been wiped out in the initial hours of the invasion.

"Message from Unity, Captain. We are cleared to use star drive."

"Roger that and thank them for me, Commander," Morgan said. "Continue on course, bring star drive to one-quarter acceleration, and hold."

"Aye, Captain. One-quarter and holding in five . . . four . . ."

He tuned out the countdown, his ears and other senses listening for the distant whine of the reactor coming to power. The matter/antimatter reactor was one of the most terrifying pieces of technology he had ever seen, and Morgan had been on a few transition jumps in his training. It was the only way to generate significant power levels, however, without resorting to alien technology that humans were still gnawing on.

The *Autolycus* had ten times the available power that the original *Odyssey* had, but still only a fraction of what was available to the new Heroics. Still, there was a trade-off for that power, as Captain Weston had realized very quickly in the last days of the invasion.

The gravity core of the Heroic Class was powerful, it was true, but its mass was measured in *planetary* multiples. Any half-blind fool with a crude gravity detection system could pick up a Heroic from a hundred AU out.

The *Autolycus*, on the other hand, only massed about as much as a small asteroid. Even if you were looking for it, the *Auto* would be almost impossible to track until you were directly on top of it. That was the way Morgan preferred his ship anyway, so while he might occasionally envy the gravity and luxury of a Heroic, the Rogue was where he belonged.

"Luna coming up, starboard side, Captain."

Morgan looked up and to the right, out the large armored glass ports that surrounded the bridge. The Moon was coming up fast, actually, and closer than one normally might expect. He checked the course the commander had put in and noted with some interest that she had elected to do a close flyby of the Moon's surface.

He didn't have a specific issue with that, honestly, but he was a little curious.

"Why so close?" he asked her, his head cocking slightly as he glanced over.

Daiyu shrugged. "I grew up wanting to see the Moon as it was seen by the early astronauts. This was a chance, and the course happens to save us fifteen percent energy over a comparable slower course."

Morgan rechecked the numbers and smiled slightly, noting that her course was using the Moon's gravity to sling them out on their escape course from Sol's gravity well. It was a neat bit of flying, actually, though perhaps not strictly necessary with the new star drive. With the older class of starship, it would have saved them several hundred tons of propellant at least.

"It's always good to practice proper ship handling," Morgan allowed, nodding to her. "Why not enjoy the view as we pass?"

"Thank you, Captain." Daiyu unstrapped from the station and drifted up and over to the large window ports so she could watch.

The *Autolycus* skimmed the surface of the Moon, coming within a few dozen kilometers and likely rattling the lunar regolith. Morgan imagined that, as close as they were flying, their air itself would rumble with the ship's passing . . . were there any air. Gravity waves didn't require atmosphere to propagate, however, so the surface was undoubtedly getting a shaking even in the silence of space.

They swept out over the lunar horizon and began climbing back into deep space, now slung outward on their way. The Moon and the Earth were in their rearview now, both visible and rapidly receding through the window ports behind them. Ahead was nothing but the black.

"Make for the heliopause, Lieutenant," Morgan ordered. "All ahead full."

"Aye aye, Skipper. All ahead full."

▶▶▶

▶Admiral Gracen stood in the center of Unity's observation dome, watching the receding light that identified the location of the *Autolycus* as the sleek ship vanished into the black. She wondered if the captain, or anyone on his crew, really understood the vital nature of their mission.

She doubted it.

It was impossible to stress sufficiently just how large a threat the Dyson Constructs of the Drasin were. She'd fought hard to get a ship assigned to hunting down any and all possible locations of the nests, and it had been a hard fight.

Too many were now convinced that with the Heroics and the new alliance with the Priminae, the Drasin could be fought ship to ship. The transition cannons were an impossible edge to beat; many in power were utterly convinced of that. Eric Weston had shut them all up with one demonstration. Using the drive of a Heroic Class ship—the *Odysseus*, naturally—he was able to disrupt tachyon reintegration, effectively "killing" inbound training warheads before they could re-form. The Drasin and the unknown aliens used the same basic drive technology as the Heroic ship, and when Eric pointed out that the same trick would work against a transition drive, well, he'd literally turned the admiral's blood cold. It was only a matter of time in her mind before the Earth's trump card was, itself, trumped.

The only defense was an offense.

Go out, find the things where they were hiding, and take the war to them *there*. Don't let them come back to Earth. Once was one time too many and one time more than anyone had a right to survive.

"Godspeed," Gracen said to the darkness above her and the receding point of light.

So much was riding on every single thing they did now. The invasion had brought the Earth in its entirety to a precipice upon which they were all now perched. One wrong move and they'd slip into the chasm below, the human race vanishing into the black without even a whimper to mark their passage.

Possibly just as bad would be to shift back, away from the precipice, and into their old habits. Fighting among themselves, ignoring the bounty of the universe around them, acting like immature children who didn't want to share whatever meager treasures they'd been able to scratch up.

No, Gracen had seen the universe, the glory and the horror, and she was in accord with Eric Weston on one thing.

They had to push off the precipice, into the unknown, and learn to damn well fly.

If we can't, I fear that our victory over the Drasin will be our last hurrah as a species.

▶▶▶

▶ Morgan was in the ship's gym as the *Autolycus* passed the orbit of Mars.

He didn't want to see what was left of the formerly red planet. It was a monument to what could have happened to the Earth if they'd been just a little less lucky. A permanent viewing station now watched the writhing mass of drones as they cooled in space, breaking up the planet and forming a new asteroid field in its place.

The Drasin had used their standard invasion tactic on Mars. They'd landed a few drones and basically let them start eating and reproducing. Unlike with Earth, there wasn't much in the way of defenders stationed anywhere near Mars, and those few that had tried . . . well, they were eliminated quickly. Before the invasion on Earth had even begun in earnest, Mars was effectively gone.

The loss of Mars actually put the situation into perspective for most people in a way that the invasion itself hadn't. Anytime someone had the temerity to suggest that it was over, all you had to do was put up an image of what was left of the red planet.

It still looked like a planet, from a distance. When you closed in, however, you could see that the color was all wrong. Closer still, and you could make out the dreaded arachnid shape of the Drasin and . . . if you watched long enough, you would see one of them move.

That usually chilled viewers enough that no matter how many people were in the room at the time, silence reigned.

Everyone who watched came away with just one sure thing in their minds.

We can't let that happen to the Earth.

Still, Morgan didn't need that reminder. He elected to spend some time in the gym, using the rotational treadmill to forestall bone loss. He didn't intend to be grounded in six months because of permanent damage to his skeleton. He had too much work to do for that.

Jogging at two times gravity was a hard workout, and actually a little on the risky side of what was permitted by regulations, but the alternative wasn't an option. Every member of the *Auto*'s crew had to meet scheduled training sessions, monitored by the ship's doc.

Otherwise they'd be transferred out the next time they got home or met an Earth or even a Priminae ship.

Even the captain.

As he jogged, he noticed Chief Doohan drift into sight nearby, just far enough away that he wasn't going to accidentally get in the way of a jogger.

"Yes, Chief?" Morgan asked, not breaking step.

"Captain," the chief said, "I understand you wanted a sitrep on engineering."

"I do. How is it working out?"

The chief didn't answer right away, knowing that if the captain were asking about anything technical, this would be an official meeting. No, he knew what the captain wanted to know. He just didn't want to talk about it.

"Chief Xiang is . . . competent."

Morgan snorted. "Xiang Feng is the leading technical expert on the star drive, Chief. You'll have to do better than that."

"He runs a tight ship, Captain. The man knows his craft." Doohan scowled. "Is that what you wanted?"

Morgan poured on a little speed, matching the turn of the wheel, and jumped up. He extended his hand, letting the chief pull him clear and back out into the microgravity environment. Grabbing a towel, Morgan wiped himself down as he considered what he was going to say.

"Chief, I know you have issues with the Block," Morgan said, holding up his hand. "Hell, they're even valid issues. When I brought you on board, you told me you could handle it. Were you wrong about that?"

Morgan could tell that, in a gravity environment, the chief would be at attention. Here, the best he could do was lift his chin and try to look stiff. It just looked awkward, but Morgan didn't think this was the time to point that out.

"No, sir."

"Then give me a sitrep on engineering," Morgan ordered, no longer any give in his voice, tone, or body language.

"Aye, Skipper. Engineering is running like a Swiss watch. All sections are green, and we're good to go."

"Excellent." Morgan clapped him on the back. "Keep it that way."

"Aye aye, Skipper."

Morgan watched the chief kick off, drifting out of the gym as he finished drying off, and wondered again whether he had chosen the right path . . . whether anyone had chosen the right path. The new mixed Navy was probably necessary, but damn, it was going to pinch for a while.

Still, there was no question, the Chinese were masters of both counter-mass, or CM, technology and space-warp drives. Morgan needed Xiang's expertise and the skill of those crew members every bit as much as he needed Doohan's reactor expertise and knowledge of the transition drive. That left it up to him to make sure everything worked and nobody slacked off, for any reason.

Morgan tossed his towel in the closest bag, tightening the loop around it to keep the contents inside, and headed out from the gym. He had to clean up and maybe catch some sleep before the *Auto* hit the heliopause.

He wasn't going to miss that, no way, no how.

CHAPTER 3

▶ Reaching the heliopause of the Sol System took only a fraction of the time it would have once taken. The new star drive provided far more effective and efficient propulsion than any of the old propellant methods. The *Autolycus* slid smoothly past the official line delimiting the gravity well of Sol and into the Oort cloud beyond.

Of course, that was all more of a technical limit than a real line in space. The heliopause was merely the point where solar winds were no longer strong enough to push out farther into space. The line had been chosen as an arbitrarily safe distance from the main gravity sources of the system for ships to be able to implement the transition drive.

Morgan pulled down the phone once more. "All hands, all hands. We are about to engage transition drive. I say again, we are about to engage transition drive."

The lights shifted, taking on a red tint as his message went out. Transition wasn't something anyone took for granted, especially not after experiencing it even once, but it was just too useful to even consider doing away with.

"Stand down the star drive," Morgan ordered. "Reroute power to tachyon transition drive."

"Aye, sir, standing down the star drive . . ."

The engineering station instantly changed as the screens went red and the waveform they showed began to collapse. The *Autolycus* was soon flying forward on inertia alone rather than surfing the standing wave they'd carved into space-time.

"Establish coordinate lock of all material in our immediate path," Morgan ordered. "Single ping only."

"Aye, Captain. Single ping."

The bridge echoed with a sound, really just a computer being helpful, since the sensor ping was composed of exotic tachyon particles and certainly not sound waves. In an instant the particles jumped out and a very few of them jumped right back, giving the *Autolycus* an idea of what lay ahead of them as they sailed through the Oort cloud toward truly deep space.

"Course clear, Captain."

Morgan nodded, not that he'd expected it to be anything else. The area might be called the Oort cloud, but it was better than ninety-nine point nine nine nine percent empty space. That last fraction of a percent, however, included a few planetoids and millions of icebergs the size of Nebraska, so it was better to check.

He keyed open the phone again. "All hands, all hands, stand by for transition drive engagement. I say again, stand by for transition drive engagement. All priority one procedures *must* be followed. There are no exceptions."

He returned the phone to its location and drew up an oxygen mask from beside his seat, looping it easily over his head but not over his face just yet.

"I want a section-by-section confirmation that all hands are ready," Morgan ordered, no smile or hint of anything other than stern discipline in his tone.

"Aye, sir," Ensign Miller replied automatically while standing watch at the intraship dispatch board. "Sections are starting to go green now."

"Good. Status on the transition reactor?"

"Online, powering up."

The checklist was slowly being ticked off, and Morgan was bound and determined to do this jump especially by the numbers. Transition effects were nasty enough in a gravity environment, but a tightly contained microgravity environment had numerous unique challenges that simply could *not* be ignored.

"All sections green, Skipper," Miller announced a moment later.

"Very good. Signal all stations, final countdown."

"Aye aye, Skipper. Countdown initiated," Lieutenant Mika said from the helm. "Coordinates for transition are good. Drive is charging. Transition in T minus . . . ten seconds."

The lights, still reddish in tint, now began to flash as an alarm sounded.

Morgan had nothing more to add. He just pulled the oxygen mask down in front of his face, sealing it over his nose and, more importantly, his mouth.

I hate this part.

▶▶▶

▶Space-time rippled ahead of the *Autolycus*, causing a wavering in the ship and the view of the stars beyond as the transition generators reached their peak and discharged through the drive. The ripple began to fold back over the sleek destroyer as its bow was suddenly rent apart. Particles tore free of the ship and spun out into space, eating away at the hull as the effect began to move back through the *Autolycus* with inevitable certainty.

Inside, those with experience looked away before the effect intersected with their decks and sections, trying not to be caught in that last interminable moment of transition while staring out into the deep black. Some things were simply not meant for the human mind.

A few were caught, of course, some out of naivete, some from bad chance, and a choice few because they were simply insane enough to enjoy the gut-wrenching terror of looking out upon a vacuum with nothing but their minds to shelter them from that certain death.

On the bridge, Morgan was one of the few who didn't look away, and possibly the only one who did so not because he was crazy enough to enjoy it, nor because he was stupid enough to be caught by accident, but simply because he didn't feel the captain should shy away from any damn thing he had ordered, be it good or bad.

Transition was certainly that. Good and bad.

The last moment of transition felt like it stretched out forever. The ship no longer existed around him, and he was just sitting there . . . frozen and immobile in the depths of space for all eternity.

Then it was over.

The *Autolycus* rushed back into existence, and with her his crew.

The sound of retching was the first thing Morgan heard even as he fought the urge himself, glad for the large oxygen mask over his face. Studies had shown that pure oxygen during and just after a transition lowered the incidence of motion sickness by a significantly large amount. More importantly, however, the flexible plastic of the mask served an absolutely vital function in those after moments.

Vomit control.

He didn't know about the *Odyssey* or other ships with the drive, but on the *Autolycus* there was no gravity of any sort. Vomit in microgravity was *not* a pleasant experience, and anything that kept it down was a good thing. The masks also served to keep the smell out of the air, which cut down on "sympathetic" upchucking as well.

"Status!" he growled, keeping the mask over his face and breathing deeply.

"Light-speed data is flowing in, Captain! We're compiling imagery now."

He could see that with his own eyes, and a lot more besides. Morgan focused his gaze out the large glass ports, looking about the local space around the ship. It was just like any other local space might be, he supposed, largely blank and incredibly boring.

There was a local star, however, ahead of them now rather than behind them as Sol had been, and he focused on that.

They'd transitioned to a small red dwarf star, not far from Earth as such things went, within thirty light-years. It had dimmed slightly over the past two decades, leaving it on the list of suspicious targets.

"Sitrep from the gravity feed!"

The *Auto* was equipped with gravity sensors from stem to stern, designed to calculate the minute deviations in the local gravity well by comparing the overall acceleration from one end of the ship to the other. By analyzing the differences in acceleration at the bow compared to the stern, they could determine the tidal effect of the well they were sitting in and compare it to what it should be based on known data points.

In theory, that information should let them detect any megastructures long before they could see them.

"Nominal, Skipper. Some spikes, but within the predicted deviation."

Morgan nodded, happy with that. That meant that they probably weren't looking at a Drasin superstation of any type.

"Launch drones," he ordered, taking another deep breath from the mask before putting it up.

"Aye aye, Skipper. Drones away."

They could see the launches from the top of the *Autolycus'* deck through the armored glass. The newly developed Hermes drones were launched via internal catapults, speeding away from the ship. The Hermes was an advanced remote instrument package mounted on a space frame that could handle multiple environments. It extended the *Auto*'s gravity trap instruments significantly by giving them a larger area to calculate tidal strength from, but also functioned as an augmenting array for a multitude of systems, from light to telemetrics.

"The star appears normal, Captain," Lieutenant Kamir, one of the ship's leading astrophysics specialists, said from his station. "No sign of any unusual effects."

"Any guess on what caused it to dim in the last decade or so?" Morgan asked, though he could hazard a guess himself.

"For now I'm thinking interstellar dust, but we'll have to measure Sol from here to confirm."

"Later," Morgan said. "After we have a better idea of what's in the immediate neighborhood."

"Yes, sir," Kamir answered, clearly pleased with the order.

Morgan understood that; it wasn't often—even in the new world they found themselves a part of—that you got a chance to study a new star up close. That would likely be changing, of course, but for the moment it was probably what Kamir signed up for more than anything else.

Unstrapping himself from the seat, Morgan drifted free and directed himself toward the forward window. The armored glass was better than ninety-nine percent clear in the visible spectrum, leaving him with a beautiful view of the local starscape. The red dwarf they'd come to see was barely different from any other star at the distance the *Auto* was sitting at, just an orange speck dead ahead of them. Morgan watched for a time, then turned and cast himself aft, gliding past the command station as he headed off the bridge.

"Commander, you have the con. Let me know if anything interesting shows up," he ordered. "Otherwise we're here for the next couple days while we survey and establish baselines."

"Aye, Captain," Daiyu said from her station. "I have the con."

Morgan slid out past the wall at the back of the bridge and grabbed a transit handle. He was pulled swiftly away.

▶▶▶

▶ The workings of a ship in space were actually quite familiar to a submarine captain like Morgan, aside from the microgravity, of course.

Morgan slowed as he arrived at one of the vertical tubes and pushed off the transit handle, dropping feet first down the tube.

"Watch out, coming through!"

The warning was just soon enough for Morgan to kick off one wall and press himself against the opposite wall of the tube as a deck chief came flying up.

The man recognized him on the way past, visibly paling and saluting quick and sloppy on the way by.

"Sorry, Skipper, didn't see you there."

"As you were," Morgan said unnecessarily. The man had already passed by the time he got the first word out.

Sub duty was, of necessity, one of the least formal—and, conversely, most regimented—of all the naval services. He wasn't going to crap on someone for being sloppy with the formalities while doing their job efficiently, but God help them if he caught them screwing up even slightly. Like on a submarine, there were just too many ways that a screwup on board the *Auto* could kill a lot of people, not just the screw-ee.

He stopped his descent three decks down, swinging out into a main thoroughfare. He grabbed another transit handle and continued his trip across the ship, coming to a stop beside the door to the main astrometrics lab. Morgan swung off the track and floated into the lab as cautiously as possible. He'd learned the hard way after the war that scientists weren't exactly the regimented or disciplined type.

Once he'd walked into a hydrosonic lab that had been retrofitted onto his old command and just turned around and walked right out. He had to order a few crewmen to go in later and disinfect the space. There was no other way he was going to go back in after what he'd seen. Given the personal nature of the scene, it wasn't something he wanted to walk in on again either.

This time things seemed mostly in order, thankfully. Sanitizing a lab in microgravity would be a real pain in the ass.

Morgan oriented himself for a moment, and then swung over to the main feed for the gravity array. He brought himself to a stop directly behind a pair of people who were poring over the intel as it came in and just listened.

"See that? I think it's the signature for a gas giant we haven't located yet."

"Yes, but we're seeing a tidal spur that suggests more than that."

"Maybe an asteroid field? Spread out enough to make detection difficult, dark enough that we can't see it on EM instruments?"

Morgan cleared his throat, startling both of them badly.

"Is there anything out of the ordinary I should know about?" he asked as they twisted around, their eyes wide.

"Uh . . . no, I mean yes. No. What was the question again?" the lady scientist stammered out.

"Is there anything out of the ordinary I should know about?" Morgan repeated himself.

"That depends on what you mean by out of the ordinary. Everything here is new data . . ."

"No, Captain." The woman cut off her assistant. "There is nothing here that comes close to matching the Drasin signatures we were briefed on."

Morgan nodded. He knew that. "What about anything else? Anything you can't explain, anything that seems out of place?"

"Well, there's a lot here that we can't identify from experience," she admitted, "but nothing that stands out as not fitting our expected theory."

Morgan considered that. "So everything fits with what you were expecting?"

"More or less," she agreed. "Certainly it's within expected deviations."

That, he supposed, was about as straightforward an answer as he could hope for.

"Thank you, Doctor . . . ?"

"Bligh," she answered. "Miranda Bligh."

"Doctor Bligh, then," Morgan said. "Thank you for your evaluation. We'll be in this system for another couple days at most. I suggest you make the most of it."

"We will," she answered. "Thank you, Captain."

"No need to thank me, I'm just following protocol. With nothing obvious to throw up any security alerts, we have to do a standard survey before moving on," he said. "Just make the most of the time, Doctor, we're on a tight schedule."

"Yes, sir."

Morgan looked over the raw feed from the instruments, a seemingly random series of numbers that he could only just barely understand. Everything counted on the feeds from the tidal detection instruments. The gravity feeds were the only lead they had on Drasin movements.

Other than, of course, planets randomly turning into asteroid belts, but we'd like to spot them before that happens if at all possible.

"As you were, then," he said, reaching up to grab a handhold.

"We will. Thank you, Captain."

This time Morgan didn't bother correcting her. It didn't really make much difference.

▶▶▶

▶ There were places on the *Autolycus* that felt wrong to Morgan. Too quiet.

His last command before transferring to the new Black Navy had been a nuclear boat, and there was always a low constant hum in the background, no matter what else was going on. The reactor didn't shut down, for obvious reasons, so even with all the sound-dampening technology and insulation possible, you still felt the reactor in your bones.

The reactor on the *Auto* was a different species altogether. The primary fuel had to be manufactured on board before the reactor could even be fired up. Most of the time the *Autolycus* ran on energy stored in high-efficiency capacitors that could power a decent-sized city for weeks. No one wanted to worry about the long-term storage of antimatter, least of all the people working and living on the ship.

What they could carry and store without too much worry, however, were the *components* of antimatter. The precursor materials were stable, compact, and thankfully extremely energy-dense. Supercooled potassium-40 could be stored easily, and all it took was the application of gamma quanta from their smaller cyclotron reactor to release antiprotons and positrons into the wild.

Combining them to form antihydrogen was the next step. Then the reactor mixed the antihydrogen stream with a normal hydrogen stream to produce energy.

It wasn't on the same level as a quantum singularity that measured its power levels in *planetary masses*, but it did the job and then some. The *Autolycus'* reactor was the epitome of Earthborn technology . . . and it was probably the last of its kind.

Like a lot of us, I suppose.

The invasion had changed a lot on Earth, aside from the obvious, of course. Certainly the death toll was monstrous, and the damage likely incalculable, but it was the intangible changes that Morgan felt most deeply.

He didn't have any family. His dad died before the war, his mother during . . . not in the fighting, just of old age. He'd never married, had no siblings. His disconnection from the world at large had made him an ideal candidate for certain types of naval duties, including the submarine fleet . . . but it had also kept him from captaining any of the boomers.

Captains with nuclear launch keys were all but required to have families at home, just to keep them on an even keel.

He'd done well in the attack fleet, however, commanding a hunter/killer sub through most of the war. He and his crew had racked up forty-nine kills by the time the fighting ended. Three of those were submersible carriers.

He still felt disconnected. Hell, more so than ever now.

Maybe that wasn't such a bad thing, though. Not out in the deep black.

For him it had always been more about the job than anything else. He didn't need reasons to do his job. Doing the job, and doing it to the best of his ability, was the reason.

Morgan checked the ship's clock and decided that he should turn in for the day. The next span of time would probably be nothing but grueling hours of boredom punctuated by relativistically long periods of sheer terror.

God, I hate the transition drive.

CHAPTER 4

▶ Morgan learned that as much as he thought he'd hated the drive before, he had to redefine the meaning of the word "hate" after each successive jump. Almost two weeks into their mission, and they'd cleared four stars from their lists.

Two had been obscured by the thick dust clouds that existed in interstellar space, one had captured a rogue planet (as best the crew could tell from its intensely tight orbit), and the last one had begun collapsing down well ahead of the predicted schedule for its type. The crew had spent a few extra days studying that one, at the request of the astrophysics and astrometrics departments, just so Morgan wouldn't have to put up with their complaints.

Scientists got really twitchy when they were staring a "revolutionary" event in the face and someone tried to tell them they couldn't study it.

Unfortunately for them, this wasn't a research cruise. Not this time out, at least.

As the relativistic effects of transition let go of him, Morgan carefully took a couple of deep breaths to clear his head and stave off the nausea. There was less gagging in the background now, he noted in the back of his mind.

Any thoughts on that were driven from his head an instant later when the *Autolycus* rumbled and shook like nothing he'd ever felt in space.

Morgan tore the mask from his face, his eyes focusing on the screens around him and then out through the armored glass to the deep black beyond.

"Report!" he ordered, still looking for the cause himself.

"We're reading multiple tidal pulls across our accelerometers, Skipper," Kamir answered instantly. "Light-speed data still streaming in!"

Morgan bit down on the urge to order a tachyon ping of the area, uncertain if he wanted to reveal their location any more than the transition effect would already have done.

"Sound general quarters," he ordered instead. "Take us to black hole stealth settings. Nothing gets out."

"Aye, Captain. General quarters!" Daiyu repeated.

The lights dimmed, shifting to red as the whole bridge began to vibrate and sink down into the ship. The view outside was obscured by the thickly armored metal sheath the bridge was designed to nestle down into during emergencies, but only for a moment as each of the windows lit up with tactical augmented views from the *Auto*'s cameras and remotes.

"Cam-plates have gone full stealth," Ensign Bonavista called from the tactical station, looking a little nervous as she fidgeted in her seat.

"Lock down all communications arrays," Daiyu ordered, going down the checklist. "I want every photon, every electron . . . *everything* accounted for. Nothing goes out!"

Morgan focused on the helm.

"Lieutenant Mika, bring us about thirty degrees to port, five degrees positive to the system plane," he ordered. "Ahead one-quarter, minimal gravitation."

"Aye, Skipper," Andrea Mika answered. "Thirty degrees port, up five. Charging the wave . . . ahead one-quarter. Feathering the throttle, Captain."

Morgan nodded tersely, settling as best he could in the straps that held him tightly to his station. He didn't know what was going on, but he'd done all he could for now.

The standing gravity wave that propelled the *Autolycus* would be detectable at a significant distance, but that could be minimized by building acceleration rather than just hammering it from a standing start. With skill, similar speed and acceleration could be reached with much smaller footprints.

All he had to do was hope that it was enough. The new course would put the *Auto* on a wide orbit of the system primary, hopefully looping up and around anything they might have been running into. Of course, all that was dependent on getting new intelligence from their scanners as quickly as possible.

"Stand by to deploy drones," he ordered. "I want them establishing a VLA around our location the second we have confirmation that we're not in imminent danger."

"Aye aye, Skipper. Drone stations are standing by."

As soon as they had cleared the space directly around them, a drone VLA, or very large array, would serve to expand their eyes in the skies by a factor of at least a thousand. However, there was no point in launching those rather fragile drones if there was something much more local to worry about.

"What do we have from astrometrics?" Morgan asked, his eyes on the short-range scanners that were showing everything clear.

"Still untangling these signals, Captain," Kamir answered. "Something has completely distorted local space-time. It's going to take hours to pull out all the individual signals from this mess."

"Great. What could do that?"

"Nothing we know of. Not even the Drasin megastructure, sir."

Morgan blinked. That was *not* what he wanted to hear.

"Local space?"

"Local space is clear, Skipper."

Morgan gritted his teeth, but nodded. "Launch the drones, deploy the VLA."

"Aye aye. VLA drones deploying."

Without a direct view of the ship's decks, Morgan and the rest of the bridge crew had to be satisfied with the augmented view projected over the windows. Red dots represented the drones as they launched away from the *Auto*, heading out from the ship to expand the resolution of their instrumentation.

"I think we've got the local primary isolated from our scans," Kamir said. "I need confirmation from astrometrics, but once I get it, we can start picking the whole system apart."

"Go to it," Morgan ordered.

With a snarled set of signals, the key was always to start with a known element, similar to working a puzzle by starting at the edges and corners. In this case, the local primary should be the largest and most stable local source of gravity, and that should give them a place to start.

"Damn it!"

Or not.

"What is it, Kamir?" Morgan asked.

"Negative match. We've got a gravity well out here larger than the known primary."

"Find it."

"Working on it, Skipper," Kamir said. "We don't have anything on our visible spectrum scanners. Switching to infrared. If there's a Dyson Construct out here, that'll show it up."

The augmented displays flickered, but nothing appeared at the target location.

"Scanning for gamma rays." Kamir cycled the system again, sounding confused.

Still nothing appeared.

The lieutenant continued to cycle through the spectrum, looking for any sign of an object where the gravity source should be, only to continue coming up empty.

"Look for Hawking radiation," Morgan ordered, a deep pit forming in his gut.

"Oh, God," Kamir croaked, switching the scans again. He sighed and slumped in place a moment later. "Negative for Hawking."

Well, at least we're not sitting on the edge of a black hole.

That would have sucked, literally and figuratively, given that they easily could have ventured far too close and been trapped for a hundred years or more before even knowing the danger. The relativistic effects of being so close to a gravity source that powerful were not to be toyed with.

"I don't understand it, Skipper," Kamir said. "There's nothing showing up on my instruments, but there *has* to be something out there. The tidal measurements can't be wrong."

"Captain," Daiyu interjected, her brow furrowed, "may I suggest we run a spectrum comparison across every frequency?"

Morgan looked confused. "Why?"

"Humor me."

He shrugged, nodding. "Alright, do it, Lieutenant."

"Aye aye . . . comparative scans running . . . wait, what?" He cocked his head, leaning as far forward as he could. "This doesn't make any sense."

"They are not aligned precisely, are they?" she asked.

"How did you know?" Kamir twisted to look at the commander, his eyes wide.

"Gravity lensing," she answered.

Kamir started swearing, colorfully and surprisingly imaginatively, causing Morgan to raise an eyebrow. Thankfully the young officer had the presence of mind to do it softly enough that his captain could pretend not to have heard him clearly.

"Lieutenant . . ." Morgan interrupted him. "Care to share with the rest of the class?"

Kamir winced, his dark skin flushing. "Sorry, Skipper. I just should have thought of that myself. I'll let the commander explain. I have work to do."

Morgan glanced over to Commander Daiyu, who shrugged casually.

"Gravity lensing is when light bends around a gravity source," she said.

"I get that. We use it for extreme long-range scans," he responded. "Just fly to the right point around a known gravity source, and you can scan very faint objects from some rather extreme distances. We're looking for other Drasin hotspots using the technique, as well as . . . other items of interest."

Which included the aliens that had been holding the Drasin's leash, though that was still classified over the commander's head the last time Morgan had checked.

"Correct," she acceded. "What you missed is that visible light will be deflected at a different rate than, say, gamma rays."

"So the scans wouldn't match. Nice." Morgan looked back to the screens. "So we have something out there that has literally cloaked itself using gravity?"

"So it would seem, Captain. So it would seem."

▶▶▶

▶ The *Autolycus* entered a long orbit around the very edge of the system, killing the warp drive and going ballistic as the ship finished deploying the VLA drones. The drones settled into matching orbits, staying equidistant from each other and the *Auto* as they began scanning and relaying data back to the ship.

A VLA combined the instrumentation of multiple scanning systems to mimic the resolution of a single, much larger instrument. On Earth the technique was used to scan the skies, originally by groups like SETI and now by every defense organization in existence as they looked for any signs of alien presence in the stars.

Being invaded had a way of changing a planet's priorities.

For the *Autolycus*, the array they could launch was a hundred times the size of anything terrestrial, giving them massively enhanced scans at relatively low cost.

Unfortunately, all that resolution was telling them only one thing.

▶ ▶ ▶

▶ "Sorry, Captain." Kamir shook his head. "Whatever it is, it's right there, but we can't scan through the gravity lens."

"That alone tells us a few things, Captain," Commander Daiyu said.

"Such as?"

"Well, any gravity source will lens to a certain degree"—she grimaced, sighing—"including the warp drive of the *Autolycus*. That is, as you can imagine, extremely classified intelligence at home."

Morgan blinked, and then whistled.

He'd known that the Block hadn't coughed up all their intelligence on the Alcubierre drive they'd developed, but this news was a nasty little bite to swallow. That meant that the Block ships could have been effectively invisible if push came to shove before the invasion.

"Yes," Daiyu said dryly, before continuing. "However, the standing wave the drive creates is limited in this application. To function as a drive mechanism, the wave must be molded, which means it will only lens fore and aft. Further, it is range-sensitive."

"Right," Kamir nodded, understanding. "The drive doesn't have the tidal strength to lens at close range . . ."

"Or at longer ranges," she continued, "though the signal will be degraded significantly there."

Daiyu tapped the screen she was floating in front of. "This, however, is perfect lensing . . . and since we can likely assume that they didn't set this up specifically for us, it must be symmetrical. That means it is *not* a star drive, but a very intense . . . possibly natural . . . gravity source."

"Natural?" Morgan asked. "What could do that?"

"A very small black hole, possibly," she said, "or something we've not seen before. Dark matter, I suppose."

"No one has ever found dark matter," Kamir objected.

"Yet the math proves it exists," Daiyu countered.

Kamir grimaced. "The math proves that something we don't know alters the formation of the observable universe. Calling it dark matter has implications I'm not comfortable making."

"Implications that would be quite true if that"—Daiyu nodded to the screen—"turns out to be caused by dark matter."

"If you two are done measuring your scientific . . . *vocabulary*," Morgan cut in dryly, "we have a situation I'd like to deal with."

"Uh, right, sorry, Skipper," Kamir mumbled, looking away.

"My apologies as well." Daiyu sighed.

"Alright," Morgan said. "So, naturally we've got a small black hole . . . which I thought we'd ruled out, by the way, or dark matter, or something completely new. What about unnaturally?"

"Hawking radiation from a small black hole might be rather difficult to detect," Daiyu added, "but it would have to be quite small. As to artificial sources . . . well, there we may as well just say it could be anything."

"She's right." Kamir nodded. "Any species with the technology to build something like this could have literally incalculable uses for it. It could be cloaking something, or the gravity might be the whole point of it on its own."

"How's that?"

"Navigation beacon?" Kamir offered. "A standing gravity wave this intense could probably be detected for light-years, even with our limited technology now that we know it's here. A species like the Priminae could likely pick it up at ten, or a hundred, times that distance."

"Okay, that makes sense."

"It could also be a weapon," Daiyu offered.

Morgan grimaced. "I like navigation beacon better."

She shot him a look, but didn't comment. "A gravity mine could tear a ship, or a fleet, apart if it were triggered properly."

"Wouldn't you need opposing waves to do that?" Kamir asked, thinking about it. "We're only detecting one unidentified source here. You'd have to get pretty close before the tidal force of this thing could spaghettify a ship."

"True. However, that doesn't mean that there aren't other, dormant systems in the area."

Morgan rubbed his face and brow, not liking the current situation in the slightest.

Of course, what's to like?

"We stay silent and black. We do not gravitate. We do not transmit," he ordered. "Helm."

"Sir?" Andrea half turned.

"I want a course ready for emergency withdrawal from the system, all military power," he told her.

"Aye, Skipper, already plotted."

"Good man . . . girl . . . woman . . ." Morgan grimaced. ". . . work. Good work."

"Thank you, sir," she smiled, turning back to her station.

He sighed, feeling the smirks and grins around him.

"Now the tricky part," he went on, barreling through the embarrassment. "I want a thrusters-only course *toward* the gravity source."

That pretty much killed the grinning.

"Captain?" Daiyu asked apprehensively.

"We still have a mission," he said, "and that thing out there counts as an anomaly. We have to identify it, whatever it is. If I understand you both correctly, the only way we're going to scan it is to get inside the effective range of the light warping."

She winced, but nodded. "Yes, Captain, that is the only way I know."

Kamir matched her wince when he looked over at the lieutenant, but also nodded. "Same here, Skipper."

"Alright then, that's what we do. We go in dark, quiet, and at a *crawl*. We do *not* gravitate, transmit, or even *fart* in the general direction of that thing. Not until we know what it is. Am I being clear enough?"

"Aye aye, Captain."

"Good. Then let's get to this."

CHAPTER 5

▶ The thrusters of the *Autolycus* flared briefly, dropping it from its stable orbit and deeper into the binary gravity well. With its stealth fully engaged, the black plates of armor that made up the ship's angular hull absorbed almost all light across the spectrum, making the ship appear as a slice of black that was as unearthly as deep space itself.

The drones followed it down, still faithfully analyzing all available data and sending the feeds back to the *Auto* via a tight-beam laser, while on board the crew pored over every bit of data in an effort to determine what was waiting for them past the horizon of the warp in space they were falling into.

The researchers and specialists were all too focused on the task at hand to become overly nervous, but many of the other crew members were eyeing whatever information they could lay their eyes on with clear and obvious trepidation. They all knew that the worst part was the waiting, but that just didn't make it any easier.

▶▶▶

▶ "We've isolated the local star, finally," Kamir said wearily, just over three hours into their descent. "The rest of the system should be easy now."

Commander Daiyu nodded, working at her own station. "And I believe that I can confirm that the anomaly is the cause of the light dimming from this star."

"Really?" Morgan looked across. "How does that work?"

"The new gravity source has been moving," she responded. "It only recently arrived in this system, and as it got closer it began bending the light away from its previous course."

That got Morgan's attention, making him shift in his seat and stare for a moment.

"It's *moving*?" he asked, more than a little incredulously.

"Yes, Captain. Twenty years ago, it would have been in deep space, not so close to the star," she responded.

"What does that do to our options?"

"Very little. Everything in the universe is in motion, so without more data, it's merely an interesting note that it is not native to this system."

"Lovely." Morgan sighed. "Do we have any idea what the range of its warp is?"

"We're tracking the tidal shift. If our estimates are correct, we'll breach the warp in another hour, perhaps two, at our current rate of descent," Daiyu told him.

Morgan nodded, unstrapping from his seat. "Then get a relief crew in here so everyone can grab coffee and food. I want my senior staff here and alert in forty-five minutes."

"Yes, Captain." Daiyu entered the orders. "You will be . . . ?"

"Officers' mess, then maybe my quarters. I'll be available on comms."

"Of course."

He released the straps and pushed up, grabbing a bar and pulling himself back and out of the bridge.

"You have the bridge."

"Aye, Captain. I have the bridge."

▶▶▶

▶ The tension on the ship was palpable.

The last time Morgan had felt a boat as twisted up as this, they'd been tracking a carrier group fifty kilometers off the Hawaiian Islands, all the while expecting a repeat of Pearl Harbor to happen anytime. Submersible carriers had been the bane of everyone's lives back then, almost impossible to track, and while they didn't pack the same punch as a surface group, they could take out a city without much problem.

Tactical nukes were nasty that way.

In the end, the Block had refrained from going that far, but more than one military base vanished in a single instant of fire and air.

Hunting a task group like that was one of the worst duties an attack sub could pull. It took days of grueling work just to track one down, all the while knowing that if you succeeded, you were as likely to die in the instant after you took down the carrier because one of her escorts nailed your ass. A lot of attack subs had one carrier kill, but it was usually the last line on their record.

That kind of tension was what he felt now.

There was too much fear on Earth now, fear that had infected his boat. The anticipation of what was coming was worse than actual action would be, but that anticipation could destroy their effectiveness when they needed it most.

Morgan made his way to the officers' mess and grabbed a sippy cup of java. If there was one thing to be despised on the *Autolycus*, it was drinking the ship's coffee. Oh, it didn't taste horrible, but there was something undignified about slurping your coffee from a cup based on a design for toddlers.

There was nothing to be done about it, though. Liquid was a bane in microgravity. So were dust, hair, and a whole host of other things that could float around and get jammed in the instruments. It was another horrible bit for morale, though. At least on his blue-water navy boat he could count on decent grub and good coffee in a real cup.

The picture of the Autolycus *and mission patch on the side of the sippy cup is a nice touch, though.* Morgan grinned as he took another sip and made his way down the length of the ship.

He caught a hand grip and stopped himself as a group of men drifted into his path, lugging crates that probably outmassed them. Morgan stayed well clear as they shifted the material past him, nodding in greeting.

"Crewmen."

"Skipper," one grunted. "Be right out of your way, sir."

"Take your time. We're not in a rush. Gear for one of the labs?"

"Yes, sir. Lab coat wanted something from storage. Hope it does some good."

"I'm sure it will."

As they got the crates past him, Morgan took hold of the transit handle again and was pulled smoothly along the main drag of the ship, heading forward.

The *Auto* was laid out like a cross between a destroyer and a submarine, with elements clearly taken from both and a few other craft elements added to the mix because of the nature of the ship's mission and environment. Like on a sub, the *Auto*'s main weapons were set forward—pulse torpedoes, the advanced laser array, and high velocity missiles (HVMs) in case the fighting got into dagger range.

Like a destroyer, however, point defense stations covered the rest of the *Auto*'s arcs, and they also had a pair of turret-mounted transition cannons just to give them a little standoff range in a pinch.

The bridge was set in the sail, which was in the aft of the vessel just forward of secondary engineering. The bridge was the only section of the boat that had a direct view of the exterior, and only when the sail was fully deployed. In fighting trim, the bridge was pulled back into the armored core of the ship, and everything felt like a sub again.

He was on his way to the primary weapons rooms, well forward of just about every other place of any importance. Most of that section was just munitions storage, a veritable warehouse of iron blocks waiting to be primed with a CM generator and solid rocket propellant to make them into HVMs, which could turn a small planet into a crater-for-crater copy of the Moon.

The *Auto* had a fully automated loading section, of course. He'd never even seen a boat that loaded their munitions by hand, outside of a naval museum. That didn't mean that there wasn't a significant crew in the weapons rooms, however.

They barely looked up when the captain undogged the door and drifted in. They were all too busy.

Morgan didn't smile, but he felt like doing so as he recognized the chief who was riding herd on the gunnery crews.

This is how it's done.

"I want every system checked again," the chief growled, drifting in the center of the room. "Inventory, fire control, software, hardware . . . hell, I'd say check your wetware if I thought you had any."

"Chief . . ." Morgan said from the door, not wanting to get in the way.

Chief Brogan glanced over his shoulder, nodding to the captain. "Skipper."

"Keeping them at work, Chief?"

"Idle hands, Skipper," Brogan answered. "You know how it is."

"Yes, I do. Are we shipshape?"

"Ready to fight, just say the word."

"Good," Morgan said, drifting over to a nearby station and checking it with a glance.

The laser capacitors were already charged to eighty percent, and they'd been cycling to keep them all within ideal operating temperatures, by the book for system maintenance under general quarters alarm.

"Well, I don't know if the word will be coming, but it's clear you have things well in hand here, Chief," Morgan said. "Keep it up."

"You know I will, Skipper."

Morgan tipped his head as he undogged the pressure door and let himself out.

If every chief I had knew the game like Brogan, I wouldn't have to worry about morale.

▶▶▶

▶Commander Daiyu looked over the scans cautiously, comparing different frequencies with near obsessiveness. As they neared the gravity source, the parallax shift between the slower frequency spectrum and the faster one was becoming more pronounced.

Radio and visible light were being bent far more than x-ray and gamma frequencies. Unfortunately there was far less of the latter to work with. The source wasn't putting out anything in the higher frequency ranges, of that she was certain—because if it had, she'd have spotted it by this point.

The tidal force detection grid on the *Autolycus* was now showing a pronounced gravity shift from stem to stern of the ship, enough that she'd noticed a distinctive drift in objects set loose on the bridge. They were drifting forward, toward the gravity source.

Soon the *Autolycus* would pass the threshold of no return on thrusters, after which they would have to power up the warp drive if they wanted to pull free of the gravity source with reverse thrust. They would still be able to sling around on thruster power, however, and snap loose, so there was no reason to raise undue alarm just yet.

Daiyu had been one of the chief military overseers of the warp drive project. Her knowledge of gravity waves was significant, but so far she couldn't quite get her mind wrapped around the data she was crunching.

It didn't fit any of the expected profiles, not for a natural object, nor for an artificial construct, that made any sense to her.

If it were a warp drive, she'd expect to see distinct fore-and-aft shaping of the wave in order to provide propulsion. Instead, the shaping, which was certainly present, was almost perfectly spherical.

Almost.

There was, in fact, a distinct distortion to the perfection that couldn't just be an accident, so it had to be by design. What was bothering her was that she couldn't figure out the purpose of the design.

"Commander, we're starting to get imagery through on gamma and x-ray bands."

Daiyu looked up sharply. "Show me."

The augmented displays projected over the now-blank windows lit up with fuzzy imagery, but it definitely showed *something* ahead of them, right at the location in space they projected the object to be sitting.

"It's not particularly reactive in either band, I see," she grumbled, glowering at the imagery.

"No, ma'am," Kamir admitted. "We're mostly building the image from what it obscures. If we went active now, we could probably get more detail."

"Absolutely not," Daiyu said, shaking her head. "Whatever this thing is, it's not natural, and if it's not natural, then it's potentially an enemy construct. We're *not* telling it that we're out here."

"Any species that advanced probably has already targeted us," Kamir responded dryly.

"The *Odyssey* was able to remain undetected in the midst of combat between two highly advanced species using techniques that I am informed have been improved significantly since," Daiyu countered. "Don't worry about them spotting us. Worry about figuring out just who, and what, *they* are."

Kamir ducked his head. "Yes, ma'am."

So far the constructed image didn't seem all that impressive, just a mostly spherical blot on the stars with some detail in areas that were reflecting natural x-ray and gamma sources as the ship approached. It wasn't much, but as the *Auto* closed in, the details were continuing to improve.

It was only a matter of time.

▶▶▶

▶ "What are you listening to?"

The man wearing the white lab coat over his issued coveralls didn't look up, or rather down. He was floating upside down—inasmuch as you had an up or a down in microgravity relative to everyone else—and gently rapping a stylus against his own skull.

"Doctor."

The speaker, a very weary and surprisingly wary woman with a strict look and tied-back hair, glared at the man ignoring her and kicked off the deck. As she drifted into range, she snapped her hand out and grabbed the stylus from him, yanking it away.

The doctor looked up, surprised. "What?"

"I asked," she growled, lifting his earphones off his head, as she braced herself with a foot and an arm, "what are you listening to?"

"Why didn't you say so?" he said, puzzled. "No need to be so grabby."

He took his stylus back and pushed the earphones down as she sighed and pinched the bridge of her nose, apparently counting to ten as she did.

"Doctor Palin . . ." Her tone was just short of a death threat.

"Hmm? Oh, just static," he said, completely oblivious. "It's the signals from the ship's instrumentation feed, converted to sound. I work best in sound."

Doctor Elizabeth Berkley just barely suppressed a sigh. She'd been dealing with Palin since he arrived on board the *Autolycus*. It felt like it had been years already, and she'd first heard the man's name *less than* a month earlier.

I can't believe this ass has a file classified so high I'm not even supposed to ask about it.

"Doctor, we're standing to general quarters."

Palin tilted his head, looking at her with mild confusion. "I fail to see how we're standing anywhere. The ship is a microgravity environment, you know."

Berkley rolled her eyes.

The man can't be this stupid. He simply can't be.

No one as stupid as he seemed to be could be breathing on their own, never mind be assigned to one of the most highly classified missions ever launched.

"Doctor Palin, general quarters means that we are to be strapped down unless undergoing vital actions."

"That's what I'm doing."

"You're listening to static," she growled. "You can do that while strapped in."

Palin scoffed. "The straps cinch up on me."

"They're for your own safety, Doctor."

"Please, Doctor . . ." Palin chuckled. "I've studied the drive system.

As long as we're in the ship, we're safely located in a microgravity bubble. It doesn't matter if the ship accelerates, brakes, or even gets knocked around a little. We're sheltered here."

"Oh, really?" Berkley asked dryly, holding up a pen in front of his face.

She pointed it in his direction and pulled it back from the doctor just as his eyes crossed to look at it. When he started to open his mouth to ask what she was doing, she let the pen go, and it dropped straight and true to ding him right in the forehead.

"Ow!" Palin yelped, more surprised than hurt. He grabbed the pen and looked at it like it had just fundamentally betrayed him. "How?"

"We're in an extended gravity well, with extreme tidal variations. Strap your idiot ass in before I toss you out of the cryptography lab and drop you down the spine of the ship until you bounce off the forward deck."

Palin stared for a moment, and then wordlessly shrugged into the straps and fastened them.

Berkley smiled beatifically at him, reached over, and put the earphones back on his head and patted them.

"Good boy. Now stay."

Palin watched her climb away from his position, moving in slow leaps and bounds in the very low gravity they were in.

I miss being in charge of my own lab.

▶▶▶

▶Commander Daiyu scowled as she looked over the new data. As the *Autolycus* moved ever closer to the anomaly, the disparity in the warping it was causing became more and more apparent across the electromagnetic spectrum.

The altered gravity waves must have incredibly short frequencies for this to be happening.

She knew that natural gravity waves had very long frequencies—on the order of dozens, if not hundreds, of light-years or more. To create a standing wave with a shorter frequency took a fair bit of technical prowess; the Block researchers spent decades trying to do just that as part of the star drive that was currently sitting in the *Autolycus*. It took a careful manipulation of fields and the collapsing of local space-time as well as several quantum effects to manage the process, and the drive was just *barely* stable on the *Auto*.

Any more power to the drive, any more mass to shove around, anything that strained the system just a slight bit more . . . and it could all collapse. Hell, it *had* all collapsed. Weston and Captain Sun had used that weakness as a strength, turning the *Wei Feng* into a one-shot superweapon.

This anomaly, however, was millions of times more massive than the *Autolycus* was or the *Wei Feng* had been. In order to control and warp space on that level . . . honestly, she didn't even want to think about the level of technical sophistication that had to take.

"We're getting a cleaner view of the object, ma'am."

"On my screen," Daiyu ordered.

"Aye, ma'am."

The screen flickered, showing a dirty image that had more artifacts and fuzzy sectors than clean ones, but her eyes widened all the same as she examined it.

"Ancestors . . ." the commander whispered, her hand snaking out to key open the intraship comm. "Captain to the bridge."

CHAPTER 6

▶ "Give me a sitrep," Morgan ordered as he dropped into the command station and looped the straps over his shoulders.

"We're almost through the space-time warping that's lensing the EM spectrum," Commander Daiyu answered. "However, I've cleaned up some of the higher-frequency imaging, and I believe you should see this."

"Show me," he said, pulling a screen to a better position.

Daiyu nodded and sent the files over to the captain's station with a flick of her wrist.

Morgan raised an eyebrow instantly, examining the silhouette. "Why do I have a sudden urge to say I have a bad feeling about this?"

The imagery was nearly spherical, and big. Really big. The parallax he was looking at made it bigger than a small moon, bigger than many small planets actually. He checked the spectroscopic readings, but they were distinctly useless at that point. The lensing effect had totally scrambled what little data they'd gotten over the hyperspectral scanners.

"Well, if it's a planet, it has to be composed almost entirely of your 'dark matter,'" Morgan said. "Nothing else would lens light the way we're seeing here."

Daiyu spared him a surprised look.

Morgan just chuckled. "Don't look so shocked. I did my reading before accepting this assignment. I know the terminology, if nothing else."

"Of course, Captain. Sorry, I just didn't have the impression that you had understood our conversation earlier."

"I didn't need to put in my two cents. Had nothing to add," Morgan admitted. "This thing can't possibly mass enough to lens the entire electromagnetic spectrum."

"Not if it's normal matter, no," Daiyu answered. "However, we both know that there are other ways of warping space-time."

"True, but the lensing was near perfect. That would seem to me to mean that it's not a drive wave," Morgan said, his eyes flicking over the data.

"Yes. However, something *is* shaping the wave, Captain. It isn't a natural formation," Daiyu said. "For one, the wave is clearly too short in frequency to be natural . . . and as a second point, we calculate the mass to be significantly less than a stellar mass."

That brought him up short, and Morgan looked over at her sharply. "No way something that small lenses light this effectively."

"Not naturally, no," Daiyu confirmed. "However, recall that I told you, our own drive is capable of lensing light. We also mass significantly less than a star, I believe you can agree."

"Right, of course." Morgan sighed, berating himself for forgetting that bit.

"The shorter wavelength that makes propulsion practical also lenses light more effectively."

"But this isn't a drive?" Morgan asked, now uncertain.

"Not in its current configuration, no."

"Then what the hell is it?"

A warning beep sounded. Commander Daiyu examined her readings carefully before turning back.

"I believe, Captain, we may be about to find out. We're breaching the lens effect."

"Screens forward," Morgan ordered. "Sound muster stations. I want everyone ready to twitch if this gets ugly."

"Aye aye, Captain." Voices echoed across the bridge as his orders were put into action.

On the screen the image remained scrambled by the lensing artifacts for another few seconds as the *Autolycus* breached the gravity wave, and then it quickly cleared up. There was a moment of silence as they stared, no one having any words come to mind as they looked on the cause of their current investigation.

It was a dark planet, if one could call it that. Not black, but more of a dull gray, and too uniform to feel natural to human eyes.

"Captain, we have hyperspectral data on the object."

"Tell me," Morgan ordered.

Kamir frowned at his instruments, shaking his head. "Strange, sir. No atmosphere to speak of, but the surface is metallic. I have a database match, but it's above my clearance."

"Send it here."

Morgan looked over the data, and then put in his own clearance and quickly read the file summary and checked the numbers.

"It's not a match, but it's close," he said finally. "The *Odyssey* recorded ships with similar composites and alloys in their encounter at the Drasin megastructure."

"I thought the Drasin didn't use metallic alloys but preferred mineral-based composites," Daiyu said.

"They do, and the Priminae are partial to ceramics," Morgan confirmed.

Daiyu didn't need long to parse just what that statement meant, and her eyes widened. "The Confederation never reported another alien species . . ."

"Yes, we did," Morgan corrected her. "We just classified it very high up the chain."

Daiyu fell silent for a moment, thinking on that. She supposed that she shouldn't be shocked by the information, but it still bothered her. The Priminae were one thing, the Drasin something else entirely, but to hide a third species from everyone?

"Fine," she muttered. "So this was built by the third group, then?"

"Possibly," Morgan allowed. "It's not a precise match, but it's clearly similar."

Daiyu accepted that, though she wasn't particularly pleased to do so. The planet, or construct, they were now approaching was clearly of artificial origin, and any information about its builders could be of vital importance. The fact that there was data being held back didn't please her much at all.

Morgan, however, had moved on.

"Start surveying it off, give me a grid, and look for anything that we can use as a landmark. Whatever this thing is, someone went to a lot of trouble to build it and set it on its way. Let's find out why."

"Aye aye, Captain."

▶▶▶

▶ The *Autolycus* slipped into a fairly tight orbit around the dark steel-gray planet, scanning using passive systems as it corkscrewed around the anomalous world. There were fine ridges, only meters deep, lining the entire surface. The pattern they made didn't appear to be a language or anything decipherable, but the marks didn't seem to be construction seams either.

"Captain?"

"Yes, Lieutenant?" Morgan asked from where he was looking over the latest hyperspectral analysis reports.

Lieutenant Kamir had spent more than his fair share of time glaring at those same reports, but right then his mind was set on something else.

"Once we slipped through the gravity wave that was lensing EM waves around this planet, we started to pick up short burst modulated radio, sir. Very low frequency, very short range, but definitely from an artificial source. Palin, down in communications, has been working up a translation."

Morgan looked up, incredulous. "Translation? We know the language?"

Kamir shrugged, looking fairly skeptical. "Palin claims to. Frankly, Skipper, I'd probably not have bothered passing it on to you yet, except that Palin was the head of the research department for translating Priminae languages, and he was on the original *Odyssey* mission."

Morgan couldn't help but be at least a little impressed. With qualifications like that, there was really only one question to ask about the man.

"Then why is he on the *Autolycus*?"

Kamir twisted his lips, sighing. "Two reasons, Skipper. First, he volunteered. Second? Reading between the lines of his jacket, I'd guess that no one else wanted him around."

Morgan grimaced. "That bad?"

"Real hard case to work with, sir," the lieutenant confirmed.

"Great. Tell me he's as good as his qualifications suggest?" Morgan asked.

"Fully three-quarters of his file is redacted at my security level, Skipper," Kamir said. "Of what wasn't, one line stood out."

"And that was?"

"Knows his stuff. E Weston." Kamir chuckled.

Morgan rolled his eyes. Captain Weston was well known as something of a tactical prodigy, but clearly he wasn't much for leaving useful notes.

"I'll check his file myself, but for now, give me the brief."

"Yes, sir."

The file appeared in the captain's folder a moment later, and Morgan opened it while keeping one eye on the survey in progress. As Kamir had said, the file was mostly blacked out, but applying his own security code cleared it up quickly.

Language genius, indeed. Morgan recognized some of the early works attributed to Palin. In fact, Morgan had worked a few of the missions referenced. During the war it was common to use submarines as intercept points to pick up coded transmissions, and the Block had some impressive codes in those days. He'd never heard how they'd been broken, but a lot of actionable intelligence had come from those missions, and now it appeared he had one of the key men responsible under his command.

It's too bad the man is clearly a prima donna.

The file was filled with personnel reports vilifying Palin, making him out to be some sort of rock-star scientist with a strong leaning toward the "mad" type. Morgan made a mental note to ensure he had a good noncom assigned to the communications section to stomp on the man if he got out of line. No way was he going to put up with that sort of nonsense on a ship as small as the *Autolycus*.

Sighing, he called up the report Palin had filed on the stray EM signals he'd supposedly decoded and, within seconds, was deeply engrossed.

Knows his stuff. Weston needs a kick in the ass if this is his idea of "knows his stuff."

Palin had already broken down the signals by categories and meanings, along with probability estimates for his translations and likely points of origin. Most of the data wasn't too far from what Morgan might expect to find around an advanced world. Actually, a lot of it seemed to be reporting on navigational hazards and similar vital yet dry bits of data.

Of particular interest, however, was one specific signal that appeared to be a homing beacon.

That wasn't the really interesting thing, however. No, the really interesting thing was where the beacon was homing from.

Or to, I suppose. Morgan noted the vectors included with the signal and looked over to Lieutenant Mika at the helm. "Andrea."

"Yes, Skipper?" She looked back at him.

"Adjust our vectors to the coordinates I'm sending you. I want a soft approach orbit."

"Aye, sir. Give me a moment to calculate," she said, looking over the numbers.

Morgan nodded, not pushing. They had time and, honestly, it was more important right then to do things *correctly* rather than quickly. Any use of thrust was a risk while they were in orbit around a planet with the capacity to create and mold gravity waves, so the less they used the better.

It took a few minutes, but Andrea got the job done as fast as he could have hoped.

"Plotted, Captain."

"Engage, softly."

"Aye, Skipper. Coming about, thrusters at one-quarter . . . no gravitation."

The screens shifted, following the nose of the *Autolycus* as the ship shifted its orbit and climbed higher from the planet. Morgan could hear the screaming from the survey labs already, but just then he was more interested in the beacon Palin had decoded than the surface of the gray planet.

"Captain, there's something out there."

Morgan leaned forward, eyes on the screens. There was indeed something right where Palin's vectors said it would be, and he was very interested in just what it was. The object was roughly the size of Luna, perhaps a little smaller, and it was holding a very high orbit over the gray world.

As they got closer, it was clear on hyperspectral scanners that the object they were closing on was similar in composition to the planet, but it was holding at an extremely odd orbit. Neither geostationary, nor remotely standard by any definition, the moon of the gray world was holding its position, as though locked there.

That's not possible. It should have degraded almost immediately, Morgan noted, both intrigued and slightly affronted by the slight against the laws of physics.

"Captain." Commander Daiyu spoke disbelievingly, as though she had had the same thought. "We're detecting a gravitational tidal point as we approach. The moon has its own stabilizing well, holding it there."

"It would have to, wouldn't it?" Morgan mumbled, a half-smile on his lips. "But . . . why?"

"I don't know, sir."

"Find me the coordinates Palin's beacon was pointing to. I want a survey of the area."

"Yes, sir."

▶▶▶

▶ The *Autolycus* slipped into a lunarcentric orbit over the vector source they'd tracked through the transmission, and in a few minutes they had high-resolution imagery complete with stereoscopic and holographic compilations.

"It looks like a landing pad," Lieutenant Mika offered with a shrug.

Morgan had to agree, though he personally thought it looked like a pad out of a science-fiction film, standing about three hundred meters over the local terrain. It looked like a pedestal, but it was a big one.

"How much space does that pad have?"

Kamir answered. "It can handle a fair-size ship. Not up to the *Autolycus'* size, of course, but easily several of our shuttles could land on it."

"You're not suggesting we deploy a team?" Daiyu asked, surprised.

"I'm thinking about it," Morgan admitted.

"The risk . . ." she said, shaking her head.

"Is high, but expected, given the nature of our mission," Morgan said. "Besides, you can't tell me you don't want to know what the hell this setup is all about."

Daiyu Li had to admit personally that she did, she really, really did, want to know what this . . . construct was.

"No," she said. "No, I cannot. In fact, if you do send a mission to the surface, I would like to volunteer to command it."

"Denied," Morgan said. "Major Phillips will lead the mission . . ."

Daiyu nodded, understanding.

"You can lead the research team," Morgan said.

Commander Daiyu took a moment to put that together, but she nodded quickly when she did. "Thank you, Captain."

"Don't get dead," Morgan ordered, and then sighed and relented slightly. "But do get us some answers, Commander."

"I will, Captain."

Morgan unstrapped from the station. "For now, you have the bridge. I want to go give the major the good news."

"Aye, Captain, I have the bridge."

CHAPTER 7

▶ Morgan gripped the transit handle tighter as it slowed, momentum shifting his feet forward. He let go and glided into the bump wall that marked where Marine country began.

He wasn't used to having a full complement of Marines on board his command. They hadn't been required on hunter/killer subs. The Marine corporal floating before him actually managed a credible salute, making Morgan look at him twice before he spotted the strap that held the man in place.

Jarheads. Morgan suppressed a chuckle. *Leave it to the Marines to go to all this trouble to look military.*

He'd never had much use for *looking* military himself, though sometimes it was necessary. It had always been far more important to *be* military. Making a show of things wasn't the way he did things, but Morgan knew that others created their morale in their own way.

"Looking for the major," he told the corporal.

"Back sections, sir."

"Thank you, Corporal."

Morgan kicked off the wall and headed back, diplomatically ignoring the corporal's breach of protocol as he reached for the intraship comm before the captain was out of sight. He wouldn't much respect any commander whose troops didn't feel the need to let him know that the old man was coming his way, but on the other hand, the kid should have known better than to do it while Morgan was still in sight.

For now they had better things to worry about, but he'd talk to the major about it later. It was never good for the jarheads to let the officers *know* just how dumb they thought they were. There was a fragile illusion to maintain there.

Morgan stopped himself at the bulkhead three sections down, rapping on the metal while holding himself in place with his free hand.

"Enter."

Major Neil Phillips was actually sitting upright behind a desk when Morgan floated into the room. An actual government-issue *desk*.

Okay, there's such a thing as taking things too far.

Morgan restrained himself from rolling his eyes at the major, but he couldn't quite help but tweak the man by intentionally orienting himself sideways to the desk.

"Captain." Phillips didn't *quite* scowl at him. "What brings you down to Marine country?"

Morgan took a moment, looking around the carefully staged room. Books on shelves that clearly *had* to be taped down. Other trinkets—including a cavalry saber mounted on the wall—and odds and ends that made no sense in a microgravity environment. Clearly, everything had to be secured so it was unmovable, but it still seemed more than a little silly to him.

He just hoped the man was at least as much go as he was show.

"I'm thinking about authorizing a deployment to the moon we're orbiting," Morgan said. "There's a shuttle landing pad with what looks like interior access."

Phillips nodded. "Recon or assault?"

"Recon and security for a tech team. Commander Daiyu will be in charge of the techs."

The major grimaced. "And the mission?"

"You."

"Permission to speak freely, Captain."

"Granted."

"I won't lie, Captain. I'm not fond of dealing with any Block agents, especially officers."

"Block, Confederation . . . forget them," Morgan told him. "Give it ten years, and no one will remember the war except for old farts in dive bars, and even fewer will give a damn."

"I'll remember."

"If that's all you remember, then you'll be one of the old farts. That's the nature of the world . . . the galaxy we live in now. Major, I need to know that you can do this mission."

"I'm a Marine, Captain," Phillips said after a long moment. "I don't have to like a job to do a job."

Morgan nodded. "Alright. Get your team ready. I want you to be set to drop in an hour if I give the mission a go."

"Sir, yes, sir."

Morgan flipped over and grabbed the bulkhead, then paused and glanced back. "I want the tech team back in one piece, Major . . ."

"What about my Marines?"

"Them too. If I wanted cannon fodder, I'd dress you up in red shirts."

Phillips looked puzzled. "Pardon, sir?"

"Never mind, Major." Morgan shook his head. "But you should brush up on the classics."

"I'll get right on that after I get back from invading the alien moon."

Morgan smiled. "That's the spirit, Major."

▶▶▶

▶ Phillips remained in place for a minute after the captain had left, considering the brief meeting carefully. It was clear that Passer was the kind of guy who wouldn't have made it as a Marine, but he seemed passable for a Navy puke.

Neil didn't much like the idea of guarding a team of techies on an alien world, but he supposed that came with the territory in the Black Navy. It was certainly a whole new galaxy, as the captain had said. The Block officer, well, she was another story entirely.

Phillips wasn't stupid. He knew that times were changing, and he was actually content to let them pass him by. The world used to make sense to him. Confederation and Block, good guys and bad guys. Now there were aliens, and the bad guys were good guys, and the Earth had damn near been *eaten*, for hell's sake.

Too complicated.

Phillips unstrapped his lap belt, drifting out of the chair that had been bolted to the floor and planting his boots on the deck. The magnetic soles clanked as they locked into place, and then again with every step he took out of his office.

"Corporal."

"Yes, Major!"

"Who's on watch?"

"Bravo squad, sir."

Phillips considered. "So Alpha just crashed, but Charlie is fresh?"

"Yes, sir."

"Tell Charlie to suit up. I want them in the shuttle bay and ready to deploy in thirty minutes."

"Yes, sir!"

The corporal vanished from sight, the sound of his magnetic boots echoing away. Phillips listened to the sound as it faded, thinking about the assignment he was on. Like the submarine service, the

Black Navy was strictly voluntary, but that didn't mean everyone who was serving in it *really* wanted to be there.

Sometimes you volunteered, sometimes you were volunteered. That was the military way.

Of course, whether he volunteered or was volunteered, Phillips was always gung ho. He was going to have to pay the captain back for the red shirt comment, though. Some things touched a little too close to home, and that was something you just didn't joke about to a Marine . . . not while you were standing in a starship, at least.

If we find any aliens, at least now I know what rumors to have the NCOs spread.

▶▶▶

▶ "Major says suit up!" Corporal Danvers bellowed as he stomped into the barracks room. "Captain wants a security team ready for a hot drop in thirty."

The Marines of Charlie squad were just starting their daily workout. They hadn't even broken a sweat when Danvers dropped the bomb.

The gunny was the first man to the lockers, grabbing his uniform and wrestling it on while floating around. Elegant the man wasn't, but he got the job done.

"We just woke up, Corporal," he growled, jamming his arm into the fatigues while bracing himself against the wall. "What the hell are we flying over that needs a hot drop?"

"Alien moon of some kind," Danvers answered. "Don't have all the details, just know that the captain wants a squad down there to run security."

"Oh, shit, man," Corporal Ian Pierce grumbled. "That means he's sending someone down there for us to babysit."

"Put a sock in it, Pierce," the gunny told him. "The captain says we drop, we drop."

"Yeah, yeah, I know it."

The rest of the team were pulling on their fatigues and listening in without opening their mouths. Pierce was the squad's designated loudmouth. Every squad was issued at least one, in Danvers' experience.

"Who's the LT on the mission?"

Danvers looked over to the soft-spoken source of that question. PFC McMillan was the squad's designated marksman. He spoke with his rifle, mostly, when he spoke at all. He was a little older than the rest of the squad, and most of Charlie listened to him despite his low rank.

"No LT assigned yet. You'll probably get one of the juniors for this run."

"Are you *shitting* me? A hot drop to an alien moon with a bunch of pukes to babysit, and we're getting a junior lunatic as command?" Pierce flung his towel into the air, an act that would have had more effect in a regular gravity environment. As it was, the sweat-soaked cloth floated around, narrowly missing two others of the squad as they ducked out of the way before it hit the wall with a splat and hung there.

"No, the major is in command," Danvers said with equanimity. "That's why I expect him to pick a junior lieutenant as second. You know he likes to see them in action before he gives them any tactical commands."

"Enough bellyaching," the gunny cut in. "We've got to suit up, so move your asses!"

The five other members of Charlie didn't hesitate. When the gunny barked, they all jumped right out the door, swung a left, and grabbed transit handles heading for the armory. The gunny paused, looking Danvers over.

"You know anything else?"

"No one knows anything else, Gunny," the corporal admitted. "That's why you're dropping."

"Just fragging beautiful," the gunnery sergeant grumbled as he hopped clear of the floor and swung out into the hall to grab a handle himself.

▶▶▶

▶ The *Autolycus* had three assault shuttles as part of her complement of auxiliaries, hardened and up-armored versions of the more common delta-winged landers favored by the Navy and the Air Force. This version had been designed for the Marines, however, and had considerably fewer amenities such as padding on the seats.

What the Copperhead Class assault lander had in its favor, on the other hand, was a significant increase in armor, redundant reactors and CM generators, and damned near infinitely heavier firepower.

The one tagged for the current drop was hanging on a rail assembly in drop position, nose pointed "down," for what that was worth, in a microgravity environment. The other two were packed away like sardines, hanging at the far end of the shuttle bay.

Pilots were already in *Copperhead One*, systems checks well under way, when the tech team arrived in the bay along with Commander Daiyu. They were in Navy-issue firmsuits, most of the team moving awkwardly in the microgravity as they maneuvered equipment cases into the shuttle and then got strapped in themselves.

The Marines were waiting for them on board, strapped in and stowed away. The dark green hardsuits looked like part of the shuttle, an impression made all the more solid by the fact that none of them moved as the Navy personnel got strapped in.

"They look like a pack of crippled frogs paddling around a pond," Pierce chuckled over the Marines' secure comm as he watched the Navy people and techs trying to get settled in.

The Marines were watching the whole thing on their enhanced

reality HUDs, something they got a big kick out of pulling on people. Looking like you weren't paying attention while you were actually watching every breath someone took was a great way to creep the hell out of people. Or, for Marines, one hell of a great joke.

"The crippled frogs are the only reason you green fools are on this ride." A cold female voice cut into the frequency. "You might want to be more concerned with doing your job rather than with them doing theirs."

Of course, the whole spooky Marine deal only worked if the person you were watching didn't have access to your secure comm channel.

Major Phillips looked over his shoulder from where he was sitting in the overwatch position of the Copperhead, his helmet clear so that his unamused expression was clearly visible to everyone.

"Cut that shit out," he told his Marines, before looking to the speaker. "Sorry about my Marines, Commander."

"Good soldiers are always like that," Commander Daiyu said lightly. "Great soldiers are reminded often that they're not as good as they think."

The gunny snorted, and then laughed softly for a moment before his link abruptly went dead. Major Phillips glared at him and the other Marines, probably a little harsher than he needed to, but he was making up for the fact that he couldn't glare openly at the commander.

Daiyu left the Marines to the major as she settled her team in, making sure that they were strapped in properly.

"Bridge just called," Lieutenant Commander Grant, the pilot, called over her shoulder. "We're clear to drop on our call. Everyone strapped in back there?"

The shuttle jumpmaster passed down the line of people and gear, checking straps. He twisted around and nodded back as he stepped into his own acceleration bolster.

"Good to drop, Katie."

"Alright." Kathryn Grant turned back to the controls and cut into the intraship comm. "*Autolycus* command and control, *Copperhead One.*"

"Go for C&C, *Copperhead One.*"

"*Copperhead One* is ready to drop. Move us into position."

"Roger that, *Copperhead One.* Stand by."

The silence was broken a couple of moments later as the assault lander shuddered and began to drop forward through the airlock in the bottom of the ship. Cycling through the lock was a ten-minute process, at the end of which the belly of the ship opened up to space and the clamps popped loose, setting the Copperhead free.

They dropped clear of the *Autolycus*, out into open space, and Grant adjusted their orientation with a light touch on the maneuvering rockets. The horizon of the moon appeared ahead of them as the Copperhead slowed its velocity and began to drop out of orbit.

"C&C, *Copperhead One.* We are clear and dropping, all systems nominal. Local gravity increasing as predicted."

"Roger, *Copperhead One.* We are dispatching drones to shadow you in."

"Got them, let's do this." Grant fired up the CM generators and dipped the nose down.

The twin reactors flared, and the Copperhead accelerated away from the *Autolycus*, heading for the surface of the moon.

▶▶▶

▶ Usually, dropping toward a planet involved watching for atmospheric windows, dealing with turbulence and friction heat, and a whole host of other variables. When the world in question was an airless moon, or really an airless anything, you just had to worry about pure ballistics.

Grant could do those numbers in her head while dead-sticking whatever crate she was flying, so the approach was a piece of cake. The Copperhead transitioned to a smooth arc as it closed on the surface of the moon, skimming close to the alloyed metal that it seemed to be constructed of, and within a few minutes the tower with the landing pad appeared on the horizon.

"Target LZ in visual," she reported. "All clear so far. No sign of surface-to-air weaponry is evident."

She leaned over, punching numbers into the lander's computer. "We're clear on this approach. Nick, get the landing systems fired up."

"You got it, Katie."

She leaned back then, looking over her shoulder. "We're good to land in ten mikes, Major."

Phillips nodded. "Thank you, Commander."

He tapped the Marines' secure comm, addressing the squad.

"You all heard the lady. Ten mikes to the LZ."

The gunny took over from there. "Pucker up and give me a Ooh rah. We've got a job to do."

"Ooh rah, Gunny!"

None of the Navy personnel were any the wiser as the Marines psyched themselves up for the op.

▶ ▶ ▶

▶ Grant circled the tower, keeping the nose of her Copperhead pointed in as she examined the LZ. Everything looked as normal as it could, given that they were looking at a towering landing pad in the middle of an otherwise barren ball of metal flying through deep space. She was tempted to give it a few more circles, but nothing new was showing up, so she decided to just get it over with.

The Copperhead settled in over the pad, rockets flaring as she carefully settled it into place. The gear took up the weight of the craft as it touched down, the suspension just barely dropping as she kept the CM on high in case she needed to bug out in a hurry.

"Green light, Nick."

"Roger that, Katie," the copilot said, flipping a switch.

The jump light flipped from red to green as the rear door dropped open and the Marines bounded out. Clad in enhancing armor, they took up security positions on the pad as the Navy and tech people got their gear in order and unloaded.

"All clear," Pierce said from where he was covering the only thing of note in the entire area, a large wall rising up from the pad with a door squarely in the middle of it. It looked big for humans, but then it was the only opening he could find, so that didn't mean so much. "Man, this place is a dreary piece of . . ."

"That'll be enough, Pierce," the gunny growled. "Can the color commentating bullshit."

"Sorry, Gunny."

The gunny just grunted, though privately he agreed with the corporal. The entire area was like some robot apocalypse nightmare. Nothing but smooth gray metal as far as the eye could see, other than the pad they were standing on and the Copperhead itself.

With the Marines arrayed around the landed craft, the Navy personnel and tech staff unpacked and unloaded their gear.

Commander Daiyu let the work proceed without micromanaging it. Her people knew their jobs well enough. She walked a little away from the group, testing the local gravity. It was lighter than Earth's, but significantly heavier than the Moon's. Movement was easy, comfortable, and a little bit of a rush.

The stars are spectacular here, she noted, looking up and around. She was aware that they were likely all warped out of their proper locations, but they looked amazing all the same, with no atmosphere to blur them and only the lights of the Copperhead to pollute her vision.

After a moment of taking in the view, she turned her attention to the only local landmark of note. There was a large door on the far side of the pad. The entire place looked eerily familiar.

I believe I've seen this in Beijing once, she thought as she carefully surveyed the pad. *Smaller, yes, but close all the same. This looks like something we would build.*

That thought chilled her slightly, a reaction she didn't want to examine too closely while she had a job to do. Daiyu focused, forcing those nagging thoughts away.

"You know, Gunny," McMillan said over the Marines' secure comm, "this place looks like something right out of a corporate headquarters back home. Looks like a human designed it."

Of course, some people didn't have those issues.

"What do you know about architecture, Private?" the gunny snorted. "Just worry about security."

"Nothing is getting within a hundred klicks of us without being spotted, Gunny."

Daiyu tuned them out, walking over to the door and examining the area for anything that looked like a latch or, more likely, some sort of interface system. She was only slightly surprised when the wall lit up on her approach, a projected hologram jumping out at her. It was an interface, she decided as she reached out to touch it.

"Whoa, Commander . . ." Major Phillips cut into her reverie. He put a hand on her shoulder, pulling her arm back. "I'd appreciate it if you let us secure the area before you started playing with the local toys."

"Do you have a computer tech with a specialty in xenocybernetics?" she asked dryly. "Because unless you do, I don't believe you can secure this."

The major glowered, but couldn't exactly refute what she was saying, so Daiyu turned back to the projection. She reached out and touched it and was again only mildly surprised to find that it had a tactile feedback feature. There were ways of doing that on Earth, of course, but most of them involved acoustic projection, which clearly wasn't the case here.

"Doctor Palin," she called, "what do you make of this?"

One of the figures in the Navy hardsuits twisted around, nearly falling over before stumbling in her direction. Daiyu opened the comm to the doctor's channel, which she'd shut off very early in the mission due to extreme annoyance.

"Oh, my, this is interesting," Palin mumbled, looking at the symbols layered in the projection.

"Is it Priminae?"

"No, no certainly not," he told her. "I see some similarities, but I believe that if anything, this is much older than the Priminae."

"They've been around over fifty thousand years as a contiguous culture, Doctor," Daiyu countered. "We don't even know how much longer they were around before they began colonizing their current worlds."

"Quite a while, I expect," Palin said, not looking away from the projection. "This technology is reminiscent of some of their older facilities, from what I understand. They don't use it much anymore, however."

"Great. Can you read any of it?"

"No," he told her lightly. "But I can tell you a few things about it."

"Such as?"

"It's human design," Palin said, "intended for use by a bipedal species, between five and seven feet tall with two primary manipulating appendages . . ."

"Hands," she offered dryly.

"Yes, yes, hands, right." He waved her off, still examining the system. "It's an interface, it was designed to be understood and utilized . . . so . . ."

He drawled off, and then just reached out and pushed a symbol without warning.

The door suddenly snapped open.

Commander Daiyu half expected the Marines to shoot him, but thankfully they restrained themselves. She didn't like the man, but he was the best linguist she had.

"*Don't* do that ever again," the gunny growled, grabbing the doctor's suit as the Marines rushed past Daiyu and Palin. "You *tell* us before you pull that shit, got me?"

"Huh?" Palin sounded confused. "Did you say something? I'm sorry. I'm busy reviewing my recordings of the interface."

The gunny pushed him away, clearly disgusted, and leveled his assault rifle as he followed his squad through the door.

"Looks clear!" Pierce called, sweeping the room with his own weapon.

Major Phillips grabbed two of his Marines. "You two stick with the Navy pukes. You're security now."

"Yes, sir."

Phillips looked into the room on the other side of the door, coming to a stop beside Commander Daiyu. "What do you think? Elevator?"

"Most likely."

"We going down?" he asked, though he figured he knew the answer.

"After we clear it with the captain, yes, I believe that we are."

"Outstanding," he said dryly, blowing out a long breath into his suit's ventilator.

CHAPTER 8

▶ "Report from the surface, Captain."

"I'll take it here at my station," Morgan said, pulling the screen in closer.

The data coming back from the surface was interesting, but nothing ground-shaking yet. The technology they'd found so far was in line with older Priminae technologies, and Palin's report matched those observations.

He was concerned with the commander's request to descend with the lift, but didn't see too many other options to deal with it. They needed intelligence, and the only way to get it was to go into the belly of the beast.

"Do we have any change on the long-range scanners?"

"Negative, Captain. We're still gathering imagery, but there have been no changes in local background radiation, no sign of movement on either the planet or the moon . . . aside from the Copperhead, of course," Kamir said. "It's as clean as we can reasonably expect it to be."

Morgan nodded absently, looking over the video and text reports from the surface. There wasn't really another play at the moment, he supposed.

"Tell the commander to proceed."

"Aye, sir."

▶▶▶

▶ On the platform, Commander Daiyu was examining the inside of the room beyond the door when the call was relayed from the *Autolycus* and the captain gave her the green light. She switched over to the Marines' secure comm, but isolated her transmission to the major alone.

"We're clear to go into the facility," she said.

"I was copied on the clearance, Commander."

She let his tone pass, knowing that the major had a problem with her. It didn't take much imagination to figure out what it was. Marines had taken some of the heaviest hits in the war, and a lot of them still had deep resentment against the Block military. It had become a culture of sorts, from what she could tell.

"Odds are we'll lose contact if we can access the interior," she said.

"I have it covered."

"Very well. Get your Marines ready. We'll activate the mechanism as soon as we finish decoding the interface."

Major Phillips turned on his heel and walked out, circling his hand in the air as he called all the Marines together aside from the two assigned to watch the techs. Daiyu watched him for a moment before returning her focus to the task at hand.

"Are we getting anywhere with the interface?"

Palin didn't turn around from where he was studying the projection that had appeared on the inner wall.

"I think this is a proto-version of the Priminae written record, Commander," he said, examining the symbols floating in the air.

"That makes this facility more than fifty thousand years old, Doctor."

"Oh, a good deal older than that, I'd say."

Daiyu frowned, trying to parse that bit of information.

"How can you possibly determine that?"

Palin shifted slightly. "Linguistic drift takes time, and if you know the cultures involved, it's easy to work out a rough timetable for it. More advanced cultures have less drift. A culture-wide communication system and modern media tend to freeze the language mostly in place. The Priminae are a *very* advanced culture."

Daiyu accepted that. She could hardly question his specialty when it wasn't her own.

"How much older?"

"*That* would be quite impossible to determine at this point," he told her. "That said, this being a protolanguage does give us some advantages. I can read parts of it, for one, and interpret other parts from that."

"How much can you read?"

"Oh, at least five percent," he said, far too cheerfully for her taste.

Five percent. Daiyu winced. She could have done with better odds, given that the success of the mission . . . and perhaps their lives . . . could very easily depend on that understanding. *Of course, they're better odds than I expected.*

"Which five percent can you read?"

"The obvious things, obviously," Palin said. "This was intended to be read, interpreted, easily. Imagine you can't read a word of English . . ."

"Easily done," she said dryly. Daiyu had actually come late to multilingual skills. It wasn't until the war that she'd learned to speak, read, and write the enemy's language.

"Well, my illiterate friend," Palin continued cheerfully, "now imagine you're in an elevator. How hard would it be to work out what the buttons do?"

"If you know it's an elevator? Not very."

"Precisely."

Daiyu nodded slowly, understanding. "So, if this is an elevator . . . ?"

"Well, if it's *not*, then it's a very strange place to put a random room," Palin chuckled.

That was true. It *had* to be some sort of transport room and, unless the species in question had developed teleportation, an elevator was the most likely.

That conclusion made her pause and look around.

Could it be a transporter room?

Daiyu shook her head. There was no evidence of teleportation technology in any of the briefs she'd been given concerning the Priminae or other nonterrestrial groups.

That would be more comforting if the intelligence I was briefed on was more complete.

Still, it seemed unlikely. Among other things, she knew the state of research into teleportation technology on Earth. It was technically feasible, but practically impossible. Quantum teleportation existed, but on a macro scale. The chaotic nature of quantum particles made it all but impossible.

So, elevator it is, she decided, looking at the display. It only took a brief glance to decipher enough, so she pointed. "That activates the system."

"Correct," Palin said. "Very simple system here. One-stop express."

He was about to say more when a tugging pulled at their suits, creating a feeling like standing in the wind, and they both turned around. The rocket exhaust from the Copperhead lifting off had blown into the room, getting all their attention.

"Where the hell are they going??" a young tech cried out.

"Standard procedure," Phillips said as he walked back into the room with his Marines. "The Copperhead will orbit the area and dust us off on demand. We're not risking the pilots and crew sitting here on the ground while we're doing whatever the hell it is you want to do."

"Never mind that," the commander said. "Are you going to leave guards up top?"

Phillips snorted. "We're actually doing this?"

"Yes, Major, we are."

Phillips sighed, jerking his thumb over his shoulder. "Evans, Longworth, you two are on post up here. Everyone else, into the elevator."

The two designated Marines stepped out onto the platform while everyone else piled in. It was a large enough room, thankfully, so there was no real crowding. Palin punched in a command as soon as they were all inside, and the doors closed, cutting them off from the exposed pad behind them.

"Going down," he said cheerfully as he punched in another command.

They all braced, expecting some sense of motion, but it seemed that nothing happened for a moment. It wasn't until the lights changed that they realized they were, in fact, moving.

"Those are numbers," Palin decided. "Distance measurements . . . meters, kilometers, maybe floors. I don't know. Some distance measurement, though."

"Do we have anything on the radiation scanners?" Daiyu asked, turning to another of the techs.

"Nothing."

Daiyu glared at the man, who looked up helplessly.

"Really, *nothing*. The only rads I'm scanning are coming from *our* gear, Commander. This room is shielded like nothing I've ever seen."

"Hmm," she considered. "That's interesting."

"It also means we're cut off," Pierce complained over the Marines' secure comm. "No calling for dustoff until we're back up top."

"We expected that," Phillips reminded them. "Our comms wouldn't penetrate as much metal as we're expecting to be buried under shortly anyway."

"Could you please use a different word, Major?" Pierce whined. "I don't like the sound of 'buried.'"

"Shut it, Corporal," the gunny ordered. "We got a job to do."

"How far down are we going?" Technician Evelyn Reach spoke up, eyeing the numbers nervously.

Evelyn was a computer specialist, one of the few on Earth with experience in Priminae computing systems. That experience was of limited use when she couldn't read the language, but it was a vital skill all the same.

"Unknown," Daiyu answered, considering the same question.

Three hundred meters to the surface, but beyond that they could keep going down and down for a long time. It depended largely on what the facility was used for. A civilian structure of some type would most likely be close to the surface, no more than a hundred meters down generally. Military facilities could be several kilometers deep, and research facilities would be as deep as needed to study whatever it was they were studying.

Without knowing any of that, however, there was no way to guess the depth they were dropping to or what precisely they would find when they arrived. No one was speaking of it, of course, but the commander had little doubt that everyone had considered the question.

Almost everyone, she supposed, glancing at Palin briefly.

Unless she was mistaken, the Marines had their weapons gripped a little tighter, fingers resting just over the trigger guards. The Navy personnel and research crew were fiddling with their instruments, and she . . . well, she was examining everybody present for signs of nerves.

We all deal with things in our own way.

The landing pad was the only feature they'd scanned on the surface of the moon, though admittedly they hadn't surveyed the entire surface yet. The question that was really bothering her, however, was the lack of security they'd seen so far. It felt more like an office building than anything else, and that just didn't make any sense.

"You see the problem with this setup, Major?" she asked softly over the officers' channel.

"Other than the glaring lack of security?" the major asked dryly. "Why no, not at all."

"The Priminae didn't bother much with security as we consider it either," she said, thinking about the reports she'd read.

The major had read the same ones. "True, but even they had biometrics and guards, such as they were."

"Well, maybe the guards just aren't around any longer," she suggested. "As to biometrics . . . how do we know we haven't been scanned?"

Major Phillips scowled, but nodded.

"If so, we must have passed muster." He grunted. "Priminae are humans genetically, right?"

"Yes, for the most part . . . and the language here is proto-Priminae," she added.

"That's razor-thin, Commander."

"We're a hundred light-years from home, traveling down into an alien moon, while looking for extraterrestrial megaconstructs that might house nightmares from beyond the stars that are looking to *eat* our planet," Daiyu countered. "Thin is a matter of perspective."

"I think we're here," Palin offered quietly a moment later, his eyes never having wavered from the display.

Everyone looked around, waiting for something to happen.

"The door ain't opening, Major . . ."

"Shut it already, Corporal!" The gunny stepped on his complaining.

"What's that sound?" Daiyu asked, realizing that she'd actually *heard* something that wasn't coming from her comm suite. She looked around. "Check atmospherics."

"We have air, Commander. Thin, not breathable, but getting thicker," Ensign Hunt said, checking his gear. "I think we're being cycled through an airlock."

"Composition?"

"Breathable once it thickens up, a little oxygen-rich by Earth standards of late, but not too far off the mark."

"No one even *thinks* of taking off their suits," Phillips ordered on the public band. "Anyone who loses suit integrity spends the rest of the trip in an isolation ward. Clear?"

"He's right." Daiyu backed up the Marine. "Leave the equipment on."

Once the air pressure reached a little over one atmosphere, Earth standard, the door slid open.

"Marines, secure the entryway," Major Phillips ordered. "Everyone else, wait here."

Pierce and McMillan led the way, sweeping their guns ahead of them as they stepped out. About a third of a second later, Pierce yelped and started swearing.

"What the hell is going on, Corporal!?"

"You've got to see this, Major," McMillan said, his voice sounding rather sickly.

Major Phillips and Commander Daiyu stepped out and instantly saw what had spooked the Marines.

"Holy shit."

Daiyu had a few other curses in mind, mostly in Cantonese, but the spirit of those was close enough to the major's selection.

They were standing on a catwalk, some sort of mesh walkway that surrounded the elevator. The walk was suspended over . . . well, nothing. As far down as they could see, there was nothing to see. The drop vanished down so far that the view just faded into a deep, dark haze.

While the Marines were looking down, Daiyu looked up. She immediately regretted it, closing her eyes as she felt her balance shift.

"Major, look up."

Phillips twisted, and then swore again.

The view above them was remarkably similar to the view below. However deep they were, it was a lot more than a few hundred meters.

"For the world is hollow and I have touched the sky."

Commander Daiyu glanced to the Marine who had spoken, reading his name from her HUD.

"Very poetic, Private McMillan."

"More than poetry, ma'am," he answered. "I can't scan anything around us. Not on visual, infrareds, hell . . . none of my feeds has anything but the catwalk we're on and the shaft we came down."

"So, Private?"

"So, Commander," he said quietly. "Where's the damn moon? Is the whole thing hollow?"

Daiyu paused, thinking about that. She cast about, looking around.

"That's a good question," she admitted. "Do we still have atmosphere?"

"Yes, ma'am," Hunt answered instantly.

Daiyu considered that, looking around as she did.

"Cavern. It has to be a cavern," she decided.

"What makes you say that?" Phillips asked, not that he disbelieved her.

"Build a shell the size of the moon, then fill it with air? Who does that?" she asked. "Besides, there's gravity here. Something is drawing us down. No, we're in a cavern."

"It's one big goddamn cavern, Commander," Pierce bitched, looking over the edge again before backing away carefully.

"This has to be a research facility," she decided. "No one would build anything like this for any other reason."

Phillips snorted. "Sounds about right. Only eggheads would build something this insane and useless."

"Insane, perhaps," she said, "but there's a use for it."

She looked around the elevator shaft to where the catwalk extended out into space, leading somewhere.

"Oh, yes, there is a use for it," she repeated. "Let's go find out what."

CHAPTER 9

▶ On the bridge of the *Autolycus*, the scene beyond the ship hadn't changed much, aside from they were now tracking the transponder of *Copperhead One* as it orbited three hundred klicks below them. They'd lost contact with the mission as soon as the landing party was inside the structure, but that had been more or less expected, and now it was a waiting game.

Waiting and analyzing.

"Captain?"

"Yes, Lieutenant?" Morgan turned his focus to Kamir as the young man shifted his seat around slightly.

"We've been examining the moon's orbit about the gray planet, sir, and it doesn't make sense."

Morgan snorted. He knew that already. The orbit wasn't remotely stable, yet it seemed to be holding like it was locked in place. "I'm assuming you have something new?"

"Yes, sir," Kamir nodded. "The gravity warping of space by the planet . . . well, Captain, we've got it mapped now. It doesn't make any sense."

"Show me."

It didn't take long for him to see what Kamir meant once he looked at the file. Oh, it helped that the *Autolycus'* computers and specialists had already done the heavy lifting on the problem, to be sure . . .

The issue remained, however, that the gravity of the gray world was clearly being shaped somehow and, worse, it was focused right on the moon. The planet should have pulled the moon right out of orbit . . . well, almost immediately.

"The moon must have its own warping effect," Morgan said, looking up.

"Yes, sir, but we're having trouble mapping it because it's part of the overall field of the planet," Kamir admitted. "The local warping is clearly unnatural."

Lieutenant Mika, at the helm, turned around as she heard the discussion. "He's right about that, Skipper. We're *not* flying anything like a standard ballistic orbit here. I'm making minute changes regularly to keep us in position."

"So the whole system's gravity has been shaped, but it's not a drive mechanism, and it seems too complicated to be just some sort of cloaking." Morgan shook his head. "Someone went to a lot of trouble to build this system. Why?"

▶▶▶

▶ The catwalk stretched out across the open space, until it vanished into the heat haze and darkness beyond their sight. It would be quite unnerving enough if it were a normal catwalk over an abyss—assuming such a thing could be considered normal at all—but the fact that there were no signs of supports holding the thing up . . .

Commander Daiyu could forgive the fear her team was showing as they moved along the walkway. She would be far more concerned if they were all reacting like Edward Palin.

The linguist was just shy of *skipping* as he walked, looking all around himself like he was at some amusement park. Frankly, he was bothering her more than the catwalk.

Even the Marines were clearly unnerved by the walk. She might go so far as to say they were terrified, but they were masking it better than most. It probably helped that they had a job to do that didn't involve staring over the edge and wondering how long it would take to hit the bottom if they fell.

"What the hell was that?"

Everyone turned to look at Pierce, who had his rifle to his shoulder and aimed out to the right and up slightly.

"What is it? What did you see, Marine?" Phillips asked.

Pierce hesitated briefly, and then shook his head. "I don't know. I thought I saw something move, but I can't find it on the playback, and my scanners didn't pick up anything."

Everyone was nervously casting about, peering out into the hazy darkness to see if they could spot anything.

"Get a grip, son," the major growled. "If your gear didn't record it, it wasn't there."

"Yeah . . . right." Pierce shook himself a bit. "Sorry, sir."

"Don't worry about it. I'm seeing every childhood nightmare I ever had right now myself," Phillips admitted. "Just keep them back in your imagination where they belong."

"I think I've got something up ahead," McMillan spoke up. "Looks like lights."

Grateful for the distraction, the group looked and, indeed, there was a lightening of the haze ahead. Now with a goal in sight, they continued with increased vigor, glad to be leaving the darkness in their rear for a time at least.

▶ ▶ ▶

▶ Guard detail was boring at best. If things got exciting, well, that usually meant that you were in the deep end and probably weren't coming back up anytime soon. Private Monroe and PFC Wilson were happy enough with the boredom when they were assigned to watch the landing pad. The tower they were on was the only visible landmark from horizon to horizon, making security detail a pretty easy job.

After deploying personal drones and generally securing the location, there wasn't much left for them to do but walk the perimeter once in a while and play games on their hacked HUDs. It was technically against regs, but hacking military-issue electronics wasn't as hard as the movies made it out to be, especially not when you could bribe the quartermaster with a couple of favors.

With all the automated tripwires and no cover to speak of for a thousand kilometers in any direction, it was a pretty low-order risk.

"Damn. How the hell do you keep beating me?"

Monroe chuckled at his friend. "You get too twisted up for the interface to follow you. Same reason your scores are always lower in tactical operations. Trust your computer, mate."

"Fricking computer geeks," Wilson swore under his breath.

Standing watch in a vacuum somewhat limited your options for diversion, of course, since you couldn't even take a break for a smoke. Not that many people smoked casually any longer, or had the balls to try smuggling cigs onto a starship. There were more restricted forms of contraband, but they were usually things that could blow a hole in the hull.

So Monroe just laughed at his buddy and swept the game from his HUD as he hefted his rifle and started the perimeter walk again.

"Damn, this is one desolate sinkhole," he muttered as he looked over the edge of the pad and out to the horizon.

The sky beyond was strange. Brilliant but strange. He guessed it was from the warping effect everyone was jabbering about, but that was over his pay grade. All he knew was that you didn't get stars and colors like this back on Earth.

The alien planet they'd tracked down to get there sat off the horizon like a slate gray disc, visible against the starlit space beyond due to its lighter color and the fact that it was eclipsing so many brilliant stars. Off in the distance he could actually see the local sun, but it was too small to be called a sun and too big to be called a star by Earth standards, so Monroe didn't know what to call it.

"Hey, Wilson, what do you think of that view?" he asked, propping his rifle on his shoulder as he looked out over the horizon of the barren metal moon.

The only response was an odd wet sound over the radio, followed by crackling static.

"Wilson?" Monroe frowned, turning around.

The suit comms shouldn't ever make a sound like static. They were one hundred percent digital. Sometimes you might lose some of the signal fidelity if enough packets were lost, but that just made someone's voice sound real crappy. It didn't sound like static.

"What the f—"

There was no one else standing on the platform with him.

Monroe's assault rifle slammed into his shoulder as he charged across the platform, lighting off his suit in full combat mode.

"Wilson! Answer me, you asshole!"

He skidded to a stop where he'd left his friend just moments earlier, sweeping the entire area with the rifle on his shoulder tracking every movement.

He was alone on the pad.

Monroe checked the door, but it was still sealed and showed no signs of opening or having been opened. It had been that way since the rest of the team headed down, presumably because the lift was in use.

That left only one possibility.

He stepped close to the edge, clearing it carefully with his weapon as he looked down for any sign of Wilson. It was a long damn way to the ground, but in a lower-gravity environment and wearing a hardened suit, it might be survivable. He really wouldn't want to find out, but it was a chance.

Just one hitch to that thought. There was no sign of Wilson's transponder on his HUD. Three hundred meters was a long way down, but it was nothing compared to the range of their suit systems.

Where the hell are you, man? Monroe wondered, cautiously looking over the side and edging around.

He leaned a little farther, hoping to spot suit lights in the darkness, when a blur of motion erupted out of the black. Monroe saw a hint of a serpentine body, a flash of teeth and claws, and then felt his ears rupture as his suit lost pressure, splattering the inside of his helmet with blood.

Ice crystals filled his HUD as he gasped for air, a pull and a sensation of falling the last things the Marine felt before the darkness took him.

In the middle of nowhere, the three-hundred-meter-tall landing pad stood alone once again.

▶▶▶

▶ "What was that?"

"What was what, Katie?"

Lieutenant Commander Grant scowled at her instruments. "I have a Marine transponder that just went dead."

"Equipment failure?" her copilot offered, not sounding particularly convinced of that possibility.

"Only if it decided to fail by going to full combat status just before going dead," she growled. "Get those Marines on the comms."

"Right."

While her copilot was working on that, Katie dipped the nose of the Copperhead and took it down. The pad was in her sights in short order as she brought the combat lander around in a tight orbit of the landmark, hitting it with the lander's floodlights.

"I'm not getting anyone on the comms."

"There's no one on the pad either," Katie hissed.

"Maybe they went inside the lift. It's shielded."

"Maybe," she said. "Hang on, I'm taking us down."

"What? Why?" he asked as they dropped under the level of the pad.

"Just want to check the base of this thing. Keep your eyes peeled."

"Right."

The Copperhead spiraled down, hitting the tower with the lights as it dropped, but nothing appeared out of place. Three hundred meters passed in just seconds, leaving them skimming the metal surface of the moon, but nothing appeared, either on their instruments or from the eyeball Mark I.

"They must have gone into the shaft, Katie."

"Yeah," she mumbled, confused. "But why the hell did one of them go operational first?"

"Ask 'em when they come out. We don't have a play. We have to wait."

Grant scowled deeply, but knew he was right. She killed the floodlights and hit the thrusters, bouncing off the surface and climbing for altitude again.

So help me, if this turns out to be some idiot jarhead idea of a joke, I'm going to have a Marine camo rug for the floor of this heap before I'm done with them.

▶▶▶

▶ On board the *Autolycus*, the lieutenant commander's sentiment was echoed, though perhaps not quite so graphically.

"*Copperhead One* reports losing contact with the surface guards, Captain."

"How?" Morgan demanded.

"Unknown. No sign of them, and no transponders are beaming. They almost have to be inside the facility, sir."

"This better not be some kind of joke," Morgan growled. "Keep trying to contact them. I want to know the second anything changes."

"Yes, sir."

What the hell could have happened? Marines are idiots, but they're not this stupid . . . Morgan thought, perhaps a little uncharitably. He'd had his problems with Marines in the past, of course—almost everyone did, in his experience . . . even other Marines. Still, for all that, they normally got the job done and didn't screw around in quite so spectacular a manner.

"Do we have any telemetry from the suit that went operational?" he asked.

"Basic data only. Video upload never engaged."

"Send it to my station," Morgan ordered.

He checked the telemetry feed they had, noting that it clearly showed the suit and weapon going operational a short time before going dead.

In normal use an armored suit and weapon were in standby mode, primarily to conserve power but also to keep the soldier inside from becoming too used to the heightened data flow that an operational suit flooded him with. Given time, a man could tune out a surprising number of things, and the last thing you wanted was a soldier learning to tune out the feeds that could save his life.

When a suit went operational, power consumption increased fivefold, and the weapon was automatically rendered "hot." There were several things that could trigger an operational state, including the soldier himself, the unit commander, or even just squeezing the trigger of the rifle.

Just because a Marine's weapon wasn't "hot" did *not* mean it was safe.

Private Monroe had independently triggered his operational status in this case, a short few seconds after PFC Wilson's suit transponder had vanished.

That's not a good sign.

It was the last few lines that bothered him most, however. Suit pressure had suddenly dropped, something that probably wasn't survivable.

"I want *Copperhead Two* ready to drop in twenty. Put a full platoon on it," he ordered.

"Aye, sir!"

Survivable or not, he *was* going to find out what happened to those Marines.

CHAPTER 10

▶ The light at the end of the proverbial tunnel was attached to a large, boxy facility that was just hanging in the middle of nowhere with no obvious support. For Commander Daiyu, this was becoming a seriously unnerving mission. For most of the rest, she suspected that they'd passed over the fear point and were now settling nicely into a form of shock that was insulating them from the reality they were looking at.

"Looks like security doors, Major," PFC McMillan reported after the squad had secured the area.

Phillips nodded, not bothering to acknowledge the obvious with a verbal response. The doors were large, solid, and secured with a massive locking mechanism that a blind man could spot.

"Everyone hold back while we check the doors for . . ." he began, only to stop when one of the Navy hardsuits skipped forward past the Marines and sidled up to the door. "Hey!"

"Doctor Palin, what are you . . ." Commander Daiyu snapped, only to fall silent when the doors automatically unlocked and slid open.

Everyone looked at the doors, and then at each other for a long moment before anyone spoke.

"Security kinda sucks here, don't it?" Pierce asked finally.

"Yeah, and not just the alien kind either," Phillips snapped at him. "Check the inside!"

"Sir!"

The Marines pushed Palin back before moving through the doors, sweeping the inside carefully. It only took a few minutes for them to clear it and report back.

"All clear. Feels like a lab inside, Major," the gunny told them.

"Alright, let's go. Easy, and no one *touches* anything without checking with the commander or myself," Phillips ordered, leaning into Doctor Palin's face. "Am I being *clear* enough?"

"Huh? What was that, Major? I was reviewing the symbols I recorded off the door."

Phillips darkened his HUD visor so his face wouldn't be seen and killed his comms before he started cursing. The suits hid the trembling, whether from fear or sheer rage, so he figured that most of the people present wouldn't realize just how close he was coming to marching the doctor to the edge of the catwalk and firing him over.

Most of the people.

"Doctor, please don't do anything else without informing me." Commander Daiyu pulled the major back, patting the shoulder of his armor. "Security, you understand."

"Oh, right. Yes, certainly."

"Thank you."

Daiyu sighed. Mixing military and researchers was rarely an easy job, though it could be amusing if there wasn't so much at stake.

"Let's keep moving," she told the major. "We still have to determine what this facility was built for."

Major Phillips took a breath, glared at Palin, and finally nodded. "Right."

As they moved farther into the facility, the doors shut automatically behind them, making a few people jump, but they continued on. Commander Daiyu was more interested in the facility itself.

It hung in the middle of nowhere, literally as well as figuratively, but once they were inside, she found herself feeling quite at home. It wasn't all that different from a secure lab space in Beijing, in all honesty. There were some things she noted that told her a lot about the facility.

It was positively pressurized, for one. That meant that when the doors were opened, she'd felt a breath of wind from *inside* the facility. That kept contaminants *out* of the facility, which meant that they were probably dealing with sensitive and highly tuned equipment. That meant that they could break things if they weren't careful, but at least they probably weren't dealing with a bio-warfare site.

Anything dealing with biological warfare, chemical warfare, or neurotoxins would likely be under *negative* pressure, so if you had a breach in the facility, the air would seep *in* and keep containment until you could patch the leak.

The walls were white, actually almost the same shade as her own lab on Earth. That likely meant that the lab had been built by a species with human-type vision. White was a very easy color for humans to spot dirt against. Not so for other species that saw in different frequencies of the spectrum.

Everything was pointing to a research facility built by humans, or close enough, with a pretty significant budget . . . because, well, a gray world and moon just screamed money to burn.

That *didn't* explain the doors or the elevators, however, and that was bothering her.

Where is the security? I find it hard to believe that no one bothered to put real locks on the facility. We could have, should have been scanned a dozen times by this point. Were we? Did we somehow "pass" security, or was it turned off before we got here?

"Major, Commander, you might want to have a look at this."

Daiyu looked over to spot McMillan standing about twenty meters farther in, staring off to one side. She and Phillips increased their pace, leaving the rest of the group behind as they caught up. What the Marine was staring at became obvious as she stopped near him.

"What on Earth . . . ?" she murmured, her eyes widening as she looked at the wall McMillan was staring at.

It was fifty meters high if it was a centimeter and over two hundred across, but the size wasn't the issue. It looked like it was made of steel bricks, set vertically, with a glowing bead between them. Thousands of bricks or tiles, and there was something *off* about them.

"Commander . . ." Phillips growled warningly as Daiyu stepped forward.

"Calm down, Major. I just need to check something."

She moved slowly, half expecting an interface to pop into existence at her fingertips, but no such luck played out. When her fingers brushed one of the steel bricks, she felt it carefully for a moment, as best she could through her suit. Then, on a hunch, Daiyu pushed the brick.

It gave under her pressure, and then popped back. Commander Daiyu wrapped her fingers around it and drew it out of the wall.

Not bricks. Books.

She flipped it over, and then opened it carefully. Inside it wasn't paper, but some form of display, similar to the OLED screens used for naval flimsies.

"They're star charts," she said, panning around the display on her book with casual gestures. The device almost seemed to read her mind, scrolling smoothly and without issue.

She handed the book back behind her to a member of the tech team who'd joined them, and then reached for another one. She pulled it down and opened it, finding another set of charts. As she absently panned through the charts, Daiyu glanced up and down the wall and was stunned.

There has to be more stellar mapping information here than everything we've ever recorded . . . by a thousand times over.

"Star charts? We came all the way down here for star charts?" Pierce laughed. "You've got to be kidding me."

"Corporal," Daiyu spoke without looking at him, "we've charted less than three percent of our own galaxy. The Priminae have better charts, to be certain, but this . . . this is treasure, Corporal. Unbelievable treasure."

"Commander," a voice said from behind her, "it's more than you think."

Daiyu half turned, seeing one of the ship's astronomers looking at the first chart she'd examined. His eyes were wide, and he was pale with shock.

"What? What is it, Sven?"

Sven Bilner looked up and wordlessly handed her the book.

Daiyu passed off the one she was holding to the major beside her and accepted the first one back, flipping it around. It wasn't a chart showing on the display, however. It was a planet.

"How?"

"Commander, you can zoom in . . . you can zoom in a great deal," Sven said. "Just tap the screen."

Daiyu did so, tapping the planet once. The image smoothly swept in, revealing more details of the world she was looking at as it did. A spectrum appeared on the side of the display, one she recognized. It was depicting a high-methane atmosphere, exactly how every single lab on Earth would do so. In fact, all of the information was present in familiar mathematical and physical constants she recognized.

It was meant to be read. Ancestors. This is incredible.

There was more, however, unless she was mistaken. The world wasn't a composite. It didn't feel like computer imagery. It looked real, *felt* real. Daiyu gasped, realization stunning her almost to the point that she dropped the device in her hands.

"Commander, what's wrong?" The major reached out to steady the device before she could drop it, but Daiyu didn't answer immediately.

"Of course," she said finally. "That's why they're shaping the warp field around this world and moon."

"Commander, you're not making any sense."

Daiyu looked at Major Phillips, laughing suddenly. "I'm making *perfect* sense, Major. We're not standing in a research lab, not the way I thought. We're standing in a *telescope*. This is an alien version of the James Webb, Major!"

The Marines mostly just looked confused, but the naval crew recognized what she meant almost instantly. How could they not? They all had to be reasonably knowledgeable about gravity wave propagation as well as stellar navigation, and what the commander had just described was . . . well, the Holy Grail.

"The planet is lensing light into the moon, which in turn lenses it further and records the imagery on these," she said, holding up the device. "Major, we're standing inside the single largest telescope I've ever imagined . . . and it might be larger than we think."

She looked over the wall, and then carefully put the first book back where she'd taken it from. "Make certain everything goes back as we found it. We don't want to accidentally destroy whatever organizational method they're using here."

She walked over to the major, taking the book he was holding. "Major, this cache may be more valuable than even the technology the Priminae gave us for the Heroics."

"I see it, Commander, don't worry," Phillips replied. "This is an intelligence coup for the century, at least. We need to date the files, however, and see just how old they are."

Commander Daiyu nodded. "I know. Most are probably of little immediate value. However, the long-term impact of this place . . ."

She shook her head. "Major, I do not believe it can be overestimated."

"Understood," Phillips said. "I'm going to detail a couple of my Marines to go back and report to the *Auto*. We may need more people down here, not to mention some way to get this information back to the ship. I assume you don't want to just pack it all up and carry it out?"

"Absolutely not!" She looked affronted. "This facility is . . . Major, this facility is irreplaceable. The best modern science says it shouldn't even exist. If we can learn to point it where we want it . . ."

"Fair enough. We have to let the captain know."

She sighed, looking wistfully at the wall behind her, but nodded. "I will go with your Marines, Major."

"Very well. We have another six hours here, max, anyway," Phillips said after a moment. "Suit air won't last more than eight, and I don't want to be down here beyond that. Not until we bring in a team to do a full workup on the atmosphere."

"Agreed."

It would take more than a couple of teams to get anything done with this site anyway, the commander expected.

Most likely they'd just do a quick survey, a few days or weeks, then turn it over to one of the Heroics, which could manage the job better in the long term.

While we are here, however, I will enjoy this.

"Pierce, you and McMillan take the commander back to the surface," Phillips ordered. "She needs to make a report."

"Yes, sir, Major."

The two Marines formed up on either side of the commander as she cast a last, and admittedly longing, look back at the wall.

Well, the faster we do this, the sooner I can get back here.

"Let us go," she said aloud, starting back down the long corridor. "The captain needs to hear about this."

▶▶▶

▶ Doctor Palin barely noticed anyone leaving as he wandered deeper into the facility.

Star charts were all fine and dandy, he supposed, but he wasn't interested in lights on a screen, or even pretty pictures of faraway planets. He was there to find the only thing that really mattered.

Language.

It existed everywhere, even in the universe itself, and Palin lived to understand it in all its myriad forms.

Mathematical formulas, chirps, words, and peacock feathers. They were all the same to him, really. He didn't care to differentiate between the value of English or the click trains of dolphins. Language had no price, in any form, and nothing else could compare.

So the doctor ignored the charts, and barely glanced at the intricate dance of what appeared to be robotic arms scanning and moving similar-looking bricks a couple of rooms over. The purpose of the facility was only a curiosity.

What he wanted to find were the records.

Journals would be simply *amazing*, something written by the builders, a note scratched by the child of an astronomer, anything. He had his own treasure to hunt, so Doctor Palin left the star charts to the others and went hunting.

▶▶▶

▶ *Lights.*

It had been a very long time since there had been lights active inside the nest.

So long, in fact, that the appearance of them now had a cautionary effect instead of the enraged reaction that had existed at one time. Over the thousands of years in darkness, even genetic memory faded, leaving behind nothing but an odd feeling when the light tore through the peace of the ancients.

It wasn't totally forgotten, however.

Deep down, in the ancient recesses of their very cells, they recognized the light.

It was something to be handled, despite caution, despite fear.

Slowly, the cavern began to move as the forces marshaled in the darkness once more prepared to charge out into the light.

The ancient sleep was at an end.

▶ ▶ ▶

▶ Major Phillips watched over the techs and the Navy personnel as they pored over the data devices one by one, carefully putting each back in the place it came from as they worked. They were looking for systems, stars, and planets they could recognize. It was a big galaxy, however, and since the stellar data was gathered from a very different angle than Earth's viewpoint, none of the familiar constellations would be of much help.

That made their current attempts somewhat less likely to be successful than finding a needle in a haystack while getting struck by lightning after hitting the Powerball lotto.

Still, they looked like they were having fun, so he left them to it.

He wasn't a fool. He was well aware of just how valuable that intelligence was. The facility itself was more valuable again, assuming they could take control of it.

What was bothering him, however, was just why the hell it had been abandoned in the first place.

Option one: It's not as abandoned as it looks. Maybe it's automated for a reason. We don't leave people stationed on the Webb, after all.

That thought didn't make a lot of sense, however, given that this facility was obviously a much more significant investment than the Webb had been. They'd somehow . . . technoformed a planet and its moon to have much more significant gravity lensing than they should have, yet not turned either into a collapsing singularity.

Phillips wasn't remotely an expert on gravity tech, but like most everyone on Earth, he'd done his homework after the invasion. Gravity tech was all the rage on Earth right now. Tech channels ran specials about it every week, so he knew the basics well enough.

So, option two . . . something forced them to abandon it, while it's still in operation? That's thin. Real thin.

Honestly, of the two, he was more inclined to believe in option one.

The problem he was having was that any species that could set something like this loose as an autonomous probe was *not* a species he wanted to piss off.

His thoughts on the subject were interrupted by a yelp that didn't come from anyone in his line of sight. Phillips looked around sharply and started swearing as he realized that he didn't see the pain in the ass from earlier. He pulled his sidearm, pointing to one Marine.

"Nickels, you're with me. The rest of you, stay put."

"Sir!"

He led the way down the corridor, checking and clearing rooms until they found the missing gray suit with the royal pain in the ass packed inside.

"Palin, you pull this again and I'll . . ." Phillips trailed off as he spotted what had caused the other man to yell.

On the floor in the corner of the room were three bodies.

Check that. Three *skeletons*, surrounded by a large stained splotch on the floor below them.

Phillips grabbed Palin and yanked him out of the room. "Get your ass back with the rest."

Nickels was still looking at the bones on the floor when Phillips stepped into the room and scanned the premises carefully.

"What do you think it means, sir?"

Phillips sighed. "Well, it means that something nasty happened here, and I only know two things about it."

"Which are?" Nickels was curious.

"It happened a long time ago," Phillips answered, eyeing the stain caused by body decomposition, "and it doesn't make any good goddamn sense."

CHAPTER 11

▶ "This place is seriously screwed up," Pierce said.

They were almost back to the shaft. The lights were visible now, and Daiyu estimated they were within five hundred meters of the elevator. Pierce, while annoying, wasn't wrong about the environment. It almost defied physics, as she hadn't spotted braces or support structures of any type.

Screwed up wasn't the expression she would choose, in all honesty, but it conveyed the idea well enough.

"I don't believe I'm saying this," McMillan said, "but I'm with you on that, brother."

"Cold-as-ice McMillan is freaked out? Oh, this is too good," Pierce laughed. "What got to you? Scared of heights?"

McMillan snorted, shaking his head inside his suit. "Hardly. I feel like I'm being watched."

Pierce stopped, half turning as the commander and the private halted behind him. "You serious? Back of your neck itching, Mac?"

McMillan nodded absently, his eyes roaming the darkness around them. "You?"

"Same."

Daiyu looked between them. "Do either of you have any evidence to support your *feelings*?"

The two Marines looked at each other, and then shook their heads. "No, ma'am."

"Then may I suggest that we continue moving while you both continue to keep an eye out for such evidence?"

"Yes, ma'am."

The trio started moving again, but Daiyu noted dryly that both Marines were no longer carrying their battle rifles at the low ready position. Both of them had gone fully *operational*, she realized, pinging on her HUD as their own full armor systems were brought online. There was a certain irony here, she supposed. Two Confederate Marines were providing security for one of the Block's top military experts on several classified technologies.

If it had been just two years earlier, she'd have laughed in the face of anyone who suggested this could possibly have happened.

She turned up her own suit's systems and started paying closer attention to their surroundings as well. She left her service pistol where it was, however, figuring that if anything was able to get past two armed Marines and kill her before she had time to draw her weapon . . . well, the odds were against her anyway.

"We'll need some serious portable scanners to map this place," Pierce grumbled.

"Field rigs with a generator boosting the scan?" McMillan suggested.

"Maybe. Those things are good to a hundred klicks. You think this cave we're in is bigger than that?"

"I dunno." McMillan shrugged. "I'm a shooter, Corporal."

"Commander?" Pierce glanced in her direction.

"I do not know, Corporal," Daiyu admitted. "Normally I would say absolutely not, but everything about this facility staggers the mind."

"Yeah, you can say that again," Pierce said.

They were walking into the bubble of light surrounding the central shaft they'd arrived at when a flutter of something in the dark made all three pause.

"You heard that, right, Mac?"

McMillan nodded. "Yeah. I heard that."

Pierce looked around. He wasn't really nervous, but he was getting antsy to identify the source of the sound. "Have eyes on the source?"

"Nope."

"Neither do I," Daiyu offered as she unclipped the catch on her holster and half drew the sidearm.

"Relax, Commander," Pierce said. "We've got this."

"When we know what *this* is, then we'll decide if you've 'got' it," she countered calmly. "For now, continue to the shaft."

"Lady's right, Corporal," McMillan offered as he swept around. "Nothing to gain just standing here."

Pierce nodded. "Let's go."

▶▶▶

▶ Phillips was as far from a cop as you got, but he'd seen his fair share of bodies that hadn't passed on peaceful-like. The ages of the ones in the office space he was standing in were pretty hard to determine, other than the fact that they hadn't died recently. They were inside, in a controlled environment, and the temperature wasn't exactly warm.

That wasn't a surprise, not if the place was a telescope as the commander figured. Heat, even waste heat, could affect imagery. Manned telescopes always tried to equalize the temperature with the outside as much as possible, just to minimize any heat haze in the transfer of light.

What it meant for the scene he was looking at, however, was that the bodies had been in a sealed, low-temperature environment. That meant decomp would have taken longer than normal, but that didn't mean as much as it might have, given that he was pretty sure he was looking at a few decades since they'd died, at a minimum.

More likely they died centuries ago.

Time in space was a relative thing, pun fully intended. Everything he saw there showed that this place had been empty for a while. The bodies were lying sprawled where they'd dropped, maybe where they'd slept. There was no sign of weapons fire, no holes, no burn marks . . . nothing. The skeletons were intact, no tool or teeth marks.

Phillips stood up from where he was crouched, pondering the scenario as best he could.

"Ensign Rivera!" he bellowed, though he really didn't have to.

"Major?" Ensign Paula Rivera was one of the Navy specialists assigned to the team. She immediately started in his direction while speaking over the comm.

"Stay put. I need you to start running tox screens on the local air," he said. "Look for any chemical that's out of place. I don't care what it is."

"Yes, sir."

"Can you scan for virals?"

Rivera was quiet for a moment. "Sir?"

"I have three bodies here with no signs of what killed them," he said. "They died a long time ago, but there are two things I know of that can hang around longer than an unwelcome houseguest. Chemicals and virals."

"I can check for anything in the air, but if I find any virals in the area, I couldn't tell you if they were the common cold or weaponized Ebola without a hell of a lot of extra time."

"Understood. Just do what you can."

"Yes, sir, Major."

▶▶▶

▶ The door was closed.

Commander Daiyu stepped close, activating the interface. It popped into existence, glowing under the touch of her hand, but the doors didn't open on command. She stepped back, leaving it active, and examined the whole instead of the part she had touched.

"Something's changed," she said. "That symbol there, it's different."

It was a circle with a point floating above it. She couldn't quite remember what was different, so she had to go to her recordings and check it against her HUD. When they had arrived, the interface had shown the circle with the point in the center.

Daiyu examined it for a moment, and then slowly looked up.

"I believe the elevator has returned to the top."

"Lovely," Pierce complained. "Can you call it back?"

"Give me a moment, Corporal, I am working on it."

That was, perhaps, not entirely true. Mostly she was working on deciphering the interface a little more thoroughly than they'd managed on the first run-through. As Palin had said, it was clearly intended to be read and understood at a glance, but that didn't mean it was entirely comprehensible. Symbols that might be instantly recognizable to the builders were occasionally puzzles with missing pieces to her.

Finally she pressed a command she believed would draw down the elevator again and waited, looking for any sign of a change.

This is going to be a long wait.

A sound of something scraping on metal brought them all up short, making them turn in the direction of the sound.

"Cover me, Mac," Pierce ordered. "I'll check it out."

"Got your back."

▶▶▶

▶ "Move! Move! Move!"

Marines poured out of the belly of *Copperhead Two*, suits already operational and guns primed as they sought out a target. Orbiting within a hundred meters, *Copperhead One* was covering the deployment, but so far there was little to cover.

"Last reports from the investigation team listed this as an elevator," a Marine lieutenant said, letting his weapon hang from its straps as he approached the doors. "Have you made any headway with the interface?"

"Yes, sir, Lieutenant," a Navy chief announced. "We're pretty sure that we've recalled it to the surface. If we're reading the display correctly, it should be here soon."

"Good. It's possible that our missing Marines are inside, but if not, we're going to have to go down and see if we can't find them," Lieutenant Ramirez said.

"Yes, sir, not a problem."

Ramirez paused, glancing up to where *Copperhead One* was circling. "*One*, you see anything?"

"Just some Marines crawling around in the dirt."

"Cleanest dirt I've ever been in," Ramirez said, "but if anything moves down here that isn't a Marine or a Navy puke . . ."

"We'll dirty it up for you in a hurry, Lieutenant. My word."

"Good enough." Ramirez refocused on the interface, noting the change. "Looks like our lift is coming up."

"Roger that. We'll keep your egress point covered."

Ramirez had no doubt of that, so for the moment he was as content as he could be just to wait for the big doors to open.

▶ ▶ ▶

▶ "Nothing here," Pierce said. "Catwalk is clear."

"Well, I know we heard *something*," McMillan said from well back, where the squad's designated marksman was covering him. "I double-checked the suit recordings. Definite metallic scrape, not metal on metal though."

"Maybe something fell," Pierce said, sweeping above him with the gun. "There's a roof in here somewhere, right?"

"That wasn't a clang, chief," McMillan answered. "It was a scrape."

"Yeah, guy can wish, can't he?" Pierce sighed, backing toward the central shaft again. "I can't see a damn thing out here. Commander, any sign of the lift?"

"I think it's been called up," Daiyu answered, "or maybe it's on an automatic return command. I don't know."

"Great. We're stuck here until it comes back down, then," Pierce growled. "This is making my skin crawl."

"Calm down. It was probably nothing," McMillan said. "Besides, we could go back to the library."

"No," Commander Daiyu said. "We wait. If there is something here, I'd rather not lead it back to the others . . . or get ambushed in the darkness."

"Lady has a point," Pierce grumbled. "Besides, it's probably nothing."

"Yeah . . ." McMillan didn't sound convinced. "Nothing."

Pierce turned around and started walking back. "Don't lose it on me, Mac. This place is creepy enough without us screwing with each other's heads."

McMillan snorted, but didn't reply as he lowered his weapon from his shoulder and glanced over to where the commander was still focusing on the door interface. He heard that same odd sound again, however, and turned back to where Pierce was still walking. The corporal must have heard it too, but hadn't reacted yet as McMillan saw the shape cut itself from the darkness and practically *materialize* right behind him.

"What?" Pierce asked, confused as McMillan stumbled backward, every system in the PFC's armor suddenly screaming. "What the hell is it?"

McMillan finally snapped out of his stupor enough to let training take over, his rifle now moving almost of its own accord. It was placed to his shoulder before he registered that he'd even moved, his finger curled around the firing stud.

"It's right behind me, isn't it?" Pierce asked with a sinking feeling even as he started to react.

"Hit the deck!"

Pierce dropped as McMillan's rifle screamed, launching heavy rounds into the atmosphere as fast as the magnetic coils could discharge. The corporal heard the impacts and reports above him as the rounds found a target even before he struck the catwalk and rolled over onto his back.

He almost wished he'd stayed facedown.

The body was serpentine, and long. Really damn long. Pierce couldn't see the end of it in the darkness that cloaked the area, but frankly he didn't *want* to see the end of it either. He swung his rifle up even as he kicked at the floor and tried to push himself away from it.

What kind of freaking snake has six legs and claws!?

His rifle screamed, joining the chorus started by McMillan's. At the range they were firing, the rounds from their weapons didn't have a chance to engage the rocket motors built into them, but that just gave them a more explosive kick when they slammed into the target and detonated.

Smoke was now obscuring the area as much as darkness, and Pierce dropped his rifle when the snake-thing reared up and brought its claws down. He scrambled backward, narrowly avoiding being eviscerated by the beast, judging from what it did to the catwalk, and then rolled over and scrabbled back to his feet and bolted with his head down as McMillan covered him.

"We need that fucking door open!"

"Working on it, Corporal," Daiyu growled, "but I do not control the speed of the lift."

McMillan stepped over Pierce as the corporal hit the ground in front of him sliding, keeping the beast in his rifle scope. The PFC was firing in bursts, mentally counting down how many rounds he had left with each whine of the accelerators. The rifle didn't even have a chance to signal it was empty before he'd ejected the mag, letting it clatter over the side and fall off into the darkness, and seated a fresh one.

The serpentine beast was snarling at him, having taken several direct hits from both his and Pierce's weapons, yet looking largely none the worse for wear. He hesitated now that Pierce was behind him and the beast was a few paces off, wondering if he should keep firing.

"What are you stopping for, Mac? Shoot that fucking thing!"

McMillan ignored Pierce, his eyes locked with the beast as it stared back. It was moving its head from side to side, as if pinpointing his position, and hissing a lot, but other than that and clambering over the catwalk, it wasn't moving in the direction of the team.

"Checking fire," Mac said finally.

Pierce climbed back to his feet, eyeing the snake-thing from over Mac's shoulder. "Are you insane? Shoot it!"

The snake let out a guttural hiss and thudded to the catwalk, unmoving.

Pierce stared blankly. "How the hell did you know it was going to do that?"

"I've seen mortal wounds before, Corporal."

"What the hell is that thing?" Pierce sighed, stepping forward to get a better look. "Damn thing creeps me out just lying there."

"You and me both," McMillan said. "Let's just hope it doesn't have friends."

"A wise attitude, Private," Daiyu said. "The lift is returning now."

"Great." Pierce grumbled, taking a moment to flip over to the Marines' secure comm and access the command channel. "Major, Pierce here."

There was no response, causing the two Marines to look at each other nervously.

"I still have their transponders on my HUD," McMillan said.

"Ditto. Keep eyes on that thing while I try to boost the signal," Pierce ordered.

"Roger that," McMillan said, walking over to the thing draped across the catwalk.

It was snakelike, obviously, with nasty, six-inch fangs protruding from its mouth. The wings were batlike, or that was as close as he could think to describe them, and it had reptilian legs. Four to the back, with a pair articulated differently to the front.

Arms? Damn, what the hell is this thing?

"This looks almost like a dragon," he said after a moment. "Uglier than the movies, and snakier than most, but still pretty much like a dragon."

"Record everything," Daiyu ordered. "But pay more attention to making sure we're not food for the next one, Private."

"Roger that, Commander," McMillan said.

Pierce took a knee, focusing on his transmission kit as he tried to get the digital signal strong enough to get a message back to the major. Unfortunately, while they still had IFF readings from the others' suits and comms, those functioned on a different band than the straight comm gear and had better range.

"I'm not getting much of a boost on the signal here," he admitted finally. "We can't leave them down here without warning."

"We wait until the doors open, then decide on a course of action," Daiyu said after a moment. "We can do nothing until then."

"And when they open, what do you plan then?"

"That," she said, "depends entirely on what, or who, is inside the lift when they open. Now remain calm, Marine, do not panic."

"Lady, I'm not panicking. I'm thinking about the rest of the team. I'm a Marine, Semper fi," Pierce growled, probably stepping on the line of insubordination, but not giving a damn at the moment.

Commander Daiyu stared at him, her face hidden behind the suit visor. She suspected that his tone would have been considerably more in line with military protocol if she had been nearly any other officer.

She took a step closer to him and leaned in. "Corporal, I really suggest you check your attitude before I choose to take official notice of it. In the absence of the major, I *am* your commanding officer, and I will not be spoken to in such a manner. Am I being clear?"

Pierce glared back, but knew that he was standing cleanly on the wrong side of the line and reluctantly backed off.

"Clear, ma'am."

"Excellent," Daiyu said, straightening up and turning back to the lift. "Now, secure the area. The lift should be here soon."

CHAPTER 12

▶ Phillips looked over the room, probably an office judging by the layout, and sighed as he pinched his nose.

"Call him back," he said finally.

"Sir?" Nickels asked, uncertain.

"The idiot who can translate this crap. Him. Call him back."

The major couldn't believe he'd just said that. The last thing he needed . . . no, the last thing he *wanted* was that idiot in the same room with him, but unfortunately it seemed that he did need just that.

"Yes, sir!" Nickels jogged off.

Bodies on the ground usually indicated foul play, but he didn't see any sign of a fight. Also, bodies were usually *cleaned up*, but whoever runs this place had just left these lying there.

Did they evacuate the place in an emergency? But from what? He pondered the situation, trying to make sense of it, right up until a stumbling fool almost bowled him over from behind.

"Oh, terribly sorry about that," Palin stuttered out, staring not at him but at the bones on the floor. "Not, uh, not used to the gravity here."

Phillips leashed in the urge to introduce the academic to the floor, instead pointing to the workstations. "There are words there. Translate them."

Palin tore his attention from the bones and looked over, only now seeing the very thing he'd been searching for in the first place. The bones were forgotten in an instant as he zeroed in on the script and symbols he saw.

"Oh, my, yes . . . oh, definitely similar to Priminae script," he mumbled, moving over to the workstations and starting to pore over language. "The precursor script is fascinating. This is going to be so much *fun*."

"While you're having fun, Doctor," Phillips said, "I want to know what happened here. Something very *wrong* happened in this room."

"Uh . . . yes, of course. I'll let you know if I find anything."

Phillips just nodded curtly and stepped out of the office, gesturing to a pair of Marines. "On this door. Watch him, don't let anything happen."

"Yes, sir!"

The major walked down the hall to where most of the geeks they'd come down with were still examining star charts. He stopped beside Lieutenant Chapman, the squad leader.

"I don't like any of this, Lieutenant," he said. "Keep the men on their toes."

"Sir." Chapman nodded. "Is there something I need to know?"

Phillips shook his head. "No, Lieutenant, just a bad feeling."

"Bodies on the floor will do that, sir."

"Calling them bodies is being generous. They've been there a while," the major said. "A long while."

"Any sign of a fight, sir?"

"None. It looks like they just curled up and died."

Chapman grimaced inside his suit. "Not the way I'd want to go, sir."

Phillips didn't say anything. It wasn't like there was a good answer to a statement like that. Personally he'd like to punch his ticket to Valhalla, or wherever warriors went when the lights went out, but saying it just felt too damned cheap. When his time was up, his time was up, and he knew that the best he could hope for was a vote in the manner if not the timing.

"Just keep your eyes open, son," he ordered. "The last time my guts curled up like this, my platoon walked into an ambush in the Philippines."

▶▶▶

▶ Edward Palin wasn't a field sort, as he himself would be the first to admit. When the chance to study more alien languages came up, however, he'd jumped at the chance and shamelessly leveraged everything he could to get himself assigned to the *Autolycus*. That meant calling in favors and making threats, but he was tired of working on the Priminae language. What was the point? They had actual native speakers available for that. His talents were hardly used at all.

Here, however, was something to sink his teeth into.

The language in the astronomical facility was likely proto-Priminae, much like Latin was proto-English, unless he was very much mistaken. He could already decipher tantalizing bits of it, but most pieces were still just the beginnings of patterns waiting to fall into place.

Palin had started his career as a code breaker, back before the Block war. During those days code breaking was generally left to computers, and usually consisted of chewing through encrypted data with supercomputing arrays. Dull, tedious work at the best of times, it was really rather disappointing after he'd spent his postdoctoral education studying some of the greatest codes in history.

Then the Chinese started using a new code, one that the computers couldn't crack. Oh, that one gave the NSA fits, he well remembered. He'd been stationed in Cheyenne Mountain by then, assigned there by the Canadian government as part of the joint monitoring plan.

Cracking the new ChiCom code became something of an obsession for the people in his division, with a steadily growing pot being offered to the person, or team, that did it. Edward Palin made his name, and several thousand dollars, by realizing that the code wasn't an encryption at all but rather was based on a dead language that hadn't been spoken for nearly three thousand years.

It took another ten years to fully break it, by which point Palin was the head of Project Windtalker, the Confederation's top-level encoding and decryption program. After the war, well, he'd gotten bored until the *Odyssey*'s first mission came up. He got himself assigned there on a whim.

Sometimes, annoying people the way he did was just as useful as having them owe him favors. The combination of the two could be quite potent, if he did say so himself.

Now he had a new challenge, however, and Palin was gleefully sinking his teeth into it with all the energy of his younger self from over twenty years earlier.

Though hopefully with a little more intelligence, he thought ruefully as he considered the comparison.

This project was actually a lot easier than Project Windtalker, given that now he had a modern language to work backward from and several key words that were clearly rooted in the same origins. Within twenty minutes Palin had started picking out words and phrases that identified the facility, based on what he knew of it as well as modern Priminae lingual patterns.

It was the handwritten notes that he found most interesting, however, and more than a little disturbing.

▶ ▶ ▶

▶ Pierce and McMillan were edgy by the time the lift was almost back to their level, since they now knew what to look for in the darkness.

Every few seconds another anomalous scan would flit by their sensors, just out of range.

"We're being checked out," Pierce said, his rifle to his shoulder as he watched the flank of the catwalk opposite from his compatriot.

"They're like a wolf pack," McMillan acknowledged, "nothing like those Drasin things. These bastards can think for themselves."

"Yeah, I just can't decide if that's a good thing or a bad thing," Pierce snorted.

Daiyu listened to their discussion while watching the door interface, splitting her focus at least three ways as she worked.

Potentially, the answer to the corporal's question could go either way. The Drasin were dangerous because they had a group mind that made decisions for the whole, while the individuals were mere drones to be sacrificed for victory. That made them both deadly and predictable, but ultimately led to their defeat at the hands of Earth's organized military . . . along with not insignificant help from the Priminae.

Had they each been a thinking and reacting soldier, the sort of mass annihilations that wiped out the bulk of the Drasin forces wouldn't have been as easily accomplished . . . if they were even possible at all.

Without more information, however, there was no way to predict what they were dealing with, other than one more xenoform that had the capacity to be a major problem.

The lift arrived silently, with no comforting beep or chime to announce its presence. The doors simply opened, taking both Marines by surprise. They spun around with their weapons at the ready, only to freeze in shock as they found themselves seriously outgunned.

"Stand down!"

The snap of command hadn't come from Commander Daiyu, primarily because as a member of the Block military her instinctive response to seeing a platoon of Confederate Marines with battle rifles aimed at her was to *remove* herself from said area.

No, it was the lieutenant in command who snapped the order out while Daiyu was ducking behind the doors and swearing under her breath in Cantonese.

The rifles were lowered quickly.

"Belay that," Corporal Pierce said a moment later. "Sorry, Lieutenant, but we've got hostiles in the area."

"Perimeter security, go!" Ramirez ordered, a gesture sending four Marines out of the lift with their weapons up and seeking targets. "Report, Corporal, what kind of hostiles?"

"That kind." Pierce pointed, his tone probably a little dryer than strictly proper for military protocol.

Ramirez had to step out of the lift to see what was being pointed to, but when he spotted the dead creature he almost jumped right out of his suit and back in.

"Holy . . ."

"We're pretty sure there are more flitting around, but they're not too keen on tangling with us right now," Pierce said. "We need more eyes on the skies while we figure out what we're going to do."

"Speaking of which . . ." Commander Daiyu entered the conversation, now having stepped back into the open. "Why are you here? We're not even close to being overdue."

"Lost contact with the two Marine guards posted at the surface, ma'am," Ramirez answered instantly. "No sign of them on the tower, or under it. I assume from your question that they didn't come down here."

"No, Lieutenant, they did not," Daiyu answered gravely, considering the situation. "This is becoming more complicated by the moment. Do you have transmission boosters?"

"Yes, ma'am, field grade comm booster."

"Set it up. I want to speak with the captain."

▶ ▶ ▶

▶ "Signal from the moon, Captain."

Morgan looked up from where he had been trying to distract himself with crew dossiers. One part of being the captain that he had never liked was the waiting when he had a team ashore. In the war it was usually a SOCOM team, often SEALs, and now it was Marines. Same thing from his perspective, however.

"Put it through."

There was a pause as the signal was patched through to his station, and he noted that he was looking at the face of his first officer through the rather bad artifacting that was scrambling the image.

"Commander, how are things progressing?"

Commander Daiyu's image didn't react immediately. There was a lag of a second or so, partly due to distance and partly due to the computer obviously fighting to compile a recognizable signal from the mess it was working with.

"It's an observatory, Captain. The gravity lensing is for an observatory," she said. "We're looking at star charts for the entire galaxy down here."

Morgan blinked.

That he hadn't been expecting. Galactic charts would be of inestimable value in their mission, and beyond that for the Earth as it continued to make defense plans.

"We have a problem, though, Captain," the commander went on. "There is a local life-form. I don't know if it's indigenous, but it does seem hostile. Two Marines are missing, and they were on the surface at the time of lost contact. Unknown if the cause was from the same life-form. I'm sending you what we've scanned on the creature."

Morgan glanced over the data packet quickly, just skimming most of it but lingering for a moment on the serpentine nature of the beast as he shivered involuntarily.

I'd almost have preferred the Drasin. I hate snakes.

"Commander, you can pull back, and we'll call in one of the Heroics to continue the local mission," Morgan offered.

He'd rather not do that, for a multitude of reasons, least of which that this was their mission and their find. That said, there was no doubt that the larger complement of a Heroic Class ship would be more suited to long-term exploitation of the find. Honestly, in the end, that was exactly what would happen.

"Would rather not, Captain," Daiyu said, echoing his own preferences, "but we're going to try to locate the missing Marines first anyway. Science team is in a lab complex, should be able to secure it. We'll stay in contact."

"Very well, Commander. We're standing by with all available resources," he said.

"Yes, Captain, thank you."

The signal cut off, though he could see that the booster remained active as the Marines' transponders were still appearing on his system.

Mostly.

Morgan frowned, noting that some of the signals were blinking in and out, despite the signal boosters.

"Do we have a location on just how far down they are?" he asked, looking around.

"No, sir, I'm sorry. We're actually trying to triangulate that now with the shuttles and drones, but interference is making a geo-lock difficult."

Damn.

"Keep trying," he ordered. "I want to know where my teams are in more than just general terms."

"Aye, sir."

▶ ▶ ▶

▶Commander Daiyu closed the comm and equalized her visor so others could see in. "Captain says we continue the mission while we look for your Marines, Lieutenant."

"Yes, ma'am," Ramirez said, glad to hear it. "We'll start setting up with the booster and see if we can ping their transponders down here."

Daiyu nodded absently, thinking about other things. "Best contact Major Phillips and tell him to secure the doors to the lab area. We don't want them running into any of the local life-forms."

Ramirez nodded. "I'll handle that immediately, ma'am."

"Good," Daiyu said, her attention focused elsewhere for the moment. "Very good, Lieutenant. See to it."

She was now more interested in the life-form, something she hadn't been able to put much of her focus on until other matters had cleared up. Walking over to it, she dropped to a crouch and examined the body more closely.

Almost wish I'd specialized in xenobiology.

Almost all higher-ranking officers in the Block, and the Confederation she supposed, had basic classes in the field now, of course. The invasion had seen to that, but the majority of the information detailed in those classes was still completely hypothetical.

The Drasin were so far from any sane evolutionary path that it was clear they'd been engineered by someone just as insane as they were. The Priminae were human, sharing genetic markers that even matched *geological* adaptations of *Homo sapiens*. Between those two extraterrestrial species that humanity was well acquainted with, there hadn't been a lot of hard facts about how life might evolve independently.

What she was looking at was certain to add a lot to those classes, Daiyu expected.

"It seems to be adapted to the low gravity of the moon, and the needs of this cavern," she said, looking around. "It's far too large to fly on Earth, but I've seen snakes that could glide over a hundred meters, easily. Give them wings and claws, and, well, I'm just as happy not to have seen the results before now."

"I'd rather not have seen them now," Corporal Pierce muttered. "How much you want to bet that those claws could cleave our armor like paper?"

That was a wager the commander wasn't remotely stupid enough to take. She'd seen what the creature did to the walkway they were standing on. Thankfully, none of it seemed to be structural damage, but even so, the armor worn by Navy and Marine personnel had to be lightweight and flexible. It was kinetic and burn-resistant, but a sharp piercing strike would perforate it easily.

"Lieutenant!"

The call over the open comm diverted all their attention to a Marine comm tech examining his equipment.

"What is it, Private?" Ramirez asked, walking over in his direction.

"I've got transponder signals on our missing Marines, sir."

"Outstanding. Where?"

The private didn't look encouraged as he pointed straight down.

Commander Daiyu, Lieutenant Ramirez, and many of the rest looked down into the depths below the catwalk and just stared for a long moment.

"Well, crap," the lieutenant muttered, forgetting to silence his transmission.

Daiyu didn't bother to call him on it. She'd been about a quarter second from saying something significantly more . . . *colorful*.

"I'll call the captain," she said finally. "We're going to need to break open the SOCOM crate."

CHAPTER 13

▶ "*Autolycus* control, *Copperhead One* . . . I have the ball."

Copperhead One snagged the hook on the first pass, and Grant killed thrust while hitting full CM to counter as much of their inertia as possible. It was still a rough ride. They were slammed hard into their restraints as the assault shuttle was stopped relative to the *Autolycus* and pulled into the ship by the trap.

"*Copperhead One*, *Autolycus* control . . . Roger that, we have you. Welcome home."

Being pulled up into the shuttle bay, not that "up" meant much on the *Auto*, was a bit of a drawn-out process. It took several minutes to secure the shuttle in its hanger, *not* its hangar . . . a literal hanger that treated her baby more like a cheap suit than the beautiful god of war it was.

"Copy, control. Thanks for the welcome, but we're on a turn-around," she said, unlatching her straps and floating free of the seat. She glanced over to her copilot. "Keep the reactor on standby. I'm going to make sure everything's loaded in."

"No problem, Commander."

She checked that they were locked, and then nodded to the jump-master, who slapped his hand down on the belly controls. The heavy doors hissed, a slight pressure differential with the ship blowing air out as the seal broke, and the doors finally pulled slowly apart.

The SOCOM crate was already in place on the other side, just waiting for the doors to open.

"Alright, bring it in," Chief Kase, the jumpmaster, ordered.

SOCOM gear was expensive, which was one reason it wasn't issued to the Marines as a matter of course, but more importantly, it often took specialized training to properly utilize. Grant didn't know what they wanted with the crate—that wasn't her job—but she hoped that they knew what they were doing.

Every ship had at least one SOCOM crate issued, mostly so that any team sent to the ship for a temporary assignment wouldn't need a second shuttle to carry their gear. The issue crate covered the basics that troopers didn't have on them.

"Get it stocked and locked," she told the chief. "We're dropping as soon as I confirm we're topped off."

"You got it, Commander."

Human gravity manipulation technology hadn't yet been shrunk down small enough to get an Albucierre drive on an assault shuttle, more's the pity, so Grant went to confirm that they were taking on a full fuel load. She wanted to be close in case the ground team needed dustoff, and only wished that she could provide close air support.

Too bad there's no way Copperhead One *would fit in the lift,* she thought wryly as she confirmed the fuel transfer in progress.

▶ ▶ ▶

▶ Captain Passer was drifting idly near the flight deck, overseeing the loading of the SOCOM crate and the refueling of *Copperhead One.* There wasn't a lot more he could be doing at the moment, as frustrating as that was. All the action was centered three hundred klicks below the *Auto* and rested in the hands of other people.

What little information they had from the moon at that point clearly showed it to be the find of the century, and that was quite likely underestimating the value of the charts they'd discovered, completely ignoring the facility itself.

Since the invasion had torn the Earth nearly asunder, a lot of things had changed, but human nature wasn't one of them. People wanted to feel like they could hit back, but against the Drasin you might as well be throwing punches at a tornado. Everyone who'd faced those things came to realize quickly that there was no justice, or vengeance, to be had there. You might as well hate a virus or an earthquake for all the satisfaction that would offer.

The people who held the Drasin's *leash*, however, were a very different story.

Among those who knew the whole story, there was something to focus on.

Something to hate.

The charts on the moon below just might be the key to finding them, and that was something Morgan practically *lived* for.

▶▶▶

▶ "Loaded and locked, ma'am."

"Thank you, Chief. Get yourself strapped in, we're about to drop," Kathryn Grant said as she cinched back into her seat and opened the comm. "Control, *Copperhead One*."

"Go for control, *One*."

"All checks are green. We are ready to drop."

"Roger that, moving Copperhead to launch position. Stand by."

She nodded. "Standing by."

The shuttle rocked a little as it was moved onto the rails of the launcher and locked into place.

"Launch on your command, *Copperhead One*."

"Roger that," Grant replied, wrapping her hand around the control stick and moving her thumb over a secured red button. She flipped the cap off it, a red light came on, and she smiled. "Launch. Launch. Launch."

She pressed the button, and a blast of electromagnetic force sent them flying out the belly of the ship.

Unlike a full catapult launch, the *Auto* just used a short pull set of rails, barely enough to get the shuttle up to hypersonic speeds if measured in Earth atmosphere near sea level. It was still enough to slam everyone back in their bolsters, and to set the moon now ahead of them spinning as Grant worked the stick and got them on course for the tower.

"*Copperhead One* is now on course for delivery of payload."

"Roger, *One*, Godspeed."

▶▶▶

▶ Commander Daiyu looked out at the stars above her as she stood on the platform set atop the tower. With no atmosphere, the stars glowed with an unearthly and steady light. It was almost eerie. She stood to one side as the Marines with her secured the platform, her eyes on the skies while they watched everything else.

Her HUD had an augmented display, so she didn't have to search for the position of *Copperhead One* when its running lights separated themselves from the other stars in the sky and began their approach.

The assault shuttle dropped fast and hit the brakes hard as it settled in low over the platform, exhaust from the maneuver plucking at her suit like a blast of wind. She waved the shuttle in and stepped back as the pilot pivoted the shuttle around and eased in.

The back ramp lowered, and she could see the jumpmaster standing in the door. He waved once, and she could see him scout the area with a turn of his helmet. Then he stepped aside, and the crate rolled out and crashed to the platform.

"SOCOM crate delivered. *Copperhead One* continuing orbit of LZ," the pilot said as the shuttle's exhaust flared, causing Daiyu to fall back a step from the blast.

"Confirmed, *Copperhead*," she said. "Thank you for the delivery."

Commander Daiyu stepped up to the crate, accessing the security and unlocking it from her suit systems. She almost could imagine the heavy thunk of the locks coming loose before the doors swung open. She gave them a push and looked over the contents with her eyes and her suit's RFI system.

"Private," she waved. "These go in the lift first."

"Yes, ma'am." The private ran over and examined the stack of devices. He grabbed the first one and started lugging it back.

She grabbed the next one and followed suit, heading for the lift.

The SOCOM chutes were obscenely expensive pieces of technology, ones that she'd have won a commendation for just a few years earlier if she had turned in just one to her superiors in the Block command.

And today I just have to ask and I'm issued a whole cratefull. How times have changed.

She glanced over at the rest of the Marines. "Two on watch. The rest of you help get the gear transferred. We need it downstairs as quickly as possible."

"Yes, ma'am!"

▶▶▶

▶ "This cavern is insane," Ramirez decided as he propped one foot on the rail of the catwalk and looked out over the expanse beyond. "Does anyone have a hit on how far it extends?"

"No, sir, we don't have anything to take a parallax reading off of, and even laser range finders aren't getting a return. It's dead space, sir."

The lieutenant shook his head. "How big does a space have to be before we don't get a hit on those?"

The corporal he was speaking to was silent for a moment. "Specs say line of sight, but that's measured by Earth standard, so we could be talking just a few klicks. I've personally painted a target at a hundred klicks with one, but I don't know the falloff."

Ramirez scowled. Even assuming a hundred klicks, he had a hard time imagining the sheer size of the space they were in. There was no bounceback in any direction, which made for the largest cave he'd ever heard of in his life. The largest on Earth was less than five klicks in length, a couple hundred meters high.

How the hell does something like this form, anyway?

"I've got a hit, sir!"

Ramirez snapped over. "You found a wall?"

"No, sir, but there's something below us."

"What do you mean?"

The corporal waved. "I mapped it. It's a small . . . island, or maybe a mountain peak. It's a hundred and twenty klicks below us. I'd have missed it, sir, except that the transponders from our Marines are near that area."

"Well, alright then," Ramirez said, satisfied. "Now we have someplace to search. Good work."

"Thank you, sir."

Now he just needed the SOCOM chutes, because there was no way in hell that he was going to abandon a pair of his Marines in the middle of a pitch-black cave on some moon that didn't even have a name.

▶▶▶

▶ Major Phillips glared unhappily at the doors that led out of the lab and into the cavern beyond. He wanted to be out there right then, part of the operation that was going down. He should have been the one tracking those Marines. They'd gone missing under his command. Hell, he'd even had to be *told* they were gone, hadn't even been the one to find out himself.

It was the lieutenant's mission now, however.

"Sir?"

"What is it, son?" Phillips asked, not turning to look at the private.

"The linguist seems to have found something."

"Oh? What did he tell you?"

"Me, sir? Nothing, sir."

"Then what makes you think he found something?"

The Marine paused for a moment, and then snorted. "He's dancing on the furniture, yelling 'Eureka!' over and over, sir."

Phillips had the nearly irresistible urge to take his helmet off just so he could palm his face in deep annoyance.

"I'll be right there," he said finally, wishing again that he could be part of the team heading down to find his two men.

▶▶▶

▶ Edward Palin loved these moments more than he loved anything else he had ever encountered in his life, the slices of time when all the pieces of a puzzle began to slide into place and everything began to make sense.

Languages were a puzzle, after all, with pieces that fit according to an innate logic that changed with every puzzle. Discovering the logic was the key to unraveling a language, because until you knew the logic you couldn't find the proverbial side pieces.

The Priminae language was incredibly complex, more so than any language on Earth, and showed what had originally appeared to be influences from both the romance languages and the languages of the Far East. He was beginning to see the true influences that had molded the Priminae language.

The proto-language was actually more complex, he suspected, with deeper inflections and meanings. Compared to what he was seeing there, Palin suspected that the Priminae were almost a regressive child race. The ancient words he was piecing together into phrases showed a complexity that he'd never seen before, not in any language he'd ever studied . . . on Earth, or off.

"Doctor!"

Palin ignored the voice, continuing his dancing.

With most languages he'd encountered, the logic was easy to follow, especially if he had just a little hint of the culture behind the logic. The Priminae had confused him, because their culture and their language had never quite made any sense to him. The complexity of the language, as well as the vocabulary they'd dug up, didn't match any of the cultural cues of the Priminae.

This proto-language, however, might just explain that.

"Doctor!"

The voice was a lot harder to ignore the second time, but Palin was well practiced in doing so. He *did* glance back and wave, however.

"Oh, hello, Major," he said. "Don't mind me."

Major Phillips stared in near slack-jawed disbelief as the doctor again turned around and went back to dancing.

"What in the name of all . . ." he grumbled as he strode forward and grabbed the doctor's shoulder. Wrenching him around, he glared into the tinted visor. "If you keep ignoring me, I *will* shoot you, Doctor."

"Pardon me?" Palin blurted, staring back.

Phillips counted to ten silently before speaking again, not quite trusting himself not to make good on his threat.

"What have you found, Doctor?"

"Found? Found?" Palin asked, perplexed. "Major, I've found the secrets of the universe. What did you think I'd found?"

"Can the shit shoveling, Doc, and tell me what the hell you're dancing around like a fool over!"

"Dancing? Oh, that?" The doctor waved casually. "I just managed to translate the memos over there."

Phillips glanced at the workstation. "Memos? What did they say?"

"Huh? Oh, nothing important. Couple standard office-type messages, one love letter home, that sort of thing."

"Nothing about . . . that?" Phillips jerked his head in the direction of the covered remains.

Palin barely glanced at it, having apparently decided to repress its existence. "Nope, not a thing."

"Then why the hell are you dancing around like an imbecile?"

"I told you, I translated them," Palin said, bewildered.

"So? You just said they're useless!"

"But they're translated . . ."

Phillips just stared for a moment, and then wordlessly shook his head and turned on his heel before stalking out.

Palin didn't spare the Marine a moment's attention.

He had more real work to do.

CHAPTER 14

▶ "Is anyone here qualified on these things?" Corporal Pierce asked as he looked at the SOCOM chute he'd been handed.

"I've done a few jumps," Ramirez said. "Relax, they're easier to handle than a civilian airborne transport. They practically fly themselves."

Pierce looked over the edge of the catwalk, into the deep black, and then back to his lieutenant. "Practically isn't the word I want to hear right now, sir."

"Corporal," Commander Daiyu cut in, "if you don't want to go, stay here. This is a volunteer-only assignment."

"No, no," Pierce said, locking the straps into his armor. "I'm in. I'm in."

Ramirez looked around at the Marines. "We've got transponder hits, almost a hundred klicks down. That means we don't have nearly as much flight time as I'd like, but it's more than enough to go down, pick up our people, and get the hell back here. Do *not* dick around down there, do *not* sightsee. Our margin for error is *not* as big as we want, trust me on this."

The Marines finished locking in the chute straps, using the armor hard points to secure themselves to the packs.

"Alright, the first part of this is just like a HALO insert," Ramirez said, looking the group over. "We're gonna drop, free-fall most of the way to our target. We don't pull the chutes until we're almost there. That'll save us some juice and give us more loiter time downstairs. Keep your eyes open going down. There are hostiles in the air, so keep your heads on a swivel and your fingers on the trigger. Do you *hear* me?"

"We hear you, sir!"

"Good," he said, planting one foot up on the catwalk rail. "Then let's do this. Semper fi! Ooh rah!"

"Ooh rah, Semper fi!"

Ramirez turned and jumped from the rail, followed quickly by the rest of the team. As the Marines vanished into the blackness, Commander Daiyu stepped over to the rail and looked down. She sighed and shook her head, mumbling under her breath.

"Sorry, Commander, what was that?"

"I said, Corporal," she spoke more clearly, "that I wish I knew if it is just your Marines who are insane, or if it is the entire Confederation."

▶▶▶

▶ It felt different, Ramirez thought on his way down, jumping in a suit.

It was so quiet, he could barely hear the roar of the atmosphere tearing past him. He wondered how much of it was the suit and how much was the lower gravity of the moon keeping him from accelerating to the same terminal velocity.

Jumping was familiar to him and the others, though jumping with his weapon in hand was a new one for him. It added a certain flair of Hollywood to the whole thing, he felt.

It also violated all kinds of regs for Marines, which was at least half the fun.

"Anyone see any sign of the hostiles?" he asked, patching the battle network together and linking everyone as he counted down the kilometers as they fell.

Negative calls came back by the numbers, but he was seeing anomalies on the network scans. There was something out there, just flitting in and out of range of their acoustic pulses. The Marines' suit scanners weren't as sophisticated as some of the gear packed by SOCOM troops, and right then he was hurting for the extended range.

"Look for enemy flyers and watch each other's backs," he ordered. "And for God's sake, don't shoot my ass!"

"You're not that bad a lieutenant, Lieutenant."

Ramirez stonily ignored the laughter, not bothering to dignify that backhanded compliment with a response. He did check his weapon's status and configuration, making sure that a round was chambered and the capacitors were hot.

"We're getting a better scan on the object, sir. Looks like a mountaintop," the comm tech said, cutting into the chatter. "Expanding larger as we get closer. I'm reading the transponders about two and a half klicks below the peak. Can I get a confirmation from another angle?"

"Confirmed. My scans match yours, Corporal," Ramirez responded, checking the information on his HUD. "ETA to target LZ is three minutes. Stay sharp. We've got a long fall left."

"Ooh rah!"

▶▶▶

▶ Commander Daiyu led her Marine guards back to the lab. There was little to be gained by standing around the catwalk and staring into the black, after all, and she wanted another look at the facility itself before they had to pull back. Once the *Autolycus* finished its initial survey there, the odds were it would be the last she'd see of the place. Another team would come in to finish up and likely claim it as a forward base and observation station.

Her specialty was in cutting-edge experimental physics, not astronomy, but she knew enough about stellar mapping to understand just how valuable the facility was to Earth at this point in time. And, she had to admit, the physics of it all had her entirely enthralled.

I hope we can find a facility schematic to explain how they're warping space-time as much as they are in such a small area.

Prior to this discovery, almost all known significant gravity lenses were natural, and generally on the order of billions of light-years away. They were scientifically interesting, of course, allowing astronomers to study galaxies on the far side of the universe in impressive detail, but they weren't the most tactically or strategically useful things in the universe.

This station, on the other hand, was more than just a technological marvel. It was a strategic gold mine the likes of which the Earth literally hadn't been able to imagine until then. To be able to peer into practically any star system in the galaxy almost as if you were there in person . . . it boggled her mind.

There were limits, of course, she thought as she walked toward the lab. The facility could only view things as they'd happened, limited by the speed of light. A system seventy thousand light-years away could only be viewed as it had been seventy thousand years ago. That was certainly an issue, as far as military advantage went, but even so the knowledge of how the system had developed over time had certain value in and of itself.

Many systems were also *far* closer than that—hundreds, thousands even—within a sphere of only a few dozen light-years.

Yet, unfortunately, she also knew that the planet and the moon were a little too far from Earth to be significantly useful in defensive operations. As a planning tool for exploration and potentially offensive missions, however . . . well, the potential honestly boggled the commander's mind.

She couldn't wait to learn more about it.

▶▶▶

▶ "We're coming up on the LZ. The mountain peak should be on my left. Can't see a damn thing, though."

Ramirez chuckled. "Pierce, in this soup, if you could see it, you would probably be about to hit it."

"Can't argue with that. Still creeping me out, sir."

"No arguments there, Corporal. Alright, break formation and hit the chutes. Don't run into each other. I want lots of room for error on this one."

"You got it, sir."

Ramirez watched as the signals of his fellow Marines spread out some, waiting until they were far enough apart that there was little chance of a collision, and then hit the power control on his SOCOM chute. The device charged a small CM field and fired retro-rockets, snapping him upright and arresting his fall as he swung below it.

"Put down on the mountain," he ordered. "Conserve power in your chutes as much as possible."

The Marines swept in, following Ramirez as he vectored in on the invisible mountaintop. It was still too dark to see visually, but they were well within range for echolocation systems to map it out.

Ramirez picked out his LZ as he entered final approach, bending his knees to absorb the impact of the landing as he hit. He landed in a run, winding up the chute until it was settled solidly against his back again, and surveyed the area with his weapon leading the way.

"Clear LZ," he called, walking across the area and taking a knee near the edge. There was nothing visible below, and he was starting to get creeped out by having to work blind, relying almost entirely on his augmented reality HUD.

"I'm down, rear sector covered," Pierce said. "Permission to detach chute to overwatch?"

"Denied," Ramirez responded as the rest of the Marines touched down around them. "Save the charge. We've got a hundred klicks to climb when we find our missing Marines, and no air support. We don't risk our return ticket."

"Yes, sir."

"Alright, form up," he said. "I've got transponder signals, fifty meters below us. Everyone better be up on their mountaineering courses."

"Hey, boss?"

Ramirez glanced back. "What is it, Mac?"

McMillan was kneeling some distance away, one hand running along the ground beneath him.

"I don't think this is a mountain, boss."

"What are you talking about?" Ramirez straightened up and walked over.

"Check the ground, boss. It's not dirt," McMillan said, tapping the ground.

Ramirez upped the pickup on his audio system, the metallic clang unmistakable. "It's metal?"

"Best bet is that it's the same metal as the outside of this moon."

"What the hell is this place?" Ramirez wondered, shaking his head. "Okay, look, it doesn't matter. We've got two Marines to recover. Leave the questions to the people above our pay grade."

"Yes, sir."

"Move out."

Ramirez got his squad deployed in a column, and they began making their way down toward the missing men's locator transponders.

"God, this is insane. I can't see a damn thing. Lieutenant, let's turn on the lights."

"Negative. Subsonics and augmented display only," Ramirez growled.

"Come on, LT, we don't even know if these things *see* light!"

"And we don't know that they can't, so shut it and do your job, Marine." Ramirez wasn't happy about working with nothing but an augmented view of the world around him either, and it was setting him on edge as he made his way down toward the transponders they were tracking.

"I think I've got stairs here, LT!"

Ramirez looked across to where the Marine was waving him on, the odd computer-generated figure looking all the stranger against the blackness it was projected against. He headed over, patting the Marine on the shoulder as he stepped past and checked the stairwell.

"Good catch, alright. I've got point. Pierce, you're on drag. Watch our backs."

"You got it, LT."

The Marines started down the stairwell, moving down three sections and maybe forty meters or more before they found a new catwalk. Ramirez led his troops around the walkway until he found a large opening that led into the structure they were walking around.

"Whoa."

"You see something, Mac?" Ramirez asked, glancing over his shoulder.

The marksman stepped forward. "This looks like the doorway access to the lab space up top, LT, but something tore the doors off."

Ramirez examined it again, and supposed that he could see what the private was referring to. The opening was a large oval with torn and wrenched edges that he wouldn't want to test his suit against, since they looked sharp as hell. It was clearly an entranceway, however, and he had a more important reason to be interested.

"Transponder signals come from inside," he said. "We're checking it out."

▶▶▶

▶ Commander Daiyu stepped cautiously into the lab where she had been directed by the Marines. Something about their body language told her something was up. Even wearing armor, they were acting distinctly odd.

"Major."

"Commander."

She looked over the room, her eyes falling on the suit her HUD identified as belonging to Doctor Palin as it danced around the far side of the room.

"I don't suppose you have any idea what that's about, do you, Major?" she asked dryly.

Phillips just shrugged, a gesture that was wasted as the armor and pressure suit mostly absorbed the motion. Daiyu recognized the movement anyway. Any spacer quickly learned to read body language in a suit. It was a vital part of the job.

"He's been like that for the past thirty minutes," the major responded. "I asked him a while ago what he found that was so exciting."

"And?"

"He said nothing in particular," Phillips said. "The dumb bastard just ignores anything you say and keeps dancing. Say the word and I'll shoot him. Myself."

Daiyu wished she wasn't wearing the suit because she really needed to rub her temples. She could feel a tension headache building.

"I'll deal with it," she said finally, wishing that she'd sent the major back and stayed with the scientists in the first place.

Riding herd on scientists working on a military project was always a bit of a challenge, because brilliant minds could be . . . not always were, but could be . . . well, eccentric was the polite term. She'd read about Einstein's infamous behavior, despite over a decade of cover-ups, and the best minds were often like that. Once they realized that they were as valuable as they were, even the most disciplined of minds couldn't quite resist testing the waters to see how much they could get away with.

Most learned quickly that there were limits. Very few people were as irreplaceable as an Albert Einstein, after all, but the more valuable they were, the looser those limits tended to be. And smart people worked out quickly how far they could push the limits, and then how they could push them even farther.

She'd read Palin's history, both his Confederation file and his Block intelligence file. Interestingly, the Block file had been *far* more complete. The Block Intelligence Division had collected blackmail material on him for years before figuring out that you couldn't blackmail someone who honestly didn't give a damn what anyone around him thought.

Edward Palin was a genius of the highest order within his field, but not interested in much of anything else as far as anyone could tell. If you weren't the subject of his current project, you pretty much didn't exist.

"Doctor," she spoke, selecting a private comm with him in order to cut out any extraneous comments from the Marines, "I need to know what you've learned."

"Huh?" Palin half turned, surprised to see her approaching. "Learned?"

"Yes, Doctor, what have you learned so far?"

He looked befuddled for a moment, as if considering her question carefully. She supposed that he might be, but she also suspected that she wouldn't recognize his thought process as consideration of any sort she might know.

"Oh, well, some grammar and vocabulary, of course," he answered. "I think I've worked out their most common symbols as well."

"That's excellent," Daiyu answered. "Have you located any information of use to us at the moment?"

"Mostly the immediate information seems to be personal letters," Palin replied, "written just before an operation was to be conducted here. Nothing beyond greetings to family and the like."

"Have you looked into their computers?"

"No. I honestly wouldn't know how to turn them on. They don't seem to have any control interfaces here that I can find."

Daiyu sighed. *That is unfortunate. The data we need will undoubtedly be inside their computer system here.*

"There is that, however," Palin said, pointing behind her and above.

The commander turned, confused. "What?"

"That, above the door," he said, absently gesturing.

"What? There's nothing above the door?"

"Not the door here. Look across the corridor."

She refocused and, lo and behold, there were indeed characters written above the door he was pointing to. "What does it say?"

"Maintenance room, more or less," Palin answered, his nose back in the work he'd been doing before.

Daiyu wanted to slap herself, or perhaps him. Either would do.

"The doors are all labeled? What room is this?"

"Oh, just someone's office, I believe. It looks more like a personal name, rather than any word root I'm familiar with."

"Doctor," she sighed, "have you been updating our language software?"

That caught Palin's attention and he looked up, almost seeming put out if she were to judge his body language, "Of course I am. I know my job, Commander. I'm also the one who wrote that software. The new database is listed under proto-Priminae."

"Thank you, Doctor. Please continue," she said, turning away.

She walked back to the major and gestured out of the office, leading him away from the occasionally manic scientist.

"Leave a guard to watch him," she ordered, "and have everyone update their language database with the proto-Priminae vocabulary and explore a little. Stay clear of any machinery. Just check and see what can be read without touching anything."

"Yes, ma'am," Phillips said, grateful to be away from the dancing fool.

CHAPTER 15

▶ "Definitely another lab complex," Pierce said as he stepped over a piece of debris and did a corner check before moving on. "The layout looks like the one up top, Lieutenant . . . just a lot messier."

"Someone did a number on this place," Ramirez agreed, "no question about that."

"No bodies, though. This kind of damage, I'd expect some casualties." Pierce frowned.

Ramirez just shrugged in his armor. "Probably cleared them out afterward."

"I guess."

They had penetrated deep into the lab complex, but there wasn't much to find. The transponder signals they were following were somewhere ahead of them, but it was a labyrinth of corridors and jammed doors they had to pry open in order to proceed.

They were mapping as they went, but while that would be useful once they had enough data for the computers to start making predictions, for the moment all it did was give them an exit strategy.

Not that I'm complaining about having that option, Ramirez thought fervently. *A good exit strategy is worth more than a good plan of attack any day.*

"Lieutenant, I've got something over here!"

Ramirez turned to the speaker. "On my way."

The Marine was kneeling over some debris that wasn't rendering clearly in his HUD, causing Ramirez to scowl as he approached.

"What is it, Jamie?"

"I think it's shards of standard-issue armor and some electronics from a vac suit, sir," she said, looking back at him. "Can't say whose."

"Shit."

"Yes, sir. There's also some kind of muck here, too."

"Muck?"

"I don't know what it is, sir," she admitted. "It's sticky, mostly liquid, and covering the parts as well as the floor. Almost glad not to see it, to be honest. I doubt it looks nice."

Ramirez grunted, figuring that was probably why he wasn't getting a good render in his suit's systems. Liquid was easy enough to render, if it stayed in place, but a sticky, viscous material that was moving with the Marine's manipulations would be hell on the subsonics they were using as their primary sensor system.

"Bag some of it," he ordered. "Transponders are just ahead."

"You got it, LT."

▶ ▶ ▶

▶ Commander Daiyu walked crisply up to the Marine that was standing at the end of the corridor, glancing at the sign on the door to confirm his report.

"Central command," she said softly. "Well, good job on finding this, Marine."

"Thank you, ma'am."

"Stand your post," she ordered. "I'm going to check out the interior. Call the major up as well."

"Yes, ma'am."

The door parted for her, again making her wonder what kind of system was controlling access. So far every door had parted for them with little problem, which left her wondering about the state of the security the builders had put in place.

Did they expect no one else to ever find this place? she wondered, though the concept felt absurd to her. That was likely due to her personal observation bias, however, and she knew it. She'd grown up, lived her entire life, in a world where secrets had to be protected. Sometimes secrets required the sacrifice of lives to keep them secure, and she'd spent her entire career either offering up her own life, or those of her subordinates, in the pursuit of impossible security.

The idea that someone would build a *supermassive* facility of this nature, then just set it loose in the universe with no security . . . felt wrong on so many levels.

Could these creatures be watchdogs of some type?

That seemed unlikely, but Daiyu couldn't completely discount anything at the moment. There were too many variables at play for that, but she couldn't follow the chain of logic that allowed someone to place vicious guardians around a secret, and then not bother to lock the doors.

No, there had to be something she was missing, and Daiyu hoped that she would find it right there in the room she was investigating.

At a glance, the command center, assuming the translation was correct, was an unimpressive room with little to recommend it. No chairs, no obvious workstations, and so on. There was an open feel to the area and what seemed to be a glassed-off section that looked out on the cavernous exterior beyond the lab facility, but it was so large and dark that the view was entirely unimpressive.

May as well have painted the walls black, she thought with some amusement.

For all of that, however, Daiyu was drawn to markings on the floor. A large circle etched in the metal drew her, and she stepped into it and waited. Nothing happened. Daiyu frowned, focusing around her as she sought out some hint of what she should do.

It was when she reached out, her hand extended past the line of the etching, that the lights flashed into existence and she felt the gentle pressure of the interface under her fingers.

Amazing system.

The doctor's rough translation database was hard at work, making sense of the symbols that appeared in front of her as she gently swept through the display, looking for anything of import. Daiyu intentionally avoided activating any of the symbols, of course, but even so she was fascinated by what little the database was able to decode.

When one bit of information swept past her, she froze in place, however, a sinking feeling forming in the pit of her gut as the translation flashed red on her HUD.

I hope that doesn't mean what the doctor's database seems to think it does.

▶▶▶

▶ Ramirez crept forward in the dark as he reached the transponder's location, probing the area with his foot and grimacing as it sunk into a slimy mound of something he didn't want to think too hard about.

"Cover me," he ordered, slinging his rifle and taking a knee.

The other Marines ringed around him, their own weapons at the ready, as he reached into the soft mass and felt around for a moment. His hand closed on a small capsule and he drew it back, examining it with his scanners before saying anything.

Damn it.

"This one was Wilson's," he announced. "Anyone have a lock on Monroe's transponder?"

No one did, so he stood back up and dropped the transponder tag into a pouch on his thigh.

"Alright, heads-up, guys," he said. "Looks like we've got one KIA now, and one still MIA. Let's spread out a bit, try and get a lock on Monroe. Do *not* get out of range of each other's cover. I don't want to lose anyone to some stupid horror video cliché. Are we clear?"

The men chuckled, but agreed.

"Good. Let's move, Marines."

"Ooh rah, sir!"

Subsonic mapping was giving him a good idea of the layout of the facility they were walking around in, and he made his way down the hall he was in until it ended at a closed door.

"Pry bar," he said, half turning.

"Here you go, sir."

The seam where the door sealed was tighter than he was used to, but Ramirez could locate it with his subsonics. He dug the bar in and wrenched hard to one side, causing an echo of a tearing sound to shudder around them. He got his hands in and strained hard, wishing that he was wearing SOCOM strength-augmenting armor, but Marines were always the last to get the good stuff.

"Give me a hand here, Mac," he grunted, still pulling.

"Yes, sir," McMillan said, throwing himself into the door. With both of them straining, they got the door to slowly move. After several moments, they had the door blocked open so they could pass inside.

"I've got a clearer signal. I think Monroe's transponder is ahead," Ramirez said as he slid into the room.

"Right behind you, sir," McMillan said, following suit.

The room was much like the rest of the facility as they entered, which was to say pretty much black. Ramirez had his weapon held to his shoulder as he moved, relying on subsonic mapping to give him an idea of what he was walking into. He was about halfway across the room when McMillan called out to him sharply.

"Freeze, sir!"

Ramirez froze.

"I just picked up an EM spike, Lieutenant, centered right below you," Mac said as he moved slowly around the immobile lieutenant. "Give me a sec, will ya . . ."

"Take your time, Private, I'm not going anywhere."

He wasn't going to move a muscle until he was certain he wasn't standing on a mine of some kind. A lot of present-generation mines had smart systems that sent up an EM signature when they armed the explosive, so it was basically first nature for a Marine to freeze if something under his feet chirped in the spectrum.

"Doesn't look like a mine, LT," McMillan said after several minutes from where he was kneeling. "If it is, then they built it right into the floor."

"Seems unlikely," Ramirez said tensely, his tone dry. "Am I safe to move?"

"No sign of EM buildup after the first chirp, and all my chem sniffers are negative for explosives," Mac told him with a shrug that Ramirez could only see because of his subsonics. "Beyond that, your guess is as good as mine, but I think so."

"What a relief." Ramirez just barely managed to tone the sarcasm down. After all, it wasn't the private's fault.

He settled his gun down on the straps and took a breath, getting ready to step off whatever it was he was standing on. As his hand swung out, however, a light blossomed in midair and he felt pressure against his fingers.

"Oh, hell," Ramirez swore, involuntarily closing his eyes as he realized what he'd stepped into.

The holographic display bloomed into existence all around him, lights snapping on as he realized that he'd somehow activated the power to the facility they were standing in.

"Watch your backs!" he called. "Lights coming on!"

His Marines spun, clearing the rooms they were in with their rifles held to shoulder ready. The suits' subsonics had done a decent job of mapping the area, but nothing quite replaced eyeball Mark I, even filtered through the armor and HUDs they wore.

Ramirez blinked away the excess light, his suit automatically dimming what was coming through to him until he adjusted, and peered at the interface floating around him.

"Anyone read this crap?" he asked, complaining really, since he was well aware that none of them did.

"Check the network, boss," Pierce advised him. "Language wizard upstairs listed a new database."

"Really?" Ramirez was surprised. He wouldn't have thought that it would be that quick.

"Yeah," Pierce said. "I'm using it now . . . kinda clunky, but it's better than nothing, I think."

Ramirez nodded absently, already loading up the translation database while trying very hard not to touch anything. The latest file was sitting at the top of the queue, so he loaded it in and slowly retracted his hands from the interface as the translations began to appear on his HUD.

"Okay, guys. I'm standing in what looks like a system command console," he said. "I need my area secured, yesterday, while I try and figure this out."

"You got it, LT."

Private McMillan called out from where he was kneeling some distance away. "I think I found Monroe, boss."

Ramirez half turned. "You mean his transponder?"

"I wish," McMillan said, drawing his hand back from a sticky-looking pool of red slag. "I think this is what's left of him. Don't know where his tag is, but I recognize his tattoo."

"Shit."

McMillan looked up, and then around. "Funny you should mention that."

"You'd *better* be fucking joking," Ramirez growled, before shaking his head. "No, scratch that. If you *are* joking about that, I'm going to string your ass up."

"No joke, not sure, but it looks like he was eaten."

"Fuck me," Corporal Pierce swore, walking over. "What the fuck eats a Marine in environmental combat armor?"

"Meddle not in the affairs of dragons," Mac said as he stood up, "for you are crunchy and good with ketchup."

He looked around at the dried mess that covered the floors, floors that had been clear "upstairs," and continued. "I'm guessing that this is all scat of those things. Guys, put your heads on swivel. I think we've stumbled into the dragon's lair."

"Just friggin' great," Ramirez swore as he refocused on the interface floating around him. "This is insanity. Okay, I think that this is security for this level . . . uh . . . I hope red doesn't mean the same thing for the people who built this as it does for us."

"Blood is red in humans, LT," Pierce said, "even if they weren't born on Earth."

"Right," Ramirez sighed. "Okay, assume the worst. I want everyone to regroup on me. We're pulling back until we've got better orders. I think we've accomplished all we can here anyway. Mac, bag what's left of Monroe."

The other nodded. They'd come down to recover their comrades or at least learn what happened to them. They had the tags of one, and the remains of another. It was a poor substitute for bringing their brothers home, but it would do as honor served for the moment. If any of them had any say in it, however, there would come a reckoning later.

"Safe to say that if anything is here, it probably knows we're around," Ramirez said. "Screw this stealth crap. Everyone go full active. We are *leaving*. Let's do it in style."

"You got it, LT. Boot 'em, people!" the squad's gunnery sergeant, Gunny Karen Scaol, responded. "On me, time to go!"

▶▶▶

▶ Light was an alien thing to the colony, something to be wary of.

It could be a harmless annoyance, but light could also burn with a ferocity that surpassed all experience of the colony, rending all before it with merciless heat.

So when the Home was suddenly illuminated for the first time in the colony's memory, they drew back and braced for the burning that happened if one was foolish enough to travel to evil places where light ruled the darkness.

The burning didn't come, however, and slowly the colony began to shift and look for evidence of what had caused the change. Moving slowly, they began to emerge from their perches and their personal lairs, sniffing out the new odors and listening for the new sounds.

The colony was abroad.

▶▶▶

▶ "Anybody else picking that up?"

Pierce twisted, sweeping the room with his gun as he spoke. Their armor had pickups designed to, among other things, triangulate sniper shots taken at a squad. At the moment, the audio trackers were going haywire and throwing up every red flag in the book.

"Hard not to," Ramirez growled as he moved with his team. "It sounds like the walls are crawling."

"I was afraid you were going to say that," Pierce moaned. "I really wanted it to just be me."

"No such luck." Ramirez sighed. "Does anyone have a vector?"

"No go, LT," McMillan answered. "The sound is echoing through this place."

"Of course it is."

Ramirez was disgusted with the lack of intelligence on hand, but he was used to dealing with that and worse. For the moment all they could do was continue on and, with a little luck, get out of the area before all hell broke loose.

That thought had barely crossed his mind before he started cursing himself blue for even daring to think about such a challenge to Murphy's law, but there was precious little he could do about it once it was out of the box.

"Step up the pace," he ordered. "I want to be topside, double time."

"Ooh rah!"

A double-time march in low gravity was probably more suited to a bad physical comedy show than a military formation, but as long as they kept upright and moving, Ramirez was more than willing to overlook his Marines bouncing off each other and the walls.

Skidding to a halt so that every man behind ran into the man ahead, however, was *not* something he was prepared to overlook.

"What the ever living *hell?*" Gunny Scaol roared, not that Ramirez blamed her since she was buried under five other Marines, and that just couldn't be comfortable, even in hardsuits.

He couldn't let her tear a strip out of the Marines just then. They had other things to worry about.

"Gunny!"

"What is it, Lieutenant?" Karen ground out, clearly talking through her teeth.

"Eyes forward."

Scaol looked forward, along with everyone else, and froze as she found herself staring at a mass of hissing serpentine creatures staring right back.

"Oh, hell," she muttered, before adding a belated, "sir."

"You said it, Gunny."

▶▶▶

▶ "What are you looking at, Commander?"

Daiyu didn't look back to the major as she answered. "I'm looking at the control mechanism for this station."

Phillips considered that for a moment. "So you can direct what star the scope looks at?"

"Far more than that, Major."

"What do you mean?" he asked, stepping forward.

"Hold back a bit, Major. I'm trying very hard not to activate certain systems here," Daiyu said. "As for what I mean, well, you can direct where the scope is gathering energy from . . . but you can also direct where the energy is *sent* afterward."

The major started to make a flippant comment, but a thought froze him, causing him to turn and look about him.

"This is a big facility, ma'am . . ." he said leadingly, "biggest telescope I've ever heard of . . ."

"Biggest one that's ever been recorded by us," she answered.

The major closed his eyes. "How much solar energy are we talking about?"

"More than enough to turn the surface of a planet to slag, Major," she answered dryly, "which is why I'm very carefully trying not to activate anything right now."

"Fair enough, fair enough. Just what is this place, Commander?"

"We're sitting on the most impressive telescope ever conceived, Major. It also happens to be a heliobeam, something no one has seriously considered building since Nazi Germany."

"Nazi Germany? Someone in World War II thought about building one of these?"

Daiyu laughed softly at the disbelief in the major's voice.

"Back then, the idea was to put mirrors into space to redirect sunlight on terrestrial targets. It's a concept that occasionally resurfaces, but the vulnerability of such a construct always causes it to be shelved."

"This thing, on the other hand . . ."

"Precisely," she said. "This facility is massively shielded, hidden from electromagnetic detection, and probably capable of deflecting almost any direct attack by using its gravity field manipulation. It also likely has a range measured in light-years, not kilometers."

"It would be light-speed limited, wouldn't it?"

"Yes, but effectively invisible. You could strike a planet with this, using high-band cosmic radiation, and render it lifeless in just a few days . . . all you have to do is adjust the focus of the system to choose whether you want to view a distant star, bake the surface of a planet, or totally irradiate an entire star system."

"Another superweapon, then." The major grimaced. "First the Drasin, now this thing?"

Daiyu considered that. "Perhaps, Major, but there is a very strong philosophical difference between the two. The Drasin are an abomination to life; this . . . this is something else entirely. Something . . . great or terrible, I do not know which."

"In my experience, Commander, the two are rarely distinguishable."

CHAPTER 16

▶ Captain Passer was reading a report as he drifted lazily in his office, one of the few bonuses of serving, or commanding, on a ship without gravity. A bonus right up until you slam into the wall for no apparent reason and suddenly realize that your ship now *does* have gravity, and that is a very bad thing for anyone with intimate knowledge of how the *Auto* was designed.

The general quarters alarm sounded as he was struggling to get up.

He flailed slightly, twisting over and covering up a groan as he grabbed for a mobile comm. "Bridge, Passer here."

"Captain, we're in a bit of a situation here," said Lieutenant Commander Conway, the ship's weapons command and control specialist and third in command, sounding quite busy.

"I damn well noticed that when I slammed into the side of my office. Why are we thrusting?"

"We aren't, sir. That's the tidal effect of the moon. The local gravity field has collapsed rapidly. If I didn't know any better, I'd swear we were sitting on a black hole, Captain."

"Are we losing altitude?"

"Negative, which is one reason why I know we're not sitting on a black hole," Conway responded, just a little too glibly for Morgan's current mood. "Hang on . . . we're reorienting the ship."

The walls began to turn as the ship rolled parallel to the tidal effect of the local gravity. Morgan walked along the wall until he could step onto the floor as the ship came "upright." While designed largely for microgravity, the smaller size of the Rogue Class ships meant that the space frame could survive a water landing in case of emergency . . . unlike the *Odyssey*, as that ship had proven in Long Island Sound.

That meant that the ship had to be designed to be walked around in case of such an event, so now safely ensconced on the floor of the *Autolycus*, Morgan hurried out of his office and headed for the bridge.

He stomped onto the bridge, glaring around as he rubbed his sore shoulder. Conway rose from the command station, nodding to the captain as he accepted the shift in command.

"Report."

"Major shift in local space-time, Captain," Conway answered. "It's clearly being generated by the moon, but we haven't been able to determine the precise cause or function of it yet. Whatever it is, it's somehow not affecting the *Autolycus* directly."

"My shoulder begs to differ," Passer responded dryly.

"That's the strange part, sir," Conway admitted. "While the ship is unaffected, anything massing less than a few hundred kilos, Earth standard, is being pulled around by the tidal effect."

Passer closed his eyes, restraining the urge to pinch the bridge of his nose.

"Is that even possible?"

Honestly, he hoped he didn't actually sound as plaintive to the crew as he did to his own ears there.

"Not by our current understanding of space-time physics. No sir, it is not."

"Great."

"However, it's not totally without precedent," Conway said. "We see a similar effect with supercooled magnetic levitation, and it's been theorized that the effect could be manipulated to single out a specific object and position it with a magnetic field. This could be the gravitic equivalent of that. However, that doesn't answer why we're not affected by the tidal force."

"Alright, chalk it up to magic supertech, and let's move on," Morgan said. "We have to deal with the situation at hand."

"Yes, sir."

"What are our accelerometers saying about it?"

Conway tapped out an order and pointed. "The origin they predict is one thousand eight hundred and fifty-nine kilometers below the surface."

Morgan scowled, the number niggling at his brain for a moment. "Isn't that near the core?"

"That is the core, precisely, Captain."

Morgan considered that, but finally nodded curtly. "Assume for now that our accelerometers are accurate, despite the exclusion effect on the *Auto*."

"Yes, sir."

"What about the shuttles?" Morgan asked, concerned.

"Similarly unaffected, Captain."

"Thank God," he mumbled, visions of the Marine deployment shuttles spiraling down to fiery graves, sucked in by the alien gravity field, still running through his head. "Are we in contact with the Marines?"

"Negative, sir. Even the signal boosters have been jammed. No idea if it's intentional or not, Captain."

"Get me comms back," Passer ordered. "Do what it takes, just get them back."

"Yes, sir."

Morgan had enough problems at the moment. The last thing he needed was to lose a massive chunk of his Marine complement, let alone some of his best scientists and his first officer, on what was their first mission off the ship.

"Sir?" The ensign standing station at the scanners half turned, sounding puzzled. "We're picking up a radiation increase, locally."

"What bandwidth?"

"Wide band, Captain . . . all frequencies, no pattern I can find."

Morgan scowled. It might be nothing, but the timing didn't have him thinking in that direction. "Targeting beam?"

"I don't think so, Captain. It's too wide an area for that. The radiation increase is all around us."

"We've got drones out, right?"

"Yes, sir," Conway answered.

"Are they registering the same increase?"

The weapons officer didn't have the answer right away. He had to check quickly before he turned back with a serious expression. "No, sir, they are not."

I hate it when I'm right. Passer scowled, considering.

"Alright, give me even armor, best deflection on all plates," he ordered.

"Aye, sir. Even armor, best deflection!"

Passer knew that would buy them some time from the rising radiation levels, especially since they hadn't gotten dangerous even with the cam-plate armor off, but he wasn't going to be feeling great about it until they knew what the hell was going on.

Oh, he could guess at what was going on. Someone, or something, had tripped the facility's on switch. That much was clear, but initial reports didn't mention much about just what the place was for, aside from being the biggest astronomical observatory in the known galaxy. *Well, the biggest artificial one at least,* he corrected himself idly. He was aware that even as he spoke there were drones being sent out to use the gravity deflection of the galaxy core to observe neighboring galaxies, which technically made the galaxy itself the largest astronomical observatory in the galaxy.

Unfortunately, nothing he knew about the concept they were looking at explained why there was a wide-band radiation increase in the local area of the *Autolycus,* and at the moment that was the only thing he was concerned with.

"Bring in a couple of the drones," he commanded. "Find out how large this rad zone is, and see if you can triangulate the source."

"Aye, sir," Conway confirmed, already going to work.

"Do we have any progress on comms?" Passer called, looking around.

"Maybe, sir," Lieutenant Kamir said, looking up, "but it'll mean repositioning the ship to put our primary array in line with the moon."

Morgan winced, recognizing just what that would mean.

"Keep working on it," he ordered, "but have the ship locked down for maneuvering."

"Aye aye, sir," Kamir said, leaning over and going back to work.

The alarm changed a few seconds later as Kamir's voice came over the ship-wide, ordering that everyone and everything be locked down.

Putting the nose of the ship toward the moon would bring them out of alignment with the current tidal flow of the moon's gravity. It would, at best, be like parking the *Auto* on a steep hill. At worst, Morgan really didn't want to speculate.

He belted himself in, getting ready for the worst.

In the end, it didn't really matter. They had people on that moon, and they had to get in contact with them.

▶▶▶

▶ "No one moves."

Ramirez's command was quiet, but sent over the command override channel so no one missed it.

"Don't twitch, don't shift your weight, don't *breathe*."

Between his squad and the only exit they knew of was a roiling mass of serpentine bodies ending in big, pissed-off-looking, toothy heads.

"Back slowly away," Ramirez ordered. "SAW gunners, take a knee."

The squad shifted slowly back, letting the squad automatic weapon gunners drop down and take point as they leveled their heavy guns downrange.

Ramirez had been tentatively pleased with the way things were going up to that point, but just as he started to give his next order, the alien creatures changed the playbook. The mass of serpentine bodies suddenly uncoiled and lunged straight at them, a screaming sound filling the air.

"Formation Bravo Nine!" he called on the fly. "Open fire!"

The two SAW gunners led the way, already in position and fingers on triggers, as their guns roared into action. Sonic booms filled the air, overpowering the screaming of the giant snakes, or dragons as some of the Marines had already dubbed them, as the big guns flung heavy slugs out at hypersonic velocity.

The air spat fire from the friction of the projectiles cutting through, and the slugs exploded as they slammed into their targets and dug deep into serpentine flesh. The air quickly clouded, filled with smoke and particulates of snake, as the roar of the guns continued to compete with the screams of their targets.

"Fall back!"

Ramirez pressed himself against the wall, clearing the way, as he leveled his assault rifle and opened fire. The heavy weapon bucked in his grip as another roar joined it from across the hall. He and Pierce held their ground as the SAW gunners turned and began to scramble back from the onrushing wave of screaming flesh.

They almost made it.

A limb with a long, curved claw like a scimitar blade slashed out of the mass, cutting the first man in two with a single stroke. The Marine went down in two different directions, blood spattering freely as his legs spun to the ground and tripped up his comrade. That was all it took, and then the attack moved to the second SAW gunner in a flash. For a moment Ramirez saw his man, and then there was nothing but pink mist in the air and coiled muscles roiling around.

"Son of a bitch!" Pierce screamed, emptying his mag and reaching for another.

Ramirez grabbed him by the back of the armor, yanking him away. "Later!"

Pierce reloaded anyway, even as Ramirez dragged him clear, and opened fire again.

"Goddamn it, I said later!" Ramirez snarled. "Save your ammo!"

McMillan appeared out of the chaos, getting a grip on Pierce as well, and the two got the pissed-off Marine stood up, turned around, and running with the rest of them.

"Up ahead," McMillan panted as they ran, chasing the rest of the squad. "The doors work. We can seal them out!"

The screaming sound increased again as they dove through the doors, the gunny slapping the control command on the interface just as they slipped past. Through the closed doors they heard screaming and scraping, like metal on metal, and the squad of Marines exchanged unbelieving stares.

"Tell me we didn't just see that."

▶▶▶

▶ Commander Daiyu was entirely focused on the interface in front of her, puzzling through the rough translations provided by Doctor Palin's database. She had quickly found that, while generally accurate, sometimes the doctor's work lacked a certain precision that was desirable when you were potentially sitting in the middle of the greatest weapon of mass destruction in the known galaxy.

The system was active, which was terrifying, but beyond that she was having a great deal of trouble determining what, or who, had turned it on.

Some of the systems appear to be running on automatic, if I am reading this correctly. However, that doesn't explain why it suddenly decided to shift from passive monitoring to more active changes in the local gravity fields.

The schematic of the moon displayed on her right was fairly clear, thankfully, she'd found. It showed a very nice depiction of the local space-time fabric, along with all the local distortions. The *Autolycus* was clearly visible in orbit, and she could see smaller blips on the projection that likely indicated the locations of the Copperheads as well.

Tracking the gravity fluctuation generated by a craft as small as a Marine Copperhead required a frightening degree of sensitivity. It was, in fact, a feat she would have considered impossible if she weren't looking right at it with her own two eyes.

I need to see calculations of the impact of the new gravity shears on photons and other radiating particles. Daiyu considered that for a moment, then snapped her fingers a couple of times.

"Yes, ma'am?"

"Get me one of our computers," she said. "I need to make calculations that I don't want my suit tied up completing."

"Yes, ma'am."

One of the perils of being the available authority on gravitic warping was that she couldn't just pass the task off to anyone else. Possibly one of her subordinates could do the calculations, but not as quickly or as accurately as she could.

There was a pattern in the fluctuations she was seeing, of that there was no doubt. The solution to it was eluding her at the moment, but only for the moment.

It wasn't strictly speaking that the actions she was seeing were impossible in and of themselves, of course. No, the problem was that they were beyond all theoretical limits of the sort of manipulations involved. Until this, all large-scale manipulations of local space-time had to be done via manipulation of mass.

The Earth-based CM generators specifically acted by shaping the way mass interacted with the universe. It offered up to a ninety percent mass shift, according to the best equations available. That is, you could increase or decrease the effective mass of any object in a CM field by about ninety percent. You didn't actually change the mass, of course—that was impossible. Rather, you merely hid or exposed more or less mass to the vagaries of the universe about you.

The Priminae technology was similar, albeit a little more efficient, but largely still relied on the same rules. They managed to accomplish far more with the same basic tool set by incorporating planet-sized singularities into their spacecraft. When you started with that much mass, you could play with a far greater range of options.

This technology, however, couldn't be doing that if her analysis of the numbers was correct.

The degree of warping she was seeing would take the mass of a stellar object, not a mere planetary one, and the systems on board the *Autolycus* would have detected anything that large no matter how deeply cloaked it was in space-time manipulations.

"Computer system, ma'am."

"Thank you, Lieutenant," Daiyu said, not looking back. She opened a direct port to the computer through her suit and fed the numbers right to it over an optical link, effectively offloading all the number crunching she'd been using her suit for and shifting her focus to other items of interest.

"Major," she called softly a moment later.

"Ma'am?" Phillips appeared over her left shoulder, as though he'd teleported there.

"I believe these are security readings, Major." She gestured at another section of the display. "They show a lot of activity in a facility below us."

The major's expression was schooled to near impassivity, but he got the point clearly enough. "Below, ma'am? The rescue team?"

"Far too much activity . . . dozens of times too much activity."

Commander Daiyu diplomatically ignored the rather colorful expletives that filtered over the comm, and actually only understood about three-quarters of them. Privately, she was rather impressed. The first thing a military person learned of another language was usually the more colorful adjectives, but the major knew several that had so far escaped her notice.

"Contact the *Autolycus*, Major," she said. "We may need more help."

"Not much more left on board, ma'am," Phillips cautioned her. "Even stripping the ship of security won't do much more than double our numbers down here."

"I am aware, but I'm loath to leave without securing this place," she said. "And I believe we may be about to have company ourselves."

She gestured to the display, showing a multitude of red dots converging on what looked to be their location. Major Phillips didn't swear this time. He was far too busy issuing orders.

▶▶▶

▶ The occasional bangs and scrapes against the door set the mood for the Marines, who were still more than a little in shock at how rapidly things had gone to pot for them.

Ramirez, however, didn't have time for a nervous breakdown. He had a team, less two now, to get the hell out of trouble. That still left eight Marines in the heat, and he owed them his full attention.

"We need to find another way out," he said simply, trying to get his own mind back in some semblance of working order.

"Well, no shit, Sherlock," Pierce said with a scowl, "'cause we sure as hell aren't going back through *that*!"

Ramirez ignored the loudmouth and his breach of protocol. "Eyes and ears. I want everyone's scans linked, and everyone on alert. We're going to get out of this. Don't lose your cool."

Orders were one way of cutting through the momentary panic that had threatened to set in. Giving his troops jobs to do would keep them from thinking too hard on what happened to their fellows, for a time at least.

The battle network was fully hot by this point, so the squad moved apart to cover the dead zones and Ramirez waited for the tactical situation to fill in on his HUD. They needed an alternative route out of the facility, so he started looking for unexplored sections that might lead to the outside. Most of what he found could be immediately discounted, but then he soon had some promising leads.

"Pierce, grab McMillan and a couple others to check out the routes I've marked," he ordered. "Watch your backs, and do *not* engage the enemy."

"No freaking worries," Pierce swore, slapping Mac on the armored shoulder and nodding off in the direction marked.

"I want guards on this door. Let me know if anything tries to get through," Ramirez said. "I'm going to check out the control room again . . ."

He paused, checking his systems. "Does anyone have contact with the team topside?"

A few negative answers left him deeply concerned. They'd lost full real-time contact on their descent to the facility they were in, but had maintained an emergency data link via the VSF channels that didn't have great bandwidth but did have exemplary range. If those were now cut off, they could be in real trouble.

"Gunny," he said, glancing over to where Karen Scaol was kneeling and glaring at the door.

"Sir?" She tilted her head in his direction.

"Get someone working on reestablishing contact with topside," he ordered. "We've lost the VSF link. I want it back."

"Yes, sir."

Orders handed out, Ramirez spared a last glance at the door he knew was the only thing between them and a nightmarish roiling mass of serpentine muscle and teeth. He suppressed a shudder, barely, and headed for the control room.

CHAPTER 17

▶ Kathryn Grant was *not* a happy flyer.

Every one of the alarms in her Copperhead had gone off for a split second before they all went suspiciously dead.

There had been a brief moment when she'd received priority alarm feeds from both the Marines on the surface—or below it, she supposed—and the *Autolycus* above her. The reason they'd gone out was simple: The communications feeds to both were cut.

"Check for jamming," she ordered, sticking the Copperhead around so she could get a better view of the skies above them.

Her copilot was working on just that when she froze in surprise and the lander rocked a bit.

"Holy sh . . ."

"What is . . . whooo boy," he said, looking up and following her gaze out and upward.

Normally they would be trying to find the *Autolycus* by a combination of general location and looking for a dim moving star against the background. Right now, that wasn't necessary. The *Autolycus* was gleaming brilliantly above them, like a newborn nova in the night sky.

"Check for weapons fire," Kathryn growled. "If they've got their armor to best deflection, they're not hiding anymore . . . and that probably means someone or something already found them."

"Roger that . . . I'm not seeing anything obvious, but there is a faint radiation increase, ma'am."

"Check it against all known nonterrestrial weapon signatures."

"No match. It's too wide-band for a laser, ma'am. Solar flare?"

"Through those gravity shears? Like hell," Kathryn replied. "The star would have had to go nova before we'd notice it inside the gravity walls of this place."

"Then I don't know, ma'am."

The problem with that was that Kathryn had no idea either, much to her ire.

"Fine. Hit the *Auto* with a comm laser. That shouldn't be jammed."

"Aye, ma'am. It'll take a minute," he said, unbuckling and moving back to the communication and detection station.

Kathryn grunted and focused on tipping the nose of the Copperhead back down and surveying for threats.

▶▶▶

▶ "Contact from *Copperhead One*, sir."

"Laser?" Morgan asked, not looking up from what he was working on.

"Yes, sir. It's oddly distorted, though, Captain."

Morgan accepted that. Almost nothing could jam a laser link, but unfortunately the gravity shears they were dealing with were on the short list. "Can you tune it in?"

"Yes, sir. So far it's a predictable distortion."

"Good. Feed them the latest intelligence we have. Ask Commander Grant to see if she can't get in contact with the Marines."

"Aye, sir."

The *Autolycus* was in the process of being locked down, but it was relatively slow going as they had to ensure that everything was double- and triple-checked for the sort of maneuvering they expected and required.

"Copperhead One is out of contact with the Marines as well, sir."

Damn.

Well, he wasn't surprised, but it was worth a shot.

"Have all stations reported in?"

"Aye, sir. We just got the last confirmation from the armory. We're locked down."

"Then turn us into the storm, Lieutenant," he ordered. "Thrusters only."

"Aye, sir," Andrea Mika responded. "Coming about, thrusters only."

The first touch of thrusters pushed them gently around as the ship began to turn in place, but in a moment they could feel the shift in gravity start. The straps from his chair bit into Morgan's shoulders as he was pressed forward, making him feel like he was sitting on a slope as Mika navigated the *Auto* around in order to bring the main radio telescope transceivers to bear on the moon below.

The *Autolycus'* normal system was quite capable of establishing communication within normal light-speed limited ranges, even punching through many forms of military-grade jamming. Their forward transceiver array, however, was designed for long-range scanning out past the limits one might normally think of in terms of human communications.

At this close a range, it would provide a very narrow arc beam that should, hopefully, be able to punch through almost any jamming and reopen communications with their ground team.

This better work, Morgan thought grimly.

He didn't have many options left if it didn't.

"In position, Captain."

"By all means, put power to the array. I want to talk to my people on the ground."

"Aye, sir."

▶▶▶

▶ *So, I was right. There is something else at work here. The numbers just don't work for any space-time manipulation technology we're aware of,* Daiyu thought, rather exhilarated by the development.

New technology, new scientific theories, had always been her reason for existence. She loved discovery more than life itself, and she could feel the momentous nature of this particular discovery in her bones.

She was so caught up in her investigations that she almost didn't notice a previously dead section of her HUD come to life.

"Commander Daiyu, *Autolycus* Actual standing by."

She froze momentarily, surprised by the voice, but quickly flicked over to the command channel.

"*Autolycus* Actual, go for Daiyu," the commander whispered softly.

"Commander," Captain Passer's voice came through, "we're using the main transceiver array to punch through the interference, but I don't know if we'll be able to keep the channel open for long. Status?"

"Captain, I am uploading all current data now," she said, sending the command before refocusing on the conversation. "We are currently studying what I believe to be a command center for the weapon . . ."

"Excuse me, Commander, did you say *weapon?*"

"Yes, sir, Captain, I believe that in addition to being an observatory, this system also functions as a very powerful heliobeam," she said.

"A sun gun. Great. That explains a lot, actually. Commander, I believe that the *Auto* has been targeted by the weapon. I need you to shut it off."

Daiyu wanted to blurt out an objection, or question the statement, but instead she turned her gaze back to the equations she was trying to solve.

"So that's what it's been doing," she whispered, her eyes widening.

"Commander?"

"I've been monitoring activities here, Captain. I do not know how, but I believe that we, or something, has tripped an automated system . . ."

"A defense program?" Morgan asked, concerned.

"Possibly. I cannot say for sure yet. I am working on it."

Morgan Passer was silent for a moment before coming back. "Work faster, Commander. External radiation is climbing on all bands. Armor is holding, for now, but we'll be forced to engage evasive maneuvering soon . . . so if you can't shut it down, I need you *off* that forsaken rock."

"Understood. Can you contact the Marine squad that went after the missing men?"

"We have their transponders. They're fainter than yours. Give us a little time," Morgan said.

"Yes, Captain. I'll get back to work."

Daiyu signed off, now turning to the interface with determination rooted in her new understanding of just what it was showing.

You are an abomination of science, she thought grimly as she began manipulating the interface. *A system of pure research corrupted by such destructive potential . . . it makes me want to cry.*

She'd been party to the creation of possibly the single most dangerous device ever built by humankind, on Earth at least, so she felt some kinship to whoever had designed the system in which she stood.

She imagined that person had likely been very much like herself, focused on the enormous potential for advancement of science . . . and blinded to the utter devastation their invention was capable of.

Of course, her invention had been partially responsible for saving the Earth from utter destruction.

Were you granted that comfort? Or did you live only to see this place become the stuff of nightmares? she wondered of her absent alien counterpart while she worked.

▶ ▶ ▶

▶ "Lieutenant, I'm getting something on the battle network," Scaol said, rushing up behind Ramirez as he glowered at the interface, trying to get it to display a map of the facility in which they were trapped.

"What is it?" he asked, not looking around.

"Transponder feed from the *Auto*, Lieutenant," she said. "It's intermittent, and just enough to tell me that they're up there, but it's more than we had."

That hooked his attention, bringing him to turn and look at the gunny. "You got the comms up?"

"Negative, sir," she said with a twist of her upper body. "Came through on standard channels. Nothing yet on the VSF."

"That's odd. They must have done something, then," he said, considering.

"Yes, sir."

"Alright, start trying to contact the ship. Let me know if you break through."

The gunny nodded stiffly. "Sir."

"Are Pierce and Mac back yet?" he asked before looking back to his work.

"No, sir. I can call them?"

"Check in," he said. "We need a way out of here."

"Yes, sir."

▶▶▶

▶ "We're still on it, Gunny. Checking the north corridor now," Pierce said as they moved forward.

Of course, "north" was a bit of a misnomer. There wasn't any magnetic field of note, and honestly he didn't know one side of the moon-sized sphere from another, but they needed some way of labeling things, so north it was. The gunny's call had come as they were starting their move down the still-darkened section of the facility, and so far there hadn't been anything much to report.

"We'll check in when we finish this one," Pierce assured the rather frustrated gunnery sergeant. The last thing any trooper wanted to deal with was an irate gunny, whether they'd had any hand in causing the irritation or not, so he did what he could to smooth things over before signing off.

The corridor was typical of what they'd come to expect so far in this giant beach ball of a moon. Dark, dusty, and crusty, and severely lacking in any kind of design aesthetics.

Not that Pierce would know anything about those, of course.

"I'm starting to hate this place," he grumbled as he took point down the hall.

They had lights this time, at least. No more point in sneaking around using subsonics, so the terror-inspiring pitch they'd been working in was now merely creepy as all get-out. After the third dead-end corridor, however, they'd gotten used to the creep factor and were moving fairly efficiently as they checked the next one on their list.

"You hate every place," McMillan snorted, amused as he walked the drag position.

The other two Marines just chuckled, not bothering to offer up anything. They knew that more entertainment was likely coming, and had no intentions of short-circuiting it, even with their current situation so dire.

"That's because we always wind up in some cesspool," Pierce bitched.

"You joined the Marines. What were you expecting? A cruise ship?" Mac replied amusedly.

He'd been in the same squad with Pierce for the better part of three years. They'd fought through the invasion in Okinawa, and he'd yet to see Pierce *like* any situation they'd been in since. Some people just liked to complain, he supposed.

Mac himself preferred to shoot.

Oh, he didn't consider himself trigger-happy by any means, but there was something about a rifle that just made sense to him. For all the technical complexity buried within his weapon, it all just . . . made sense. Get a bearing and range to target, adjust for environmental conditions, squeeze the trigger. Problem solved.

He had an application to sniper school in for after this tour, and a bit of time on the *Autolycus* should pretty much guarantee him a slot.

Assuming they lived through their current predicament.

"Something's tripping the motion scanners . . . hold up a second," Pierce said, fist in the air.

Mac stopped, bracing himself slightly on the wall as he brought his rifle up. The two Marines between them dropped to a crouch to clear his line of fire.

"What have you got, Ian?" Mac asked softly, though he probably could have shouted it without alerting someone closer than a meter away, given the insulation of his suit.

"I don't know. It's fuzzy."

That didn't surprise Mac in the slightest. Motion trackers weren't the most reliable forms of detection they had. Generally only useful inside as security devices, few motion systems could penetrate a sheet of paper, let alone a wall, and they quailed in terror before a stiff breeze. With advanced instrumentation, however, they had some limited field utility.

In this case, Pierce was using short-range radar systems with backscatter x-ray technology to look through some of the walls. Pulses fired every few seconds and were quite draining to a suit's power supply, each pulse slightly weaker than the one before it. Any unexpected changes between the two pulses would show up as an alarm.

Unfortunately, the pulses could be rendered worthless by the wrong type of material in whatever you were scanning through. Mac figured that if anything was the wrong type of material, it was probably some alien metal alloy no one had seen before.

"It's gone," Pierce said finally, waving them up.

The four-person squad started moving forward again, deeper down the corridor. Pierce was checking their position against the map they'd been compiling, trying to determine their location relative to what they knew of the facility they were exploring.

"I think we're coming up on the end of the line, just around the corner," he said finally. "Stay alert."

"Ooh rah," the other three grunted softly as they followed.

As they rounded the corner, Pierce again raised his fist and the team stopped and deployed as before. Ahead of them they could see another door, sealed shut. According to the maps being compiled by their armor computers, it should lead to the outside.

"Alright, camp here," Pierce ordered. "I'm going to send word back to the lieutenant."

▶▶▶

▶ "Sir? Pierce reports that he may have a way out."

Ramirez nodded curtly, stepping out of the center of the interface, logging everything he'd seen to his armor's memory. He just hoped it was worth something, because some good had to come out of this damned mission.

"Alright, let him know we're coming. Pull the guards from the doors last, but let's move quickly."

The gunny nodded. "Yes, sir."

While she was off to get the rest together and ready to move, Ramirez checked the communications queues and was thankful to find a dispatch waiting for him.

Whatever is blocking the communications must not be strong enough to totally shut down all bands, he thought as he opened the files and examined the briefing.

The current situation had changed a lot since he'd taken his men over the rail, but it didn't look like his mission had changed. He had to get his squad back, regroup with the major and others, and then likely pull back off the moon.

Most likely it would fall to a full incursion force to take and secure the facility, not to mention whatever was on the primary planet of the system.

"We're ready, sir."

"Thank you, Gunny," Ramirez said, refocusing. "Let's move out."

"As you say," Gunny Scaol answered, gesturing to the men. "Move out!"

CHAPTER 18

▶ "External radiation is still climbing, Captain," Kamir said, glancing up. "Our drones indicate that the beam is being tightened as well, sir. We're being targeted."

Of course we are, Morgan thought grimly.

He could see that easily enough. There was no question that the presence of the *Auto* had been detected, and whatever was running the facility below them had taken offense to their presence.

A heliobeam.

It was such an obscure technology that he'd had to look it up, to see if there was anything in the theories that would be of some help. It had been a wasted few minutes of research.

The concept was simple enough, of course. Children used it, burning paper or ants (depending on how they'd been raised) with magnifying glasses. Here before him was the largest artificially created magnifying glass in the galaxy, or he hoped it was at least, but it *was* just that.

Okay, not *just* that. The facility was actually several gravity lenses working in conjunction with one another, doing more than just focusing light—actually sucking it in from a distance, creating a lensing system that affected radiation across the spectrum on an order of efficiency that every one of his scientists swore should be impossible.

The results spoke for themselves, however.

The hull of the *Auto* was heating up, even with the cam-plate armor set to best reflection. Nothing too dangerous yet, but the *Autolycus'* cooling systems were already beginning to become compromised. Internal temperature was up three degrees across the board, and the heat pumps couldn't keep up.

They were redirecting cooling to the dark side of the ship, but at best that effectively halved their radiative cooling capacity, and since they were currently sitting nose into the beam, it was actually a lot less than that.

For the moment it was a slight issue, not even really a comfort problem, but in a few hours the ship would begin to experience severe problems if it kept up. Habitation cooling was the least of their problems. If the reactors weren't kept in proper temperatures, they'd first lose efficiency, and then they'd lose containment.

The first was survivable. The second wasn't.

"We've completed all queued uploads and downloads from the moon, Captain."

"Can you confirm that the Marines received the briefing packet?" Morgan asked.

"No, sir. We sent it, twice, but we didn't get an error check response. We know they received something, but we can't be sure it was intact."

Morgan sighed, settling in as best he could as he felt the straps press into his shoulders.

"That's the best we can do, I suppose," he finally decided. "Alright, Helm, level us out."

"Aye, Captain, bringing the nose up."

The ship creaked and groaned in ways that Morgan was certain no starship ever should, but it slowly righted itself, relatively speaking, and both captain and crew breathed more than a little sigh of relief as they felt themselves settle more easily into their stations.

"We're perpendicular to the tidal pull, and the beam, Captain," Lieutenant Mika said finally, her hands coming off the controls.

"Good," Morgan said. "Inform engineering that I want cooling redirected to the dorsal side as soon as possible."

"Yes, sir," Conway answered. "They're probably already on that."

Morgan grunted, but didn't object. The truth was the truth, and the engineers knew their business better than he did. That was a fact.

It wouldn't hurt to remind them, however, since that was his business.

"Andrea," he said, leaning forward, "I need you to start calculating escape maneuvers."

"Sir?" The lieutenant looked puzzled.

He supposed that he shouldn't blame her. After all, there should be nothing too complicated about escaping the local area. Just power up the drives, warp space-time, and fly out. Nothing simpler.

Morgan doubted it would go so easily, unfortunately.

"We've been target-locked by an alien war machine," he said softly, not wanting his voice to travel too far just then. "Maybe it lets us go, maybe it doesn't. Right now it just wants to toast our belly a little, but we're floating over a gravity generator capable of warping light. I want to have options for getting out of here, and, if that proves infeasible, I want options for evading the beam. Get to it."

"Aye aye, sir."

Morgan settled back, not quite glowering at the screen.

This was the part he hated most about commanding a ship of any sort, whether a submarine or an interstellar cruiser.

The waiting. Waiting while other people's lives were on the line, put there by his orders, their fates no longer in his hands . . . indeed, his fate now lay in theirs.

That was a feeling he never got used to.

Morgan hoped he never would, either.

▶ ▶ ▶

▶ When Ramirez and the rest arrived, Pierce had a field scanner up against the door.

"Are we clear?"

Pierce looked over and nodded. "Clear, LT."

"Okay. I've checked the map, and Corporal Pierce is right. This should link to the outside," he said, looking around. "We're going to head through and pull chutes straight for topside, no dicking around. These things have us outnumbered, and as much as I wish it were different, we're not in any position to take them on right now."

The unspoken message was clear enough that everyone nodded, though none of them liked it.

There wouldn't be any time for payback, or retrieving their fallen. They'd been there and done that, and while Ramirez was willing to risk a lot to possibly save a pair of his Marines, he wasn't going to risk the whole squad to retrieve bodies.

"We'll be back," he said simply. "Don't doubt that. Another day."

Everyone repeated his last two words softly, nodding.

"Semper fi. Ooh rah!"

The assembled Marines belted it back to him automatically. "Ooh rah. Semper fi!"

Ramirez nodded to Pierce, who already had a hand on the door control interface. The corporal flicked the command icons and the doors slid open, letting the Marines loose as the squad surged through, weapons up and seeking targets.

The room opened up, leading out to another set of doors just twenty meters on. A quick check of their dead reckoning nav gear told the Marines that they were almost outside.

The point Marines cleared the room, including looking up and around, and then waved the rest on as they headed for the doors. They moved as a group, shuffling more than marching, with guns and hands resting on the shoulders of the man ahead, everyone looking for the trouble they were sure was coming.

"Clear," Pierce said at the door, stepping to one side to activate the projected interface before glancing back at Ramirez.

"Go for it, Pierce," Ramirez confirmed, nodding stiffly in his helmet.

The Marines spread out, covering the doors as Corporal Pierce tapped the command to open the door. The slabs of metal slid apart, opening onto the black of the great cavern beyond, and Ramirez felt his heart slow just a bit as he let out a breath he hadn't been aware he was holding.

Despite everything their dead reckoning navigation said, he'd been half afraid that somehow the door was going to lead to another interior section of the alien facility.

"Alright, Marines, let's go home."

The attack came just as they were crossing the boundary, a shriek slicing the air and shadows descending right after the drag Marine stepped out of the facility and the doors started to close behind him.

▶▶▶

▶ "We have movement outside, Major."

Phillips redirected his attention from where the commander was still engrossed in the intricacies of the alien interface. He turned to see the private standing there, his body language more than a little nervous.

"Identification?"

"None as yet, sir," the private answered. "Whatever it is, it's just skirting the edge of our detection radius."

Phillips didn't like the sound of that, not one bit. For whatever it was to be skirting the edge of detection meant that it *knew* where that edge was. He stirred himself, pivoting on his heel, and started toward the door.

"Stay with the commander," he ordered.

"Sir!"

Phillips marched stiffly back to the entrance of the facility, noting that the majority of his squad of Marines were already laid out in defensive positions in case something came through the door.

Good.

"Report," he said aloud as he walked into view.

"Not a lot to report, Major. It looks like the same creatures from earlier, but they're holding back," the Marine on watch said. "Damned if we can get a good glimpse of them."

"What scans are you using?" Phillips asked.

"Everything we've got, sir."

The major nodded. "Go to passives."

"Sir?" The Marine looked at him askance, knowing that passive scanners would slash their range to a fraction of what they could normally detect objects out to.

"Passives, Sergeant," Phillips ordered calmly. "After that . . . patience. Tell me the second you spot anything."

The sergeant nodded slowly. "Yes, sir."

▶ ▶ ▶

▶ "Scatter!"

Following his own order, Ramirez threw himself aside and hit the ground on his back in a rough skid as he brought his rifle up. The heavy weapon barked into the dark, joined by a half dozen others in nearly the same instant.

They were lying in wait, Ramirez realized, his body reacting on automatic as he tried to figure a way out of the mess they were in.

"Frag out!"

The lieutenant just had time to roll his rifle over to cover his face before an airburst fragmentation round detonated, overwhelming the screams of the aliens for a moment, driving the enemy back.

"Clear the deck!" McMillan called, taking a knee as he switched his weapon selector back from explosive to high-velocity penetration rounds.

His marksman's rifle roared in a slow staccato as he pivoted and fired with deliberate motions.

Ramirez rolled back to his feet. "Form up behind Mac!"

He grabbed the nearest Marine by the back of his armor and pulled him behind the marksman, who was unloading steady rounds into the air at targets only he could see.

Ramirez piggybacked on McMillan's systems to get an idea of what they were up against and cringed at the number of bandits the marksman had tagged. They were moving around unpredictably, the sound of their wings and the low hiss the serpents made coming from all directions, and he couldn't be sure if the count was right, high, or low. All he knew was that it was a whole load of trouble.

He hauled the closest Marine to his feet, bellowing orders as he moved.

"Suppression fire! Put airbursting rounds up. I want the skies cleared!"

"Frag out!"

Ramirez covered automatically, though there was little risk of a blue-on-blue strike with the issued airbursting munitions. They were designed to proximity detonate in midair, sending shrapnel up and out, not back down at the shooter.

"Clear a hole! We need to get topside!" he ordered, checking the packs on each of the Marines as they fired.

After he cleared them, Ramirez half turned to where Mac was slugging a new mag into his rifle without breaking his target lock.

"Can you hold them for a minute?"

"I've got you covered, LT," the PFC reassured him without pausing between shots.

Ramirez nodded, running back down the line, slapping the Marines on the packs. "Get out of here! Move it!"

Counter-mass generators whined as the packs lifted off, lines to their armor snapping taut. The rockets flared bright against the lightless void they were fighting in. One by one the Marines started to rocket off, yanked away by the CM chutes.

"Thirty seconds, Mac!" Ramirez ordered.

"Roger that!" McMillan called, letting another empty mag hit the ground at his feet. He fished a replacement from his kit, slugging it home as he flicked his eyes to the armor HUD and activated his own chute.

The momentary distraction cost the marksman as a screaming serpentine shape broke from the darkness on his left side and slashed toward him. At the last second, McMillan recognized the threat and threw himself back in a desperate attempt to avoid contact.

It failed. He was sent sprawling through the air, landing hard on the ground in a roll as liquid splatter soaked the ground around him.

Seeing stars, the marksman twisted over onto his back and brought his rifle up. The weapon slammed back into his shoulder comfortingly as he opened fire again, still dazed and trying to clear his head and his vision. He got to his knees, and then fell over as he again tried to fire.

"Mac!" Pierce screamed, hitting the ground in a slide, his own rifle roaring on automatic fire as he came to a stop next to the private. "Mac! Talk to me!"

"Get out of here, man. I'll be right behind you," McMillan mumbled, getting back up so he could aim his weapon.

Ramirez was by his side then, weapon roaring. "Jesus, Mac, get your arse out of here! We've got you covered!"

"I'm fine, LT! Just let me get to my feet . . ."

"Mac, damn it," Pierce snarled, slapping his pack and initiating an override to his chute. "Just go!"

The CM chute jumped away, his line snapping tight, and McMillan felt himself being yanked as he began to climb. He was fifty meters up and still ascending before he looked down to see if he could spot his comrades below, and he finally noticed the burnt orange chemical foam covering the stump of his right leg.

Oh, he thought numbly. *That's why I couldn't stand up.*

On the platform below, the last two Marines were readying their own departure.

"I can get his leg," Pierce said, tensing to bolt across the deck.

"Leave it," Ramirez ordered. "We're hours from medical treatment. No way they'll be able to reattach. Just go!"

"But, LT—"

"GO!"

Ramirez didn't wait for the corporal to obey the order. He overrode Pierce's suit and triggered both their chutes at once. The retro thrust slammed them down into the boots of their armor, and then they were climbing away from the roiling mass that had claimed the platform.

Unfortunately for both of them, they were close enough to watch as the serpentine creatures glared up at them, screamed, and launched themselves into the air.

"Frag out," Ramirez called as he took a range to his targets and started pumping smart rounds down into the creatures' midst.

▶▶▶

▶ "Got another one."

Major Phillips checked the tag and nodded. "Good catch, Private. They're getting closer. Looks like they can sense a lot past the normal human spectrum."

Since shutting down their active scanners, the Marines had spotted more and more of the aliens as they braved getting closer to the facility. They couldn't be certain how many of the snakelike beasties there were out beyond the range of their passive scopes, but they knew that the number was a lot higher than any of them were comfortable with.

Of course, a single fifteen-meter-long flying snake was well beyond their comfort zone, never mind accounting for its friends.

"Major? What's going on?"

Phillips half turned, nodding as Commander Daiyu approached. "We're surrounded, Commander. Local fauna, very hostile and lethal."

"We've met," Daiyu said, glancing out past the Marines. "The latest update from the *Autolycus* doesn't look good, Major. They're under assault from the heliobeam."

Phillips scowled. "Can they hold out?"

"Not for much longer without risking the containment on the reactor," she answered. "The beam is compromising the ship's cooling systems."

"My Marines are coming back up," Phillips said, "but they're being pursued. We'll have to make a run for the lift and meet them there."

She nodded. "I'll get the research team together."

"Roger that. I'll organize the breakout."

As Daiyu left, the major turned back to the assembled Marines. "You heard the commander. Weapons and systems check. We exfil in ten."

"Sir, yes, sir!"

CHAPTER 19

▶ "Pack up your equipment," Daiyu ordered as she swept into the midst of the researchers. "We are evacuating back to the *Autolycus*."

Most of them started moving instantly, having expected that command. Two, however, did not. Daiyu was unsurprised at one of the two. Doctor Palin was proving to be a pain in her posterior, no matter how talented he was. The other, however, was her own aide, a civilian scientist named Richard Hawkins.

"Richard, it is time to leave," she repeated herself, nudging his suit lightly, wanting to move on to the task of motivating the linguist.

"Commander, I think we have a problem," Richard told her.

"I am aware that we have problems, Richard, plural. That is why we are withdrawing back to the ship."

"No, that's just it. I don't think the ship is under attack."

Daiyu frowned, distracted enough to pause and give him her full attention. "They report rising radiation levels increasing the heat on the hull. That qualifies, Richard."

"I think we're just looking at waste energy, possibly being used to get a location lock on the ship," he said. "Look at what the facility computer is showing in this section."

Daiyu looked over the display, leaning in as she saw what he was pointing out.

"The system is still charging," she said, puzzled.

"That's not all, Commander," Richard said, gesturing to another section. "Tell me I'm reading that wrong."

She turned her focus to the section indicated and put her entire attention on it, trying to determine what he was talking about. It didn't take her long to recognize that she was looking at a real-time rendering of space-time around the local moon/planet system.

"Is that . . . ?" Daiyu trailed off, almost fearing the answer.

"I think so, yes."

The system clearly showed the presence of the *Autolycus* in orbit around the moon, and she could see shears in space-time forming all around it.

"We're trapped," Daiyu said, with some finality. "The *Autolycus* doesn't have the power to warp space-time shears that steep."

"That's what I thought," Richard said quietly. "I'd hoped I was wrong."

"No, you are not," Daiyu said. "I have to try to contact the ship."

▶ ▶ ▶

▶ In the dark, Ramirez relied on his HUD and the suit transponders to keep track of his Marines. They were ascending as fast as their chutes could manage, burning fuel at an ungodly rate despite the maximum use of counter-mass. He had run the numbers twice already, however, and was confident that they'd make the walkway with room to spare.

Unfortunately, they had pursuers.

The alien serpents were lithe in the air, but not spectacularly fast as they climbed. That gave the Marines the advantage for the moment, but there was something bothering him that Ramirez couldn't quite put his finger on.

It wasn't until a proximity alarm went off on one of the Marines' suits that he realized just what it was.

Oh, fuck me, he mentally swore as he looked up. *I forgot that we probably didn't have all of them in our rearview.*

"Watch for attack from above," he called, a moment too late.

The darkness was lit up with the flash of rocket-propelled slugs cutting lines across the abyss, the shrieks of the attacking serpents punctuated by the staccato roar of explosions flashing in the night.

"They're everywhere!"

"Suck it up, Marines!" Gunny Scaol snarled, her weapon roaring. "Nowhere to go but through!"

Fighting while hanging off the bottom of a CM chute was a precarious and dangerous situation. Even with their weapons slaved to their battle network, relying heavily on IFF signals to keep them from fragging each other with blue-on-blue strikes, the incidental shrapnel of a near miss could still wreak serious havoc with the only things keeping them aloft.

But the chutes could take light hits from shrapnel. They'd been designed to take worse, as had the armor the Marines' suits were constructed of. It was when the serpents were suddenly among them that things turned ugly in a very real way.

The sound sent a chill through Ramirez, right to his spine, even before he recognized what it was and what it meant. Deep down, he didn't need to know exactly what made the sound to know it was a bad, *bad* sound.

The last time he'd heard anything remotely like it had been on board a ship, back on Earth, when a rookie river pilot gunned the engine before the lines were secured. The cable snapped, sending three men to sick bay, and one home in a box.

For a moment he didn't know how he could have heard anything like that on an alien world, in midair of all places. Then he looked up to the lines attaching him to the chute that was holding his life suspended a thousand kilometers over God alone knew what.

"Son of a . . . !"

The gunny was swearing up a storm, and Ramirez couldn't blame her. She was dangling by one cable, spinning around as her chute fought to maintain altitude control against the force of her flailing. Her weapon was hanging useless by the strap as she reached up to grab the cable.

"Belay that noise, Gunny!" Ramirez ordered, hoping she'd listen to him.

It was likely a testament to her indoctrination at Camp Pendleton more than any respect she had for him, but Scaol froze and stopped her swearing just as ordered.

"Cover the gunny." Ramirez tagged a pair of nearby Marines, issuing the order. "Everyone else watch for any others on a flyby. Clear?"

"Clear! Sir!"

"Damn thing sliced right through a carbon core wire, LT," Scaol croaked, sounding like she'd just danced with the specter of death, which, of course, she had.

"I saw it, Gunny, just hang tight . . ."

Ramirez winced. He really could have phrased that a little better.

Karen Scaol chuckled. "Yes, sir. Be here if you need me, sir."

"I know you will, Gunny."

The squad was literally hauling ass, accelerating vertically as fast as the chutes could manage, but the sheer depth of the darkness around them made it feel like they were in the tightest of confines, with enemy soldiers waiting to leap out from any side. Ramirez cursed the black, knowing that no matter how deadly or big the serpents were, they had no chance against a Marine fire team that could see them coming. But these conditions were another story.

So far, active scanners hadn't been terribly useful, and passives had execrable range. Their warning on an attack was less than two seconds, barely enough time to react if you were already leaning the right way. No time at all if you were caught out of position.

Ramirez had been in jungles that offered a lower chance of ambush than the open air they were currently flying through.

He looked over, his eyes on the black skies but his mind on his squad. "Pierce. What's Mac's status?"

"He's holding on, LT," Pierce said, from where he was pacing beside Mac. "Caught the shakes, but still breathing."

"Shock or coming down?" Ramirez asked, wondering if the man was about to crash from losing his leg, or if he'd already crashed from the adrenaline surge of the earlier fight.

"Both, LT."

Fuck, Ramirez thought, just remembering to keep his mouth shut. He didn't want to convey any negative thought to the injured man, but shock combined with a comedown from a battle state could be ugly. "Keep an eye on him."

"No need to ask."

A blare of fire to his left made Ramirez twist around, reorienting as best he could to be in position to intercept an attack. When nothing materialized, he had to fight back an urge to snap at his men and tell them to stop wasting ammo.

It was going to be touch and go whether they'd make it back topside with any bullets left in their guns, but at the same time he didn't dare blunt their reaction time with orders.

He checked his altimeter, noting that it was functioning based on dead reckoning navigation since none of the other systems were remotely reliable. They had another forty klicks, vertical, before they reached the catwalk.

Whoever built this freak of a place was certifiable.

He didn't know if they had some design reason to build a place the size of a moon, fill it with air, and then populate it with frigging *dragons* of all damn things, but he hoped so. Because otherwise, whoever built the place was a goddamned psychopath.

"Incoming!"

Everyone was still reacting as the shriek dopplered through their midst and that damn sound rang out.

Twice.

It was a damnable thing. Ramirez barely caught a glimpse of Pierce as he plummeted into the black, but his voice didn't fade. Radio traveled much faster, and farther, than sound. His moment of panic came through clear as a bell as Pierce fell, cut loose from his chute, which was now rocketing upward.

"Shit!" Ramirez swore, making a gut decision before the actual thoughts had time to even appear in his brain. He cut power to his own chute, retracting it to his back, and hung in the air for a brief moment before pitching over and diving for the abyss. "Gunny! Your squad!"

"LT!" Scaol called. "You don't have enough fuel!"

▶▶▶

▶ The heat was starting to become noticeable, Morgan noted as he wiped the sweat from his forehead and looked over the intelligence they were still receiving from the teams below.

It had started as a straight-up exploration of an alien artifact, granted not something to be taken lightly, but the whole mission was rapidly turning into a clusterfuck of rather epic proportions.

I'm starting to understand just how Weston was able to screw up his first mission so damned badly, Morgan thought wryly, with more than a little self-deprecation in his mental tone. He just hoped that his first mission didn't result in another invasion of Earth before the costs were tallied.

"Sir, there's a priority message from Commander Daiyu. Not sure how she got it through. Must have used an ultralow-frequency pulse."

Morgan nodded absently, already opening the mail system. ULF signals had good penetration when dealing with broadcast obstacles, but they were generally considered too slow to use, as their speed drastically reduced the information you could put into a signal.

The message was, as expected, short. The contents, however, were explosive.

Oh, damn. If the commander was right, and he had little reason to doubt her, they were in a lot deeper trouble than he'd realized.

"Weps," he said, calling out to the weapons station, "I need a tasking for one of our drones."

"Yes, sir. Location?"

He tapped in the coordinates and sent them. "To your station, Weps."

Ensign Bonavista glanced down, and then actually did a double take before hesitantly looking over her shoulder. "Captain, these coordinates are away from the moon. There's nothing out there."

"Then we won't have a problem, will we, Weps?"

"No, sir, I suppose we won't."

She turned her focus to the job at hand, and Morgan just shook his head in the background.

We can only hope. We can only hope.

▶ ▶ ▶

▶ "Commander! We're ready to move," Major Phillips said. "Have you got the eggheads ready yet?"

"We have a problem, Major," Daiyu said softly. "You had best come through and see this yourself."

It took a few moments for the major to work his way back through the facility to where Commander Daiyu was once more locked into the holographic interface that controlled the alien technology. He scowled under his helmet, knowing that whatever was going on, he wasn't going to like it.

"Give me the bad news, Commander," Phillips managed to say without sighing, knowing that something had just screwed their plans up but good.

"The system isn't fully online yet," Daiyu said. "However, it is powering up and has already erected gravity shears on all sides of the *Autolycus*. We're running the numbers now, but I do not believe the ship can survive passing through those shears."

Phillips closed his eyes, counting off a few numbers so he didn't say something in front of a superior officer that he might regret later in his career.

"Understood," he said after a few seconds. "How do we shut it down?"

"Working on that, Major," she told him, not looking back. "In the meantime, see to your wayward Marines."

"Yes, ma'am."

Phillips recognized the dismissal for what it was and turned on his heel, striding back out. He reached the entrance to the facility in just a few seconds, noting that everyone was ready to break out according to the plan.

"Plan's changed!"

Phillips listened to the griping for a moment, letting them get it out of their systems more than anything, and then cut in again.

"Quit your bellyaching! We've got jobs to do, and we're going to get them done. Anyone who thinks otherwise can transfer to the Air Force when we get home. Until then, you're Marines. By God, act like it."

"What's the sitrep, Major?" the sergeant of the group asked.

"Looks like we may have to figure out how to pull the plug on this place," Phillips said. "Eggheads and the commander are on that now. Our immediate problem is getting our guys back. Where are they?"

"Twenty klicks from the catwalk, about a klick that way." The sergeant pointed toward the shaft in the distance.

"Alright, let's get them leaning in this direction. I want them to withdraw here and hunker down until we know what we're doing," Phillips ordered. "Let's organize some cover for them when they get back up here."

"Yes, sir," the sergeant nodded, turning back. "Cranston! Mitchell! Jones! Miram! Fall out, you're with me. The rest of you, keep this door secured and be ready in case we have trouble on our ass when we get back."

"Yes, Sergeant!"

"With your permission, Major?"

"Granted, Sergeant."

Sergeant Towers nodded curtly, and then pivoted and walked his squad out the door and into the black beyond.

▶▶▶

▶ Gunny Scaol was *pissed.*

Flying by a glorified Tinkertoy was bad enough, but being twisted and turned around bodily because you were being hauled behind said Tinkertoy by a lone cable just *sucked.* She wasn't prone to motion sickness, the Corps had seen to that over the years, but her current situation was pushing that particular asset of hers to its limits.

"Ten klicks to the catwalk, Gunny."

"I can read the HUD, Marine," she growled. "How is Mac?"

"I'm alive," the marksman said, his voice trying to make a liar of him.

"I can read those numbers, too," Scaol replied. "Have anything useful to add?"

Mac chuckled weakly. "No, Gunny, sorry about that."

"Yeah, well, can probably cut you a little slack. You did save our butts down there," she told him. "Just don't die until I get a chance to repay the favor."

"Yes, Sergeant, whatever you say."

"Fuel check," she said, not having anything better to do at the moment. She sure as hell couldn't aim in her current circumstance, and firing blind would probably get someone killed.

The fuel numbers for the squad showed on her HUD instantly, clearly listing everyone in the red, but enough to get them the last ten klicks to the catwalk. Her eyes focused for a moment on the lieutenant's numbers, which were better than the rest of the team because he had more fuel at the moment, but he was more than a hundred klicks below them, and there was no way he had the numbers to make it back.

Goddamn, LT, I just got you trained up proper.

CHAPTER 20

▶ Arms at his sides, Ramirez had little to do other than wonder whether he was crazy, or just stupid, as he dove through the black abyss after his lost corporal. Without the battle network and HUD connected to his suit, there wouldn't have been a chance in all hell of his finding Pierce, but with it he almost didn't have to *do* anything himself in the attempt.

It was almost too easy, just making micro-adjustments as he dove, noting that Pierce had reached terminal velocity and was in a stable fall. He could almost forget that he and Pierce were dropping through hostile air because, for the moment at least, the dragons seemed to be following the rest of the squad and not hunting stragglers. The recon Marine was fully HALO trained, so there was no worry about him panicking further, though Ramirez was actually more worried about the exact opposite reaction.

A man could do stupid things when feeling fatalistic about his situation.

"On your nine high, Corporal," he said as he adjusted. "I've got you."

"Begging the lieutenant's pardon, sir, but who the fuck has *you?*"

He's definitely not lost it. That's good, at least.

"Let me worry about that."

Pierce didn't say anything for a moment as the distance between the two closed, finally speaking up again as Ramirez was only a few seconds from contact.

"You should have left me, sir. No reason for both of us to go down." Pierce said the last part laughing openly.

"Get it? Go down?"

"I get it. Now shut up and brace."

Ramirez hit the corporal in the shoulders, trying to bleed velocity as quickly as he could without wasting fuel. The impact sent them both spinning, tossing them apart, but also had the effect of equalizing their rate of descent. After stabilizing their spin, Ramirez banked back in and caught up to his corporal again, this time not letting go once he caught him.

"Got you," he said, pulling straps from his armor links and latching them together.

His chute detached from his back, paying out the line as the CM generators pulsed to full power and the rockets roared and stopped their descent.

"That's great, LT. *Now what?*"

Ramirez twisted around, instinctively looking for somewhere . . . *anywhere* . . . to put down, but in the black abyss they inhabited, that would be asking for far too much.

"Go active," he grunted, tuning his own armor up to full active scans. "Look for something to land on."

"In this soup? Fat chance," Pierce sighed, but his armor was fully active a moment later as well.

Suit-based radar was of limited range, generally used only as part of the battle network to prevent blue-on-blue strikes, but it was still reasonably effective. Unfortunately, it relied on something being out there to detect and, so far as either Marine could figure, that just wasn't the case.

"Alright. I'm taking us back to the facility."

It was quiet for a moment before Pierce responded. "Boss man, between those monsters and a fall to my death . . . you can just drop me off here."

"Shut it! I'm not losing anyone else on this damned mission, you get me? We're going back and locking the whole place down. The systems respond to humans. I think we can keep those things out."

"Didn't work so well for whoever built this place, LT."

"You got a better plan?"

"We could hope for a soft landing?"

"We're going to the facility, Corporal."

"You're the boss, boss."

Ramirez sighed.

Corporals.

▶▶▶

▶ The catwalk showed up on their suit sensors before anyone could see it, giving Gunny Scaol time to get everyone drifting in the right direction before they actually made it back.

"Land in waves," she ordered. "I want full coverage at all times. Don't give those fucking things a chance to sneak up on us!"

"You best go first, Gunny."

Scaol bit back a scathing response. Normally she'd tear a strip off a Marine that told her to take cover before her squad. But damn it, she was a hanging duck at the moment, and he had a damned point.

"Right," she said, gritting her teeth. "I'll lead in."

Her chute was on proverbial fumes as she dropped to the catwalk, then cut it loose and let the piece of kit fall to the walkway. She got her weapon back in hand, propping one foot on the expended chute, and signaled the others in.

"Bring 'em in, boys," she ordered. "I've got you covered."

Night-vision systems were naturally limited by available light, or whatever radiated energy their detection system was based on. In the Marines' case, they used a combination of active and passive sensors that were generally enough to see a thousand meters off like it was bright daylight.

In the black abyss they were fighting in, however, the range of the passives was measured in tens of meters, not hundreds, let alone a thousand. The actives were better, but even those were limited to the cone of radiating energy they could project, which barely gave them a hundred meters if they had luck on their side.

If they were looking in just the right direction at just the right time, Scaol knew they could spot and pot one of the alien beasties before it became a threat. The problem was that all too often it seemed like the dragons could tell when they were being watched and would hold back.

To her, that said that the dragons could see the night-vision beams when they were active, and had enough sense to avoid charging right into them.

Bully for them, but it gives us a real problem, she thought as the Marines under her command started landing on the catwalk around her.

She noted the IFF of a PFC tech specialist landing a few meters away and strode over and slapped him on the shoulder.

"Mercer, we need to chat."

"Uh . . . yes, Gunny, what is it?" the Marine asked, nervously looking around.

"These bastards can see us. We need to see them."

PFC Mercer looked confused, but nodded. "Uh . . . yes, Gunny."

"What about those screams, Mercer? Our sonics should be able to pick those up."

Mercer nodded slowly. "Right . . . you mean triangulate their approach?"

"Can you do it?"

The Marine took a moment, clearly thinking, and Scaol left him to it while she finished securing the landing zone. Everyone left was on deck, securing the zone while they waited for orders from the major or the skipper himself.

She got her squad squared away, checking ammo levels and redistributing rounds until everyone had at least a mag in their gun and one in their pouch, all the while keeping one eye on the two blips still showing on her HUD.

Telemetry from Pierce's and the lieutenant's suits was mostly dead, but she could still read the locator beacons for each.

She couldn't tell if the Marines were still alive, but the two beacons were together and ascending slowly. Scaol chose to take that as a good sign, for what it was worth. At the moment no one had the fuel to mount a rescue op—not that the last one they'd tried had worked out so well—so the LT and Pierce would just have to make do on their own.

"Everyone loaded and mobile?" she asked, looking around. No one said otherwise, so Scaol just continued on. "Keep a perimeter. The major is still in the facility on this level along with everyone else. Not much point hanging here, so let's go meet up with him and the others and see if we can get a briefing. Come on, Mac, I've got you."

Her somewhat depleted team accepted that easily enough, especially because by the time they'd gotten squared away, the squad the major had sent out reached their location. Scaol pulled McMillan's arm over her shoulder, and they set out in turn with Tower's fresh squad providing cover.

This is going to be one fucked-up report.

▶▶▶

▶ "Well, that's problematic."

Captain Passer's comment went largely unnoted by those around him. Those who were in earshot were too busy looking at the data feed from the drone they'd just lost to pay him any mind.

"We've been isolated, Captain," Kamir said, examining the data. "I have no idea how they did it, but we're surrounded by several shearing points in space-time."

Morgan nodded. "That confirms the commander's report, so it seems we've sailed into deep waters this time. Keep drones along the periphery. I want to know if those lines move."

"Aye, sir," Kamir nodded.

"Conway, you have the bridge," Morgan said, unstrapping.

"Aye aye, Skipper, I have the bridge," Conway said, shifting to the central command station as the captain vacated it.

"I'll be in engineering if anyone needs me," Morgan said on his way out.

Moving around the ship with a light gravity pull was an interesting change. The transit handles were useless; they weren't designed to hold weight vertically, though they probably could. He'd look like a damn fool hanging on to one for dear life as he was hauled around the ship, though, and that was not an option Morgan was entertaining.

Feel like a jarhead, stomping around in magnetic boots. With local gravity being somewhat . . . unpredictable, everyone had pulled on pairs of the unwieldy boots just in case something changed. Ship operations had to go on, come hell or high gravity.

The *Auto* wasn't a huge ship, however, so making it from the bridge to main engineering only took a couple of minutes. Once there, he found the two people he needed to speak with, subtly ignoring one another as they tended to their stations.

Xiang Feng and Doohan had their reasons for disliking each other, but he didn't have time to play to their paranoia at the moment.

"Chiefs, to me," Morgan ordered, jerking his head toward a side office before turning and walking into the room without looking back.

The two engineers looked to where he'd gone, and then glared at one another for a brief moment before they dropped what they were doing and followed.

Morgan was waiting for them in the small conference room, with the display table already folded out of the wall. He looked between them and shook his head as they stood about as far apart as they could manage in the confined space.

"Don't let me hear of you two letting this bullshit get in the way, or I'll lock you both up until we get home."

Neither engineer quite knew how to answer that, so both kept their mouths shut. Morgan seemed satisfied with that response, or as close to satisfied as could be expected.

"Here's the situation," the captain said after a moment, laying it all out for them.

The two engineers had more than a passing familiarity with the notion of asymmetric gravity fields, though Doohan would concede—if pressed, with a lethal weapon—that his counterpart was the expert on the subject. Still, the shearing forces detected around the *Auto* seemed to fly in the face of modern quantum physics and their understanding of how space-time was shaped.

"We need options," Morgan said after finishing his summary. "Chief Doohan, can we transition out?"

"Not a chance, Skipper." The Canadian shook his head. "If we try, we'll scatter our atoms across thirty light-years of space, I can all but promise you that."

"He is right," Xiang said reluctantly. "I have read the briefing files on the transition system. It is a miracle that it works as well as it does in near-neutral gravity. This is far beyond its capacity."

"Can your warp drive get us out of this?" Doohan said.

The Chinese engineer shook his head. "No. This shearing force is too strong. Even if my engines could push us through it, I do not believe the hull would survive."

"So we're trapped," Morgan sighed, not surprised. He was far from an expert, but he knew the capabilities of his ship, and her limitations.

"What if we overcharged a warp field?" Doohan suggested. "Blow out one of our shuttle drives and try to collapse the standing wave?"

"No, shuttle drives don't have the power," Xiang said. "Maybe our main drive could do it, but we'd be dead in space afterward."

"Not if we can build enough speed to get to escape velocity," Doohan corrected, "or close enough, at least. If we can sling ourselves far enough out, we can still transition even without the warp drive."

"Possible. We will need to be certain of the math," Xiang said pensively.

Good, at least they have an idea, Morgan thought, stepping back. "I'll leave the details to you. In the meantime, I'm ordering our entry team to try to turn off the alien weapon while they have access to the machine's interface. If you come up with anything else, let me know."

With that, he left the two engineers arguing over a physics problem, each now apparently oblivious to the other's nationality.

As it should be.

▶▶▶

▶Commander Daiyu scowled openly at the interface she was standing before, willing it to tell her something different than what it was currently insisting on.

While security on some levels of the facility was apparently totally open, it was clear to her that the people who had built the ancient construct had at least the common sense to put layers of locks on the weaponized section of the station.

She had been able to locate the shutdown sequence, at least, she thought, but activating it was another matter entirely.

Unless I miss my guess, all changes have to be physically initiated at the fire control station . . . and that is not here.

She swore in Mandarin, wishing she could strike the offending computer, but the ethereal nature of the projected interface made that effectively impossible.

"I may not know what you said, Commander, but I recognize a nasty epithet when I hear one," Major Phillips said as he approached from behind her.

She glanced back, sighing. "Yes, well, I am far from . . . happy, at the moment."

"Commander, none of us are happy." He grinned for a moment, and then sobered up. "Still, it would be better if you didn't lose your temper in front of the others. Bad for morale, you know."

"Are you saying that your Marines can't handle a few curse words?" she asked, lightly amused.

"Oh, they can handle those. Just don't say 'em like you mean 'em."

"I will keep that in mind."

"So what caused those nasty words to spill out, as if I actually wanted to know?"

"You may not want to know, Major, but I am very much afraid that you need to know," Daiyu said wearily, shaking her head. "We cannot deactivate the system from here. It must be done at the physical fire control system."

"And this is . . . ?"

"A library interface, at most," she said, waving a hand dismissively. "I would guess that the security is so low because civilian researchers were expected to come and go, accessing star charts at regular intervals."

Phillips grunted. "Explains a bit."

"Indeed."

The Marine major looked over the display. "Any idea where the fire control system is?"

"Unfortunately," she told him dryly, flicking a hand against the interface until it shifted, "that appears to be it there, in relation to the facility we're in now."

Phillips growled, shaking his head.

The imagery was clearly a facility located deeper inside the moon, the very one that his Marines had just returned from. Those who had returned.

"It figures. We've got four KIAs listed in that place, two MIAs, and one of my best men is missing his right leg. Going back down there is a *bad* idea, Commander."

"With the *Autolycus* isolated and unable to escape this system," Daiyu said, "and the alien weapon warming up, I'm not certain we have other options."

Phillips groaned. "What I wouldn't give for air support."

"We'll need to retrieve the rest of the operations package," Daiyu decided, "and whatever else you need from the ship."

"And we need to do it yesterday," Phillips muttered. "This isn't my first cattle drive, Commander."

She stared at him for a long moment, mildly confused.

"What an odd expression. Why would cattle drive anywhere?"

CHAPTER 21

▶ The two men tumbled to the metal ground, sprawling with as much finesse as . . . well, as a Marine, actually. The CM chute that had been carrying them crashed to the ground beside them, its fuel exhausted and batteries on slim power.

Ramirez groaned as he rolled over onto his back and lay still. "You alright, Corporal?"

"I'm alive, LT," Pierce said. "Better than I expected."

The lieutenant snorted at that. "No shit. You mean you didn't think a nosedive into a bottomless abyss was a ticket to a long and healthy life?"

"LT?"

"Yeah?"

"Shut up."

Ramirez chuckled, figuring that if there was ever a time to relax regs a little, it was probably right after a hundred-kilometer dive into a black abyss. He took a few breaths, and then sat up and looked around.

With his scanners operating entirely in passive mode, there just wasn't a lot to see, but the area around him was empty up to a dozen meters out or so.

"How much air do you have left, Pierce?" he asked, checking his own system.

"Not enough. Half hour, maybe forty minutes."

"Yeah, I'm not much better," Ramirez confirmed. "Well, let's just hope those things don't carry anything contagious."

"I'm not exactly concerned with their hygiene or health, boss, it's the teeth and claws that have my more immediate attention."

"Yeah, no shit," Ramirez said softly. "Still . . . I'm going to pop the tab on this tin can, save the canned stuff for later, in case I need it."

"You sure?" Pierce sounded wary. "It'll mean isolation if we get back."

"The odds of us getting back, in the next forty minutes, are pretty damn slim. I'll take my chances with the air in here."

Ramirez shut off his suit's air supply and popped the seal on his helmet, the air hissing out and condensing slightly. He took a hesitant breath, but didn't smell anything besides the slightly charcoal hint of the suit's filters, and so he began breathing normally.

"You've got a point," Pierce said, popping his own seal a moment later.

"Alright, we've got no juice for the pack . . . but your pack is still mobile and in range," Ramirez said, "so we have that."

"Does it have enough to get us topside?"

"Not even close."

"Figures."

"I think we can use it as a relay to get back in communication with the rest," Ramirez said. "I'm having it sit about halfway up."

Pierce nodded, looking around. "You do that. Meanwhile, we're still in monster central, I hope you realize."

"Don't use any active scanners," Ramirez ordered. "We don't know what those things see with, but it's clear that they can spot some of our actives."

"Roger that." Pierce pulled a small cylinder from his belt. "I'm going to pop a flare and toss it over that way. It'll give us some light, but hopefully will attract anything away from us as well."

"Just let me get some cover here," Ramirez said, crouching down behind a wall of some kind.

"Roger that," Pierce said, moving to cover himself before popping the flare and tossing it overhand a good distance away.

The magnesium flare ignited in the air, casting light and shadows all around them as they ducked down and as far out of sight as they could. The indirect light was dim enough that their passive light amplification systems were still reasonably effective, and the two Marines scouted around quickly.

"I've got nothing," Pierce said.

"Ditto."

"I see a sealed entrance about forty meters that way," Pierce gestured, "but we know those things have a way into at least part of the facility."

"Better inside than out here," Ramirez decided. "Those things can swoop in from any angle right now."

"Yeah. Move in three?"

Ramirez nodded, and then both spoke at once.

"Three!"

The two Marines bolted across the open ground, rifles leading the way, but they were moving too fast to aim at much even if something jumped right out in front of them. They skidded to a stop at the doors, both men frantically pawing at the air as they tried to trigger the command line interface they'd seen elsewhere.

"I've got nothing over here, boss," Pierce said, feeling around wildly.

"Nothing here either." Ramirez hesitated, and then made a snap choice. "Breach it."

"On it." Pierce slung his rifle, pushing it around behind his back as he dug out a breaching strip.

Breaching strips were basically rolls of duct tape with a high-explosive-shaped charge integrated in the material, offset so as to allow the charges to be packed more tightly. Pierce tore off a few strips and secured them to the door while Ramirez covered him, then attached a remote detonator to the resulting configuration of tape and explosives and stepped back.

"Fire in the hole," Pierce intoned, not particularly excited, though the warning was mandatory.

The soft poof of the explosives detonating was mostly directed inward as the plasma jet of the shaped charge sliced through the doors, leaving a large chunk barely hanging there. Pierce stepped up, kicked it in, and waved to Ramirez.

"Time to move, man."

Ramirez backed in through the hole, following Pierce as he kept up the rear.

It probably wouldn't do much, but once he was on the other side Ramirez put the chunk of door back up to block the hole, and then quickly taped a couple of frag rounds to either side and retreated before setting them to proximity detonate if anyone without a friendly IFF moved the chunk of metal.

He retreated back to where Pierce was kneeling by a branch in the corridor and looked around. "I don't have this place mapped. We landed on a lower level than we've explored. We're going to be doing this blind."

"We could turn on our subsonics," Pierce offered halfheartedly. "That's what they're designed for."

"No way. Those things were on us last time, and we don't know how they locked in on us. We do this the old-fashioned way."

Pierce snorted. "Great. Bouncing off the walls it is."

The two Marines headed deeper into the dark corridors of the alien facility, relying entirely on their passive light amplification and thermal systems. Unfortunately, since the aliens seemed to be reptilian, or as close to it as an alien got, thermal was largely ineffective.

"Any luck with that relay you set up, boss?" Pierce asked softly as they walked.

"Not yet. It's still looking for a strong signal," Ramirez said.

"What kind of loiter is left on it?"

Ramirez checked the numbers. "A few hours. Without a load the system is pretty efficient."

"Great. How close would it get us to the catwalk?"

"We'd fall to our deaths before we even had it in sight," Ramirez said dryly.

Pierce winced. "Well, let's not do that."

"I wasn't planning on it."

▶▶▶

▶ Sweat was trickling down his back as Morgan leaned over the console and examined the current feed from the external scanners. The hull temperature was up several degrees now, despite all their best efforts at cooling, and the temperatures had penetrated through the ship.

"Can we redirect cooling through the scanner sails if we extend them in the shadow of the ship?" he asked, looking across the bridge for the answer.

"We do run coolant through those sails, sir, but it's not going to give us much compared to the heat we've got building up."

Morgan just waved one hand. "Do it. I'll take what I can get. Have the chiefs found us anything to break us clear of this trap?"

"Not yet, sir," Kamir answered. "The best they've got right now pretty much involves turning us into a floating barge with less maneuverability than Unity Station."

Morgan sighed, rubbing the sweat from his eyes.

"Let's chalk that up as plan B then," he said dryly.

Being stranded in space might not be the death sentence it seemed. They had an FTL burst transmitter on board that should be able to bring in some help, if not from one of the Heroics then at least from the Priminae merchant fleet, but the idea of having his ship towed back to port on its first mission wasn't something he wanted to entertain unnecessarily.

More importantly, marginally perhaps, but still, was the fact that no one could confidently say that a burst transmission would make it out of the strange gravity fields that were corrupting the entire system they were in. So both for his personal ego, and the lives of his crew, Morgan was determined to investigate every possible alternative before resorting to one that left the *Autolycus* dead in space.

"Commander Daiyu has retrieved the rest of the SOCOM deployment crate we delivered to the surface," Lieutenant Commander Conway said. "Her last report from the surface was that they had located the fire control system for the weapon."

"That's all well and good, if they can do anything with it," Morgan said. "However, I'm not confident enough of that to leave it entirely to them."

He looked around the bridge, at the section commanders of every major and most minor sections of the ship, leveling a stern glower at all of them.

"Find us a way out of this rat trap, before the weapon we're orbiting decides it's time to clean house and reset."

▶▶▶

▶Commander Daiyu and the Marines finished plundering the SOCOM crate of everything it had left, as well as whatever else the Copperheads had been able to supply them with. Critically important, they had fuel cells for their depleted chutes, and more ammunition than when they had originally landed.

Given the nature of the threat, every man and woman among them had little doubt it was all going to be needed.

Daiyu herself had spent the time in the lift both going up and now heading back down, reviewing everything the Marines' scanners had recorded about the alien creatures.

They were large serpentine creatures, almost fifteen meters long, with wickedly effective curved claws on their forward limbs and a more complicated wing system than she had originally credited them with. While they had the almost *traditional* batlike wings that the Marines had noted at first, she spotted something in the recordings that showed the creatures in flight. They weren't held aloft merely by the two large and leathery appendages sprouting from their bodies.

In flight the aliens actually flattened out, their entire length becoming a lifting body as they *slithered* through the air. Snakes on Earth could do that, certainly, but nothing remotely of this size.

An effect of the lower gravity here, she supposed, *likely combined with the higher oxygen content.*

Phillips was speaking quietly to McMillan in the corner. The injured Marine was propped up against the wall but refused to sit down.

"We're leaving all the noncombatants we can in the facility we originally located," Phillips said, "but we can't spare you any Marines."

"I don't need a leg to hold a fixed position, sir. I've got this." McMillan was adamant. "Go finish the mission, sir."

The major nodded, his helmeted form seeming to search the corporal for a long moment.

"Semper fi, Marine, I'll see you when I get back."

"We'll be waiting, sir."

"Is everybody else clear on our mission?" Phillips spoke as he stepped to the front of the lift and turned to face them as they once more descended to the mouth of the abyss.

"Sir! Yes, sir!"

Daiyu blinked at the overenthusiastic and disturbingly in-sync response. Marines were disturbing on so many levels, she felt, largely because they often seemed to be raw trainees fresh from graduation even when she knew damn well they were experienced veterans of multiple campaigns.

She suspected that many of them relished that very contradiction and, as for those who didn't, they just went along.

"I'll review anyway," Phillips said, glaring around at everyone as if daring them to object.

No one took that bait, proving to her that these Marines were at least slightly more intelligent than the average trainee.

"We've located what the commander believes is the fire control mechanism for this entire facility," Phillips said, "so we are going to take, secure, and *hold* that position while the eggheads try and disarm this damned thing."

"Ooh rah!"

"And if we happen across a pair of wayward Marines in the meantime," Phillips growled, sounding almost disgusted, "someone show them the way home."

"Semper fi, sir!"

▶▶▶

▶ Pierce cleared the corner, dropping to one knee as Ramirez swept around him and began to proceed farther in.

"Mic check," Ramirez mumbled. "Are you hearing that?"

"The creepy scrabbling noise that totally *doesn't* sound like giant rats scraping the other side of the walls?" Pierce asked. "Nope. Totally not hearing a thing."

"Shit."

Pierce tapped his helmet lightly, shaking his head. "Man, it bugs me how little shows up on thermal, boss. Are you sure these things are working?"

"Yeah, the temperature in here has just equalized," Ramirez answered.

"I've never seen anything like it before."

Ramirez sighed, but didn't blame Pierce for being creeped out. Actually, he was a lot more creeped out than his corporal, because he knew enough about the tech to understand what he was seeing and just how . . . not impossible, but unlikely, it was.

"That's because, unless I miss my guess, no one has been down here for a *very* long time," Ramirez said. "There's no sun down here, so the heat is coming from an internal source, something steady and pervasive. Everything has either come up, or dropped, to a steady temperature. Thermals are next to useless in this."

"Our kit can scan *footprints* from an hour ago," Pierce said, looking behind him to check. Indeed, his own and the lieutenant's footprints were glowing faintly in the scanner.

"That's why I said I don't think anyone has been down here in a long time, and those creatures . . ."

"Dragons," Pierce interrupted.

"Those *creatures*," Ramirez stressed, glaring over his shoulder, "seem to be cold-blooded. They scan as mostly ambient temperature, same as everything else."

"There's operating equipment in this place. There should be heat sources all over."

"Quantum logic circuits," Ramirez said. "It was in the brief on the Priminae technology. Doesn't generate heat. Power is . . . formed at the site of usage, so there's no conduits, no heat loss."

Pierce snorted, but didn't know near enough about the subject to say anything. It all sounded like voodoo to him, but his job wasn't to figure any of it out. He was a knuckle-dragger and a shooter for this run, so he supposed he didn't need to.

"Still creepy as hell," he grumbled.

You don't know the half of it, Ramirez thought darkly, not interested in spooking his subordinate.

He didn't know how long it would take to completely equalize the temperature of a place the size they were dealing with, but he suspected it was a *long* time. Decades would be far too short, if his guess was right, and centuries might not even be enough.

To his mind, at least, whoever had built the massive *planetary* system they were currently exploring had to have abandoned it centuries or, more likely in his opinion, millennia earlier.

They were stalking around in a long-dead monument to someone who was apparently capable of building *planets* in their spare time. None of that was calculated to leave him at ease, so the less said about the snake monsters—Ramirez was consciously forcing himself not to call them *dragons*—the better.

A teeth-jarring screech of something hard against metal shook them both from their thoughts as the two Marines tried to triangulate the location of the sound. Systems in their suits were designed to locate a sniper's position from the sound of a shot being fired, but it was far more effective in the open air than the confines of the tight corridors they found themselves in.

About the only thing they could tell was that it came from ahead of them, which they'd already worked out for themselves no thanks to any fancy electronics.

Ramirez shifted his grip on his rifle, thumbing the power dial up to maximum. At close range the electromagnetic accelerator in the weapon was the only source for kinetic stopping power at his disposal, since the scramjet rounds wouldn't have time to kick in. There was little need to conserve power in the rifle's fuel cells in that case, so it was time to go for broke.

"CQB, Pierce," he said softly.

"Already shifted, boss."

CQB, or close quarters battle, meant exactly what the wording said. Their gear had various settings to make it more effective at the ranges they needed in any given situation, and right then it was pretty clear that if anything happened, they were going to be looking in the cold dead eyes of their enemy.

That led him to give an order that, while technically still on the books, he'd never heard given in his entire career . . . nor had he *ever* heard of it being given.

"Pierce," he said softly, "fix bayonets."

The corporal gave him a surprised look, but obediently reached down and slid the thick blade from his ankle sheath, the metal on metal hissing in the dark, and twisted it onto the front of his rifle. Ramirez did the same, checking his ammo count for the fiftieth time as he did so.

When the bullets ran out, the blades would be all they had. Arguably, a good sword might actually be more effective in the close quarters they were going to be fighting in, but he'd left his saber back on the *Auto*, and had never sharpened it to a fighting hone anyway.

The two armed and armored Marines moved slowly to allow their night-vision systems to give them the best possible view of the immediate area before proceeding onward.

▶ ▶ ▶

▶ Standing on the catwalk, looking out over a black abyss that felt less real than she knew it should, Commander Daiyu looked over the Marines and specialists readying themselves for the jump. They needed the civilians. They were specialists in xenotechnology, xeno-communications, and various other branches that could prove vital to the mission, but none of the military personnel were enthused about having any of them along.

Daiyu herself wished that they could do what needed to be done with telepresence, but communications were spotty at best given the ranges involved, and the alien technology that permeated the entire moon/planet system was clearly playing a role in limiting their trans-missions.

That meant the Marines would have to be escorts as well as sol-diers, and that was a load they were just going to have to shoulder.

"You all know our target. A fair few of you have been there once already," Major Phillips told everyone. "We're looking at a hundred-kilometer drop, straight down into a hostile abyss. Don't stray from the group, don't get fancy. Stick with your partners, and don't try to override your CM chutes."

This time, with so many barely qualified or completely unquali-fied people along for the trip, they were going to have to slave many of the programmable chutes to a central program. It wouldn't ensure perfect safety, not in a hostile environment, but anything that kept them from misplacing a scientist whose only previous experience with free fall was floating around his lab on the *Auto* was going to be a good thing.

"Civilians, stay in the group. If something happens, do *not* get separated from your guards. The Marines are there to keep you alive, so don't make their jobs any harder than they have to be."

Phillips looked the whole group over, nodding finally with a degree of satisfaction. It wasn't the team he'd have preferred in a situation like this. Honestly, the team he'd have preferred would be a Marine expeditionary force with air support and a firebase as backup.

"Alright, by the numbers, then," he ordered. "First squad . . . jump!"

Four Marines hopped the rail almost before his order was given, vanishing into the night below.

"Second squad . . . jump!"

Private McMillan watched as the Marines and the Navy personnel vanished into the darkness, then waved to one of the civilian researchers left behind.

"Come on, give me a hand . . . or leg, I guess," he said, with a hint of dark humor in his tone. "The sooner we're under cover, the better."

▶▶▶

▶Ramirez twitched as he rounded the corner, his focus shifting to his HUD as a set of lights appeared from nowhere. The momentary distraction nearly cost him his head as a flash slashed at him out of the darkness just as Pierce kicked his legs out from under him.

As the lieutenant crashed to the ground, Pierce threw himself back to evade the slash. The razor-sharp claw cut deep into the metal of the wall as he hit the ground on his back, his weapon barking three times.

The air filters on his suit were enough to eliminate most chemical and biological weapons known to man, but the faintest whiff of the chemical explosives from his trio of shots still managed to permeate his air as the backwash of the exploding rounds swept over him.

The snake screamed—Ramirez didn't know if it was pain or anger or both—and vanished back into the dark.

"LT, you okay?" he demanded, his eyes searching the dark in vain.

"I'm breathing, Corporal," Ramirez said slowly. "Thanks for the save."

"Anytime," Pierce said, "but mind telling me what had your head up your ass?" Pierce winced, climbing back to his feet. Pierce's description, while hardly flattering, was apt enough.

"I've got friendlies on the IFF, coming down fast," he said. "They just appeared right then."

Pierce snorted. "You've got some shit hot luck, LT. Good and bad."

"Tell me about it," Ramirez said as he began to edge forward, looking for signs of his attacker. "Damn. I don't see a body."

"Scared it off at least," Pierce shrugged. "I'll take it for a win."

There would be no arguments from Ramirez over that, not since they were both still breathing. Still, the lieutenant didn't much like that they were trapped inside with the damn things. He had been holding out some hope that the area of the base they were in hadn't been infested. *So much for that.*

Still, it was better than countless angles of open sky to try and defend against, at least when you could see more than a few meters out.

"If help is coming down the pipe, shouldn't we pull back and meet them?" Pierce asked.

"Hang on. I've got a lot of new material sitting in my queue." Ramirez winced as he saw the long list of file names and briefings that had been sent back to his suit from the relay drone. It was all information that was automatically shared across the entire network on a peer-to-peer basis, some of it marked important for him, most of it thankfully not.

Pierce nodded, stepping past him. "I'll cover you while you do your homework, boss, but we need to make a call on that ASAP."

"Roger that," Ramirez said, already skimming the summaries and looking for anything that seemed to stand out.

Well . . . He whistled silently a moment later. *That qualifies.*

"Okay, we're deeper in the shit than we thought," he muttered.

"Oh, joyous day," Pierce replied. "Lay it out for me."

"Eggheads figured out that this thing is more than a telescope. Apparently it's also a really big magnifying glass."

Pierce frowned, confused. "Uh . . . I sort of thought that was a telescope."

"Yeah, but no one put it together until after we dropped," Ramirez muttered. "You ever fry ants with a magnifying glass?"

"Oh, shit . . ." Pierce swore, and then paused as a thought struck him. He swore again, before asking, "The *Auto?*"

"Under a beam now, and they're trapped by some kind of gravity reef." Ramirez shook his head. "I don't understand it, but we've got a team dropping on our heads, looking for the off switch."

"Do they know where it is?"

Ramirez was already checking the image captures saved by Commander Daiyu, comparing them to the mapping they'd been doing on their own. He looked up the corridor, and then back down it. "I think we're in it."

"LT, if the ship is under attack, let's not lead with 'I think,' okay?"

"Better than 'Watch this,' " Ramirez replied.

"One damn time," Pierce protested hotly. "One damn time, and I never hear the end of it . . ."

"Come on, I think it's this way," Ramirez said, nodding down the corridor.

Pierce continued to grumble, but he shouldered his weapon and followed suit as the lieutenant started trekking into the darkness.

CHAPTER 22

▶ A night drop high over the Earth was one of the most thrilling and spectacular sights Daiyu had ever experienced. The lights of the civilization below, the slight curve of the earth, and the endless night sky above and around her were nearly her idea of heaven, if such a place were to exist.

Falling into an endless black abyss, trusting only her instruments and the previous reports of Marines who hadn't all managed to return from their own tumble into infinity . . . that was a nightmare that could only compare with hell, a place she was well aware *did* exist.

There was nothing to it but to gird her shaken courage and fall by the numbers though, since the job had to be done and she was one of those in position to see it through. The lower facility was slowly rising up to meet her as she felt the roar of air pluck at her armor, slight nudges from her chute keeping her on target and out of the way of everyone else.

Their formation was relatively loose by military standards, far looser than the precision guidance their networked equipment would enable them to maintain, but the major had decided to stick with it to allow more room for error. She was acutely aware that, while Phillips was more qualified than she, he wasn't exactly a HALO jump specialist himself and he was likely almost as nervous as she was.

Normally she might be amused by that fact. Now, though, it just gave her chills. The drop alone was terrifying, not to mention what might be waiting to jump out of the darkness at them . . .

▶▶▶

▶ "Captain," Kamir said, his tone almost hesitant as he stared at his screen like it might be lying to him.

"What is it, Lieutenant?" Morgan asked calmly, nudging the younger man just enough to get him talking.

"Scanners are showing something odd, I think," the officer said, tilting his head one way and then the other as if the angle of his glance might make a difference in how the screen display appeared.

"Well then, Lieutenant," Morgan said, his tone now sterner, "out with it."

"Aye, sir," Kamir said. "It's the gravity shears around us . . . I've been mapping them, and we just now got around to mapping the shear beneath the ship, and it's . . . it's weak, Captain."

Morgan shifted in his seat, the loose belt he had looped over his shoulder sliding off as he leaned forward. "Be specific."

"It's a fraction of the strength of the other shears around us, sir. Less than ten percent. I'd have to check with the chiefs, but I think we could blow through it."

"Do it. Call the chiefs."

Morgan managed to keep his personal disgust out of his voice so as not to intimidate his officers, but he was more than a little angry that this was the first they'd realized that the field was uneven around them. He checked previous orders quickly, grimacing as he realized that it was clear that no one had even considered looking *under* the ship to see if there was a way out.

Damn it! I'm a submariner. I think in three dimensions for a living! I should have spotted that. Get your head in the game, Passer, or this will be your last space command.

▶▶▶

▶ The volume and, well, the volume of cursing emanating from the chief's office in engineering would have been of more comfort to many in the crew if they understood a word of it. Unfortunately for them, it was Chief Xiang who was swearing up a storm, and his preferred tongue was Mandarin.

Hearing Chinese swearing echoing through engineering wasn't especially comforting to the relatively large majority of those who had been fighting against Block forces only a few years earlier.

Chief Doohan was one of those himself, but he refused to let the Block-head get to him as he strode into the office and glowered at the ranting man.

"What in the damned hells are you on about?" he swore, his Canadian accent coming out a bit as he got angry. It wasn't much really, just enough to make him almost say "aboot" at the end of his question, while he also just managed to check himself before adding an "eh" to the end. "You're scaring the nine hells out of the kiddies outside, Xiang!"

Xiang took a deep breath, visibly steadying himself before speaking.

"Apologies, Chief Doohan," he said slowly, deliberately. "New scanner data just came in from the bridge."

Doohan winced. "How boned are we?"

The phrase puzzled the Chinese man for a moment, but he got enough to understand from context and waved off Doohan's concern.

"We are in better shape than we were. I am just . . . frustrated . . . that we did not see it before," Xiang admitted, looking incredibly annoyed with himself.

Doohan leaned forward. "What is it?"

"We are in a bubble, yes?"

"Right, I can see it put that way," Doohan admitted. "So?"

"It is not self-sustaining. It must be powered from the outside," Xiang explained. "So consider, if you are keeping a bubble inflated from the outside . . . where does the air pressure come from?"

"Well, from . . ." Doohan trailed off, grimacing. "From an opening you can pump the energy into. Below us?"

"Very good, Chief." Xiang smiled sardonically. "Unfortunately, we all missed the scientific answer, and it was one of the young crewmen on the bridge playing with *robots* who found it. I am most put out."

Doohan winced, now understanding why his . . . *colleague* . . . was swearing up a storm in the middle of engineering. They'd all been so focused on trying to solve the problem, they'd gone and forgotten to *define* it in the first place.

"Oy," he groaned, leaning on the wall. "We're not gonna live this one down too soon. What do the numbers look like?"

Xiang slid a portable screen across to him, still cursing occasionally under his breath. Doohan caught it easily enough and flipped it around to have a look.

"Huh. This is interesting," he said after a moment. "There's a projection feed from the moon. I can see the gravity walls holding the energy in a coherent form, but it looks like they might be weak enough to punch through. How close do you think we'll have to get to the moon?"

"Close," Xiang said with finality. "Possibly too close, but that remains to be seen. I've been working the numbers, and I believe we can do it without destroying my engines."

Doohan quirked his eyebrow at that, but didn't comment. It was a fair comment. The gravity drives were built in factories outside Beijing, and Xiang had accompanied them into orbit and personally overseen their installation on the *Auto*. They *were* his engines, almost as much as the transition drive was Doohan's.

Almost.

"Alright, let's get our people moving on this," Doohan said, hesitating before sighing and saying something he would have sworn that he'd never have said, normally. "Your team takes the lead on this. I'll have my guys back you up. Just tell us what you need done."

Xiang nodded his head slowly. "Yes . . . yes, let's begin."

▶▶▶

▶ "Down!" Pierce screamed.

Ramirez hit the deck, not bothering to look at Pierce or wonder what had happened, and was rolling even before he felt the impact. Pierce lunged over him, leading with the ten-inch blade attached to the front of his rifle and driving it deep into the serpentine monster that had almost got the drop on Ramirez.

The snaky bastards had learned quick, it seemed, and weren't screaming right before they attacked. He wasn't sure what that was about in the first place. Maybe they were using some kind of echolocation, but the fact that they were trying to be sneaky wasn't a good thing.

Pierce twisted his rifle around, not wasting his ammo as he sought to inflict killing force with nothing but the fighting knife and some leverage. The snake was doing its part, certainly screaming now, as it twisted and fought in an attempt to get away from the stabbing pain. The Marine doggedly chased after it, however, slashing and stabbing until the snake slumped to the ground and lay twitching.

"Thanks," Ramirez said, climbing to his feet.

"No problem," Pierce answered, slamming his blade into the snake's head to stop the twitching, and then looking around. "Where are we?"

"Best guess? The fire control section the others are aiming for is just up ahead," Ramirez said. "I'm worried, though. These things are getting worse in here."

"Tell me about it," Pierce muttered, checking his weapon and noting that he'd actually twisted the blade mount a bit. "Much more of this, and one of these things is going to take my blade and run with it."

Ramirez grunted, not having much to say to that. The rifle and blades were made about as strong as anything of their size and dimensions could be. Twisting the metal around like that shouldn't be possible, but he'd seen enough to stop saying things like that.

Someone out there, or in here, is listening, and the perverted bastard just loves making me eat those words.

"Next time, I'm carrying my damn saber," he said finally, stepping over the snake as he prepared to take point and push on.

Pierce chuckled. "You want to carry an antique sword into a fight, boss? Really?"

"Be better than this." Ramirez held up the bayonet end of his rifle, shaking it a bit. "If we're going to be running around alien worlds, maybe a good long blade isn't such a bad idea."

"Just pack a machete, boss, it'll be less hassle."

The duo worked through the bowels of the alien facility, ignoring most of the branching corridors and rooms they encountered in passing as they zeroed in on the location the commander's intel download identified as the probable fire control system. Securing the safety of the ship was now the mission priority, followed by survival and extraction. Both of those goals were best served by reaching the fire control system, meeting up with the commander, and shutting down whatever ancient weapon they'd tripped while stumbling around in the depths of that abyssal hell of a moon.

"Is that light up ahead?" Pierce asked, his suit sensors starting to make out actual definition in the distance, something that hadn't happened since they'd moved out of the area of the flare he'd tossed. It was the first hint of light, other than their own suits and equipment, they'd seen since jumping.

"I think so," Ramirez admitted, "but look at the shadows."

Pierce did, and just barely kept his swearing down to reasonable levels as he realized that the shadows were *crawling* in seemingly random directions. That was something shadows didn't do, not with a steady light source, and that meant that those were *not* shadows.

"Oh, hell."

▶▶▶

▶ "Motion trackers are reporting movement all through the facility," Phillips said as he signaled a stop to allow everyone to regroup. "I think I know why we didn't run into any of those things on our way down."

"I didn't think we had anything that could scan that deep," Daiyu admitted a moment later, after catching her breath.

The suits had some basic power amplification, but her recent exertions were taking their toll on the woman who had spent most of her career overseeing lab coats in sealed facilities rather than mucking about in the field. She checked her own HUD, mirroring the major's, and saw what he was seeing. It didn't look good, from what she could tell at least.

"We don't," the major grunted, "but we've got a good link to Pierce and Ramirez now, as well as the portable scanners that were dropped in the first incursion down here. They're extending our reach considerably."

"How close are the things?" she asked.

"There are some hints of movement near us," Phillips admitted, "but they seem to be congregating on our wayward Marines' position."

Daiyu scowled. That was both good and bad, and then very bad depending on how one looked at it. Certainly, it was good that they had a clear shot to their target, but as they got closer, the resistance would grow. As for the very bad, well, there were two men down there who were low on everything but enemies.

"Major, I believe we'd best pick up our pace. Otherwise we'll be short two more men on this trip, and I rather think we've lost enough . . . don't you?"

"Damn right, Commander," Phillips nodded, flipping his hand slightly to signal the others. "We're *moving*, people. Keep it tight, keep it right, and don't give those snakes a chance, or they'll take a body part you may not want to part with. Move out!"

"Ooh rah!"

The team moved out on command, the Marines wedging mostly forward, but leaving enough men to cover the flanks and rear of the group as they proceeded into the depths of the facility. There was light there, in the corridors the Marines earlier had left through, but it was sporadic and left many shadows for things to hide in.

Phillips glowered inside his helmet, wondering what the hell it was with alien worlds. Every time humans ventured out, they seemed to find monsters looking to eat them, or everything, or, well . . . whatever. It was, frankly, a depressing statement on the state of the universe, in his mind.

I thought space was supposed to be full of intelligent species with high-tech spaceships and shit that we could fight. Instead I'm on a damned big game trophy hunt, and I don't even have the right tools for the job!

Honestly, who would think that the biggest threat to his Marines would be *animals*, of all damned things.

▶ ▶ ▶

▶ The pair of Marines looked at one another for a moment, their expressions lost in the darkness and the tint of their helmets, but the meaning and intent were clear enough.

"This is gonna suck," Pierce said, his tone entirely as certain as his words.

"Have a better idea?"

"We retreat and see if we can find a tropical island to retire on somewhere on this forsaken moon?"

Ramirez shot him a second look, shaking his head. "You ever heard of a tropical island with no sun?"

"Spent time on a few where we were shelled so often I didn't see sunlight for three days. That count?"

Ramirez sighed. "Probably not, but maybe it should."

The two fell into an easy silence as they contemplated the situation again, their eyes on the roiling shadows that moved seemingly of their own volition.

"So," Pierce spoke again casually, almost conversationally, "how many rounds you have left?"

Ramirez's eyes flicked to his HUD briefly, checking what he already knew. "Eighteen. You?"

"Twenty-nine."

Neither man bothered to mention that it had taken a minimum of three rounds, in their best encounter, to kill one of the snake beasts. They both just counted up the rest of their munitions and came to the same conclusion at once.

"We're screwed."

Ramirez supposed that he should probably play the cheerful lieutenant, try bolstering his man's attitude, but in all honesty he didn't think it would work on Pierce under the best of circumstances. Trying that act now might just get him fragged on general principles.

"Pull back and wait for reinforcements," he halfheartedly suggested.

"Sorry, LT, have you been checking the motion sensors we dropped?" Pierce asked, his voice *way* too light.

The chance of a clean withdrawal had come and gone with the activation of those sensors at their backs, showing them to be clearly surrounded.

Ramirez sighed. "Yeah, but I thought I should offer."

"If we're going to die, LT, I'd rather do it charging a mission objective than turning tail. Let's do this."

Ramirez laughed lightly. There wasn't really anything else he could do. Cursing wouldn't get him anything, and his pride wouldn't let him sob, so his chuckles trickled out of the unsealed helmet and echoed lightly off the walls surrounding them. He checked that his recorders were all on and dumping data back to the others. At least there would be a record of what was about to happen.

"Well, belly up to the bar, Marine, 'cause this is one happy hour we'll not soon forget," he said, seating his rifle to his shoulder as he took the lead position.

Pierce fell into the drag slot, covering the left side over Ramirez's shoulder while keeping an eye on the sensor signals for signs of attack from behind.

"Right on, LT. Let's rock."

▶▶▶

▶ Major Phillips watched the tactical display floating in front of his face as the two Marines started the battle they'd trapped themselves in. He would have torn a strip off them for so stupidly walking into a trap like that, but with only two of them, they didn't exactly have a lot of options. Probably they should have stayed outside rather than let themselves get pinned down in the corridors, but honestly the serpents moved too fast in the open sky.

It wasn't a fair fight in the enclosed corridors, not with his Marines being so low on ammo, but it was a lot closer than out in the open where visibility was measured in dozens of meters and the enemy could fly fast enough to cross that distance in a second.

"Godspeed, Marines," he said softly, not transmitting.

"Can we do anything for them?" Commander Daiyu asked, her voice coming over a private channel.

Phillips shook his head. "We don't have the corridors mapped, so we can't send a supply drone on ahead. All we can do is get there ourselves as fast as we can."

She nodded. "Then let us be on our way."

"Right you are, ma'am," he said over the group channel, waving his hand forward. "Step it up, Marines! Ooh rah!"

"Ooh rah!"

The roar of the Marines' unified call made the Navy personnel and the researchers with them jump, but Daiyu was already urging them on.

"Get moving," she said. "We have work to accomplish."

CHAPTER 23

▶ Captain Passer looked over the numbers, a dark light glittering in his eyes as he considered them. Chiefs Xiang and Doohan had pulled out the stops, best he could tell, getting him the projections as fast as they had.

Took them both working together, too, judging from this, Morgan noted with some amusement but more satisfaction.

He didn't care if they hated each other, but they had to put that aside in a crisis at the very least. In theory the transition drives were not in any way linked to the gravity drives, but in practice it was very bad form to have two top-rated engineering chiefs at each other's throats when they were assigned to the same boat.

"Have the numbers been analyzed, Mr. Kamir?" Morgan asked, looking up to where the astrophysics specialist was sitting at his post.

"Aye, Captain," Kamir answered confidently. "We estimate better than ninety percent chance of this working, sir."

"And the other almost ten percent?"

"Depends, sir," Kamir admitted with a slight flush. "Worst case?"

"Please."

"Gravitic inversion," Kamir answered candidly. "We blow our engines."

"That would be bad," Morgan said dryly.

"Very low probability, Captain," Kamir rushed to say. "Less than three percent."

Morgan nodded, having read the numbers. He really just wanted to know that they'd been checked by other eyes.

"Very well . . . Andrea, lay in the course, if you will."

"Aye, Captain," Lieutenant Mika said, her shoulders twitching as she tapped in the commands.

"Give me the ship-wide," Morgan asked.

"You're on ship-wide, sir," Lieutenant Commander Conway said from where he was strapping himself in.

Morgan nodded, not bothering yet to follow suit.

"All hands, this is the captain," he said. "We are about to attempt a breakout of the gravity field we're currently held by. These maneuvers may involve violent turbulence, so please ensure that everything is secured for possible acceleration. All hands are to report to their duty stations and stand by for orders."

Morgan signed off the channel, and then glanced over at Conway. "Signal general quarters."

"General quarters. Aye, sir."

The alarm sounded in the background as the bridge crew got down to work, focusing on what was to come and trusting the rest to those who knew their business.

"Course prepared, Captain," Andrea said from the helm.

"Alright, ease us out of orbit, Andrea," Morgan ordered, nodding to her back.

"Aye, Captain, retro thrust firing . . . we are dropping out of the sky, sir."

Morgan smiled thinly. "Just watch that sudden stop at the end."

"Aye aye, sir," she grinned. "Watching the sudden stop."

▶▶▶

▶ Orbiting a planet, or any significant source of gravity, was a lot like constantly throwing yourself at the ground and figuring out how to miss. Without enough speed, you were certain of only one thing: You weren't going to miss.

As the *Autolycus* fired its retro thrusters, it swiftly bled off orbital velocity, and the gravity of the moon took command of the ship and began to inexorably draw it down. The process started slowly, but in the airless void of the space over the moon, it accelerated quickly and there was no terminal velocity for the ship to reach. Ten meters per second became a hundred, and a hundred quickly turned into a thousand.

The *Autolycus* struck the gravity shear beneath the ship at over three hundred meters per second and accelerating, and the tidal force of the gravity variance caused the ship to creak and groan like an ancient sailing vessel in high seas.

"Any time you're ready," Morgan said tersely, listening to the sound of his ship creaking around him. Sounds that no spacecraft should *ever* make were echoing in his ears, and he very much wanted them to stop.

"Roger that, Skipper," Andrea said, tapping in a command. "Engineering, the captain is getting impatient up here."

They could all hear Doohan's snort over the comm. "Tell him that the laws of physics operate on their own schedule, Andy. He can sooner order the moon blue than change 'em."

Andrea flushed slightly. "We're on an open comm, Chief. You just told him yourself."

▶ ▶ ▶

▶ In engineering the chief cringed, a truly horrible grimace crossing his visage before he forced himself to move on.

"Right, then," he said. "As I was saying, Captain, we're just about ready now, sir."

Captain Passer's amused tone filtered through the comm quite well, much to the chief's chagrin. "Excellent, Chief. On your own time, then."

Doohan sighed, casually waving a hand to where his counterpart was clearly straining something in a very nearly futile attempt not to laugh his ass off. Knowing that Xiang wouldn't bother even *trying* not to laugh at him if the comm wasn't open, Doohan made a note to get revenge. Someday. In some way.

For now, however, they had work to do.

"Chief Xiang," he said sharply, "it's your ballgame."

Xiang got himself under a better semblance of control and nodded. "Yes, Chief Doohan. Initiating warping of space-time."

The hum that filled engineering, and indeed much of the ship, seemed to originate from everywhere and nowhere as the big space-time engines started sucking power from the *Auto*'s twin reactors. Enough power to run several cities, and not small ones either, coursed through the system and began to physically manhandle space and time itself, twisting the gravity shear the ship was flying through and slicing a channel right through it.

The *Auto* ceased its creaking and groaning as Andrea put the ship's nose down and used the thrusters to accelerate through the temporary channel, flying right at the face of the moon below. Fast quickly became breakneck speed, the gray face of the celestial satellite spinning as the *Auto* fought the contradictory pull of the gravity shears around it. Everyone with a view to the outside held their breath long enough that the moment registered on the ship's life-support computers.

Then they were through.

From the outside, it was hardly spectacular. There was nothing to see other than a ship flying through space—albeit it straight at a rather large moon and at a rather uncomfortably fast pace—but still only that. Inside, however, the instant the *Auto* exploded through the rift, there was a tangible change in the hum of the warp drive and a sudden feeling of lightness as microgravity returned to the starship, three hundred kilometers above the moon's surface.

And falling.

▶▶▶

▶ Andrea Mika tapped one single command, automatically loading the preset flight control program she'd already prepared, and prayed that she'd gotten the numbers right.

It was necessary to keep a human hand on the controls, because preset programs—even advanced AI systems—crashed at least twice as often as a live pilot who was actually present. Still, sometimes events that required adjusting in flight happened too fast for human reflexes to follow. Plunging toward the surface of the moon with just barely three seconds to pull the ship up and keep from slamming into the ground was one of those times.

The *Auto* kicked in full retro burn at almost the last possible moment of its descent, but Andrea had known that would be at best a time-buying effort. It was the gravity drive that she and the others were counting on, but it needed precious seconds to equalize and warp space for flight after having been focused on breaching the shear they'd just flown through.

The nose of the *Autolycus* came up, rockets firing madly from all points on the ship, as the gravity drive finally came into play. Space warped visibly about the ship for a moment as the drive strained against momentum, and the sleek lines of the *Auto* wavered as if seen through a heat haze. The ship drew more and more power from the reactors, leaving those who had a line of sight to the instruments with a falling sensation in their guts. Finally the bubble coalesced, and the *Auto* began to accelerate upward even as momentum continued to drag the crew down.

Hearts pounding, every soul on board with a view of the instruments watched as the *Auto* bottomed out within two kilometers of the surface, the gravity warp of her drives kicking up dust and debris that had long since settled there from the moon's travels through interstellar space.

Andrea took back manual control in an instant, bringing the *Auto* up to a safer altitude of about thirty kilometers and steadying the ship in flight as everyone else began to shake off the terror of the plunge and get back to work.

Captain Passer slumped a little in his seat, no mean trick in a microgravity environment, and let out a deep breath he'd barely realized he was holding.

"Nice job, Andrea," he said. "Good flying."

"Thank you, sir," she answered, taking a cloth from where it was tucked into the cushion of her seat and wiping away the cold sweat before it could ball up and float off her brow.

She was grinning for all that, however, knowing that she'd just done something that would likely wind up in the instruction books.

Probably with a heading that read "Things NOT to Do," but what the hell, she'd take it.

▶▶▶

▶ Morgan watched with half his attention as Andrea set the ship into a station-keeping orbit, albeit an extremely *low* one. On Earth they'd actually have to watch out for commuter flights at this altitude, but that didn't seem like much of a problem in their current circumstances. With the gravity drive, it made only a little difference how close they were to the surface. Mainly it was an energy sink to fly this low, but compared to being trapped in the gravity cage and *cooked*, he'd take what he could get.

"I want every scanner wired and running, maximum power," he ordered. "No sense hiding now, so let's be sure we can see what's coming our way."

"Aye, sir," Kamir said instantly as he bent to his task.

Morgan considered their position, and debated what he should do about it. The problem was that he just didn't have enough information about the weapon system they were dealing with. Were they inside its range? Or could it still target the *Auto* this close to the moon's surface?

Too much depended on things he had no data on, and that was enough to drive a man like Passer to drink.

"How many drones do we have left?"

"We lost three during the passage, Captain. The rest are with us."

Morgan nodded. "Alright. Deploy them around the ship. I want a perimeter. Let me know if we get even a hint of another gravity cage being set up."

"Aye, sir."

"In the meantime," he ordered, "get everyone back in contact while we're clear of the gravity interference. I want to know what the hell is going on down there."

"Aye aye, Skipper!"

▶ ▶ ▶

▶ The Copperhead wheeled around, circling the tower as Lieutenant Commander Grant worked the stick and throttle with expert motions to keep one eye on the plummeting *Autolycus*.

"Holy lord in heaven," her copilot mumbled. "Can they even *do* that?"

"Apparently they can," Grant answered as the glittering shape of the *Auto* leveled out at the last second, turning its death plunge into a sweeping flight that was bringing it closer to the tower. "I'm going to have to get Andrea to show me her coding for that move."

The man in the seat beside her shot Grant a look of unadulterated terror, knowing full well that his CO would be all too eager to adapt any crazy maneuvers over to the Copperhead. He was saved from trying to come up with a response, however, when their communications channels came fully back online with new telemetry feeds from the *Auto* streaming in.

"Dump our records into the *Auto*'s computer," Grant ordered, her eyes flicking down and seeing the same thing he was. "No way to know how long we'll have clear channels."

"Yes, ma'am."

The *Autolycus* was flying low, barely thirty kilometers up, but she could understand the reasoning. They'd busted clear of the gravity trap they were in, but it would take more than that to scare the skipper into abandoning the people he had on the surface. That made flying under the enemy radar the next likely maneuver to attempt.

Katie Grant just hoped the gamble paid off, because if the alien weapon could focus that low, then the ship might just get caught with nowhere to run to, since there was no way it could survive another swan dive like the last one.

Not without blowing a hole in the surface of this moon, at least.

"We've got orders coming in, Katie," Nicholas Reese, the copilot, said. "Captain wants us to RTB for fuel."

Grant grimaced, checking the reactor levels.

The Copperheads could actually fly for days without refueling, depending on how deeply they drank from their reactors. The issue usually wasn't fuel, in reality, but cooling. In space there was surprisingly little heat loss, since the most efficient mode of cooling was through heat transference and in a vacuum there was simply nothing to transfer the heat out with. That generally left radiating heat as the go-to method for a ship like the *Auto*, but Copperheads didn't have the kind of mass and surface area to make that work for them.

In order to maintain safe temperatures in their reactors, the most effective method was to use liquid coolant and eject the superheated fluid into space. That was, however, fairly mass-intensive, and was thus reserved for combat power draws.

They'd been mostly station-keeping so far, so *Copperhead One* still had near full levels of coolant and little need to refuel.

"Inform the *Auto* that we're still good to go," she said. "*Copperhead One* is mission capable."

Nick nodded, speaking softly into his mic.

"Skipper says get back in the barn," he told her a moment later, shrugging apologetically. "No one is coming up for a while yet. He wants flight crews refreshed in case we need to run a prolonged mission when they do."

Going unspoken was the fact that, if the *Auto* had to bug out, they'd be leaving fewer people behind if the Copperhead crews were on board. Grant didn't like it, but orders were orders, so she started working out the numbers for the return shot as she tiredly nodded and secured her own mic.

"Roger that, *Autolycus* control, *Copperhead One* RT . . ." Grant trailed off as some of her instruments started flashing where they really shouldn't have been flashing.

"*Copperhead One*, please say again. Did not copy your last."

"Stand by, *Autolycus* control," Grant said. "We have something happening here."

"Roger, *Copperhead One*, *Autolycus* control standing by."

"What is it?" Nick asked, now noticing the telltales flashing on his side as well.

"We've got something pegging off our antiradiation scanners like crazy, but I'm having issues locking it down. See if you can't localize the signal," Grant said, flipping a few switches as she banked the craft over to see if she could spot anything with the most reliable scanner she had on board, the eyeball Mark I.

"I don't know what's going on, Katie," Nick said, his head down as he worked furiously at the computer. "Threat board is lighting up, but I'm not seeing anything on it!"

"Remind me to get those instruments overhauled, 'cause I'm seeing something from here," she answered grimly, twisting the stick and dipping the Copperhead over to the other side. "Over your right shoulder, Nicky."

Nick looked right and down, his eyes widening as he spotted what she'd seen. Swarms of black craft were coming right out of the moon through a previously unopened rift. The only thing keeping Grant from fighting down an immediate panic was that the swarm didn't seem even mildly interested in her Copperhead. It was arrowing straight for the *Autolycus*, like it had a mission.

No doubt it does, she thought as she opened her comm mic again. "*Autolycus* control, *Copperhead One*."

"Go for control, Copperhead."

"Patch to *Autolycus* actual, clearance code Cerberus."

That left a brief pause on the other side, and she could almost imagine the moment of panic the comm specialist on the *Auto* was having. He came back a moment later, though, and his voice didn't *quite* crack when he spoke.

"Roger that, Copperhead. Patching to *Autolycus* actual, code Cerberus."

A brief scramble on the line was replaced in a couple of seconds by Captain Passer's voice coming through clear and even.

"What do you have, Commander?"

"Looks like a swarm of combat drones, if I'm guessing right," she said. "Coming up out of the moon just below the tower we've been monitoring. No count possible. They don't show on instruments, but they're coming your way and it looks like they have an axe to grind."

"Roger that. Thanks for the heads-up." Passer took a breath. "Belay the order to RTB until we determine how big a threat these are."

"Yes, sir. Good luck."

"Thank you. *Autolycus* out."

"Keep an eye on those things," she ordered, speaking to her co-pilot. "I want to know if they so much as twitch in our direction."

"Roger that," Nick said emphatically, not wanting any more to do with the black swarm than he absolutely had to have. "Damn, those bastards are fast . . ."

"No kidding," Grant grumbled, keeping an external camera on the swarm as it raced beneath them. "Why is it that every time we come out this far, we run into swarming monsters from the freaking abyss?"

Nick shrugged. "It makes sense in a grim sort of way, Katie. That's the direction technology is going in, even back home. If we hadn't outlawed armed drones by international treaty after India and China started selling them on the open market, we'd probably be buried in swarming robots ourselves."

"Oh, make me feel so much warmer and fuzzier, why don't you?" she muttered sarcastically.

"Anytime, Katie. I live to please. You know that."

Her response wasn't fit for the ears of children, adults, or any living species known to mankind.

▶▶▶

▶ "Get them on camera," Morgan ordered. "I want to see these things myself."

"Aye, Captain, but it's not easy. We can pick up a heightened radiation signature, but nothing specific. We're tracking based on optical motion scanners, but those are having issues with shadows at the moment. A few more seconds," Kamir said from where he was hunched over his system, working furiously.

Morgan didn't bother responding. It wouldn't make the man or the machine run any quicker, and he had other problems to deal with.

"Secure from best reflection armor," he ordered. "Black us out. They're tracking us somehow, but as long as they can't seem to turn that heliobeam on us, I want to make it as hard on them as possible."

"Aye, Captain, going black."

The lights inside the ship darkened noticeably as its armor changed frequencies, not so much because the illumination might "leak" out somehow, but because brighter lights did give off a more noticeable electromagnetic signature. It wasn't much, but every joule counted when you were dealing with scanners that could track a ship amid the stars themselves.

"Battle stations," he ordered next. "Arm point defense. Release all safeties."

"Aye aye, Skipper."

"Got the swarm on scanners, Skipper."

"Put them on screen, Lieutenant."

"Aye, sir," Kamir said, sending the signal to the wraparound screens.

The bridge crew leaned against their straps, as though that would offer them a better view, to see the image of the dark crafts skimming against the background of the moon's surface. The vessels flitted haphazardly, seemingly on collision courses with one another, but from the lack of debris Morgan assumed that they were under better control than it appeared as they charged forward toward the ship.

We must be under their defensive screen, he supposed as he watched the approach.

That didn't surprise him. A weapon like the heliobeam would work best at specific ranges. Probably extremely far out, light-years even in a vacuum, but there would have to be a minimum range as well, given the nature of the focusing technology involved.

I'm more surprised that it was able to target us as close as it did, Morgan decided as he considered the new form of attack.

"Have we determined the size of the . . . crafts?" he asked, uncertain what to call them.

They were likely drones, run by a central computer somewhere, he supposed, but that wasn't certain, and they really could be any number of things. The Drasin that had ravaged the Earth certainly qualified as living creatures, likely even sentient ones, not that anyone had ever managed to *talk* to one of them, so he wasn't going to make assumptions just yet.

"No, sir," Kamir said, "we have few references for size, and they're staying low against the surface, keeping us from getting anything concrete. Best guess right now is that each is between thirty and three hundred meters across."

"That's one hell of a wide range, Lieutenant," Morgan growled.

"Aye, Skipper, I know it. Working on bringing it down, but since they're absorbing active scanners damn near as well as our own black hole armor settings, we can't get any sort of hard lock. We've painted the moon itself, which is how we're getting enough data to make guesses, but without known points it's hard to determine just how high they're flying over the surface. We need more data, and we're not going to get it from here. Not in time, sir."

Morgan grimaced, knowing that the young officer was right.

"Fine," he said after a moment. "Put me on with *Copperhead One.*"

CHAPTER 24

▶ "Get down!"

Pierce hit the ground instantly, his brain barely registering his reasons for doing so even as he pushed back off the deck and rolled to his knees.

Vaguely, in the corner of his mind, he recognized Ramirez slamming bodily into a snake that was trying to flank him, digging the bayonet and twisting as the lieutenant screamed some inarticulate battle cry. It was all a little unreal, honestly. Pierce had long since given up on the idea that this was actually happening.

He surged up, leading with his own bayonet-tipped rifle as another of the snakes slid into his range.

Both of them had long since fired their last shot of ammo. Even their service pistols were strewn somewhere behind them, empty and discarded like the useless lumps they were. The rifles, tipped with ten-inch-long steel blades, remained.

Behind them, around them, the floors and walls were coated in a mixture of blood and whatever it was that the aliens counted as the same. His suit had been perforated a dozen times, slashed open and left to hang like some useless and bizarre fashion statement, but they'd actually made progress.

He wasn't sure what they were progressing to, exactly, but they were still moving, so they were still alive.

He threw his weight into the lunge, driving the snake to the ground before jerking his weapon back and stabbing it in again and again. Honestly, Pierce didn't know if any of the strikes were lethal, but pain did seem to affect the serpents. They pulled back from particularly nasty fights, clearly unused to the feeling, or at least unwilling to entertain it longer than they must.

Pierce supposed, in some idle section of his brain, that the little piece of information would mean something to someone, beyond the obvious. For now, however, it just meant that the two Marines would occasionally be rewarded with some time to catch their breath.

Now, with no serpent slashing at him or trying to coil around him, Pierce panted and looked over to check that Ramirez was still kicking beside him. The lieutenant was also somewhat the worse for wear, his own armor slashed open, and he'd managed to lose his helmet at some point. Pierce wondered what the unfiltered air smelled like, but a glance around him at the moment made him decide not to ask.

An abattoir, even an alien one, wasn't something he cared much to breathe in if he could avoid it.

"You okay?" he asked. Probably the singularly most stupid question of his career, but honestly what else could he ask?

Ramirez shot him a look that made it pretty clear that just about anything would be less stupid, but the lieutenant nodded anyway.

"I'm breathing. I'm good," Ramirez said, panting deeply. "Where are we?"

Pierce checked his HUD, which was miraculously still operating.

"Another hundred meters of this to the target room," he said.

Ramirez shook his head. "I don't think I've got another ten in me."

"You've made it this far, LT," Pierce chuckled, his laugh coming out as a dry rasp. He checked his water, but his suit was dry. *Hope the others have extra when they get here.*

Ramirez nodded, pulling off part of his armor from where it was hanging loose and obstructing his range of motion. "Yeah. Right. Just another hundred meters."

Left unspoken was the fact that once they got there, neither man knew what to expect. What they did know was that they would have to secure the target area against intrusion by a very great many pissed-off fifteen-meter-long snakes with wings and claws.

Frankly, Pierce was starting to reminisce fondly about fighting the Chinese and Block soldiers at the tail end of the war. Hell, he'd gone head to head with the Drasin when those alien bastards invaded, and they were looking pretty good at the moment as well.

A hiss of movement decided it for them, however, and both men pushed themselves upright and moved shoulder to shoulder as they leveled their weapons again.

As the snake head lunged out of the dark, both Marines screamed "Ooh rah!" and drove their bayonet blades into its face.

Pierce briefly entertained the idea that the creature seemed surprised by the reception, but then he was far too busy fighting to care.

▶ ▶ ▶

▶ "Another dead end," Major Phillips growled, glaring at the empty lab or office space or whatever it was sitting in front of them. "Someone map us an alternate route!"

"On it, Major."

"I've got two Marines fighting for their lives down there, a ship under attack above us, and we're running around like rats in a goddamn maze," he yelled, not honestly certain what part of that was pissing him off most.

"Anger will do none of them, or us, any good, Major. Control yourself," Commander Daiyu ordered in no uncertain tone as she finished mapping the current area into their cloud system and got ready to move again. "We will arrive when we arrive, not one moment sooner. Our only task right now is to ensure that we do not arrive any later than we can possibly avoid, and we are doing so."

Phillips had always intentionally avoided expressing, or even *feeling*, any given opinion about the commander or, indeed, any of the other former Block officers that were stationed on his ship. It was unprofessional, and it was unproductive, but by that point he was honestly beginning to despise the cold woman who was commanding this little farce.

Men were fighting for their lives below them, the ship was under threat above them, and she was more interested in recording the damned alien architecture.

Alright, even in his current state of mind he knew that wasn't true. He'd met officers like her before, people who just turned off their emotions and did the job. He didn't like any of *them* either.

Blasted cold fish left everyone around them feeling like they were expendable.

A fighting man needs to know that someone else cares if he lives or dies. That's the way of things. When the dying starts, a man doesn't fight for his flag, his country, or his honor. A man fights for his brothers and sisters in arms, for leaders who prove they give a damn, and for family back home. The last thing my men need is some ice queen directing them to die for a mission they couldn't give a fuck about.

Unfortunately, he had no say over that.

Not until she did something worth fragging her over, he supposed.

Phillips firmly put *that* thought out of his mind. He was being monumentally unfair to the woman at this point, and more importantly, there was time to worry about that when the opportunities presented themselves.

He had no doubt whatsoever that they would do just that, and soon.

"We have another track, Major," a private said, sliding a new path over to his map.

"Good man," Phillips said, accepting the route change. "Commander?"

"Lead on, Major," Commander Daiyu said calmly. "I will follow."

Phillips nodded curtly, laying out the formation as he got his men under way. They were backtracking twenty-odd meters to another branch of the facility. Hopefully this one would lead down to the next level where his two missing Marines were.

Their transponders were now strong on his IFF screens, but they'd been getting less and less telemetry from them as their armor and electronics were damaged in the fighting. Only the distributed nature of their systems kept him from assuming, to himself at least, that the two were likely KIA.

For now, they were still fighting. Ramirez was entirely out of comm, his helmet apparently destroyed along with chunks of his armor, but Pierce's armor was still filing reports and movement data. Without the map updates from Pierce, the odds would have been strongly against them being able to find a connecting path. Phillips would have been forced to take his squad down and around the facility to enter through the lower access, exposing them to attack from the skies.

That was something he was deeply glad he hadn't had to do.

Now you two better hang on. We're coming for you.

▶ ▶ ▶

▶ Ramirez grunted, nearly losing all the air from his lungs as he was slammed into the wall, barely keeping his unprotected head from bouncing off the unyielding metal surface. He slid to his knees, propping himself up with his rifle as he gasped to refill his lungs and looked wild-eyed around him.

They'd popped off flares as the fighting intensified, and gave up on trying stealth, so both he and Pierce were now using full suit lights. The field of battle, such as it was, was now cluttered with scraps from their armor and slick with blood and fluids from both Marines and snakes alike.

He realized, however, as he scrambled back to his feet, that something was missing from the scene.

"Pierce!"

"A little busy here, boss man!" the corporal snarled, stabbing his bayonet into the snake closest to him, eliciting a scream from it before it retreated again. "What?"

"How many kills you think you have?" Ramirez asked.

"What?" Pierce asked incredulously. "What are you, trophy collecting? I don't know, been too busy to count. Has to be a pile, though."

"Oh, yeah?" Ramirez jerked his head around. "Where's the bodies?"

"Well they're right around . . ." Pierce actually paused, stunned as he realized that there were no bodies anywhere in sight. The moment of distraction could have cost him, but Ramirez had expected it and threw himself in to fight off one of the serpents trying to take advantage.

"See what I mean?" Ramirez asked afterward, panting more than a little.

"What the hell, boss?"

"Haven't you noticed, Pierce? They're toying with us now," the lieutenant said tiredly. "I think once we started fighting back with blades, it became a game to them."

"Those sons of . . ." Pierce started swearing, fluently and color-fully, in multiple languages as he tightly gripped his rifle. It was one thing to be swarmed by alien beasts looking to eat him, but for them to play with their food was just flat-out insulting!

"Calm down, Pierce. At least this gives us a chance. We might be alive when the others get here."

"Yeah, but . . ." Pierce was still fighting with the injury to his personal pride. Sure, he wasn't normally a knife fighter, and he hadn't fought with bayonets since Parris Island, but by God he'd never been ignored in a fight, no matter what weapon was in his hand!

"Keep pushing to the target," Ramirez ordered grimly, "and don't interrupt the enemy when he's in the process of making a mistake."

Pierce set himself, nodding unconsciously. The snakes sure as hell were making one big mother of a mistake if they were underestimating a pair of fighting Marines in their midst.

Their last mistake, if I have anything to say about it.

With that thought firmly in mind, Pierce girded himself and slipped into position on Ramirez's left flank. They could see the muscled serpentine forms roiling around them, just at the edge of the shadows, occasionally caught in the beams of their suit lights. It looked like the darkness itself was alive, and all either man wanted was a full load out and an artillery firebase on call.

Instead, with nothing but empty rifles fixed with bayonets, the two Marines roared against the blackness and then charged.

▶▶▶

▶ The sonic boom of the rapid-fire burst echoed slowly away as the serpent slumped to the ground in the corridor ahead of the group. They barely paused to look, having gotten their fill of such things some time earlier. Marines, officers, and civilians alike picked their way through the mess and headed down the ramp that led to the deck below.

They were all in fully active combat mode. The major hadn't seen much advantage in stealth after reviewing the reports from earlier. That gave them a slightly better warning time than earlier encounters had benefited from, but it was still too close for comfort by far.

Phillips had ordered the lead and drag teams to slave their rifles to automatic fire, letting the computers have control over the fire systems. That meant that if anything crossed their barrels that didn't respond to an IFF challenge, the computer would put a burst in it. Generally it was a tactic that was frowned upon, since soldiers normally operated in areas populated by untagged civilians, but in this case, he figured it was almost a tailor-made solution.

"We're getting closer," the commander said as she stayed close to his left side, a step behind his stride.

Major Phillips grunted. "I hope so. This place has me turned around, and I can't even make heads or tails of the maps we're compiling."

"The internal structure is . . . complex," she said with a bit of a grimace. "And . . ."

When she trailed off, Phillips took note. He obviously didn't like Daiyu, but he didn't know her to be particularly the type to shy away from saying . . . well, anything, really.

"And what?" he asked finally, not taking his eyes off the darkness they were proceeding into.

"I'm not certain that the interior is actually . . . well, possible," she said finally.

"Pardon?"

"Major, we're in the center of a station that is actively warping space-time," she said, her tone lecturing. "Some of the internal dimensions as they show on our scanners don't match up with the ones we've mapped before."

"Are you actually saying this place is . . . what? Bigger on the inside than outside?"

"Possibly, but it's more likely at this point that the warping is affecting our instrumentation," she admitted. "Barring further information."

"Thank God."

The major could handle a lot. Give him a charging enemy, or a nice insurrection to deal with, and he'd be fine. But he wasn't sure he wanted to deal with wrapping his mind around a space that was larger inside than out. It seriously harshed his worldview.

"In either case," she continued, "it means that we can't trust our dead-reckoning systems to map the interior cleanly."

"Great," Phillips grumbled. "One more problem for the list."

"Sir, motion trackers are starting to trip out ahead of us."

The major suppressed the urge to groan and rub his face, since the helmet he wore would prevent it anyway and he'd rather not look like a total imbecile in front of his men. The hits, as was normal in his experience, just kept on coming.

"Alright, put your heads on a swivel and keep those guns on automatic," he ordered. "If it moves and isn't screaming our codes, turn it to paste."

"Yes, sir!"

▶▶▶

▶As best the two Marines could tell, they were in sight of the target location, though in the deep inky darkness of the moon's interior, the term "sight" was of rather flexible meaning.

"There's a door," Pierce announced, better able to see in the darkness since he still had his helmet with its night vision optics mostly intact.

"Push for it," Ramirez added, "and pray the room is solid enough for us to barricade the door and hold the threshold. Otherwise this is going to be one short occupation."

"Horatius at the bridge, LT, I can dig it."

Ramirez rolled his eyes, but didn't comment. He didn't have the breath to speak and run at the same time for the moment, and his subordinate's questionable enthusiasm and recollection of the classics were the least of his concerns.

They still had their rifles in hand, bayonets fixed, but the awkward spears were little more than a mild deterrent as best he could tell. The snakes seemed to respect the blades more, but at the same time it was very clear that the lengths of steel were little more than annoyances to the serpents.

The Marine lieutenant felt like he was being played with, a feeling he didn't like when it was coming from other men, and that he liked even less when it came from giant snakes that could eat him in two bites.

Fighting off a few more of the increasingly sneaky attacks, the two Marines made the door and managed to get the mechanism working with a minimal bit of fiddling. Ramirez sent up a brief thanks to the builders, who had clearly understood one of the fundamental lessons learned by every soldier who'd ever had to fight door to door. Doors were both the bane and the blessing of existence. When they worked the way you wanted, when you wanted, you could ask no more of life. Most of the time, however, the evil blasted things were clearly possessed by the devil and intent on nothing but murdering you and your compatriots by stubbornly refusing to open, or close, or whatever it was you needed them to do.

"Shut it! Shut it!"

"Working on it," Ramirez growled, trying to navigate the alien interface system in the dark while Pierce stood guard at the door with his better night vision. The wall lit up as Ramirez found the spot, and then he slammed his hand down hard on the holographic image, only mildly surprised to feel it resist his motion for a moment before he punched through and hit the wall.

The door ground to a close, and the two Marines slumped on either side of the portal, combat tension still running high in them both as they took a fleeting moment.

Finally Pierce looked around, his suit lights and NVDs both on full. "Whoa."

Limited only to his and Pierce's suit lights, Ramirez tried to spot what the corporal was seeing, but didn't.

"What is it?"

"See if you can find the lights for this place," Pierce said. "I'm not sure what the hell I'm looking at."

"Right."

The lieutenant reactivated the interface and started trying to decipher the symbols without the reference tables provided by Palin. Luckily, as the language expert had repeatedly said, the system was designed to be read at a glance. He found the obvious symbol for lights and hit that, turning around as clean white illumination flooded the room.

"Oh. Wow."

And what a room it was. It seemed to stretch on forever as they stood there on a large overlook platform, surrounded by a railing and what looked like interface stations at regular intervals.

"Hey, boss," Pierce spoke up softly.

"Yeah, Corporal?"

"Is it just me, or does this room look bigger than the whole damn facility we're standing in?"

"It's not just you."

"Well, that's good news and bad news," Pierce said sarcastically, "but at least I'm not due a trip to the head shrinker."

"After seeing this, Pierce," Ramirez said quietly in response as he walked to the edge of the platform and looked out and down, "I think we're both going to need time with the head shrinker."

"Well, crap."

Down, a few hundred or perhaps a few thousand meters, Pierce spotted a glowing, pulsing ball of light. He didn't know what the hell it was, but it looked impressive.

"Yeah," he said after a moment. "Yeah, I think we've found what we were looking for."

"You know what that is?"

"Not a clue, but I bet you it's what we're looking for," Ramirez said firmly. "Does this look like anything less than the control room for a sci-fi superweapon to you?"

"It's missing the evil overlord's throne, but other than that . . . ?" Pierce shrugged. "Sure, why not?"

"Well as long as we can keep those snake-things out . . ."

A long, slow rattling sound cut him off, and the Marines exchanged worried glances before sweeping their weapons up and readying themselves for a fight.

"Next time, boss? Just keep your mouth shut, okay?"

Ramirez had an impression of motion from above him, and only just started to get his weapon up when it felt like the whole damned moon fell on him and everything went black.

CHAPTER 25

▶ The Copperhead banked low to the surface of the moon, a maneuver not strictly needed in the vacuum of space, but Grant was dragging the ship's belly on the surface and wanted a look at the targets above her with her own two eyes.

They were black, generally unimpressive in shape, but since they were designed for use in an airless void, there was no need for anything special, she supposed. Unfortunately, the lack of requirements for aerodynamics and other design considerations made it rather difficult for her to determine if the objects were combat drones, missiles, or something else entirely.

"*Autolycus, Copperhead One,*" she said into her comm. "Are you receiving?"

"Roger, *Copperhead One, Autolycus* actual here. We are receiving all feeds, five by five," the captain's voice came back. "We're analyzing the feeds now. They look about twenty meters across the beam, thirty forward to aft. That fit what you're seeing?"

"Aye, sir, that sounds about right," Grant said, one hand lightly caressing the plastic shields covering her weapon controls. "Should I splash a few?"

"Negative. We'll handle that, *Copperhead One*. All point defense systems are online, but we're going to see what they're up to first. Pull out of the area. You're not going to want to get caught in the backlash."

"Roger that, Skipper," she said, kicking in retro thrust and bleeding speed to make the alien drones, missiles—whatever they were—lose her before she tipped the nose of the Copperhead up and stood the drop ship on end.

As they were rocketing back to altitude, Grant glanced over at Nick. "Creepy things."

He nodded. "Yeah. It's pretty clear that they were designed by someone who didn't even consider that they might see use in an atmosphere. We don't build 'em like that."

"Just as well," Grant said, kicking the Copperhead's twin reactors to full power, slamming both of them hard back in their bolsters. "Creepy-looking things."

▶▶▶

▶ "They're ten minutes out at current speed, Skipper," Lieutenant Commander Conway said, checking the readings from his station's side panel.

"Understood," Morgan said, looking over to the helm. "Helm, stand by to change course. Eighteen degrees starboard, full military power."

"Aye, Captain," Andrea answered instantly. "Eighteen starboard, full military power, at your command, sir."

"Engage."

The ship rumbled to life instantly, like a waking giant readying itself to take on the world. The nose of the *Auto* shifted over as her big reactors warped space and brought her about.

"Inbound bogeys are shifting course to intercept, Skipper," Conway said quietly.

Morgan nodded absently. "Helm, take us thirty-six to starboard."

"Aye aye, Skipper. Thirty-six degrees to starboard, turning now."

The horizon of the moon tilted in the screens as the *Auto* turned in the opposite direction.

"Bogeys have altered to intercept again," Conway said.

"Record for transmission," Morgan said, this time speaking to the computer.

"Recording."

"Unknown vessels, this is the Terran starship *Autolycus*. You are approaching on an intercept course. Break off, or we will be forced to consider your actions hostile and will react accordingly. I say again, break off your approach or we will open fire," Morgan said, tapping the screen by his right hand when he was done.

"Recording complete."

"Translate to Priminae, loop both versions. Transmit on all Terran and Priminae frequencies."

The computer went straight to work, translating the wording even as it started broadcasting the English version. Morgan let it run, shifting his attention to more pressing matters.

"Redesignate all bogeys to bandits."

"Aye aye, Skipper," Conway said, sweeping his fingers across his controls. "Redesignated."

The yellow warning icons on their boards were now an angry red, flashing a warning that anyone from Earth would recognize at a glance. Morgan waited a few heartbeats, willing them to turn away even though he honestly didn't expect anything of the sort.

Finally, for the record, he asked, "Have the bandits changed course?"

"No, sir," Conway answered instantly.

"Very well, Helm, put our nose into them. Tactical, light 'em up," Morgan ordered.

"Aye aye, Skipper."

▶▶▶

▶ The *Autolycus*, now no longer attempting to avoid contact with the inbound ships, turned her nose into the oncoming squadron as her primary laser array charged. As the ship came to bear on the oncoming vessels, the targeting beams flashed out to localize and analyze the materials that made up the hulls of the selected targets.

In seconds, that information ran through the *Auto*'s computers as her multispectral scanners analyzed the reflection off the bandits' hulls, and a laser frequency was selected by the computer. That information was sent to the Class IV laser array, and the primary beam weapon of the Terran ship jumped to full power.

A carefully tailored beam from a Terran Class IV laser could slice through pretty much any material it had ever been tested against. Only Terran adaptive armor and Priminae force shields had ever been proven effective defenses; the targets this time were too small to house the latter and clearly had no adaptive capacity to speak of.

When the lasers reached their targets, alien vessels were incinerated nearly instantly, material ablating away instead of burning in the absence of air and creating a trail of glowing material like embers from a bonfire as craft vanished from the heat.

Eight craft simply . . . "went away" under the glare of the *Auto*'s laser before the rest scattered, peeling away from the center with remarkable precision.

▶▶▶

▶ "That's an automated evasive pattern," Conway noted absently as he watched the scene.

Morgan nodded. "Yes, it is. Geometrically perfect, and very stupid. Point defense, splash them."

"Aye, sir, with pleasure."

Morgan noted the hint of genuine feral glee in his tactical officer's tone and decided to speak with her later. It wasn't that he disapproved of it, exactly, but since the invasion of Earth, there was a strong undercurrent of vengeance that did not bode well for the future in his opinion.

He'd seen it too many times in the past. People looking for payback did things that they would later come to either regret . . . or justify by any means they could. Either were bad outcomes.

For the moment, however, he focused on the plots that were echoing on his personal station as the ship's point defense HVM batteries opened up.

Replacing lasers and cannons for PD duty, the HVM banks used counter-mass technology to hide the one-ton mass of the kinetic projectiles from the laws of the universe, and then accelerated them to two-thirds of light speed before dumping the full mass back into the sidereal universe. The impact of one was enough to vaporize solid nickel-iron asteroids, meaning that very few constructed designs could stand up to them.

The alien craft were clearly not of a type that could withstand them and, as their predictable evasive patterns continued, the *Auto*'s point defense batteries continued to pick them off with ease that was honestly starting to make Morgan more than a little *uneasy*.

"Kamir, step up scanning," he ordered. "Watch our back."

"Aye, Skipper." The lieutenant nodded, shifting his focus.

Morgan didn't know if there would be trouble coming from another direction or not, but it was better to look first than to react after taking a hit.

The bandits were too close, and a fair size too small, to be effectively engaged by the *Auto*'s primary weapons now that they were evading, predictable as their maneuvers were, but the point defense systems had so far proven effective. His concern, however, was that while they had eliminated fully a third of the bandits in the first attack, that left a lot more to go, and they were splitting up and converging from wildly varying vectors.

So far, they had shown no sign of any offensive weapons.

To someone with less experience, that might seem like a sign that they weren't dangerous, but Morgan had seen too much in his time, and he had visions of suicide boats coming up alongside his sub while he had been in port in Japan.

That assumed they weren't just highly maneuverable missiles, of course, which he supposed was nearly the same thing.

"They're re-vectoring, Skipper, coming in from a hundred-and-twenty-degree arc. Point defense is becoming overtaxed. Projections say that at least twenty-five percent will make it through our defenses," Conway said tensely from beside him.

"Understood," Morgan said, considering his options.

He could charge the enemy formation, though that seemed counterintuitive. It would allow him to control the duration of the *Auto*'s exposure to the enemy forces, however, punching through their formation and coming out the other side while they were still working to bleed velocity.

Unfortunately, that strategy could be undone by a single hit if the enemy was using antimatter warheads. He didn't think they were. The burning material would have been *much* more energetic during the early engagement, but the point was that he didn't know *what* they were packing, and that made direct contact a foolish move.

"Signal the Copperheads," he decided, tapping his finger at a point on his plot. "I want them to do a little job for me."

▶▶▶

▶ "*Two, Three,*" Grant said as she flipped switches. "Form up on my position."

The other two Copperhead assault ships responded while she was checking off her instruments, confirming the orders.

"Weapons free, Nick, we're going in."

Beside her, Nicholas was flipping up banks of switch covers, bringing all the safeties off the Copperhead's weapons as Grant finished her preflight checklist. She barely spared him a glance, knowing that he'd get the job done, and instead looked over her shoulder to where the Marine jumpmaster was standing.

"Better strap in, Chief. This is going to get *fun*."

The Marine nodded, pushing himself into his bolster and strapping himself down. He knew enough to want some security around him when the lieutenant commander was grinning like that.

Grant looked back to the front, sharp eyes picking out the shadow of the targets as they moved against the black sky. It wasn't easy, as dark as they were, but when one eclipsed the stars beyond it, she could follow its progression with only a little difficulty. Between that, her own instruments, and the feed from the *Auto*, they had little fear of losing track of the targets.

"Bandits dead ahead," Nick said from beside her. "Locking them up."

The Copperhead wasn't remotely an air, or space, superiority fighter. It was designed to land troops in hostile environments, however, and that hostility was occasionally expected to come from above, so the designers had made certain that they included air-to-air and space-to-space capability in the design.

Grant powered up the Copperhead's tactical scanners, having to link with the *Auto* to get solid locks on the alien craft as they vectored in to the main ship. The Copperheads had little trouble haloing the craft, however, and the three assault landers spread out slightly as Grant initiated the final attack run.

"Hang tight, and if you have any prayers, now would be the time."

She grinned, more than a little maniacally, as she nudged the

276 • EVAN CURRIE

throttle up and sent *Copperhead One* rocketing in, with the other two ships following close behind.

Linked as they were with the *Autolycus* and one another, the combat network ensured that they each targeted the precise alien craft the captain wanted them to. When the link went hot and the final order came down, the Copperheads loosed their own version of hell.

▶▶▶

▶ "Vector for the port side of the enemy formation, ahead all flank," Morgan ordered, his eyes on the plot.

"Aye aye, Skipper. Ahead all flank."

The *Auto* was warping space hard enough that she'd need a full inspection when they got her home, but he didn't want to chance a prolonged close-range encounter with unknown craft if he could help it. The bow was aiming right into the HVM fire of the three closing Copperheads, letting them hammer the enemy formation right where the *Auto* was going to break through, while their own point defense batteries took out the flanks.

They're determined. I'll give them that much, Morgan noted, his eyes on the formation.

There was little enough doubt in his mind now that he was dealing with drones or missiles and not craft flown by living hands. Not that he'd really thought otherwise before, to be honest, but the reactions of the craft were too geometrically perfect to be anything else. It was clearly some sort of automated system, and likely not one intended for taking on serious military targets.

That didn't mean he was going to let them close with him if he could help it.

Blossoms of shrapnel and light erupted ahead of the *Auto* as the Copperheads did their job, hammering the drones with close support fire. The smaller HVMs packed a fraction of what the *Auto*'s own point defense systems did, but they were enough to do the job just the same.

"All hands, brace for impact!" Morgan called as the *Auto* entered the engagement envelope of the alien craft, in the most dangerous part of the maneuver.

If anything slipped up there, there would be consequences.

Collision alarms rang out on all decks as the *Autolycus* accelerated through the enemy formation, shuddering as her HVM banks fired on near continuous autofire. As they swatted the enemy craft from the sky port and starboard, at first the maneuver looked perfect by the numbers, but as the *Auto* entered a specific range the pattern of the attacking craft abruptly changed.

Morgan recognized it instantly as a terminal guidance maneuver and swore, but there was no time to make changes.

"Hit them with everything we have!"

The point blank weapon emplacements of the *Autolycus* opened up in response to the command, hammering into the missiles angling directly in to slam into the ship.

"Some of them are going to break through, Captain!" Andrea called.

"Warn damage control teams," Morgan ordered. "Lock down the compartments. Command or damage control access only."

"Aye aye, Skipper!" Conway answered instantly. "Ship is on lockdown!"

Emergency doors sealed the bridge off. All through the ship, similar doors slammed shut to seal compartments off from one another in order to prevent explosive decompression from running rampant from one side of the *Auto* to the other in the event of a worst-case scenario.

"One's breaking through! Get it! Get it!"

Andrea was shouting orders over her comm as she tried to coordinate the close-in response, but it was too late. She didn't even have time to announce the coming strike, not that anyone missed her yelling as the strike rammed home. The bridge crew winced as one when the alien craft slammed into the *Auto*, expecting to feel the results of an explosion shake the deck below their feet.

Instead, off in the distance, a deep, reverberating sound like a giant gong echoed through the insulated decks.

Morgan and Conway looked at one another, confusion clear on both their faces.

"Clang?" Morgan asked, incredulous. "What the . . ."

It was Conway, a former officer on a destroyer in the war, who paled and cut the captain off as he yelled into his comm.

"Marines to deck seven, section P thirteen! I say again, Marines to deck seven, section P thirteen! Stand by to repel boarders!"

Morgan, initially shocked by his officer yelling in his face, paled as the implications struck him. He didn't know if Conway was right, but it was better to be sure.

"Are we losing atmosphere from that section?"

"Not certain, Captain. If we are, it's a slow leak."

"Damn it." Morgan didn't know if he should be happy about that or not, but it felt like one of those good news/bad news things to him.

"We're through, sir! The Copperheads are coming about to pace us, Skipper," Kamir announced. "We could slow to pick them up . . ."

"Negative! Maintain flank acceleration. Do *not* let those things catch us now that we're ahead of them," Morgan ordered, knowing that the enemy craft would have to dump a ton of delta-V before they could try to overtake the *Auto* again. In that time, the ship could be thousands of kilometers away, even limited as they were this close to the surface of the moon.

"Yes, sir."

"Get me the Marines on deck seven. I want to know what they find down there."

▶▶▶

▶ Lieutenant James Orlon held up a fist as his team reached the sealed door of section P thirteen, waving his tech sergeant forward to the keypad controls. While the sergeant went to work on the door locks, Orlon looked back at the rest of the team.

"Scanners say that we still have air on the other side of this hatch, but if any of you lose suit integrity at any time, I want your ass *out of there*," he ordered firmly. "Saving your sorry ass could get someone else killed. Got me?"

"We got you, sir!"

"Alright. Sergeant, are we ready?"

"Ready to go, sir." The sergeant nodded, his hand over the controls as he waited for the order.

"Pop the hatch."

There was a small hiss of pressure equalizing as the hatch snapped open, totally ignored by the Marines. They hit the door full force and slammed it into the wall as they burst through it.

They skidded to a halt, bumping into one another when, instead of an enemy they could engage, they found that half the compartment was covered in a black slime that seemed to be moving.

"What the hell . . ."

Orlon pushed his way through, swearing at his men until they got some semblance of discipline back, and stared at the scene himself for a moment. He had to will his mouth to stay shut rather than spout off the same crap his men were whispering; instead he took a breath and calmly activated the officers' comm channel.

"Captain, you'd better have a look at what I'm seeing here."

CHAPTER 26

▶ "Holy . . ."

The word was a hushed whisper, even over the network comms, but it summed up the feelings of the Marines and the naval officers as they walked through the halls of the alien structure, eyeing the mess around them.

There were scraps of armor and marine combat kit scattered randomly along the floor as they made their way forward. Some type of ichor practically coated the floor and walls. In places it was mixed with blood, which didn't give Phillips much hope for recovering his Marines. The fact that they'd been injured enough for him to see their blood in the mess he was walking through was not a good sign.

Commander Daiyu was more interested in the ichor, he noted, as he saw her talking quietly with a pair of the researchers they'd brought along in hopes of actually figuring the damned place out fast enough to help the *Autolycus*. Phillips waited until they were done before getting the commander on a direct comm.

"Anything useful?"

"Immediately? Likely not," she said, "though I'm not certain. The alien blood has a genetic structure we can test with our kit."

"So?"

"So, Major, that means it's quite close to Earth genetics. Our equipment is designed to analyze DNA structures, blood types, and so forth," she said, looking around. "Like the Priminae, these things are more closely related to us than seems . . . likely."

"Right. I'd heard about the Prim," he said, shrugging. "Humans in space. Go figure."

"Not human, Major. The Priminae are not genetically human," she corrected. "Similarly, I doubt these things are actually related to any species on Earth."

Phillips frowned, absently waving his Marines forward as the group got under way again. "I'd heard that the Priminae were genetically human."

"No. Your Doctor Palin, who did the initial test, was in a hurry. He did not have time to do a full gene scan," she explained. "What he did was scan for known human genes, the one percent that separates us from animals, and the Priminae matched every single one."

"Right?" he asked leadingly.

"When they did a full gene scan, they found that in the other ninety-nine percent, the Priminae don't match humans at all," she said. "The so-called junk DNA was all different. Priminae clearly evolved on a world other than Earth. They had reptilian DNA, fish DNA, and so forth, just like we do . . . but it was *different* than ours. They evolved on a world similar to ours, but different."

"That"—Major Phillips shook his head—"seems unlikely."

"It seems *impossible*," she hissed, "however it happened. The question now is, just how did it happen? It is almost enough to make one believe in God."

The major glanced in her direction, his tone neutral as he spoke. "You have a problem with God?"

"No, Major, but I do not believe in anything without evidence, and so far in my life I've not yet seen any to support the existence of a supreme being," she said simply, "though this comes closest."

"Really? How?"

"In order for two species to evolve nearly identically on completely different worlds, Major, would require intervention . . . or the stupidest degree of chance I've ever considered." She shrugged. "Still, it doesn't require *divine* intervention. That doesn't rule it out, of course, but it doesn't stand as evidence of divinity, I'm afraid."

"If you say so, Commander."

The major wasn't about to start a religious debate in a combat zone, especially since he wasn't entirely certain of his own beliefs. He'd seen a lot of things, and some of them had felt truly beyond anything normal to him, but he also understood what she meant about evidence.

"So these things have DNA, then?"

Daiyu nodded. "Yes, which may mean that they were seeded from the same source as Earth."

"Does that information have any value to us right now?"

"Possibly," she said, considering. "It means we should have an idea of their limitations, vulnerabilities . . ."

"That's useful. Anything specific?"

"Well, poisons should have similar effects as they do on us, as would most weapons," she answered. "I would suggest treating them like large wild animals on Earth."

That was more than he had been expecting, though much of it he had already figured out for himself. The problem was, aside from a couple of anti-materiel weapons, they didn't have anything particularly good for hunting.

"If they're based on the same construct as us, how do you explain the flying snake motif?" he asked, his tone wry, mostly just to continue the conversation as they made their way through the blood-and-gore-covered corridors.

Whatever else, those two Marines put up one hell of a fight down here, he thought as he examined a scrap of suit armor coated with whatever it was that passed for blood in those snake-things.

He supposed, from what the commander was saying, that it *was* blood, but that felt wrong somehow. Viscerally wrong.

"Earth had some quite large flying animals in the past, and even modern snakes have been known to glide long distances," Commander Daiyu answered him, clearly more focused on the conversation than what they were walking through. "So it's not entirely out of line that something like this might evolve here, in a lighter gravity world . . ."

"A world with no sunlight," he said. "How does that work?"

"I suspect that there is as much sunlight here as the designers choose to allow," Daiyu responded, "and while it may be dark now, it's still quite warm, so there is energy to be had. Life is adaptable, Major. If there is energy to be had, life will find it and take it for itself."

Amen. That was one thing he wasn't going to disagree with her on. He knew how hardy even the nominally fragile human species was, able to adapt and not only survive but *thrive* in some of the harshest climates imaginable. There was no reason to think that these things were any less hardy.

The group paused while the recon team picked up a discarded service pistol, its slide still locked back on the empty chamber.

"Lieutenant Ramirez's service piece, sir. Fired dry," the Marine holding it said.

The major wished the soldier had something more to say, but the scene spoke well enough for itself.

Two Marines ran out of ammo and went on fighting—not at all unusual from his experience, he was proud to say. The nature of the foe made the story worth telling, but finding the two Marines alive would make it worth singing about.

"Keep moving," he ordered. "They're up ahead, and so is our objective. If they fell trying to secure, we finish the job for them. If they didn't, then we owe those two drinks when this is over. Semper fi."

The Marines all echoed his final two words as the group got under way again. The quiet of the corridors was now made all the darker and more disturbing by the evidence of battle lying around them.

"Where are they?" one of the Marines hissed, edging his rifle around as he looked for targets in the darkness.

"If we lose their transponders . . ." began another.

"Not them." The Marine cut his fellow off. "The snakes. They attacked Pierce and Ramirez relentlessly by what we've got here, but I don't see no bodies. Did they drag off their dead?"

"It could be," a Navy man spoke up from the center of the group. "I haven't seen any sign of flora, and without it food could be scarce. They may eat their dead."

"Oh, that's just friggin' lovely," the Marine bitched.

"Shove a sock in it, Marine," the gunny growled. "None of us are exactly happy to be here, but we have a job to do. Get me?"

"Got you, Gunny."

Gunny Scaol spared a moment to glare over the group, making sure no one had an idea to start up that particular conversation again.

The major switched to the officers' channel, turning to the commander. "Please keep your scientists from creeping out my Marines. They get hard to control when they're jumpy."

Daiyu just nodded tiredly, turning to the Navy team and clearly speaking to them on another channel that he wasn't currently monitoring.

Phillips checked the map, for what it was worth. The computer had tried to render the surrounding area, but the display was so horribly out of alignment that it looked like something out of an early three-dimensional video game, from when the designers didn't actually bother with measuring the appropriate dimensions and just let the magic of virtual space solve all their problems.

They were perhaps a hundred meters from the last transponder location for the missing Marines, which was also roughly the reported location of the command and control interface for the heliobeam. According to the map, they were also about to walk through a solid wall and over a chasm that, as best he could tell, didn't even exist . . . so he was taking the hundred-meter measurement with a grain of salt or two.

Still, the map and the evidence of carnage pointed to one thing, and that was that they were more or less on the right track.

Good enough.

▶▶▶

▶ There was movement in the darkness.

His head was groggy. He could barely think, but the rattling hiss to his left only served to emphasize the sensation that he felt run down his spine. Ramirez couldn't see a damn thing; the lights where they were, if there were any, were all off, and his suit was pretty much dead. He could almost imagine that he could see something moving in the darkness, however, and he actually *could* feel something moving.

"Pierce," he hissed softly. "Pierce, are you here?"

With no answer forthcoming, Ramirez shifted slightly as he tried to work out what kind of shape he was in.

Arms and legs are intact, at least, he noted, supposing that was good news. The bad news, however, was that he wasn't getting much range of motion from either. *Am I tied up?*

Without light, and unable to move, he couldn't figure out a way to determine the answer to that question, so he decided to act as though he was.

I think I can reach my knife.

The flip blade clipped to his armor straps wasn't much of a weapon, but it had a six-inch steel edge that could cut most things a man needed cutting. He pulled it clear and flipped it open with his right thumb before stabbing it out toward whatever was holding him in place.

There was a tearing sound, followed by a louder one as he pulled the blade up, and then Ramirez was falling.

"Oof!"

He hit the ground like a lump, and the knife skittered away in the darkness, much to his personal shame and annoyance.

Great, my last weapon, such as it was, and I lose it because I couldn't get my damn fist shut.

A rattling hiss to his right caused him to twist around, his eyes seeking out motion in the darkness.

Ramirez knew he wasn't alone. He could feel the presence of others . . . the movement in the darkness around him. He couldn't see, and could only sporadically hear, but he could *feel* it.

Of course, that left him with the question of just what he was supposed to *do* about it.

No weapons, no armor, no visibility. Oh, yeah, I'm boned.

Stumbling around would do him no good, that much was clear, so Ramirez sat down and started to pick apart what little there was left of his armor. The combat firmsuit used a distributed network of power cells and components, partly for situations like this so that the suit would be harder to take completely offline. He found one of the cells and pulled it from the armor, and then hunted around for anything he could jury-rig to emit light.

Doing that by touch in the dark was far from a simple task, but it was mostly an exercise in patience more than something truly difficult. Marines were responsible for general maintenance of their own suits, just as they were for their own weapons. He couldn't strip a suit down to components and reassemble it in three minutes blindfolded, but he knew his way around the system just the same.

The hardest part was finding a light emitter, but he figured he didn't need much. He pulled some of the suit's trouble indicator lights and wired them into the power cell in just a couple of minutes, lighting up the quantum dots and casting a red hue around him.

He picked the dots from the warning indicators because they'd light up red, hopefully keeping his night vision intact, for all the good it would do in total darkness. Looking around him, however, at the area bathed in red light, Ramirez started regretting the choice.

Oh shit, oh shit, oh shit.

The walls around him, if he could call them that, were *moving*.

Ramirez cast about, looking for his rifle initially. But it wasn't anywhere he could see, so he instead started hunting for the small flip blade. On his hands and knees, moving as slowly and quietly as he could, he searched the floor futilely until he heard a sound that wasn't the depressingly creepy rattling hiss that he was rapidly becoming used to.

"Pierce?" he whispered, recognizing the moan for what it was. "Where are you, man?"

His only clue was a glint of a reflection beneath one of the slowly twisting masses of muscle that seemed to make up the walls of the room they were in. He gingerly started to pull at the immensely muscled form to uncover the corporal.

"Lieutenant?"

"I'm here, Corporal. You alright?"

Pierce groaned again. "Suit says I'm good. I think the suit is lying."

Ramirez snorted, but didn't bother answering. "Okay, help me get you free."

"Free from what?" Pierce looked down, and then suddenly tensed up and started to kick and struggle. "Holy hell!"

"Calm down!" Ramirez ordered in a whisper as the rattling hiss grew louder and more agitated. "They're not attacking us right now, and I'd like to keep it that way, seeing as how we're not exactly armed."

Pierce stiffened at the order, but at least he wasn't fighting anymore. He took a moment to review his situation as best he could without panicking, and found that not panicking quickly got harder and harder the more he reviewed his situation. He was wrapped in the thick coil of muscle that belonged to one of the snakes, one larger than any he could remember seeing, and all around him the room seemed to shiver with a faint rhythmic rattling.

"Hey," Ramirez said, clapping his hands in front of Pierce's face, "focus on me. Me. Not this shit."

Pierce nodded shakily. "Yes, sir."

"Okay, push out while I pull," Ramirez ordered, putting his arms around the huge moving tube of pure muscle, planting his foot right in the middle of the roiling mass, and pulling.

They both grunted with the exertion, but slowly the serpentine body lifted from Pierce, and the corporal was able to slip loose and drop to the ground beside Ramirez. With some relief, Ramirez let the snake go and stepped back from the wall.

Pierce was panting as he looked around, starting to hyperventilate. "Oh shit man, oh shit man, we're dead. Game o—"

Ramirez backhanded him across the helmet. "Snap out of it, jackass. We're not dead yet, and I'm not going to let you make it happen any faster than it has to."

Pierce swallowed visibly—no mean feat in a mostly intact firmsuit—but nodded.

"Yes, sir."

"You packing anything?"

"Have an eight-inch fixed blade in my boot, but that won't do crap against these things by itself."

Ramirez nodded, knowing he was right. Just then, however, he needed to keep the Marine busy, or the man would start to think too much about the situation, and that was not a good thing.

"We may need it anyway. Alright, start scouting this place. We need a way out."

Pierce nodded. "Yes, sir."

▶▶▶

▶ "Secure the room. I want field scanners assembled, look for any sign of my missing Marines," Phillips ordered, standing in the center of the large platform that overlooked what logically shouldn't even exist. "Commander, what the hell am I looking at?"

Commander Daiyu shook her head, standing at the rails and looking out over the abyss and down at the pulsing ball of light that seemed so impossibly far away.

"A tesseract, possibly?" she offered, not sounding convinced.

"I'm going to need a bit more than that, Commander."

"I don't know, Major. We may be looking at an internal space larger than the area that contains it," she said, "or we may be experiencing an extremely sharp gravity gradient."

The two officers were standing at the epicenter of furious activity as their respective commands set about doing the jobs they had made their way down this far to do, but suddenly it all felt like a sideshow to both of them.

"I don't know much about the science, Commander, but I've done the basic reading," Phillips said slowly, "and shouldn't there be some major issues with a gradient that sharp?"

"Indeed." She nodded. "We should have spaghettified already."

The major winced.

That was one of those words associated with gravity technology that just sent chills down his spine. It sounded innocent enough, almost comical really, but it described a gravity field so intense that the tidal force would pull so much harder on one part of the body that you were literally run through the universe's equivalent of a pasta maker.

However, since he felt fine and wasn't in the process of having every bone in his body split over and over again, he firmly put the image out of his head.

"So let's assume it's not a gradient that sharp," he said. "That leaves a tesseract, yes?"

"Maybe," she answered, but shook her head. "But I'll assume that something simpler is happening here, however. I think that the gravity fields have affected our scanners and mappers far more than we realized, and we're at the bottom of the facility instead of the center as we predicted."

The major tilted his head, considering that, then nodded.

"Sounds good."

Any solution that didn't require him twisting his gray matter into knots to understand was a solution he could stand behind, as long as it didn't turn out to be catastrophically wrong.

"Let's get to work, then."

"Yes," Daiyu said, tearing herself away from the view, "let's."

She walked back to what they'd earlier identified as a control vector, similar to the ones they'd located in the other facility above.

"Have you translated the script?" Daiyu asked, loath though she was to interrupt the irritating language expert.

Doctor Palin looked up, seemingly surprised that there were other people in the area. Daiyu honestly wouldn't be shocked if he had forgotten that he was part of an expedition.

"Yes, yes, it was easy," he said simply, waving absently at her. "It's on your cloud directory. Now, if you'll let me get back to my real work . . ."

Of course, he was also clearly a genius with languages.

She accessed the cloud folder and found the new matrix there, waiting to be loaded into her translation applications. She did so without delay, and then turned her focus to the control system.

As was normal, and reasonable, it was clearly designed to be deciphered. Easy-to-comprehend symbols made up the most obvious controls that lit into existence as she stepped into the interface field. Power, light, and various other common registers were easy enough to make out. In fact, she probably could have worked those out herself with little enough trouble, they were so clearly marked.

There is definitely security here, but it seems more focused on . . . She scowled, uncertain what she was seeing.

The system was clearly checking something, but whatever it was, she seemed to pass the test as the interface blossomed into existence around her. The tactile holographic system presented her with a wide range of options, most of which were quite different from the interface she'd used topside.

Daiyu set herself to finding the controls for the heliobeam or, failing that, determining any way to clear the *Autolycus* to freely leave the moon's orbit without becoming trapped by gravity gradients.

While she was working on that, and the rest of her team was spread out trying to decipher the rest of the technology, language, and varia of their surroundings, the Marines were considerably more focused. They were assembling a field network node, a transceiver system intended to boost network connections even under enemy jammers, in hopes of getting a lock on their two missing comrades.

It was a job of a few minutes. Most of that time was spent unpacking the components before the node was brought online. The powerful transceiver could slice through stone, metal, and even enemy jamming through its use of spread-spectrum technology, so when it came online, their own systems instantly recognized the difference, and the local networks cleared up in a blink.

Initially, however, there was little sign of the two missing Marines.

"Damn," Phillips grumbled, one foot planted on the railing that edged the platform they were on. He was staring out over the abyss, but inside his helmet he had the system running a wide-angle, full-spectrum scan for his missing men. "Where the hell are you two?"

▶▶▶

▶ "We're in a damn snake pit, Lieutenant. I mean, right in the freaking middle of one," Pierce said as he finished his survey of the area. "I can't find the walls, just more snakes."

"At least you still have your armor and helmet," Ramirez growled. "You do *not* want to know what it smells like out here, so stop your bitching."

The corporal was, probably wisely, silent in response to that.

"We need to find a way out of here," Ramirez continued. "Before these things decide it's time to let us in on what they brought us here for."

"What do you think they did bring us here for?"

Ramirez shrugged. "Midnight snack?"

Pierce shuddered, visibly through his armor, no less. "Not funny, boss."

"Who's joking?"

A rattling hiss, louder than they had heard earlier, cut off their back-and-forth. Both men twisted toward the sound and, in the red light cast by their makeshift lamp, the wall seemed to open as a flood of black, writhing snakes the size of pythons spilled down onto the floor and began to spread out like the most terrifying oil spill imaginable.

"Oh," Ramirez said dully.

"'Oh'? 'Oh'? What the hell do you mean, 'Oh'?" Pierce was again clearly hyperventilating.

"We're not a midnight snack," Ramirez said.

"Not a . . . that's good, right? So what are we?" Pierce asked, taking slower breaths as his armor systems redlined and basically ordered him to calm the hell down.

"Baby food."

▶▶▶

▶ "Got one!"

The major pivoted on his heel, marching instantly toward the scanner and the techs surrounding it. Technically he didn't have to, but he preferred to look men in the eyes, or as close as he could manage, when talking to them.

"Where?"

"Straight down, sir."

Phillips checked the scans, and then looked down at the floor for a moment before cursing and marching back to the rails so he could lean over. The system had finished its calculations by that point, and he could see Corporal Pierce's transponder tag showing up on his HUD as being about eighty meters below, somewhere behind an outcropping.

"I need volunteers for a retrieval squad," he said. "Straight drop with chutes, pack heavy."

CHAPTER 27

▶ "I need information, and I need it *now*," Morgan growled as he looked at the black substance the Marines were seeing in section P thirteen.

"We don't have any, sir," one of the ship's exobiologists said over the comms. "Whatever it is, it doesn't register as biological. It's not in my bailiwick, Captain."

"Well whose is it in?"

The man was flustered, but at the moment Morgan couldn't bring himself to care. His ship had been attacked, potentially invaded, and no one could tell him by what.

"Sir, all I know is what it isn't. It's not biological, it doesn't seem to be mechanical or electrical. It reads as elementally neutral according to everything we've got here. Sir, by everything I have, it's just some black oily residue. It's not even flammable."

Morgan shook his head. To his mind, that was all very interesting, but it was also far too good to be true.

"So you're telling me that whatever that warhead splattered all over the interior of my ship, it's not *dangerous*?"

The exobiologist started backpedaling. "Um . . . no, uh, sir. I'm just saying . . ."

"Listen, I know it's not your specialty. I don't *care*," Morgan said. "Call who you need, and find out whose specialty it is. But I want to know *what in the hell* that stuff is doing on my ship!"

The man nodded wildly. "Yes, sir!"

The comm link went black, leaving Morgan to sigh and slump in his restraints.

"You were a little harsh on the white coat, sir," Conway offered softly from beside him.

Morgan nodded. "I know. Maybe I'll even apologize. Eventually. Not today, though, and not while we're in the middle of a crisis."

"Yes, sir."

"Get him some help down there, though," Morgan ordered. "He's not wrong about it not being in his bailiwick. Send him, I don't know, chemical engineers?"

"How about a weapons specialist, sir?" Conway suggested. "Specifically, someone with experience in theoretical weapons tech?"

"Who do we have?" Morgan asked, thinking about the crew roster.

He knew all of their primary specialties, but he didn't know of any that quite fit the bill.

"Doohan used to design weapons for the Fed, during the war. He got into transition engineering as part of the team that designed the t-cannons," Conway answered.

Morgan whistled softly, appreciatively.

Transition cannons, or t-cannons, were pretty much the epitome of theoretical weapons technology. Using the technology that allowed the *Autolycus* to hop between the stars with near infinite speed, a t-cannon could transition a nuclear warhead and send it instantly across several light-minutes to a place where it would re-form and detonate. Faster-than-light delivery of warheads had changed the entire field of battle in the Drasin war, and it was still considered the ultimate trump card.

"Send him," Morgan said, "but for God's sake, give him some security. He's our chief transition engineer."

"Aye aye, Skipper."

▶▶▶

▶ Chief Doohan had to push his way through the crowd of Marines and naval personnel standing around outside the affected compartment. He was in an environmental suit, with full combat HUD. Not as bulky as a firmsuit or a hardsuit, but enough to give him some protection while working around hazardous materials. He just hoped that the alien stuff he was coming to check on was aware of that as well.

"Make way, damn it. Man has a job to do here."

He nodded his thanks to the Marine who'd taken control, carving out a pathway to the dogged hatch. Doohan glanced at it briefly, and then back to the Marine.

"Hatch stays sealed unless in use, sir. You go through, we lock you in."

Doohan nodded, understanding. "Do what you have to do, Marine."

The Marine undogged the hatch, pushing it open. Doohan slipped through and heard it swing shut and lock behind him as he looked over the scene. The interior of the compartment looked rather like an oil spill, to his mind, but he'd been told that the material didn't read as flammable . . . or even particularly chemically active.

"Anything new?" he asked as he dropped his equipment case, not bothering to look at the few people standing around working. The one who was doing the least at the moment would answer him, or he could wait.

"Not a thing, Chief," a Navy lieutenant said, walking over and also wearing an environmental suit. "The slime just sits there."

"I doubt that, Lieutenant," Doohan said, pulling out a multi-tool. He powered it up and checked the general readings of the area. "Huh. Electrical readings are down from normal for this compartment. Do we have any shorts reported?"

"Not that I know of . . ."

They didn't. Doohan had logged into the ship's network while he was speaking, ignoring the answer the officer gave. The lieutenant was speaking largely out of habit, but also to make himself feel like he was contributing.

Electrical activity was indeed low for the compartment, but not radically so. Doohan noted it, and then moved on. There wasn't much he could determine from the passive scans, unfortunately, which meant he was going to have to take some chances.

The trick if you were about to cut corners was to cut them as intelligently as possible; otherwise what you were working on might blow up in your face, literally in some cases.

A low-powered active scan gave him more information on the substance, enough to know that while it might be chemically neutral, it wasn't electrically neutral in the slightest. There was a hell of a lot of activity going on down there, at or below the level of the electrons.

"We may be looking at a quantum material," he said. "It seems to be gathering energy from the surroundings."

"Trying to drain the ship's power?"

"No, not specifically at least, though it's likely leached a few kilowatts from us by now," Doohan admitted. "That's not its avenue of attack."

"So it is a weapon, then?"

"Son," Doohan laughed, "it was delivered by a missile that slammed into us after we made every attempt to communicate and avoid impact. Of course it's a weapon."

Even if it wasn't a weapon, he wouldn't dare start thinking that *yet* anyway.

"So what is it?"

"Well, I don't know yet, but if we're lucky it's just a quantum explosive, not much worse than antimatter."

"Lucky?" The lieutenant croaked the word out.

Doohan chuckled, going about his work. "I've seen some projections for quantum explosives . . . scary stuff."

Whatever it was, however, he was pretty sure it wasn't a quantum explosive. He was familiar with the theoretical designs for such things, and this didn't match. There was something about the building electrical charge that bothered him more than he thought it should.

Doohan scooped up a bit of the slime out of the main puddle of goop, coating the leads of his scanner, and checked the readings carefully. There was a growing energy reading from the material, nothing he could get a good scan on directly but the halo effect was easy enough to see.

It's definitely charging to something, but what?

He sighed, checking the time, and made a snap decision as he stepped back from the goop and then sent an electrical charge through the leads of his scanner into the sample.

This is the dumbest thing I've ever done, but at least it's all being recorded for posterity, he thought as he watched the sample, grinning.

"Watch this," he said.

"Watch what?" the lieutenant asked, walking over, clearly not getting the joke.

The sample writhed under the power being applied, and then suddenly doubled in mass as the leads of his scanner *vanished*. Doohan killed the power instantly, then ripped the remains of the leads out of the scanner and threw them across the room.

"What the hell was that!?"

Doohan ignored the officer, already on the comm straight to the captain.

"Skipper? We have a problem."

▶▶▶

▶ The *Auto* was hurtling along in what was perhaps the lowest orbit on record. Barely thirty kilometers over the surface of the moon, not daring to slow down since the remaining missiles were still in close pursuit, though thankfully not gaining.

They'd left the LZ behind some time ago, but were probably only minutes from flying over it again and regaining temporary contact with the Copperheads and hopefully the landing team. For now, however, Captain Passer's main concern was the substance that had coated the interior of one of the ship's compartments.

"It's a quantum machine," Doohan said, "similar to nanotechnology, though much simpler in function. With an application of power, it can break down quantum bonds directly, and then use the energy from that to convert available mass into more of itself. Unlike nanotechnology, which never really worked the way it was projected to, this material is actually capable of . . . well, for lack of a better term, alchemy. It can alter the properties of matter directly at the quantum level. I've never seen or heard of anything like it, Skipper."

"What's it doing on my ship?" Morgan asked tersely.

Doohan grimaced. "Charging, sir."

"And when it's charged?"

"We become an orbiting blob of black goop, Skipper."

Morgan was glad for the straps holding him into his seat, because otherwise he likely would have done something rather un-officer-like.

"Get it off my ship, Chief," he ordered softly instead.

"That's a problem, Skipper," Doohan admitted. "I don't think we can get it all, and if we leave *any* of it . . . well, we may as well have not even tried in the first place."

"I am not losing my command to a *slime mold*, Chief. Find a way."

The chief nodded reluctantly. "Aye aye, Skipper."

The comm went black, leaving Morgan to close his eyes and restrain himself from doing anything blatantly obvious like rubbing his face. It was bad enough that he had little doubt his officers could tell he looked like someone had just sucker punched him in the gut.

"We could abandon to the moon," Conway offered softly. "There's breathable atmosphere and . . ."

"Last option, Lieutenant Commander, not even on the table yet," Morgan hissed.

"Yes, sir."

There has to be another option, Morgan thought grimly. *I'm not losing my first space command like this.*

He hoped that he wasn't being stupidly stubborn, but he just couldn't give in to the idea that he'd lost. He was still breathing, his ship was still flying. The game just wasn't over yet.

Morgan unsnapped his restraints, pushing free of the bolster.

"Captain?" Conway looked over, confused.

"You have the bridge, Commander."

"Aye, Skipper, I have the bridge."

"Just keep us ahead of those damn things," Morgan said. "I want to check this personally."

▶ ▶ ▶

▶ "Captain on deck!"

"As you were," Morgan said as he drifted through the rather crowded compartment.

He didn't have any problem getting through, though, as people pressed themselves hard against the sides to give him room.

"Any word from inside?" he asked the Marine at the door.

"Not since I let the chief in."

"Alright, pop it."

"Sir?"

"I said pop the door, Marine," Morgan ordered. "I want to see this personally."

"Sir, I'll have to dog it behind you, regs . . ."

"Whatever." Morgan waved the Marine off. "Do what you got to do, I'll signal when I'm done."

"Yes, sir."

The Marine, clearly reluctant, popped the hatch and let his captain walk into the room filled with the unknown, likely hostile, substance. Morgan pitied the man slightly, but not enough to not pull himself into the room and let the door swing shut behind him.

Chief Doohan was the first to realize just who had entered the area, and he was *not* happy.

"Skipper, with all due respect, are you out of your goddamned mind? What the hell are you doing here?"

"Wanted to see it for myself," Morgan said, amused that the officers were clearly edging away from the noncom who was chewing out the old man in front of everyone.

Not many people could get away with doing that on a Navy ship. In fact, just about no one could short of a two-star. Under certain specific and admittedly extreme situations, however, a chief was among the few with the guts and experience to toe the line his captain had etched invisibly in the dirt between them.

"There's nothing here you couldn't have seen from the bridge, sir."

"No, but I think better when I've seen a problem with my own eyes," Morgan answered absently as he looked over the mess. "Besides, if this crap goes off, is the bridge going to be spared?"

Doohan winced, but didn't answer. There was nothing he could say at that point that would win him the argument, not that he'd been likely to win a war of words with the skipper anyway.

"Talk to me. What about blowing the section?" Morgan asked.

"Heat from the explosives is just as likely to metastasize the goop, sir." Doohan shook his head. "If we have time, I'd cut the entire compartment free with laser torches, but that would take days."

"Great. So what are our options?"

Doohan winced. "Abandon ship, sir?"

"As I said before, I am *not* losing my ship to a slime mold, Chief. Give me another option."

"Captain, I don't think we *have* any other options."

Morgan slumped, seeming to fall into himself slightly due to microgravity.

"Chief, are you sure?" he asked softly.

"Captain, I'm as sure as I can be."

Morgan nodded slowly, not wanting to believe it. Really not wanting to believe it, but there was a line he refused to cross as captain. When your best people told you something, you either had to take them at their word, or assume you knew better. The latter was *not* an option in this case.

"Alright, I'll start preparations," he said quietly. "How long do we have?"

"Still projecting that, Captain, but the larger the pool of substance, the more power it has to absorb to activate," Doohan replied, equally quietly. "I think that it deployed incorrectly, sir."

"Oh?"

"Yes, sir, I suspect that it was intended to spatter more, on the exterior hull. With smaller patches, absorbing power becomes less intensive, and they can activate quicker and become self-sustaining on a quantum level. I think our armor is softer than what it was designed to penetrate. It punched through and spilled the whole patch right here."

Morgan snorted. "Saved by inferior armor? You're kidding, right?"

"It happens. A high-velocity round can punch through weak armor and right through the target without dumping much energy into it, giving you nothing but a clean hole. Better armor can slow the round down enough that it sprawls inside the body, dumping all its energy and tearing the target to shreds. We got lucky."

"This kind of luck we can do without," Morgan said. "Keep working as long as you can."

"Aye aye, sir."

Morgan turned away, moving hand over hand to the door, which opened on his approach. The Marine on the other side looked a lot happier to be letting the captain out than he had been letting him in.

If only you knew, son.

▶▶▶

▶ The muster stations alarm was sounding through the ship, cutting through the tension people were feeling and then cranking it right up to an eleven.

The order to muster stations could mean a lot of things, but damn few of them were any good, so as the crew dutifully went about their orders, the rumors started.

However close those rumors came to the truth, and however tense the crew was, none of them matched up to the dark depression settling in on their captain, though he tried faithfully to keep it from any who saw him.

CHAPTER 28

▶ "Ow! Damn it!" Ramirez started swearing, yanking the snake off his leg and tossing it away. "Son of a . . . that *hurt*!"

"You got bit. What did you expect?"

The lieutenant glared at the corporal, who was still relatively snug in his armor as the roiling mass of serpents spilled around where the men had pushed themselves into the farthest corner possible.

"You think those things are poisonous?" Pierce asked, eyeing Ramirez with worry.

"I don't know," Ramirez admitted, shrugging. "Doesn't matter, does it? We're not getting out of here without a miracle."

"Yeah, I . . ." Pierce paused, blinking as his HUD lit up, and then he slowly grinned. "LT, you are a freaking good-luck charm."

"Huh?"

Pierce put his comm on an open channel, broadcasting what he was hearing.

"Corporal Pierce, this is Lieutenant Hyde. Are you alright?"

"Hell no, I'm not alright!" Pierce snarled. "Me and Ramirez are about to become snake chow in here!"

"The lieutenant is with you? Excellent. Duck and cover, we're going to blow our way in."

"Watch your ass. The walls are covered in snakes," Pierce advised.

"Negative, corporal. The walls *are* snakes. We see them. Get ready for an adventure."

"Oh shit!" Pierce tackled Ramirez to push him away from the wall, covering him with his own body.

He didn't have to explain. Ramirez knew what was coming as they toppled into the writhing pile of snakes. He clapped his hands over his ears and blew out all the air in his lungs just as the thunderclap from hell rolled over them.

They rolled over, both men getting bit but largely ignoring the smaller snakes as they blearily looked to the newly smoking hole in the wall across from them. Out past the now bleeding and twitching serpents, three Marines were hanging down from what looked like a rock outcropping, rifles aimed in their direction.

"Begging the lieutenant's pardon," Pierce said as he picked Ramirez up by the back of his undersuit, "but it's time for hauling *ass*."

They ran, mostly stumbling in all honesty, toward the hole in the wall as an ungodly rattle erupted behind them. Neither man wanted to look over his shoulder as they vaulted the twitching meat and landed outside the prison they were escaping, yet both risked the glance.

"Oh, *hell no*! Momma's pissed that we are *not* hanging around." Pierce swore, turning his back on the great snake head coming at them. He shoved Ramirez ahead of him, and then continued to spin as he bodily *threw* the lieutenant out and over the edge of the abyss right at the Marines. "Gunny! Catch!"

Ramirez screamed openly and loudly as he flailed across the intervening space, slamming nearly headlong into the armored figure of the gunny as she closed her grip on his right arm. He was pale and shaking, but actually more in control of his faculties than he honestly would have expected.

"Thanks, Gunny," he croaked out, twisting a bit to get a view of what was behind him.

"Don't," she said, firing her rifle with her off hand as Pierce, too, leapt out over the abyss. "You don't want to see it."

Pierce slammed into Lieutenant Hyde, holding on for dear life as Hyde, too, fired as best he could, now swaying from the impact.

"Up! Up! Up!" Hyde ordered. "Climb the hell out of here!"

The rockets on the Marines' chutes flared, yanking them back and away as the massive head of a snake ten times the size of anything they'd seen already lunged out at them, just missing. It screamed at them, and then slowly began to unwind from its hidey-hole and curl its way up the rock after them.

▶▶▶

▶ "Everyone, get ready. We've got trouble coming our way!" Major Phillips ordered, rallying the rest of his Marines.

He wished that he had more than the comparative handful left, but they'd not landed a full division, unfortunately. The rescue of the two missing Marines had clearly pissed off the snakes below them, which was problematic.

He supposed that maybe they should have waited, given Commander Daiyu more time, but that was in the past now, and they had the present to deal with.

"Cover the commander and the rest. We *need* to get those systems under our control!"

He did his best not to sound like it, but Phillips was worried. They weren't exactly loaded for bear at the moment, certainly not well enough equipped to stand off any serious assault. On the other hand, for once they had some real-world visibility. The area they were in had actual ambient light, and that meant that a lot of the disadvantages from earlier were mitigated.

The only question now is, will they stop coming before we run out of ammo?

The three Marines he'd sent below were coming back up at a full burn, along with the pair of wayward sons they'd picked up. On their heels, they were likely bringing all the serpents of hell.

There was a time when they'd sing songs about this, Phillips thought as he triple-checked his rifle and settled into position near the rail. *Too bad the Corps doesn't issue us a bard right along with the rifles and armor.*

"Commander," he said aloud, "you might want to hurry up just a little."

Commander Daiyu glanced out at him from where she stood amid the holographic interface. "I am working as quickly as I am able, Major. Hold them back."

Phillips didn't have a response. Honestly, he didn't know what the hell she thought he was going to do, so he just focused on the task at hand.

The commander, in turn, refocused on her own.

The heliobeam controls were inextricably tied into the controls for nearly everything else, which made some sense, she supposed, as they were all linked through the same primary effect. The gravity controls were the center of the entire facility, its entire reason for being, in fact, which made her the best person available to negotiate the protocols built into the system.

The problem was, in part, that the builders were so far beyond her knowledge that she may as well be some Neanderthal on the plains in comparison. Only the fact that they clearly intended the system to be used and understood made it even possible for her to do what she was doing.

Daiyu drew up an image of the moon/planet system that apparently constituted the heliobeam itself. In miniature, any astronomer would recognize the design of the system as a very basic refracting telescope, using the planet as the primary lens and the moon as the focal lens, bringing the light and energy to a pinpoint deep inside the structure.

She couldn't tell if the moon was entirely constructed, or if the builders had somehow grabbed a real moon or planetoid and used it as a construction base. Whatever the answer was, the outer shell was just that, a shell that extended hundreds of kilometers above the surface and, if she was reading it correctly, served to focus the gravity manipulation correctly.

By any measure, it was a stunning construction.

Why they chose to infest it with dragons was a problem she was still stumped on.

The roar of rifle fire pulled her attention away briefly, but Daiyu forced herself to keep working. Whatever the others were up to, she couldn't help them in any other way than by saving the ship they needed to return home on.

These controls modify the warping of space, she noted, lightly touching the system and watching the focus of the space-time warp alter.

She had limited manual control over the system from where she was standing, but what she needed was access to the automated systems. Daiyu located and entered into the defensive section of the interface, and was rewarded with a glaring red image of the *Autolycus* orbiting the planet.

There you are, she thought as she lightly tapped the ship and brought it up closer. *Now how do I clear the threat board?*

She was thinking slowly and deliberately before touching *anything.* One mistake at this point might just cause the system to tear the *Autolycus* in two, though she doubted it. If it could do that, it probably would have already, instead of trapping the ship and heating it up with the heliobeam. Still, she didn't dare cut corners here and now.

She found a row of commands lighting up as she examined the profile of the *Auto*, and a brief examination gave her some hope. The system was complex, certainly, but it was simpler by far than she had any right to expect.

This looks like specifications for the ship . . . displacement, perhaps? Power rating is nearly Priminae standard results. I'm surprised it can even detect that the Autolycus *has a reactor system.*

Certainly before the war it had been very clear that the alien groups they'd located largely considered Terran ships to be harmless due to their extremely low power curves. That was a lesson that burned those aliens badly before they got their heads on straight.

Commands. Designation . . . hostile. Daiyu opened the "hostile" section and found a history of the ship's actions, noting that it had initially been judged as merely "unknown" and hadn't earned hostile status until the captain escaped the gravity cage.

Interesting. The heliobeam couldn't have been intended to damage the ship, then, could it?

She wasn't sure, but she supposed that it could have been some sort of scanner. Against a ship that was lightly armored and had no energy shielding, such as the *Autolycus*, it was just possible that the alien scanning beam registered as a weapon.

For all that it didn't matter now. She had to work with what was, not with what could have been.

Come on, where are you? The Autolycus *is not hostile, damn it. There has to be a way to redesignate it here.*

As she was mentally running down the system, a new section opened up and Daiyu blinked.

She was looking at a profile of the *Autolycus* and it was asking her a question, but the translation wasn't clear.

"Doctor!"

Palin looked up absently from a short distance away, completely oblivious to the rifle fire around him. "Yes? What is it? I'm working on the local language, if you don't mind."

"Doctor, what does this say?" she demanded, jabbing her finger in the direction of the image of the *Autolycus*.

"Humm," Palin hummed absently, leaning in and through the projected interface, snickering a little. "Oh, that tickles . . ."

"Doctor . . ."

"Hmm? Oh, right . . . well, let's see, it says, Subject Hostile, Yes or No?" Palin said, reaching out absently and punching the "No" section.

Daiyu almost drew her service pistol and shot him.

She likely would have, if she hadn't been so caught up in the image of the *Autolycus* changing from red to a pasty off-white. The system seemed to shift, colors fading, and everything that had been screaming at her since she activated the interface was now mostly quiet.

"Is . . . is that it?" she asked, feeling a little let down.

"Is what it?" Palin asked, curiously manipulating the interface. "Oh, this is interesting. Oh, yes . . ."

"Doctor, is the ship out of danger?" she asked.

"Well, it's no longer being targeted by the station," he answered. "However, it's still a starship, so I would say . . . no?"

Honestly, she was surprised that no one else had shot him by this point.

"Doctor, is the ship cleared by the local facility?"

"Yes."

"Thank you," she grumbled, stepping out of the interface, heading for the Marines and Major Phillips. "Major, I think we're done!"

She didn't notice the doctor step into the interface and continue playing around behind her.

"About damn time!" Phillips stepped back from the abyss, turning to her direction. "We've retrieved my Marines, our ammo reserves are down by over half. I was about to haul you out of there by the scruff if you'd taken much more time. Marines! Fall back to the door!"

Daiyu ignored the major's comment about hauling her anywhere. It didn't matter any longer. She instead drew her service pistol and fired three rounds into a snake that had popped over the rail, issuing her own orders to her crew. "It is time to leave. Please follow the directions of the Marines. They will ensure your safety."

The Marines were pulling back, shielding one of their own, who was running around in his skivvies. Daiyu briefly wondered how they were going to get him into a lander, but decided to worry more about that when it was an actual problem of the present.

Instead she focused on gathering her team, pulling them away from whatever fascinating little puzzles they'd located. There were a *lot* of fascinating little puzzles on the large control deck, and all pointed in more or less the same direction.

That was when she realized that she was short one annoying doctor of advanced linguistic studies.

Her descent into the filthiest corners of the Chinese language would have bought her either a reprimand or a commendation from her superiors in the Block, depending on when they'd heard it.

"Palin, what in the *hells* are you doing?" she growled, stomping in his direction. "We are leaving this place!"

"One moment," he said, holding up a finger without turning to even look at her.

Commander Daiyu slowly and deliberately holstered her pistol, glowering at the back of the doctor's neck.

"There are no more moments," she said. "It is time to go."

"Almost done," he told her, still working at the interface.

"Doctor . . ."

"Got it!"

She didn't quite have time to ask him what he had "got" when a hissing sound startled her into jumping and drawing her weapon again. She wasn't the only one. Several Marines turned and locked their rifles on a pedestal that had risen out of the floor. On it was a glowing dodecahedron, looking like some ethereal jewel.

Doctor Palin hopped out of the interface, deftly grabbing the object as he headed for the door with the rest. "Well? Come on, time to go and all that, right?"

"I am going to shoot him. I know it, I just know it," Daiyu gritted out as she stalked after him, the Marines closing ranks behind her as they covered the Navy officers and researchers retreating to the door.

"Not if I get to him first," Phillips growled. "What the hell is that thing he grabbed?"

"No idea, but we can ask later," she said. "We have more pressing matters at hand."

"Agreed," Major Phillips said. "I think we pissed off a whole nest of those damn dragons. It's going to be one *hot* extraction."

"Oh, excellent. It's been so boring up until now."

▶▶▶

▶As soon as the rifle fire died down, the dragons spilled over the rails like an angry wave right out of someone's darkest nightmares. The rattling hiss of the dozens of them, not to mention the larger momma dragon, echoed after the group as they retreated down the corridors as quickly as the Marines could push the researchers along.

"Point, watch yourselves. Don't get distracted. We know these things have ways into the corridors," Phillips advised, noting that many of the Marines at the point position were consistently looking back to see if the group was closely pursued. "Drag team will handle pursuit."

Herding cats had nothing on herding Marines, but the major thanked all the gods, real or imagined, that he wasn't trying to herd researchers. The commander was looking like she was seriously considering fragging the language doc but, while he wouldn't blame her, it wouldn't look good on either of their records, so he hoped she would hold back.

"I've got comms back, sir!"

Phillips blinked, checking his own combat network, and realized what Lieutenant Hyde was talking about. They were receiving telemetry data from the *Auto* and the orbiting Copperheads.

"What's going on?" he asked, more rhetorically than anything. "I'm showing better signal strength than we should have on the surface."

"Oh, that?" the annoying doctor looked up. "I just had the station put our frequencies on a repeater."

Major Phillips stared at the man for a long moment, stifling the first words that came to his mind.

The man isn't a Marine, for obvious reasons. Don't treat him like one. Ever.

"Thank you, Doctor," he said aloud, only his tone giving away his annoyance. "However, in the future could you please let us know when you do something that affects the whole group?"

"Hmmm? Oh, certainly. Certainly."

Phillips desperately wanted to keep this fool from coming on an away mission ever again, but he *had* actually done something really useful. Phillips couldn't figure out why he was so frustrated.

Damn it, I've never met anyone that does this to me.

"Keep moving," he ordered finally. "We need to get the hell out of here."

▶▶▶

▶ Being chased by a horde of angry dragons had a way of motivating a group of people to a degree Phillips had rarely seen in his career. It had taken several hours to make their way down through the corridors. It took less than thirty minutes to fight their way back up.

Alright, it helped to know which direction they had to go at each junction, but it was still pretty impressive.

"Get the chutes on, everyone who doesn't have one," he ordered as they reached the stash point. "I want to be out of here and on our way topside ASAP. Hyde, can you take Ramirez?"

"I'll get him strapped in, sir," the lieutenant promised, grabbing a harness from a compartment on his chute and tossing it to the unarmored Ramirez.

"Time to go!" Phillips yelled back to the two Marines guarding the entryway. "Get that door shut and hope it holds!"

One of the Marines triggered the shut mechanism and the two broke and ran, sprinting for the launch point as the first of the Marines and researchers lifted off, their chute rockets flaring. The major covered his team as the rest got strapped in and took off, standing alone as the last man on the field for a few seconds before he tripped his own chute and was yanked up into the sky.

The door burst open, a roiling mass of angry serpents spilling out onto the field. He held his fire, hoping they wouldn't see him, but it was a forlorn hope as one looked up and launched itself into the air, followed shortly by the rest.

Phillips opened fire, using short bursts to try to thin the herd, but for all the good it seemed to be doing, he may as well have been tossing spitballs.

"Incoming!"

It was going to be an air battle, all the way up.

CHAPTER 29

▶ "Holy hell, what's going on?" Grant blinked as half her instrument panel came to life. Suddenly she was back in full contact with both the ship and the teams under the surface. "*Copperhead Two, One* here."

"Go for *Two*."

"Did your network just come back?"

"Roger, *One*. We're running one hundred percent online as of . . . thirty seconds ago?"

"Thank you, *Two*," Grant said, tapping a couple of commands.

The Marines' transponders were showing them a *long* way below her, moving fast. They were all showing hot, with shots fired. That wasn't good, but at least she could see them again.

"*Autolycus* control, *Copperhead One* here."

"Go for control, *One*."

"Are you reading a full network capacity? Our systems are going one hundred percent."

"Roger, *One*."

"What's going on?"

"We don't know, *One*. We're a little busy here at the moment. Captain has ordered muster stations. Something bad is happening. Will advise when we have time. Control out."

Grant looked over at Nick, who looked back at her, and then the two looked over their shoulder to where the jumpmaster was sitting.

"Don't look at me," the Marine said. "I don't know what the hell is going on either."

"Doesn't sound good," Nick said, shaking his head. "Man, that's our ride home."

"Can't worry about that right now," Grant said firmly. "We've got Marines on the ground in a running firefight. We need to be ready to pick them up when they get topside."

"Roger that," Nick said, starting a checklist. "Prep for emergency dustoff?"

"Got in one, Nick. Let's make sure we're ready when they need us."

▶▶▶

▶ "Start getting nonessential personnel to the escape pods," Morgan ordered quietly as he settled back into the command station.

Conway looked at him, eyes wide. "Excuse me, sir?"

"Do it," Morgan said again, taking a deep breath. "Doohan doesn't think he can clear the section, and when it goes . . . the ship goes with it."

Conway closed his eyes, swearing under his breath. Morgan ignored it. When you got news like that, you were allowed an epithet or two.

"Aye, sir. I'll start moving them as quietly as I can," Conway said. "News is going to spread fast, though."

"Let it, just don't start a panic. Move the civilian researchers first. That'll keep them from tripping us up later."

"Yes, sir."

While Conway was working on that, Morgan continued to work.

His job wouldn't end with the *Autolycus*, though it would certainly be the end of his career.

"Captain," Andrea said, catching his attention. "The enemy drone ships have backed off."

"What?" Morgan blinked. "That doesn't make sense. Are they mirroring our course? Hoping to catch us on the flip side?"

"No, sir. They're withdrawing and returning to the tower."

"What the hell?"

"There's more, sir. We've got full tactical network communication back up. In fact, it's cleaner than it should be. Full contact with the ground team."

"Okay, someone did something, and I don't think it was us. Get me Commander Daiyu."

"Aye, sir, patching to your comm."

"Commander . . ." Morgan tried to sound calm.

"Captain," Daiyu returned, sounding rather the opposite. "We're a little busy here."

"Do you know why our comms are back?"

"Mission accomplished, Captain. The ship can now leave orbit," Daiyu answered. "The comms are the result of Doctor Palin playing around at the end. We're on our way back up."

"You may want to reconsider that, Commander. We were attacked. It could be serious."

"You don't know?"

"The weapon hasn't . . . detonated, but it is building to full deployment," Morgan answered hesitantly. "Commander, get yourselves to a secure place and establish a perimeter. We may be sending people down to you."

"This place is hostile, Captain. We've rather annoyed the locals," she answered, rifle fire in the background making her point for her.

"Still better than what we're facing, Commander. I'm sorry. I know this isn't what you want to hear."

"Very well. We'll establish a base in the observation labs," Daiyu said. "Good luck."

"You as well."

The comm ended, and Morgan considered the conversation for a moment before he keyed open a comm to Chief Doohan.

"Chief, is the goop still charging?"

"Yes, sir, why?"

"No reason, Chief." Morgan winced. He'd hoped that maybe the weapon would have been turned off, much like the missiles had been recalled. *No such luck.*

"Captain, we've an idea down here . . . but it's a little insane," Doohan said, sounding like someone was pulling his teeth.

Morgan blinked. "Insane how?"

"Well, Captain, we could blow the compartment with an antimatter charge."

There was literally nothing Morgan could think to say to that. Insane didn't cover it. Insane didn't *begin* to cover it.

"Chief, are you *high* on something?" Morgan demanded, hissing his next words. "That's not insane, it's suicide!"

"I think we can control it, sir."

"Chief, damn it, you don't 'control' an antimatter explosion. It just vaporizes *everything*," Morgan said. "You can't shape something like that."

"No, you're right, we can't . . . but an antimatter explosion won't charge this goop either. It'll annihilate it."

"And everything else!"

"Not if we draw the right amount of antihydrogen from the reactor, Captain."

Morgan looked over to where Conway was staring back at him, near stark terror on the younger man's face. He didn't blame him. There were some things you just didn't play with.

On the other hand . . .

He closed his eyes. "Go for it, Chief."

"Yes, sir."

The comm closed, and Morgan turned back to Conway. "Get people moving to the pods faster."

Conway nodded silently but enthusiastically.

Fuck it, Morgan thought darkly. *If we're going out, let's do it in a blaze they'll see ten light-years away.*

▶▶▶

▶ On *Copperhead One*, Grant was monitoring the Marines' chatter on the ground. They were hard-pressed, but had fought through the tunnels without losing anyone, mostly by staying ahead of the dragons, as they kept calling them.

Now that she had access to the full network, she could pull up images of the beasts in question and yeah, she had to admit . . .

"Dragons" works.

They sure weren't snakes. Whoever heard of snakes with claws and wings?

It was when the Marines got out in the open that the story started to shift. It sounded good at first; they were getting strapped in and hooked up, and the team was lifting off by the numbers. As the last of them left the field, however, the major called in a warning, and it became clear that things weren't going so well at all.

"Damn." Nick shook his head. "They're outnumbered, and those chutes are pigs in the air."

Grant nodded, knowing it was true. The chutes were excellent for ground mobility, letting a soldier hop across a battlefield like nothing else, but against an airborne threat? They were a damn near lethal liability.

SOP was you didn't use chutes, except for infiltration, unless you were fighting under a friendly sky.

"Those things don't have guns. They'll be fine," the jumpmaster said, his voice sounding less certain than his words.

"Maybe," Grant said, considering the situation. "Maybe not."

She keyed up an overhead map of the surface.

"Katie, what are you doing?" Nick asked, nervous.

"Just checking something."

She looked at the image of the tower, focusing on the lift access.

"Katie, we'll never fit," Nick said, having flown with her more than long enough to follow her thought process.

"No, not there. But what about here?" she asked, flicking the image over, showing the still-open area that the enemy missiles came from.

"You don't even know where that leads," he warned.

"It leads down," Grant said, a feral grin on her face as she twisted the stick to the right.

The Copperhead banked right, dropped its nose, and dove for the surface.

"Katie!"

Nick's voice was lost in the whoops of enjoyment from both the Marine in the back and the pilot at the stick.

▶ ▶ ▶

▶ Morgan Passer was once more outside the sealed hatch that led to the contaminated section of his ship, facing off with a Marine who desperately wanted to deny him entrance. The Marine was, again, going to lose, but there was something gratifying about the man trying even when he knew it was futile.

"Is the chief inside?"

"No, sir."

Morgan nodded, expecting that Chief Doohan was off drawing antihydrogen for his cockamamie plan. Honestly, he did *not* think it stood a chance in hell of working, but he was about to lose his ship anyway, so what the hell?

Better to go out in a blaze of glory than a blob of goop.

"One side! Magnetic containment unit coming through!"

That was one order Morgan hurried to obey, even on his own ship. An explosives expert with antihydrogen in hand outranked *God*.

"I hope you know what you're doing, Chief," he murmured as Doohan carefully came through the crowded hallway pushing a crash cart with two magnetic containment jars bolted to it.

"Haven't blown up anything I didn't mean to in years, Skipper."

"You're *not* making me feel any better, Chief."

Doohan just grinned maniacally. "Not often I get to do something this crazy, Skipper. May as well enjoy. Scot, you're recording this all, right?"

The nervous engineering crewman nodded, holding a hand cam. "Y-yes, Chief."

"Good. If we live, this is going to be legendary."

Morgan sighed and desperately resisted the urge to facepalm. *I should have known he'd enjoy this way too much.*

"Just don't annihilate us all, Chief," he said. "When I die, I sort of want *something* left, even if it's just expanding gasses."

"No worries, Skipper, there will be plenty left of us if this goes wrong. It's a straight ticket to pure energy." Doohan chuckled. "And from there we'll scatter across the galaxy over the next seventy thousand years. Can't think of a better way to go, no rotting in a hole in the ground for me."

"Chief, please stop talking like that until *after* we've survived this. You're making me scared to let you play with that stuff."

"More than you were already?"

Morgan considered that carefully, and then held up his thumb and forefinger a few millimeters apart. "Little bit."

Doohan laughed openly. "Smart man. Don't worry, this isn't my time yet."

"See to it that it isn't, Chief." Morgan nodded to the Marine. "Well, let him through."

"Yes, sir."

The hatch was opened, letting the two men and the incredibly dangerous substance through. When it closed behind them, Morgan let out a sigh of relief that was, he knew, entirely pointless. If the chief was wrong, that hatch would do *nothing* to protect him, but what could he say? He just wanted that nightmare fuel out of sight.

▶▶▶

▶ "Where the hell is she going?"

The copilot of *Copperhead Three* was scowling openly at his instruments, as if they had just betrayed him.

"What? Who?" the pilot asked, glancing over.

Orbiting the tower was a job any of them could do in their sleep, and sometimes it felt like they were doing just that. You could easily get so caught in the routine that you almost dozed off while still wide awake.

"Katie. She's taking her lander in low. Check it out."

The two leaned forward, frowning as the icon for *Copperhead One* came in low near the tower, skimming the surface as it buzzed the opening that the missiles had come from. Both men blinked and stared as the Copperhead paused briefly, and then dropped neat as can be right into the opening.

"What the hell . . . ?"

"She didn't just do that, did she?"

"*Copperhead One, Three.*"

"Go for *One*," Katie's voice came back, "but I'm a little busy here."

"What the hell are you doing?"

"Looking for a way inside."

The two men exchanged glances, and then stared back at the screen.

"You're *what*?"

"You heard me. *One* out."

The pilot blinked, shaking his head. "I'd say she's off her rocker, but then we all knew that a while ago."

"Think she'll find a way?"

"Maybe. Keep watch."

The copilot frowned. "You don't want to follow her?"

"We can't. If she bites it, we need to be out here to pick up anyone who gets to the surface. Let me know if she finds a way in."

"Yes, sir."

CHAPTER 30

▶ "Here they come again!"

Phillips swore, his stomach lurching into his throat as his chute cut out hard, putting him into free fall to avoid the attack from above. Then he was snapped hard as the rockets roared and left him strung out like the tail of a particularly violent kite.

He managed to muscle his rifle on to target as a blur swept past him in a narrow miss and unloaded a burst at close range. The hissing scream rent the air around him as the serpent went into a death spiral, twisting violently in the air as it clawed at the great gaping wounds torn in it by the rifle fire.

They'd come under air attack almost immediately after liftoff and lost two Marines and three of the researchers in the first skirmish. Since then it had been a battle just to gain and maintain any altitude as the snakes got above them and dropped out of the black like true nightmare fodder.

The chutes were programmed with minimal maneuvering ability, but the snakes were born to fly. There was no way they could take them in the air. He couldn't even remember how long they'd been trying, but he did know that the chutes were running low on power.

Soon they either would have their feet on something firm, or they'd be taking a tumble into the abyss.

Phillips wouldn't have bet money on which just then, no matter what odds were offered.

He put his chute into a hard climb, looking to gain as much altitude as he could while the snakes were coming around for another run. Unfortunately, it was clear that the enemy was smarter than he'd given them credit for.

"Another pack, coming in from above!"

Damn it. They've split their forces!

He twisted in place, trying to bring his rifle around, but it was too little too late as the huge teeth gleamed in the limited light from his suit.

Phillips jerked in place, shocked, as he was suddenly struck all across his body.

He blinked, and then looked out again and saw the headless body of the serpent dropping from sight.

What the hell?

His comm channel came to life a second later.

"Major, Marines, this is Mac on overwatch. I have you covered."

▶▶▶

▶ Splayed out on the catwalk, McMillan could almost imagine that he wasn't missing his leg as he looked through the powerful optics on his anti-materiel rifle.

Almost.

The pain wasn't the tipoff. He'd felt worse in the past. It was the way the balance had shifted and he couldn't adjust the way he normally could. He'd manually tuned down the pain meds his suit was administering in favor of keeping a clear mind, but he didn't have access to turn them off entirely. The drugs slowed down his target acquisition, kept him from identifying new threats as quickly as he'd prefer.

That wasn't going to stop him from putting twenty-millimeter rounds on target, though, not while his mates were in trouble.

"You're clear from above for now, Major," he said as he sought out the next target on his list.

He'd grabbed a heavy rifle, practically an artillery piece, from the SOCOM kit. It packed enough of a punch to deal with the flying snakes and then some. Almost as important, however, was that he could quickly acquire targets over the battle network. If the Marines in the fight saw a target, it was as good as dead.

The rifle slammed back into his shoulder, another depleted uranium round reaching out over three kilometers to "touch" a snake's midsection. The impact cut the beast in half, sending it tumbling away into the abyss as he looked for another target.

The icons of his fellow Marines danced across the rifle's optics, lights in the darkness fighting to avoid being snuffed out. The dragons were represented by red, of course, when they were identified. Most of the time he had to locate one and designate it himself before the system would recognize it. Then if he didn't splash the bastard right away, he could easily lose it to the night and have to start all over again.

He preferred not to let that happen.

The big rifle hammered his shoulder again. Another twenty-millimeter round heading downrange to splash a target.

Mac was in his element, leg or no leg, for what he supposed might be the last time of his life. He was determined to make it count.

▶▶▶

▶ "Climb! Climb! Climb!"

Major Phillips hadn't expected the last-minute save, but he'd take any miracle he could get and be happy for it. He directed the squad to head for the catwalk, hoping they all got there before their chutes ran out of power.

With Mac on overwatch, the squad got a bit of breathing room. Bolts of lightning from the darkness were an incredibly terrifying thing to have happen to any attacking force, even these snake-things. Unfortunately, unlike most human forces he'd know that would have some sense of self-preservation, the serpents seemed merely a little setback.

So, after the third or fourth strike from out of the black against them, the snakes started to realize that certain angles of attack were safer than others, and the pressure began to build again.

Still, the team was making real headway again, and now had to worry about covering less area as they flew on.

The difference in his Marines, however, now that they had a trusted sniper on overwatch, was remarkable. He could hear it in the comm chatter, much of the earlier terror now completely gone.

Knowing you had someone out there looking out for you, well, that just seemed to bring them all back to life in a way.

"Watch your back, Hyde," a Marine called. "Got a snaky little prick trying to sneak in behind you."

"I see him," the lieutenant answered, his rifle roaring. "Guess he thought he was safe from Mac around that side. Too bad, so sad. Adios, sucker."

"Don't get cocky," Phillips ordered over the comm. "They still have an advantage over us in too many ways for us to start celebrating yet. Make for the catwalk, best speed."

The group did as ordered. Well, those in active control of their chutes did, at least. The rest just followed along, slaved to the officer's commands, because neither Phillips nor Daiyu trusted some of them not to fly off on their own for no particular reason anyone would later be able to determine.

The snakes were not content to let it end there, however, and the pressure continued to mount as the pack tested the limits of their prey's defenses. Soon they were coming in five, ten, even more at a time, and while Mac continued to pick off as many as he could, his actions were a drop in the bucket as the firefight intensified.

Major Phillips was grinding his teeth, the frustration building as he could even *see* the distant light of the topside facility and the catwalk he knew it illuminated. They were *so* close, but the snakes kept herding them, picking off stray flyers, and all too often escaping unscathed.

No matter how many creatures the squad killed, it seemed like there were dozens more to take their place.

"We've played their game too long," he said finally, knowing that some of the chutes were running on literal fumes now. They were minutes from cutting out and sending men and women plummeting to their deaths. "We have to make a run for it, no more turning. If one of those snake bastards gets between you and the catwalk, cut through the son of a bitch."

The order was acknowledged, though most knew that it wasn't much of a plan. Odds were probably low on any single one of them making it, but at least some of them would, and that was better than what would happen if they kept playing tag with the snakes in the creatures' own element.

The chutes flared, pulling for the catwalk with Marines, Navy personnel, and researchers dangling on their lines like bait in shark-infested waters. Rifles roared as the snakes tried to cut them off, only to find that their prey had apparently lost all sense of fear.

The first action confused the snakes more than anything, causing many of them to pull back and get chopped to ribbons as a reward for their hesitation.

They regrouped, however, coming back around, and this time it was clear that they weren't going to be surprised again.

Phillips' HUD counted them off as they were identified, the numbers starting with the first one he spotted. Then the second appeared, then three more, eight more, twenty . . . and the numbers kept climbing. His heart sank. He didn't expect to see daylight ever again as he charged into the maws of the monsters, his rifle firing itself dry.

A roaring whine shook the air around them as spotlights turned night into day wherever they touched, and a rotary cannon exploded to life from behind them. As the snakes were torn to shreds under the firepower, Phillips twisted to see the lights of *Copperhead One* closing on their position from above and behind him.

"We have you covered, Major. Get your people on board."

"Katie, I've never been so damned happy to see one of those ugly beasts in my life, and I served in the Pacific during the war." Phillips opened the comm to his team. "You all heard the lady. Get ready to pack in!"

The Copperhead pulled ahead of them, rear doors open as the chief stood to one side with a heavy machine gun on a gimbal mount rocking in his hands.

▶▶▶

▶ The twenty-millimeter autocannon roared and shook in his hands as the chief covered the first of the retrievals cutting their chutes loose. It fired cold, the heavy accelerator barrel barely glinting as the rounds exploded from its depths. In the light of the Copperhead's cabin, however, the weapon blew rings of smoky condensation with every shot, as the rounds broke the sound barrier and left brief vapor cones in their wake.

Men scrambled aboard, struggling with their chutes as they tried to get out of the way of the next person while working with unfamiliar systems.

"Toss 'em out!" he ordered. "They're on fumes, and we don't have room for everyone as it is!"

The Marines nodded, kicking their chutes clear as the next pair arrived. Researchers this time, so the Marines physically pulled them in while the chief kept up the cover fire. The snakes were testing the Copperhead's defenses, but he was determined to show them the error of their ways.

Two by two, the Copperhead retrieved the flyers in order of how badly they were hurting for rocket fuel. The major packed in somewhere in the middle of the pack, cutting his chute loose as soon as a Marine grabbed his arm.

"Welcome aboard, sir," the chief yelled over the racket that he was making, the shots of the machine gun rattling everything, even the sound-insulated armor. "Pardon me for not saluting."

"Chief, you save my butt like this and you can flip me the bird if you like," the major grinned.

Phillips nodded quickly and got clear, letting the next pair come in as he pushed through to the front of the Copperhead, leaning in between the pilots.

"I'm not going to ask how you got down here. I probably don't want to know, but you have my thanks, Commander," he said, leaning in a bit as he braced himself.

Katie flashed him a grin. "We were getting a little bored flying around up there, Major, so no prob."

Something *massive* dove past the front of the Copperhead, and Grant had to yank hard on the stick to avoid contact, literally. The assault lander pitched up, rolling left, and then leveled out as people started yelling from behind him.

"What the *hell* was that?" the copilot demanded, shocked.

"It was a *big* mother of . . ." Grant mumbled, twisting the Copperhead around as her head moved on a swivel, looking for whatever the hell it was. "Major?"

"I don't know, Commander. We saw one big one, but I'd swear there was no way that thing could fly," he said, shaking his head. "It was too damn big."

"That thing looked like it could swallow *us*," the copilot blurted.

"Calm down, it wasn't that big," Grant said, looking over her shoulder. "Chief, are we still loading?"

"After *that* maneuver?" The chief's incredulity was clear. "It's going to take a minute to line up for the rest, you know that!"

"Damn!" she swore, leveling the Copperhead out. "We've got something out there, Chief. Get them in here!"

Phillips leaned in. "No way you have room for everyone, Commander. No way."

"Well, then we'll just have to cover the rest to the catwalk."

The major nodded. "Like the way you think, Marine."

Grant nodded, acknowledging the compliment as she gently worked the stick and brought the Copperhead around in a search for the object they'd seen. It made her nervous, sharing the sky with something *that* big.

"Negative radar contacts, thermal is clear . . ." she muttered, shaking her head. "Thermal is *never* clear . . ."

"They seem to be cold-blooded," Phillips offered. "Everything in here is pretty close to ambient temperature."

"Weird. Still, I can't find that thing on any . . . Holy shit!" she swore, retrofiring the Copperhead's rockets as they came face to face with nightmare fuel on steroids, their lights illuminating bits and pieces of something right in front of them.

The wingspan on the big one had to be thirty meters, and the coiled body looked close to five in diameter. It wasn't big enough to eat the Copperhead, despite impressions, but Grant suddenly wouldn't care to make bets on what kind of damage it could cause.

The serpent lunged at them and she danced the ship sideways, avoiding the lunge, and answered with her forward rotary cannon. The first couple of rounds hit, drawing a scream that felt like it shook the Copperhead, but the serpent vanished into the darkness before she could get the kill.

"Eyes out! Eyes out!" Grant called. "Call out if you see . . ."

"Three low!"

Responding to her copilot's warning, she banked hard to the left, away from the attack, and then twisted her nose into it just as the serpent loomed massively large in their view, then vanished over them before she could fire.

A thud and the shaking of the Copperhead let them know that it hadn't disappeared entirely.

"It's on us," Phillips said, looking up.

"No shit, sir," Grant grumbled. "Chief, we've got a hitchhiker!"

"I can hear it," the chief called back. "What's it doing?"

The answer to that came as a horrible screeching sound prefaced an explosion of sparks from the side of the craft.

"That did *not* just happen!" Grant swore, eyes wide.

"What? What happened?"

"Something just cut out half my avionics," she said, "but they're *armored* . . ."

"Can you stay aloft?" Major Phillips asked.

"No problem. This thing is damn near bulletproof, we have backups . . . but if we lose too many more . . ." She shook her head. "No damn way. No way I lose my ship to a damn *snake*! Everyone hang on!"

"Commander, what . . ."

The major was cut off as he had to literally hang on to keep from bouncing around inside the craft like a rubber ball. The Copperhead pitched over and broke into a dive, becoming inverted. He could hear people hit the roof behind him, but he was too busy keeping himself in place to worry about them.

"Commander . . . !" he called, his eyes wide under his helmet.

"Try holding on through this, you bitch," Grant said through gritted teeth as she put the Copperhead into an inverted roll and started to pull significant negative gees.

As she was starting to redout, all the blood in her body rushing into her head and eyes, Grant heard an ugly scraping sound reverberate through the craft. Suddenly they jerked upward as though they'd just lost a significant weight.

She rolled back over, sighing as the red receded. "Lost the bitch. What were you saying, Major?"

"Never mind, Commander." Phillips sighed. "Do we have a location on the rest of my team?"

"Yes, sir, we're vectoring back now. They're almost to the catwalk," Grant said.

"That thing is still out there," Nicholas said from the copilot's seat, drawing their looks. "Hey, I'm just saying."

"Don't remind me," Grant mumbled. "I can't believe a snake cut my avionics."

They returned to the stragglers, swooping in and providing cover fire again as a few more dragons tried to pick off an easy meal. With the Copperhead packed to the gills, they restricted themselves to a support role as the rest of the Marines and naval officers made it to the catwalk.

They were joined there by those who had been left in the topside facility earlier, as they tried to work out what to do next.

"Can you cover them to the lift?" Phillips asked.

"Sure, but . . ."

Whatever Grant was going to say was lost as the Copperhead

slammed to one side, rocking them all hard enough to make them see stars.

"Son of a . . ." Grant growled, struggling to keep control as the ship spun out over the catwalk. She did *not* want to plant her ship onto a bunch of Marines. That would completely suck.

"Queen bitch is back!"

"I figured that out myself, Chief!" she called over her shoulder. "Little busy not *crashing* here!"

She got the ship out over the abyss and away from the Marines and officers, barely keeping control as she did. The Copperhead's reactors were screaming in response to her demand for more power as she fought the machine for control.

"Oh, God!"

Looking up, they all saw what prompted Nick's scream as a muscled coil of the serpent wrapped around the cockpit glass and started to *squeeze.*

Then lights exploded from outside as heavy cannon fire roared and shook the air around them. They all heard screaming, unearthly sounds that sent shivers down all their spines, and then the coils slipped away and the Copperhead leveled out.

Grant breathed slowly for a long moment, nodding out at the lights beyond her cockpit as she reached for the comms.

"*Two, Three. One.* Glad you could join the party."

The pilots of *Copperhead Two* and *Copperhead Three* chuckled at her as they orbited the wounded but still sightworthy *Copperhead One.*

"Thanks for the invite. Sorry we're late."

CHAPTER 31

▶ "Are you sure this is going to work, Chief?"

Doohan chuckled, shaking his head at the naive question from the crewman. In the man's defense, he clearly had enough faith . . . and guts . . . to volunteer for the job, but it was still a pretty stupid question.

"Of course not."

The younger man nodded, pale and shaking as he manipulated the bottle of antihydrogen.

"That's what I figured."

Okay, Doohan noted as he worked, *maybe the kid isn't as naive as I thought.*

Two bottles of, literally, the most dangerous substance in the universe were enough to scare him deep to his core, but when faced with what was possibly the second most dangerous substance he'd ever encountered, what else could you resort to but the first?

The two men looked over the black goop that had begun to expand out into the rest of the compartment. It was still going slow, but now that it was moving he knew that it was only a matter of time before the material metastasized, and when that happened, not even the antimatter would save them.

"What now?"

Chief Doohan nodded, knowing that was a good question.

He could try to get fancy, but honestly didn't think it would work even if he tried. Antimatter wasn't any normal explosive. You couldn't "shape" it the way one could lesser materials. Given a few months, and one hell of an energy field . . . something from one of the Heroic Class ships . . . then maybe he could do something.

As it was? Not hardly.

"Easy, son, just hand me the first bottle," he said, extending a hand.

The crewman nodded and gingerly passed him the first of the two containment bottles. Doohan carefully held it, judging its weight, and then pitched the bottle underhand into the center of the goop.

The crewman nearly passed out.

Doohan grinned. "Relax. The containment can handle more shock than that. Give me the other one."

Despite shooting Doohan a look that clearly considered him to be completely and totally *insane*, the crewman handed him the second bottle.

Doohan repeated his action, picking another spot to give the two the best chance, and then nodded. "Time to go."

The crewman needed no convincing of *that*. They double-timed it to the door and passed through as the rippling goop behind them expanded a little more. Dogging the hatch behind them, both men bolted for the next section, not trusting that hatch to hold.

The Marines were waiting for them there, letting them through before securing that hatch as well.

Neither engineer stuck around. Both kept running.

The Marines looked at one another, then after the running engineers, and didn't bother to speak before they took off at a dead sprint themselves.

▶▶▶

▶ "Chief reports that he set them," Conway said, looking over at the captain with more than a little trepidation.

Morgan nodded. "Good. When will they go off?"

"I asked him that," Conway said, grimacing.

"And?"

"And he said he wasn't sure, whenever the goop got around to eating the bottles."

I will not whimper. I won't, Captain Passer thought to himself as he closed his eyes and lowered his head.

Morgan took a deep breath. "Is everyone in the pods?"

"Yes. All nonessential crew are ready to abandon if this doesn't work," Conway said. "Stations are currently manned by volunteers only."

"Good," Morgan said, and then looked over at the other officer. "We don't both need to be here, Conway. Get to a pod."

"That's funny, sir. I was about to tell you the same thing," Conway returned, making no effort to move.

Morgan snorted, but honestly there was no time to argue the point. If the man wanted to remain at his station, then so be it.

"So now we just sit here and wait," Morgan said instead of following up. "Not even a countdown."

"Pretty inconsiderate of him, if you ask me," Conway offered. "You'd think it'd be easy to rig a failure point on something containing *antimatter.*"

"Not as easy as you'd think," Morgan admitted. "Those bottles are built to be damn near . . ."

The ship suddenly lurched to one side for an instant before a shock wave shook the bridge and rattled them all around like they were ball bearings in a maze. For a long moment afterward, there was silence as everyone looked around at everyone else.

Finally, Conway broke the silence.

"You were saying about the bottles, sir?"

"No one likes a smartass, Commander," Morgan said dryly.

"Sorry, sir."

"C-Captain?"

Morgan looked up to where Andrea was covering tactical and comms stations. "Yes?"

"Message from *Copperhead One*," she said, swallowing and taking a deep breath. "Copperhead flight requests permission to come aboard . . . and *Copperhead One* actual wants to know what the hell that explosion was."

Morgan snorted, and then started to snicker, and finally was laughing helplessly. If he hadn't been strapped in, he would have wound up on the floor. If they had gravity, of course.

"Tell them . . ." he started, pausing to take a deep breath, "tell them . . . permission granted, and that explosion was Chief Doohan playing around with antimatter."

"Y-Yes sir," Andrea said, shaking her head and sending the message.

A moment later she stiffened, looked back at the captain and then at her controls with clearly indecisive and conflicted emotions on her face.

"What is it, Andrea?" Morgan asked, still smiling.

"Copperhead flight acknowledges my signal and officially retracts their request to come aboard, sir."

Morgan clenched his fist to his forehead, just barely keeping from laughing again as he got control of himself.

"Tell them to get their ass on board," he said finally. "I want to put at least a few AU between us and this place before we signal home."

"Yes, sir."

▶▶▶

▶ The decks of the *Autolycus* were a relief to see, and Commander Daiyu felt herself begin to relax for the first time in what felt like an eternity. She was gliding along one of the internal tracks, limply letting the transit handle pull her along to her destination.

Debriefing was going to be horrid, but it could wait a little longer.

By the time she arrived, the captain was already there along with a few people from the ground mission.

Daiyu nodded to each as she settled in, just trying to relax as much as she could.

"I've briefly examined the mission files," Captain Passer said, "and I want to congratulate you. You did well on a mission that became extremely taxing in ways you couldn't have predicted. We'll do a full debrief later, but I want your impressions before I send an FTL signal home."

Everyone nodded, understanding.

FTL signals were power-intensive, and not to be wasted on a ship like the *Auto*. One of the Heroics could, almost, chat casually with FTL, but they literally had power reserves measured in *planetary masses*. On the *Autolycus*, with its puny fusion reactors, you wanted to craft your messages with extra care.

Daiyu spoke first. "The planet/moon system is an invaluable construct, Captain. The observatory aspect alone is . . . priceless. The weapon, well, I would not advise it be left to another's hand."

"Agreed."

"The ecosystem should be studied," the team's exobiologist said enthusiastically. "A complex apex species like the dragons has to have a huge pyramid of life below it, but we didn't see any sign of it . . ."

"We stayed mostly within alien facilities," Daiyu reminded him. "Little chance for life to grow there."

"That's exactly my point. There must be *amazing* fauna and flora deeper down in the moon's . . ."

"Yes," Morgan held up his hand. "I'm sure. For now, however, let's remain with tactical and strategic benefits."

"Yes, sir, sorry."

"We can't overestimate the value of the facility, Captain," Daiyu picked up again. "It is quite possibly the single most important find . . . ever. The information held there alone is incalculable."

Morgan nodded. He understood and even agreed. He just hoped it would be worth the lives it had, and would, cost.

"Very well. I suppose I have enough for the message," he said. "You all need some rest. The ship is secure, go grab some shut-eye and . . ."

"Excuse me, Captain?"

"Yes, Doctor?"

Palin smiled blandly at the captain. "I thought you might like to hold on to this."

Morgan watched as the doctor pulled a glowing geometric object from a pouch, resting it on the table. Everyone stared at it for a long quiet moment, the same question echoing in each one's mind.

"What is that, Doctor?" Morgan asked, finally, for all of them.

Palin shrugged, and then yawned.

"Fire of the Gods, Captain," he said as he pushed off and floated out of the room. "It's the Fire of the Gods."

EPILOGUE

▶ The *Odysseus*, lead ship of the Heroic Class, dwarfed the Rogue Class *Autolycus* by a factor of fifty at least. Side by side, the two ships were an odd match as they drifted in the outer system that contained the heliobeam worlds.

Captain Passer walked the halls of the *Odysseus*, enjoying the feel of gravity again as he made his way to his meeting. The wide halls felt luxurious, but almost decadent, too. He smiled tightly at his own thoughts as he arrived at the conference room and was admitted by the Marine guard.

"Ah, Captain Passer. It's good to see you're still in one piece." Eric Weston rose from his seat, crossing the room and extending his hand.

Morgan took it. "Thank you, Commodore."

"Please, Eric will do here," Commodore Weston said. "I have to say, you stepped in it just about as deep as I did on my first mission."

"Let's hope not," Morgan said with some feeling. "We lost eighteen people on that moon. I would rather keep it at that."

Weston nodded soberly, agreeing.

His first mission had led, arguably, to an all-out invasion of the Earth. Of course, the chances were that the invasion had been coming anyway. It was just a matter of counting down the days, but not everyone saw it that way.

"Yes," Eric said, "we can but hope. Still, you accounted well for yourselves."

"I have good people."

"I know the feeling," Eric said. "Well, let's be about it, then, shall we?"

Morgan agreed and slipped down into a chair.

"I reviewed your report, of course," Eric said. "As has the admiralty. We'll get you patched up and good to return to Earth. There's a dry dock waiting for you there."

"Thank you, sir."

"Not going to take credit for that," Eric chuckled. "As long as you haven't compromised the hull too badly, or fractured the ship's spine, they'll fix you up good as new. I have to say, intentionally popping a couple antimatter bottles? That was risky, Captain."

"No more than letting that goop eat my ship."

Eric nodded darkly, knowing well enough the feeling of seeing something actually *eat* your ship. It wasn't a pleasant memory.

"True," was all he said aloud. "We've discussed the . . . data you retrieved. Did you bring it?"

Passer nodded, setting a case on the table and popping it open. He picked out the glowing gem within and handed it to the commodore.

"Beautiful, isn't it?" Eric asked as he turned it over. "And nearly identical to Priminae long-term data storage. Our optical interface should be able to ready it. Are you certain of what it contains?"

"Some of it," Morgan nodded. "Doctor Palin was certain, at least."

"Palin." Eric smiled. "You're lucky to have him."

"Some of my officers would disagree," Morgan said, a wisp of a smile on his own face, "but he did pull some rather impressive tricks out of his . . . hat."

"Yes, well, he does that," Eric said, as he set the gem on a reader and checked the response. "Interface is compatible. It's Priminae technology . . . or a precursor, I suppose. They haven't changed their technology in millennia."

"I still find that hard to believe," Morgan admitted.

"We all do. Huh." Eric blinked. "It's an *old* format, but readable. Here we go . . ."

A holographic image of the galaxy leapt into being between them, and both men examined it closely. Some sections were lit up, and with a few deft motions Eric brought them in closer to see that specific stars were marked clearly.

"Precursor facilities . . ." He breathed. "This . . . confirms a lot of theories, Captain."

"Such as?"

"We've often thought that the Drasin . . ." Eric tapped a few commands into the reader and was rewarded by the image shifting, showing one of the Drasin in profile, along with a marked star beside it. "We've often thought that someone was holding their leash . . . Here, a . . . prison? The Drasin were stored here."

Eric sat back, shaking his head.

"Someone out there accessed one of these facilities, Captain, and in it they found the Drasin. They used them as a weapon against the Priminae, and against us. We cannot ignore that."

Morgan nodded, completely in agreement.

"Before the *Odysseus* was dispatched, the admiralty authorized a new long-term mission for the Rogue Class," Eric said. "It's contingent on what we find here, but I think I can confirm it now. You're no longer going to be hunting for Drasin facilities, Captain."

"We're looking for the people who used them?" Morgan leaned forward.

"No, that's my job," Eric said firmly. "You're now in charge of Operation Prometheus."

"Sir?"

"You said Palin called this the Fire of the Gods, right?" Eric asked, nodding to the gem in the reader.

"Yes, sir." Morgan understood the name now.

"Our enemies, whoever they are, used one of these facilities against us," Eric said. "No more. Never again. We want you to go out and steal fire from the gods, find these facilities, confirm they're intact, and secure them until a task force can arrive to take control."

"Steal fire from the gods?" Morgan laughed lightly. "I like the sound of that."

"You accept, then?"

"Commodore, when my crew and I are done, the gods will have to bum a light from *us*."

AUTHOR BIO

Evan Currie is the bestselling author of the Odyssey One series, the Warrior's Wings series, and more. Although his postsecondary education was in computer sciences, and he has worked in the local lobster industry steadily over the last decade, writing has always been his true passion. Currie himself says it best: "It's what I do for fun and to relax. There's not much I can imagine better than being a storyteller."